HER SAVAGE SCOT

THE HIGHLAND WARRIOR CHRONICLES
BOOK ONE

CHRISTINA PHILLIPS

PHOENIX 18 PUBLISHING

Cover Art by Kim Killion Publishing
5/2026

ISBN 978-0-6487568-6-6

For Iris and Derek, with love

CHAPTER 1

KINGDOM OF DAL RIADA, PICTLAND.
SPRING, 843

Connor MacKenzie stifled the irrational urge to flinch as Maeve Balfour, possibly the most beautiful woman in the great hall that evening, drifted her fingers across his. He attempted without success to ignore the blatant invite in her seductive hazel eyes and instead downed his tankard of ale. God, he was tired. All he wanted was for this victory feast to end so he could fall into oblivion in his bed.

Alone.

Lies. What he wanted was to sink into Maeve's welcoming heat, feel her arms around him and forget for a few precious moments the bloodied images imprinted in his brain.

But their liaison could no longer continue.

"You look tense, my love." Maeve offered him a smile that during the last year had never failed to rouse his interest. Tonight was no different, except tonight everything was different. "Come to my chambers later," she whispered as she raised her goblet to her lips. "There's no chance of MacDougall catching us now."

Corrosive guilt cramped his gut and strangled the heated lust that threatened to override good sense. "The man's not cold in his grave yet, Maeve." The hypocrisy of his words choked him. He'd held Iain MacDougall in contempt during his life. Why did death suddenly elevate his status?

He'd been a bastard to every soul he owned. His wife included.

A blush heated Maeve's aristocratic cheeks. "Aye. And I won't pretend despair when all that fills my heart is relief. You know how it was, Connor. He lost my respect long ago."

"I know." Briefly he squeezed her fingers and recalled how hard Maeve, as a young bride six years ago, had tried to win the love of her arrogant lord. How MacDougall had abused her and bedded any female unlucky enough to catch his salacious eye. "But I saw him fall." Saw the Norsemen behead him. No matter how much he'd despised the man, no warrior deserved such a barbaric fate. "He was still my countryman. And I failed to save him."

Maeve studied the cut of lamb she'd barely touched before picking it up between thumb and forefinger and slinging it to the prowling dogs. "Does this change things between us?"

Appetite lost, he shoved his plate aside. The raucous laughter and jeers around the long table hammered into his brain. The stink of ale and sweat and canine drenched his senses.

The memory of Maeve in his arms haunted his twisted conscience.

"How can it not?" He glanced across the table at his half-brother Fergus who was stuffing his mouth with one hand and fondling a dull-eyed slave girl with the other. "You know it does."

He turned to the young woman by his side, but from the corner of his eye saw Fergus stumble to his feet and drag the reluctant girl from the hall. Weary disgust roiled Connor's stomach. There were women aplenty who'd share Fergus' bed, yet he found more pleasure in taking those who had no rights of denial.

"Aye." Maeve's voice was soft, as if it were no great revelation to her. "But I hoped—I prayed—it wouldn't." She offered him a smile that magnified his guilt, illuminated his self-loathing. "You honored me with fidelity this last year. That's more than my husband ever did. I can wait until you're ready."

Aye, he'd been faithful to his mistress. But Maeve had given him what he needed. A warm body to slake his need. Pleasing conversation to soothe his mind.

And the safety of knowing she would never—*could* never—demand any more from him.

He had no more he could give.

THE CHILL NIGHT air of the keep was a welcome respite after the stuffy confines of the crowded hall. He dragged in a great breath, filling his lungs, clearing his head. Dunadd, the royal stronghold of Dal Riada, and the center of existence for its surrounding chattels and farmsteads dominated the hilltop. For three hundred years, the stronghold's formidable ramparts had repelled enemy attacks from both the Northumbrians in the south and the Picts to the northeast. But now they faced a new invader. One who dared to stake their claim on the Scots' islands heritage, who dared to look across the firth of Lorn to the heart of their kingdom.

Light spilled from the narrow window slits behind him, illuminating Fergus as he dropped a couple of coins into the girl's hand and staggered back. She curled her fingers against her breast and huddled against the stone wall, making her way back toward the massive timber doors.

Then she stilled, like a rabbit sensing a predatory fox, as she became aware of Connor's presence. Biting back a curse, he stepped away from the wall to allow her unimpeded access, but she remained frozen, obviously expecting him to take his turn with her. And even though it had been weeks since he'd lain with Maeve, the thought of slaking his pent-up lust with an intimidated slave was enough to cool any ardor that still heated his blood.

"Get back to the kitchens." His voice was unintentionally gruff and she flinched, sinking into the shadows of the ancient stone. And who was he to tell her what to do? She'd obey her master. And if serving the warriors' every need was her order, then she had no choice in the matter.

He waited until she scurried away before striding toward Fergus who turned and offered a welcoming leer.

"Alone, little brother? You need to learn how to enjoy life more." He adjusted his plaid then rolled his shoulders, clearly well satisfied.

"We have different definitions of enjoyment." Connor narrowed his eyes as he stared down from their mighty hill toward the firth and beyond, where the Isle of Iona braved the western ocean. Where the Scots had so recently beaten back the Norse invaders who cast their shadow across the outer islands like a hell-borne plague.

Fergus slapped his shoulder and attempted to pull him into a bear hug. The drunker Fergus became, the more inclined to familial intimacy he became. It didn't mean much when Connor still bore the scars from his brother's childhood beatings.

But, after all, Fergus was his only brother. Buried deep inside, somewhere, lay the tattered remains of his boyhood hero-worship. And it had been thirteen years since Fergus had dared lay hands on him in anger.

"If you can't find pleasure in bedding every beautiful woman you come across, then you might as well tether your balls in another marriage."

Connor grunted, disinclined to discuss such matters. Fergus didn't take the hint.

"Not that a wife would keep my cock leashed." Fergus grinned at his wit and aimed a less-than-steady punch at Connor's chest. "But such unnatural chastity comes easily to you." He staggered and steadied himself against Connor's shoulder. "Tell me. How many whores have you had these last four years?"

"None." Connor shoved his brother upright. He and Maeve had been scrupulous in their efforts to keep their affair private. Neither had wanted to arouse MacDougall's suspicion. Not because he feared the other man's fury, but because he had no intention of allowing such knowledge to besmirch Maeve's reputation.

MacDougall would have dragged her naked by her hair through the filth of the middens had he discovered her infidelity. And in the challenge to avenge her honor, Connor would have run his sword through the bastard's heart.

And marriage to the widow would have been the inevitable conclusion.

"Then it's a wonder," Fergus said, "how you manage to lift your sword, considering the exercise you must inflict upon your wrist in pursuit of self-gratification."

Sometimes it was easier to agree than argue when Fergus floundered in ale-induced stupidity. Especially when Connor had no intention of enlightening him as to the error of his convictions. "Aye."

THE SHARP TANG of salt from the sea flavored the westerly breeze as Connor strode toward the stables the following morning. Clouds scudded across the pale-blue sky and rain threatened on the horizon, but it would take more than a spring thunderstorm to prevent him from leaving.

His hillfort in the east of Dal Riada, small as it was, had been neglected too long.

"Connor." Ewan MacKinnon, fellow warrior, lifelong friend

and the only one aware of his attachment to Maeve, hailed him from the stronghold. Connor turned, raised a hand in greeting and waited until Ewan reached his side. "The king wants to see us."

"Do you know why?" Connor abandoned the stables to fall into step beside his friend as they returned to the stronghold. God, he hoped the king didn't have another imminent battle plan in mind. He'd die for his king, but he'd like a short respite first. The thought of returning to the killing fields without so much as a week of peace knotted his guts.

Treacherous thoughts. Ones he would never utter. But still they polluted his mind.

Ewan shrugged and looked as grim as Connor felt. "Can't be the Norse back already. Probably the Picts this time."

Slaves were clearing the great hall of the remnants of the previous night's feast, and a couple of dogs fought a bloody battle under the high table as he and Ewan passed through on their way to the king's inner sanctum. A couple of older warriors, eyes hard, expressions of stone, emerged from the sanctum as Connor and Ewan approached. An aura of secrecy and intrigue clung to them as palpable as the mist that obscured the hilltops at dawn.

Through the open door, their king waved them in. As Connor went down on one knee and bowed his head, he knew he wouldn't be returning this day to the place he called home. The war room vibrated with scarcely concealed anticipation.

"Connor. Ewan." Kenneth MacAlpin, King of the Scots, flicked his hand in an impatient gesture, ordering them to rise. Four of the king's advisers flanked him, staring at Connor and Ewan as if they were cockroaches they'd like to crush beneath their heels.

They probably would. None of them had forgotten that, until four years ago, both Connor's and Ewan's fathers had been MacAlpin's most trusted of intimates. But along with so many others during that bloodied battle of '39, their lives had been lost defending their king. And their noble positions had been filled with those less scrupulous.

The king folded his arms and leaned back against his heavy timber desk. "If we want continued success against the Norsemen, we need the Picts' allegiance."

Connor refrained from glancing at Ewan, but only just. Of all the things he'd expected the king to say, it hadn't been this.

"I can't see them deferring to a Scot." Especially since they didn't even formally recognize MacAlpin's kingship of Dal Riada. "Why should they offer us their trust?"

"Wrad is dead," the king said.

Connor waited, but it appeared MacAlpin considered that explanation enough.

"Why does the death of their high king affect us?" Ewan said, clearly as much in the dark as Connor. "Their heathen tribes will only fight among themselves again until they elevate another to the position."

The king bared his teeth in a feral smile. "They won't. Because in accordance with their customs of inheritance, the kingship of Fortriu now belongs to me."

This time Connor did catch Ewan's eye. "I can't see the Picts agreeing without bloodshed."

"They don't have a choice." The king strolled around his desk and glanced at the map that covered its surface. "My birthright is unchallenged through the bloodline of my royal mother."

"And claiming Fortriu will secure the loyalty of all the Pictish clans?" Ewan didn't sound convinced and Connor agreed. While there had been intermittent peace between the two peoples over the last three hundred years, trust had never taken root. And to mean anything, loyalty had to be freely given not extracted by brutality.

He caught the guarded look that passed among the king's advisers. As if they knew how the king intended to exact such loyalty. Connor's gaze sharpened on the king, who appeared absorbed in studying the borderlines of the seven Pictish kingdoms that swallowed up the land northeast of Dal Riada.

There was more at stake here than the claiming of a matrilineal heritage.

"Marriage will claim their loyalty." The king finally looked up, iron purpose glinting in his eyes. "Their daughters and our warriors. And a Scot ruling the supreme kingdom uncontested."

Aye, he could see that working. In theory. In practice he doubted the Picts would so easily give up their royal daughters. "But what if they don't want such an alliance?"

The king tapped his finger on the map and Connor and Ewan dutifully stepped forward. "The northernmost clans are most affected by the Norse. Fidach is weak and relies on the neighboring Ce." He jabbed his finger at the relevant clan territories. "Rex Bredei mac Lutin of Ce has at least two if not more daughters. He's the one we need as our ally. Assure him of our undivided support against the barbaric Norsemen in return for political favor. Once we've secured his eldest daughter in marriage, our hold on the north strengthens."

"Who does my liege consider worthy of such marriage?"

"A man," the king said, "who will beget heirs without delay."

Unease trickled along Connor's spine at the piercing glare MacAlpin arrowed his way. Surely the king wasn't suggesting *he* was to be married to this foreign princess? Connor's ties to the king were absolute, by virtue of his heritage and personal actions.

But he didn't possess royal blood. Why would any Pict king agree to such a union for his daughter?

"It's a pity," the king said, never taking his eyes from Connor, "the eldest Princess Devorgilla of Ce has a reputation as a cantankerous shrew. She's also reclusive and, I fear, has the countenance of a belligerent hag."

And MacAlpin expected him to *impregnate her?*

The king continued, apparently deriving perverse pleasure from cataloging every possible fault he could. "It's likely her first husband welcomed death with open arms as a chance to escape her scolding tongue."

"How old is the princess?" Ewan sounded horrified, as if convinced he might be the recipient of such a foul bedfellow.

The king gestured and one of his advisers stepped forward. "She's no longer young. She's been widowed many years now. But our sources reliably inform us she is not yet past child-bearing."

The information didn't alleviate the unsavory image forming in Connor's mind. His own lady mother was not yet past child-bearing age.

"As two of my most trusted warriors," the king said, "I charge you with the task of delivering this proposition to mac Lutin." He held out his hand and an adviser passed him a scroll, the scarlet wax proudly displaying the elaborate royal seal. "It's doubtful whether he can read, but he'll recognize the authenticity of my credential."

Connor took the proffered scroll. "If mac Lutin accepts the terms." And of course he would accept the terms. What man wouldn't want to rid himself of a daughter past her prime, a daughter with a reputation that would repel most suitors? A daughter who, far from spending the rest of her life as a drain on his resources, would give him legitimate reason to call on the Scots as allies in time of war? "Do you want the marriage undertaken at Ce?"

Among heathens. But since he had nothing but loyalty for his king invested in this marriage, what did it matter where the ceremony took place?

A frown slashed the king's brow. "How the hell can it be undertaken in Ce? Your task is to win mac Lutin's favor, secure the princess as our bride and bring the entire royal family back with you. I'll not trust the Picts to supervise a marriage of this import."

"The entire royal family?"

"Aye." The king's sharp-eyed gaze bored into him. "We'll be celebrating more than a wedding. It will also be the ideal opportunity to discuss my coronation at Fortriu. I doubt any of the minor kings will want to miss *that*."

A politically sensitive wedding, a potentially contentious coronation and obviously MacAlpin was inviting the other Pictish royal clans as witnesses. A suffocating weight compressed his lungs. Far from serving out the remainder of his days fighting for his country's freedom and receiving comfort from the arms of an undemanding mistress, he was to become a stud for his king's machinations.

"When do you want us to leave?" He hoped his revulsion wasn't apparent in either his expression or voice, but the king's eyes narrowed.

"You disapprove the plan?"

"No, my liege." Just because he personally found it abhorrent didn't blind him to the potential gains they could make in forging such strong connections with the mighty clan of Ce. "In principle we stand to gain a great deal by such an alliance." And then he chanced voicing his dissent. "But I have reservations the King of Ce will accept my offer."

Seconds passed, the air thick with distrust. Then the king's frown faded, and he laughed, a short bark of amusement that appeared to flummox his advisers as much as Connor.

"God Almighty, boy," the king said, flattening his palms on the map and leaning across the desk. "You didn't think I had *you* in mind for this marriage, did you?"

It had been many years since anyone had dared call Connor *boy* without risking a bloodied nose. MacAlpin might be seventeen years his senior but that hardly qualified him to utter such term of abuse.

His status, however, gave him the authority to say whatever he wished.

Connor mentally gritted his teeth and ignored the scarcely

concealed sneers crawling across the advisers' smug faces. His king was above censure. The same couldn't be said for the fawning minions he now surrounded himself with.

"So that was the reason for your reticence." It wasn't a question. It sounded like a revelation, and a welcome one at that. Connor glowered, yet instead of striking him for such insolence it only made the king laugh again. "And what of you, Ewan?" The king finally transferred his attention to the other man. "Did you think you might have been chosen for a royal bride?"

Connor didn't have to look at his friend to know compressed anger simmered beneath his surface. He could feel it vibrating in tightly repressed waves.

"My liege," Ewan said. It sounded as though he forced the words between gritted teeth.

The king shoved himself upright. "I have no doubt either one of you could charm even Princess Devorgilla of Ce into your bed if you so much as smiled at her. Alas, it takes more than the famed Scots charm and a hard warrior body to tempt a king to part with a daughter." Again, amusement flared across his face. Amusement and… something else. Something so fleeting, so bizarre he had to be mistaken.

Relief?

"To hook a king, we have to offer royal blood." Once more MacAlpin's attention focused on Connor. "Your half-brother, Fergus."

"Fergus?" He'd watched his brother escape matrimony countless times over the years. But no amount of charm or bargaining would release him from this duty.

His brother could be a bastard, but he didn't deserve to be shackled to a heathen shrew. Then again, Fergus didn't believe in fidelity. It was unlikely this marriage would change his mind.

"His mother's connection to me through our grandfather gives him enough royal prestige." The king let out a breath. "And by God, he's sired enough bastards to prove his virility."

Connor ignored the dull ache that knotted his chest at the king's careless comment. Fergus produced bairns as easily as he changed bed partners and didn't give a damn about any of them.

If nothing else, he would soon ensure the Pictish princess was with child.

CHAPTER 2

THE KINGDOM OF CE, PICTLAND

*A*ila, Princess Devorgilla of Ce, shivered in the early morning chill and pulled her woolen cloak more securely across her body. Once, long ago, she hadn't needed any protection against the harsh Highland elements. But the frost that had entered her heart nine years ago had never truly thawed. And the remnants flowed through her veins, stealing any hope of warmth even on the most glorious summer day.

And although it wasn't yet summer, today was certainly beautiful. Drun, her elderly deerhound, leaned heavily against her thigh and absently she draped an arm around his neck as she inhaled a great breath, savoring the scents of spring grass and fresh earth, her face turned toward the sun. With her eyes closed, she listened as the morning chorus of blackbird, song thrush, wren and chaffinch filled the air; the faint bleating of lambs echoed in the distance and the bark of the hunting dogs sank into her consciousness.

Familiar. *Safe.* Her home, where nothing fundamental had changed for more than two hundred years.

She opened her eyes and glanced into the far glen. The palace of Ce-eviot, the royal stronghold of the land of Ce, commanded an unparalleled view of the surrounding countryside. No enemy could advance unseen nor breach the mighty hill's ramparts without detection.

Yet a faint tremor of unease fluttered through the pit of her stomach. Frowning, she turned and, shielding her eyes against the early morning sun, looked south, where in the far distance the twin mountains of the mythical Earth goddess dominated the landscape.

Nothing. What had she expected? Not only was Ce-eviot protected by its elevated position but also by the two dozen or so outlying hillforts. Their defenses were legendary. Next to Fortriu, they possessed the most impenetrable palace in Pictland.

But the strange disquiet lingered. A haunting, unwelcome sensation that reminded her of other times when such intangible intuition had attacked without warning.

Shivering, and this time not from the brisk spring breeze, she turned to make her way down the slope toward the tranquil stone monastery. As always, no matter how she tried to ignore them, her glance snagged on the nearest ancient standing stones that formed part of the massive circle surrounding the holy sanctuary. Her ancestors had used the heathen power of the stones as a conduit to the old gods. And when she was a girl so had she. The recollection of what she used to believe in, who she had once been, caused her to stumble on the uneven ground. Without thinking, she steadied herself on the immense boulder that towered three times her height, the boulder that displayed sacred carvings that predated the origins of their palace by more than two thousand years.

Instantly the comforting mountains, glens and woodlands vanished, sucked into a vicious vortex of screaming wind and howling rage. Breath choked her throat and tears stung her eyes, but she couldn't drag her hand away from the intricate symbols etched over the entirety of the stone.

Her heart hammered and terror snaked deadly tendrils into

her paralyzed brain. Why had she touched the cursed symbols? Images of slaughtered warriors slashed across her mind, crimson blood spraying, the stink of decay twisting her stomach.

Primeval warning pounded through every beat, every breath, a warning she didn't understand, couldn't understand, *didn't believe in.*

Fiery pain catapulted through her fingers as she wrenched her hand from the stone and cradled it with her other. Such a spiteful punishment from a redundant goddess who Aila had long since discarded. Teeth clenched, she concentrated on regulating her heartbeat and calming her erratic breath, as Drun whined in sympathy and pressed his great head against her waist.

It was only a memory of the cursed Vikings. Yet the thought lacked conviction. With loathing, she glared at the serpent, symbol of the goddess Bride, as it coiled around the cauldron carved deep into the face of the boulder.

I don't need you anymore, Bride. The thought glowed with impotent fury and smothered anguish. *You failed me.* What use were warnings when they came too late? What use were visions from the ancients when they did nothing but torment the living with impossible dreams? Dreams she would do anything to see fulfilled but that were now forever beyond her reach.

Bride was dead to her. Still cradling her stinging hand, Aila stamped down the slope toward the monastery, where Bride had been reincarnated as a mortal. Fallible and as such, more easily understood.

More easily tamed into the tapestry of the new religion.

Aila pushed open the timber door and entered the tranquil sanctum, but before the familiar peace could soothe her soul, a discordant thought pierced her mind.

The blood-soaked warriors had not been Vikings.

～

THE DARK STRANGER, his face obscured by swirling shadows, came to Aila again that night. Somewhere deep in her mind she knew this was a dream, the same way she always knew these were dreams. And, as always, she didn't try to resist no matter how much she knew she should.

He cradled her face between his calloused palms, his touch gentle but assured. They were no longer in her bedchamber but somewhere she had never been before, not even in her previous dreams. A secluded glen, and the last rays of the setting sun turned the mountains a fiery crimson, as orange sparks glittered across the rippling surface of the nearby loch.

She flattened her hands against his naked chest and the heat from his skin warmed her in a way she had never been warm in the real world for too many years. His heart thudded beneath her palm and the vibration echoed through her blood, fanning the embers that glowed deep within her.

He trailed his fingers along the column of her throat. Erotic tingles of desire rippled over her exposed flesh, causing tremors across her shoulders and along her arms. His teeth flashed in the twilight at her reaction, but still she couldn't see his face.

She had never seen his face in all the months he had come to her.

"Who are you?" she whispered, but the words were only in her mind because she didn't want to know who he was. Her secret lover was but a figment of her dark pagan imagination.

In the black of night, she did not care.

Again, he smiled as if he could hear her thoughts after all. But he didn't reply. He had never said a word and although a part of her longed to hear his voice, mostly she was relieved. Talking to a dream-lover was one step too close to the edge of madness.

Slowly he unbraided her plaits until her hair cascaded over her shoulders and covered her breasts. He slipped her gown over her arms and her hair brushed against her nipples in a tantalizing caress.

He held her hands and tugged her to the ground. The grasses were soft, like shredded silk, and as he laid her on her back, the softness embraced her as though she sank into the downiest of feathers.

As he loomed over her, his fists planted in the grass beside her shoulders and his calves scarcely touching her thighs, she speared her fingers through his black hair. But even as she pushed his hair back, hoping for a glimpse of his face, he lowered his head and drifted kisses along her throat.

She buried her fingers in his hair, cradling his head, as his lips worked their dark magic. His hot breath teased her sensitized skin and delicious quivers spiraled from wherever his mouth touched, wherever his breath grazed.

He shifted lower, keeping a whisper of distance between them, and his mouth ensnared her nipple. She gasped, reared up, but still couldn't feel the hard ridges of his chest against her. Instead, she felt him smile against her breast, and sharp darts of pleasure arrowed straight to her core.

Restlessly she shifted. She wanted to wrap her legs around him, but he kept her trapped between his thighs. But he didn't smother her with his hard, warrior-toned body, didn't crowd her with his need. She couldn't escape him, but she wasn't his prisoner. He existed only to pleasure her, and her hands fell to his shoulders, her nails clawing his unyielding flesh.

His tongue flicked across her sensitive peak, a wondrous torture. He cupped her other breast, his thumb mimicking his tongue. She wanted to tell him to suck harder, to pinch her nipple, but the words locked in her throat.

He relinquished her breasts and they throbbed with unfulfilled need as he slid farther down her restless body. His breath singed her belly and his fingers teased her waist and hip, trailing seductive ribbons of fire across her trembling skin.

Feverishly she reached for his face. She wanted to kiss him. Kiss him properly on the mouth but he resisted her efforts as he always did. Burning frustration tore through her, but only for an instant as he lowered his head and sprinkled kisses along the seam of her thigh.

He parted her slick folds and slid a finger against her swollen clitoris. Her hands fisted in the grass, her eyes closed, but she couldn't contain the throaty moan that escaped. He circled her sensitive bud, the pressure mounting, unbearable, his uneven breath a sensuous whisper across her damp cleft.

The tip of his tongue glided over her clit. Wet flesh, hot breath and the shocking graze of teeth caused sharp tremors of desire deep inside her. She gripped his hair and tried to pull him up, but he was as immovable as rock and his tongue continued to tease and torture without mercy.

She wanted more. The frenzied thought pounded through her mind and deep in her dream, deep in this secret world that wasn't real, she faced the truth. She wanted him inside her.

With one last blaze of fiery orange, the sun sank behind the mountains and the grass swirled around her in myriad tiny whirlwinds. Her heart slammed against her ribs in denial, but she couldn't hold on to her secret lover. Couldn't hold on to the dream any longer.

The time for dreams is over.

The feminine voice floated through her mind and Aila clenched her teeth in a desperate effort to reclaim the moment, but it faded farther from her grasp with every frenzied heartbeat. Consciousness and cold reality beckoned her and biting her lip to prevent any sound from escaping, she opened her eyes.

The first pink tendrils of dawn slid through the timber shutters, illuminating the sleeping figure of her cousin beside her. Raw frustration rampaged through Aila's blood, no matter how she tried to dampen the lust sizzling between her thighs. A scorching reminder that her wicked dreams, while already fading, affected her just as wantonly in the waking world as in that nighttime cocoon.

She clutched at the tangled bed linen and tried to regulate her erratic breathing and racing pulse. Although the details of her dream were as insubstantial as the early morning mist that gathered in Highland glens, she longed to be back in her mysterious dream-lover's embrace.

Perhaps he would come to her again this night. His visits had become more frequent of late and although she knew it was wrong to wish for those dreams, it made no difference.

No one would ever know of them.

It's time to awaken. The voice was inside her mind yet was surely not her thought. An eerie shiver crawled over her exposed arms and she hastily pulled her furs up to her chin. Perhaps she wasn't as fully awake as she imagined. And then the voice whispered through her mind again, as ethereal as a half-forgotten dream. *A new day awaits.*

THE FOLLOWING afternoon Aila flexed her aching fingers and stared idly through the large arched window as one of the resident peacocks strutted across the grass, displaying his magnificent feathers to his adoring harem.

Two hours earlier one of the monks, Uuen, an incurable gossip, had informed both her and her young noble students of the arrival of a band of Scots. Flanked by a dozen of their own warriors from an outlying hillfort, the Scots were now being entertained at the palace to await the king's return.

As she watched her little sister Finella skip across the grass toward the monastery Aila's mind drifted back to the Scots' unexpected arrival. Doubtless it was connected to the death of King Wrad, whose demise was the cause of her father and younger brother's absence. Did the Scots think to take advantage of the loss of their high king? To try to drive a wedge between the remaining kingdoms?

If so, they would be disappointed. The Picts learned from their mistakes. And fighting each other when their numbers were so depleted was no longer a viable option.

Finella finally reached the window and indicated, by a series of urgent hand gestures, that she wanted Aila to come outside. Aila glanced at her young charges and wished, not for the first time, that her sister displayed some talent for illumination. But Finella couldn't draw or paint to save her skin. Her artistic skills centered on exquisite needlework and with a small smile, Aila trailed her fingertips over the elaborate threadwork of her gown.

"Dismissed," she told her students, who heaved a collective sigh of relief. She only taught those with talent, those who showed eagerness to learn the intricacies of artistry. But if they wished to remain under her charge, she required absolute diligence from them. She stood for no foolishness during her lessons.

Stepping outside, she drew her cloak around her and watched Finella as she raced toward her, dressed in nothing more than her brightly colored gown. As always, her sister had managed to elude her appointed companions.

"Aila." Finella spun to a halt, grabbing hold of Aila's arm to stop herself from toppling over the peacock that ruffled his feathers in clear annoyance. "Did you hear? The Scots have arrived!"

"I heard." She wrapped her arm around Finella's shoulders, and they strolled toward the copse which was a good distance beyond the bronze-smith's forge, a favorite place of hers from childhood. Drun, her faithful shadow, hobbled by her side. "And are they the hairy savages you've always imagined?"

"Oh no." Finella's green eyes widened in awestruck astonishment. "Truly the men are quite beautiful. Although they dress a little oddly and speak with a strange accent, they're scarcely savages. Why would Mamma say such things?"

Finella took everything said to her as the literal truth. Aila smothered a sigh. Had she ever been this naive at ten? They all knew the Scots were savages and the Vikings were devils. It didn't mean they necessarily looked any different from the most noble of Picts.

"A handsome face can hide a corrupt heart. Remember that, Finella." And then her curiosity got the better of her. "What do they want, do you know?"

Her sister shrugged. "Mamma is not inclined to be civil since they refuse to state their business to her. They're here to see Papa." She glanced up. "Mamma is so irate, she plans a great feast this eve to *show them*." Finella raised her eyebrows, clearly not quite understanding their mother's logic. "Will you be there, Aila?"

"No." Her mother didn't need her support, not with her own mother and various visiting relations as allies. If the Scots believed they could bully the queen, they were going to be gratifyingly slaughtered this night by feminine Pictish wit.

That would be worth seeing. She'd watch from the hidden staircase.

Finella heaved a sigh. "I can't stay. I only wanted to tell you about the Scots. I had to pretend I needed the garderobe. Mamma won't let me out of her sight." Her eyes widened in obvious excitement. "She's afraid the Scots will steal me away." The possibility didn't appear to worry her in the least.

Aila didn't blame their mother for her concern. What honor did foreign Scots possess? As a Princess Devorgilla of Ce, Finella always needed to be protected, within the ramparts of the palace and beyond.

"Then you should return." She wheeled around and pointed her sister in the direction of the palace. There were many peasants who toiled at various tasks in the immediate vicinity. Aila knew Finella would come to no harm before she was once again safely within the palace walls and under the protective mantle of her ladies. But she would take no chances. She beckoned one of the men over with orders to accompany her sister back home.

Only when Finella disappeared inside did she turn and make her way toward the secluded copse tended for its vital supply of timber. None of the Picts' round houses or forges intruded in the area. With a sigh, she sat by the edge of the nearby stream and wrapped one arm around her knees and the other around Drun.

She hoped the Scots didn't intend on staying long after her father and brother returned. But they were not expected home for at least a week. Could she avoid their unwelcome guests for that length of time?

Drun, his head in her lap, thumped his tail on the lush grass and awareness trickled along her spine. She was no longer alone. The certainty gripped her, as tangible as the rough fur beneath her fingers.

She had been so concerned about ensuring Finella's safety from the Scots it hadn't occurred to her she should also consider her own. It had been years since she, as befit her status, had her every step shadowed. There was no need when she spent her days teaching in the monastery. And since none of her people would ever dare to creep upon her unawares, that left only one scenario.

Stiffening her already rigid back, she flung a haughty glance over her shoulder, a look designed to intimidate. Instead her breath caught in her throat as an eerie shiver of familiarity prickled her skin and for one dizzying second her heart ceased beating.

He stood on a ridge just a few feet from her, a huge, towering Scot, dark hair whipping across his face in the fresh breeze. A great swathe of blue, green, and black plaid wrapped around his waist and hung over his left shoulder and a broadsword was attached to his leather belt.

A foreign savage from his wild hair to his unadorned boots. And she couldn't move a muscle to defend her territorial rights.

"Forgive me." He spoke in Pictish and his deep voice with its beguiling accent shattered her paralysis as her eyes widened at his breach of protocol in addressing her without invitation. "I didn't mean to startle you."

"Then perhaps you shouldn't approach with such stealth." Irritated by the way her heart refused to calm its erratic flutter, she angled her jaw in an unmistakable gesture of disdain.

He didn't retreat. Instead he began to descend and even though he kept his distance, her heart kicked painfully against her ribs.

She was simply irked that he dared to approach her. But no matter how hard she tried to make herself believe that, she couldn't ignore the sudden constriction in her breasts. It was unnerving, unexpected, and not entirely… unpleasant.

"I didn't know you were here until I almost fell over you." He shot her a disarming smile. For one unbelievable second her lips almost curved upward in response, before she remembered who he was. Who *she* was. And sent him a frosty glare instead.

That didn't appear to touch him. "Do you have any objection if I join you? I could do with a few moments of quiet."

She most certainly did object. It was bad enough he had invaded her solitude. That her treacherous body found his company enticing. Words of dismissal trembled on the tip of her tongue as, for the first time, she caught his gaze.

The words faded, forgotten. His eyes were beautiful, a strangely captivating gray that reminded her of stormy Highland skies.

Disoriented by such a fanciful notion she watched as he sat on the bank of the stream, clearly having taken her silence as acquiescence.

Did he truly not know who she was? Was that even possible? Her fingers toyed with the delicate fringe of her silken veil. Once again, she had forgotten to secure it with one of her gold circlets and the material had long since slipped from her head to drape around her shoulders. The Scot likely did not even realize she was a widow, never mind the eldest Princess Devorgilla of Ce.

Everything she believed in demanded she end this encounter instantly. But what did it matter if she stayed here for just a little longer or kept her identity from him? Never before had she come across someone—a man—who wasn't fully aware of her rank. It might be… interesting to pretend, for a few short minutes, that she was an ordinary noblewoman.

She didn't intend to join in any festivities her mother planned for their guests. He would never discover her deception.

Unnerved by the strange turn of her thoughts she buried her warm face in Drun's rough fur. But even severing eye contact with the Scot didn't serve to change her mind.

~

CONNOR WATCHED the young woman nuzzle her dog and somehow couldn't drag his fascinated gaze away. He'd told her the truth. He hadn't known until a moment ago that she'd settled by the stream. But he had seen her vanish over the ridge. And had decided to follow her with the sole intention of making her acquaintance.

To hell with that. He was interested in more than mere conversation with this woman, although he wasn't sure why. Several noblewomen had already made their interest in the Scots plain. Ewan was, even now, enjoying the delights of two eager young ladies. If all Connor wanted was a quick tumble, there was no need to seek out yet another woman—who might not even be searching for extramarital intrigue.

But even the veiled offers and sexually charged flirting of four of the queen's ladies hadn't managed to diminish the oppressive atmosphere of the royal household, and so he'd made his excuses and left. There would be plenty of time that evening during the feast the queen intended to hold to choose a willing bed partner.

God knew, he needed relief.

Yet for now, he'd wanted a moment of solitude. But something about this lone woman and her injured dog had snagged his interest in a way nothing had come close to in too many years.

So he had followed her, unaccountably more aroused by her cloak-swathed figure than any of the queen's magnificently gowned ladies.

Forearm resting across his knee, he allowed his gaze to roam over her striking hair. He'd never seen anything like it before. An intriguing blend that looked dark gold from one angle and light auburn from another, loosely braided in two long plaits that fell over her shoulders. A vibrant green length of silk concealed her neck and the richly woven cloak wrapped around her body as if they were in the midst of winter instead of an unseasonably warm spring.

She was obviously of the aristocracy. And undoubtedly married, even if she didn't wear the traditional veil over her head as the women of Dal Riada did.

But was she loyal to her husband? Or, like many noblewomen of his acquaintance, looking for illicit excitement outside the shackles of a loveless marriage?

Yet she gave him no encouragement. No sign she was aware of why he'd followed her, why he now sat beside her. Why he waited for her response.

Had he stumbled across one of the few women at Ce-eviot uninterested in enjoying a brief affair with a visiting Scot? And then she raised her head and looked at him.

Eyes as green as her silk regarded him in frank assessment, as if far from being a reticent wife she fully reciprocated his interest. His doubt vanished as a surge of lust speared through his groin.

God, he'd not been so instantly aroused by a woman since he'd been a raw youth.

"My name's Connor MacKenzie of Dunbrae." He offered her a

half-smile, a clear indication of his interest but not too overt to startle should he, by some grievous mischance, have misread the signs. And if that was the case, he could only hope the weight of his plaid disguised his unabashed erection, since if this woman wasn't offering what he imagined, then she'd likely swoon in horror.

Unlike his brother, he wasn't used to seducing complete strangers. If Fergus was in his place, then this woman would be in no doubt of his intentions. And, most likely, would already be in his brother's arms whether she was married or not.

Bizarrely, the notion irritated him. And the woman still hadn't responded.

Neither had she looked away. Unaccountably fascinated by her open regard he stared back, noting the dark lashes that framed her exceptional eyes, the delicate features of her face, and the oddly fragile air that emanated from her heavily swathed figure.

"Aila," she said at last. She no longer sounded aggrieved. "Of Ce."

It was hardly an invitation to share her bed, but it was, at least, encouraging. "Do you live at the palace?" Although to his mind it was nothing but a glorified stronghold. "I didn't see you there this afternoon." There had been a dozen or more of the queen's ladies, who all apparently had urgent need to be in her presence at the Scots' arrival.

"No, I wasn't there." Her lips twitched. Clearly, she was fully aware of his line of thought and found amusement at her peers' salacious curiosity. "I teach in the monastery."

Her casual words, so unexpected, staggered him. Everyone knew the Picts held on to the old pagan ways, despite their outward show of support for Christianity. He'd seen the stone monastery and had briefly wondered at its purpose in this far-flung heathen land. Could they have been mistaken? Had the Picts abandoned their old gods in favor of the only God?

And Aila taught in their monastery? How could a woman teach in a monastery? They were sanctuaries of learning, but no matter how intelligent she was, a woman did not teach.

A thought so horrific punched through his mind that his lust instantly evaporated. Was Aila a holy bride? Wedded to the church? Had he been contemplating seducing a virgin of the Lord?

Then she smiled at him, and it wasn't the smile of a woman who had turned her back on the world of earthly pleasures. It illuminated her pale face, caused her eyes to sparkle with secret mirth. As if she had guessed his trail of thoughts and found them amusing.

He wished he could say the same. Her smile caused his blood to heat with renewed lust, and unwarranted anticipation thundered through him. But he still couldn't straighten out in his mind the thought of a noblewoman teaching in a monastery. And he certainly couldn't wrap his brain around the possibility that she was a bride of Christ.

"And your husband doesn't object?" It was blunt. But at least it would clear up his confusion. Because no matter how desirable Aila of Ce was, he wouldn't risk his immortal soul if she was, indeed, beyond the touch of any mortal man. Even if his damn cock had other ideas.

Her lashes swept down, hiding her eyes and the dog whined, nudging his great head against her waist. Again, her hair captured his attention and he imagined loosening the shining tresses from their bindings, spearing his fingers through the auburn-gold silk, and burying his shaft in her welcoming warmth.

He stealthily shifted on the uncomfortable ground. But his erection refused to diminish. Hell beckoned if Aila was, after all, wedded to the church.

And this time he wasn't thinking only of his immortal soul.

"My husband died nine years ago." There was a quiet pride to her voice and acidic disappointment seared his gut.

A widow. It made no difference, now, whether Aila returned his interest. He would as soon take an untouched maid to his bed as he would a widow, for either would expect more from him than he could give.

"I'm sorry for your loss." More than she would ever know. But as she gazed toward the copse, he couldn't help another glance. Couldn't help but admire the delicate profile of her face. Couldn't help but think she had been widowed while still a bride.

Why hadn't her king arranged for a suitable remarriage? No Scotswoman of noble blood would be left unattached. It was unthinkable.

The Picts couldn't be that indifferent to the security of their warriors' widows. Or was that why she worked in the monastery? Because she had to earn her keep?

CHAPTER 3

$\mathcal{A}$ila risked darting the silent Scot a glance. He was staring into the trees, seemingly lost in thought, a frown darkening his brow.

Her breath quickened as she dragged her heated gaze over his profile. He was too far away for her to reach out and touch, yet he was physically closer to her than any man, aside from her own kin, had been in nine years.

A savage Scot he might be, but he had been touched by the ancient gods when it came to beauty. Hair so black it reminded her of a raven's wing, and although it was shorter than that of Pictish men—barely reaching his shoulders—the wind-tangled mass fascinated her.

Her fingers tightened in Drun's fur as the outrageous notion of sliding those same fingers through the Scot's—through Connor's—hair whispered through her mind. And instead of strangling the thought in its infancy, she lingered over it, savoring the novel sensation. The realization that, unbelievably, the thought of touching another man no longer sent waves of revulsion plundering through her heart.

Acidic guilt speared through her, an ancient pain she'd lived with for more than a third of her life, yet now clouded by the passage of so many years. Involuntarily she sought the comforting weight of her cross. Was it so wrong to find another man intriguing? Connor would be gone soon. She would never see him again. Why shouldn't she have a little fun while he remained? Practice her long unused skills of flirtation on him? At least he, unlike her shadowy dream-lover, would respond.

She clawed through her mind, trying to find a subject to engage his interest. At fifteen she'd had no problem talking to anyone, male or female, whatever their rank. For a second her younger self mocked her for the reclusive woman she had become. For the woman who couldn't find a single thing to say to the man by her side.

The man who appeared more than content to remain staring into the copse. Had she misunderstood the heat of appreciation in his voice when he'd spoken to her? The gleam of approval in his eyes? Connor had told her he'd wanted quiet and she hadn't believed him. But perhaps he'd told her the truth? Because he certainly gave the impression of a man wishing for nothing but his own company now.

The breeze rustled through the grass. If he wanted to be alone then he could leave. This was her special place and if she wished to talk—then she would. She drew in a quick breath and fancied she caught an elusive hint of wild Scot warrior on the breeze.

"How long are you staying in Ce?"

He turned to her and again she was entranced by his stormy eyes. The frown vanished and a half-smile tugged at his lips as if far from wishing to be alone he had only been waiting for her to resume the conversation.

Perhaps that was it. He'd offered his condolences on the death of her husband and had then assumed she no longer wished for his intrusion.

And up until this moment, that was exactly how she always felt.

"Until our business with your king is concluded."

She dearly wanted to know what his business was, but if he refused to confide in her mother, the queen, he certainly wouldn't confide in her—a woman whose rank he was entirely oblivious to.

No matter. Her father would tell them both upon his return.

"I hope," she said, feeling daring and lightheaded and inexcusably young again, "you're not here to provoke war, Connor." How easily his name slipped from her tongue. How easy it was to slip back into the meaningless banter she'd so enjoyed before her premature widowhood.

His eyes crinkled, as if he found her banter equally enjoyable. "War is the last thing on my mind, Aila." She liked the way he said her name in his strange accent. He made her name sound exotic —foreign. She tried without success to ignore the delicious tremors that quivered through her and spilled, like magical stardust, into her bloodstream. But it was hard to remember why such feelings were wrong when his deep voice, hypnotic eyes, and irresistible smile made her feel so right.

Had Scots always been so disarming in their manner? She'd been a child, younger than Finella, the last time any had visited Ce. And then the encounter between their two peoples had been anything but amicable.

"What is on your mind, then?" *Reckless*. What was she saying? But how exhilarating it felt to flirt with danger, to tease with words and a glance. Until this moment, she hadn't even realized how much she'd missed such amusing interaction with a delectable-looking man.

Her ever-present guilt streaked through her heart. Reminding her that she was alive, and while she might no longer deserve death, she certainly didn't deserve a second chance at happiness.

And for the second time that afternoon, she smothered the guilt. Time enough to repent for her moments of pleasure after Connor had left Ce.

For the first time in nine years, she was looking at a man who was looking at her with desire in his eyes. She knew her behavior was unforgivable. She should declare her status and shatter this enchanting spell, but the words lodged in her throat.

Because the truth was, she wanted to hear him say he desired her. Wanted unbiased proof that someone—a stranger—could look at her and see the woman beneath this chilly facade, the woman who yearned to live once more.

"What's on my mind?" He repeated her question and the breath stilled in her breast as anticipation scrambled through her stomach. This was madness. She was behaving like a thirteen-year-old maid, yet she couldn't help herself.

"Yes." Was that really her voice? He would think her shameless. And she didn't care. She had not enjoyed herself so much since—she couldn't even recall.

Connor offered her a smile that looked more pained than passionate. "I'm wondering what it is you do in the monastery, Aila."

She continued to stare at him until the meaning of his words lodged into her brain with the force of a newly crafted arrow. Heat rose in her cheeks, a humiliating burn that radiated throughout the rest of her body.

She had misinterpreted his interest. Mortification paralyzed her and the overwhelming desire to flee flooded her senses.

But she was a princess. With grim determination, she remained motionless, desperate not to show how badly her error had shaken her confidence. Pride, forged through countless generations and refined to an art form during the last few years, surged through her. Rescuing her and preventing any from seeing even a hint of her true thoughts.

Thoughts she had no right harboring in the first place. But that knowledge did nothing to soothe her wounded feelings.

"I'm an artist." He would never guess the wretched turmoil beneath her calm facade. Obviously, she had been too long on her own, ensconced within the familiar love of her family, to judge with any accuracy a man's intent.

While her mind imagined they had played a double-edged game of words, Connor had imagined no such thing.

CONNOR SAW the fiery blush sweep her pale cheeks before it faded just as rapidly. It was the only indication she gave of understanding, in humiliating detail, the reason for his tactical withdrawal.

If he had any sense of honor, he'd make some godforsaken excuse and leave. They both knew attraction sizzled between them. Both knew that, up until mere minutes ago, he would have acted on that attraction had she given him the slightest encouragement.

She had. And he, with as much finesse as a blundering ox, had retreated.

His arse remained rooted to the ground, as his gaze remained fixed on her averted face. And his cock, damn it, refused to accept she was forbidden fruit by virtue of her widowed status.

"An artist?" Why was he prolonging this torture? It was clear she wished him gone. Any woman would wish him gone after having rebuked so gentle an advance. He should seek out one of the married women in the palace, one whose warrior husband accompanied their king, and slake the fire in his blood. The lust-fueled fire that was blinding his good sense when it came to Aila.

She looked at him and inclined her head in a regal manner.

"An illuminator, to be precise." There was no residual hint of breathlessness in her voice. No censure. She was coolly polite, as if the libidinous undercurrents of their previous conversation had existed only in his lascivious mind.

Her cloak slid down her arms to pool around her waist and her vibrant emerald gown exposed her slender frame. Without her protective cloak, the extent of her fragility was potently obvious. She looked as though one robust gust of the famed Highland wind could sweep her away.

Something tightened in his gut. Linked to the lust that still seethed through his blood and yet, somehow, apart.

He ignored it. With more success than he managed to ignore his cursed erection.

"An illuminator?" Mentally he cringed. Was he condemned to repeat every word she uttered? But not only was he finding it difficult to concentrate on her side of the conversation, what he did manage to focus on didn't make sense.

Women, to his knowledge, simply did not undertake the craft of illumination. Clearly, they were at cross-purposes.

She offered him a tight smile that didn't reach her eyes. Her stunning green eyes, that no longer sparkled with mirth.

"My husband taught me the art while I was still a child. I do what I can to ensure the memory of his many achievements lives on."

He watched her as she absently caressed the dog, as her disinterested gaze shifted from him and focused on the trees on the far side of the stream.

Not for the first time her words confused him. Had she not been married to a warrior? The thought gnawed at him. It was scarcely comprehensible. She was of noble blood. She would, undoubtedly, have married one of similar status.

The art of illumination was a craft held sacred by learned monks. How, then, had she ended up with a man of the church? He'd heard of such couplings where husband and wife regarded each other as brother and sister. A marriage devoid of earthly passion, dedicated to the worship of pure, spiritual love.

Not only was she widowed, she was probably a virgin widow. Double the reason to make good his escape. Yet he remained, unable to tear his fascinated gaze from her.

"And you teach others this craft?" But why did she teach? And again, he couldn't imagine why her father or king hadn't arranged a more suitable second marriage for her.

Once more she inclined her head. As if she were a queen and he a lowly subject undeserving of verbal response.

It was glaringly obvious she wished him to leave. His gaze dropped to the dog, who was staring at him with glazed brown eyes. It began to slowly thump its tail on the ground, fully aware of Connor's regard.

Aila gave a scarcely smothered sigh and flattened her hand on the dog's head, clearly willing it to be still.

"Time to go, Drun," she said and as the dog laboriously raised its great head and struggled to its feet, he rose and went toward her.

She stared at his proffered hand as if he offered her a writhing snake. After another second's hesitation, she gripped the gaping edges of her cloak together in one hand and placed her other in his.

Her hand was small, fine-boned, her fingers slender and faintly stained by the tools of her trade. But as her skin brushed his palm, awareness sizzled in his blood and thundered through his chest. As if, instead of a touch as light as a butterfly, she had wrapped her naked body around him and knocked him forcefully to the ground.

Slowly he curled his fingers around hers. Never had his hand so utterly dwarfed that of a woman. His sun-darkened skin stood out in stark relief against the paleness of hers as though she rarely ventured into the outside world, never mind spent any time enjoying the warmth of the sun.

He risked glancing at her face as with utmost care he pulled her to her feet, but her lashes were lowered, shielding her eyes. She clasped her cloak about her at her breast and appeared not in the least affected by their touch.

"Thank you." Her voice was cool as she withdrew her hand,

and he flexed his fingers, trying to eradicate the lingering awareness that clung to his flesh.

"With your leave, I'll escort you back." Aye, because it made perfect sense to spend as much time as he could in the company of this woman. A woman who was not only out of bounds for a brief sexual fling but happened to arouse him to agonizing heights with the slightest touch of her hand.

She didn't even glance at him. "As you wish."

He stared at her retreating back as she made her way up the gentle slope. As dismissals went, it was blatantly clear. Why then was he compelled to follow her? After all, he was the one who no longer wished to continue with a liaison. Wasn't he?

It was a good question, but he couldn't answer it. And instead of turning in the opposite direction, which was the logical course of action, within a few strides he was by her side.

She shot him an oddly furtive glance. The confusion in her eyes, in that one fleeting second as their gazes meshed, sliced into him like a blade. It was obvious she found his continued presence inexplicable.

That made two of them. It wasn't as if he enjoyed self-torture.

The silence screamed between them. He might not be a seasoned seducer of women, but he'd never been tongue-tied around one. He might have been thirteen years old again, and in the presence of a temptress from one of his night fevered fantasies.

Breath hissed between his teeth. Never had his fantasies involved a virgin widow. He'd be damned if he'd start now.

"Hey, boy." He offered his fingers for the dog to sniff. Aila shot him another glance, but there was no confusion in her look this time. It was clearly disapproving. He ignored her obvious wish for him to remain mute. "He's a great age for a deerhound." He'd never seen a dog with so much gray fur and rubbed the creature behind his ears.

"Drun is eleven." Aila glanced at his hand and frowned, clearly wishing Drun might savage him. "I've had him since he was eight weeks old."

"And no doubt he was a great hunter until he retired." He glanced at the dog's ungainly back leg. It looked as if it had been broken in several places.

Aila sighed and one arm escaped her cloak to wrap with loving protection around the dog's neck.

"He would have been the best." She could have been speaking of a favored child, such was the heartbreaking pride in her voice. "But he was never given the chance." She stopped walking and kissed the top of the dog's head. "Were you, my love?" Her voice was soft, gentle, as though she spoke not to an animal but to her beloved.

With a stab of unease, he recalled how Maeve used to call him *my love*. And immediately wondered how it would feel to have Aila look at him with desire in her eyes, to hear her whisper those words as he held her in his arms.

This was madness. She *had* looked at him with desire. And he'd rejected her. He wasn't so arrogant as to assume she would offer herself a second time. And even if she did, it would make no difference.

He only had liaisons with married women.

s Aila threaded a length of glittering blue stones through her cousin Elise's golden hair, she tried to ignore the tremors of agitation that twisted through her stomach every time she thought of how she'd flirted with Connor MacKenzie.

Her only comfort was the knowledge that he was clearly oblivious to her attempts at flirtation. Had he guessed her intense mortification, he surely wouldn't have insisted on accompanying her back to the palace or continued to speak with her as though nothing was amiss.

He had spoken of Drun. Of Ce-eviot's numerous forges. The impressive size of their villages and the palace's incomparable location. It had been a relief to leave him at the palace's gates, so she didn't have to continually respond to his questions or see the half-smile that quirked his lips whenever she happened to glance his way.

"My lady." Floradh, her elderly servant who sat on the ancient oak chest, its intricate carvings hidden beneath many embroidered coverings and cushions, paused in her task of mending a gown. "Why don't you attend the feast this eve? See how many savage Scots Lady Elise can tame with her wondrous smile?"

Aila caught her cousin's reflection in the oval polished-silver mirror and Elise flashed Aila a smile, the smile that could halt a warrior at ten paces and cause him to forsake any good sense he might once have possessed.

Would Connor fall for Elise's charms? Aila didn't doubt it. Elise, unlike her, knew exactly how to enchant a man.

"At least watch from the hidden staircase," Elise said. "The Scots are well worth watching, I assure you."

"I have no desire to watch a pack of Scots make fools of themselves with my countrywomen." Specifically, Connor MacKenzie. Although she had no problem watching other guests embarrass themselves. Indeed, the more foolishly they behaved the more entertaining the night.

For a brief moment, she remembered how much she'd once enjoyed participating in such festivities. But that was long ago. So long ago that the thought of once again joining a feast and having dozens of curious eyes glance her way, of having to make light, inconsequential conversation with strange men, caused her stomach to contract with unformed terror.

And because of her widowhood, because her health had been compromised for so long in her past, her parents didn't insist on her attendance.

She glared at the rich tapestries adorning the walls of her chamber, for once not admiring the vibrancy of the hunting scenes or the delicacy of the details. All she could see were Connor's stormy-gray eyes and his black hair whipping across his face as he stood looking down at her, holding out his hand.

Elise turned to look at her and, with difficulty, Aila dragged her attention from the memory of how Connor MacKenzie's touch had caused illicit desire to streak through her. How degrading. She hoped she never saw him again.

"I, on the other hand," Elise said, "will find great delight in watching the Scots make fools of themselves." She stood up and twirled in front of the mirror, her sapphire-blue gown a perfect match for her eyes. In the glow from the fire, she looked younger than her twenty-one years, as if she had not a care in the world.

But then Elise always did look happier when apart from her elderly husband. To know her cousin was shackled to a man where there was not only a lack of love but also mutual respect grieved Aila to the core of her soul.

She hoped Elise *did* make a magnificent conquest this eve. Just so long as it wasn't Connor MacKenzie.

"I intend to enjoy my six months here without my mother's eye upon me," Elise said and then leaned in close to whisper in Aila's ear, "or having to undertake the onerous duties expected of a wife."

Aila smiled, as Elise clearly expected, but not once had she found the duties of a wife to be onerous. And although for the last nine years the thought of ever taking another man had filled her with a nauseous combination of alarm and terror, her strange, erotic dreams didn't frighten her at all.

They had shocked her at first when they started last midwinter. But now she shamefully craved those dreams, not only for the sensory pleasure but also because her dream-lover fascinated her.

Her dark-haired, stormy-eyed, dream-lover.

The comb slipped from her suddenly nerveless fingers. Hastily she sank to her knees onto the exquisite Persian rug, hiding her face so Elise couldn't see the blood that rushed to her cheeks.

It was only sheer coincidence. She was superimposing Connor's looks on her shadowy stranger and it didn't mean a thing.

She had to change the subject. Her mind had been occupied with Connor ever since she had left him at the palace gates, and it was infuriating. Not least because she knew he wouldn't have spared a second thinking of *her*.

"I'm glad you are here, Elise." They had virtually grown up

together and despite the five-year difference in their ages, had always been close. "It's been too long since you last stayed in Ce."

"Four months and three days. How fortunate the lure of the sea entices my husband more than I could ever hope to do."

Aila caught her cousin's gaze. Elise didn't look unduly concerned by the knowledge. After all, she wasn't the only one of their friends tied to a man where love didn't factor into the arrangement. But even so, it didn't prevent Aila's sense of injustice at the unpleasant choice of mate her cousin had been given. How different Elise's marriage was from her own brief one to Onuist.

"There." Elise straightened her veil. "Now I'm ready to show our barbarous guests an eve of Pictish refinement."

"Tell me every detail when you return tonight." *Unless the details involve...* She strangled the thought before it could take hold. She didn't care if Connor fell under Elise's spell. He could fall under a charging horse for all the difference it made to her.

AFTER AILA HAD EATEN her solitary meal in her antechamber, she stood in front of the fire, warming her hands that didn't need warming and attempting to ignore the rising sensation of frustration flooding through her.

She hadn't been this restless since she'd been a young maid. She had the inexplicable desire to do something, go somewhere, and yet her thoughts were tangled, and nothing made sense.

"My lady?" Floradh's voice pulled her back to reality and she turned to her servant, who was looking at her with an odd expression on her face. "I didn't wish to say anything in front of Lady Elise, but did the Scot offend you earlier this day?"

Aila smothered a groan. She should have guessed her oldest servant would discover a Scot had escorted her back to the palace. Like Uuen, Floradh didn't miss much that occurred in Ce-eviot.

There was no point denying or pretending ignorance. Either would only cause Floradh to assume something illicit had transpired. "No. He merely accompanied me back to the palace."

"Because, my lady, no Scot can be trusted." Floradh's voice rose in agitation. "You shouldn't walk alone while they infest our land."

She had no intention of allowing Connor—of allowing the visiting Scots—to dictate her movements. But Floradh thought only of her safety, and so she battened down her resentment.

"It's been nine years since we last fought the Scots," she reminded the old woman. "They are not our enemy." *At least not at the moment.* But peace between various clans and peoples was so tenuous in Pictland, who could say how long it might last?

Floradh didn't look convinced but appeared resigned to allowing the matter to rest. "Shall I warm the bed for you, my lady?"

Aila glanced at her bed and another wave of restlessness swept through her, fueling her simmering resentment. "No." The decision came instantly, and she swung away from the fire. "I'm going to watch the feast."

"My lady?"

Aila halted by the door and glanced over her shoulder. Floradh was holding out Aila's cloak, a bemused expression on her face.

Aila stared at her cloak, uncomprehending. How had she forgotten to take it? She never went anywhere without it. But then, usually as soon as she moved away from a fire the tips of her fingers would chill and shivers trail over her arms.

With a sense of disbelief, she realized that tonight that hadn't occurred.

Irritated, and not sure why, she snatched the cloak and slung it around her shoulders, for once its familiar weight not wrapping her in a cocoon of comfort. She pulled open her door, waited for dear, faithful Drun to limp outside, before jerking it shut with a satisfying thud.

The stone corridor was chilly, but strangely the cold didn't penetrate into the marrow of her bones. She hesitated, unnerved, before thrusting the thought aside and taking one of the torches from its sconce to light her way. A dark shadow detached from the wall and she stifled an impatient sigh. "I am quite safe by myself."

"My lady." He was of the peasant class but, as all men born within the boundaries of Ce-eviot, he would have received adequate training in case of war. "The queen's orders."

Of course it was the queen's orders. Her mother's opinion of the Scots was scathing, and she wouldn't trust them not to ravish her daughter should they stumble upon her in a dark corner.

Suddenly feeling less inclined to indulge in something that, in the past, had given her hours of secret pleasure, she turned her back on her hulking bodyguard. The staircase she used for her solitary hobby wasn't the main one. It was a narrow, strategically constructed one, hidden between the thickness of the outer and inner walls of the palace. And it curved directly around the feasting hall, giving her a perfect view through the spyhole that had been cut into the massive stone hundreds of years ago.

She settled her shoulder against the wall, tried to ignore the unwelcome presence looming several steps above, and peered down into the hall.

The feast was well underway. Remnants of the first courses littered the high table, where her mother and senior royal relatives sat on ornately carved chairs, and the long table, where everyone else sat on plain benches.

And directly in her sight, as she gazed down at the long table, sat Connor.

Next to Elise.

And he appeared fascinated by the younger woman's animated conversation.

Only years of hiding her innermost emotions prevented her from slumping against the wall. Why did it matter that Connor found Elise so charming? Everybody else did. Especially men.

It was no great surprise. She'd known he would fall for her cousin's sweet charms.

Drun nudged her waist, sensing her distress and she buried her fingers in his rough, comforting fur. Drun, who knew everything there was to know about her, and whom she could trust with her life never to reveal.

Dearest Drun. Until today, whenever one of her melancholy moods attacked, his loyalty had been enough. But until today, her melancholy had only been stirred by memories of her past, never by her present. And most certainly never by a Scot.

Damn Connor. Damn all the Scots. Why had they come to Ce? Why had he found her by the stream this day?

~

CONNOR TOOK a long swallow of mead before turning to the woman by his side. Her bright-blue eyes sparkled with mischief as she regarded him over the rim of her goblet.

"I was always taught," she said in his language, "that Dal Riada was a heathen, barbarous village located on a barren rock."

"I fear you are sadly in need of some further education on the matter."

Her eyes widened. They were beautiful, clear, and deceptively innocent. But for some annoying reason he kept seeing Aila's captivating green eyes instead.

"Connor MacKenzie." Her voice was a breathy caress. "Are you offering to teach me of your savage Scots ways?"

He laughed. And froze as an eerie sensation of being watched crawled along his spine. His warrior instincts sharpened and under pretext of rolling his shoulders, he glanced stealthily along the table.

Nothing appeared amiss. His men were enjoying themselves but, under his orders, were not overindulging in wine or mead. They might not be at war with the Picts, but neither were they yet allies.

But still unease washed through him. As if eyes unseen bored into him, assessing him. And found him wanting.

He banished the thought. His conscience was clear when it came to Aila, even if he regretted causing her a moment's distress. Far better that than starting something that could be all too easily misinterpreted by her—or her kin.

And where was she? The hall was all but bursting at the seams with noblewomen of all ages—but Aila had yet to make an appearance. God, he hadn't upset her to such a degree that she couldn't bear to be in the same chamber with him, had he?

"Connor?" Elise, the exquisite blonde beauty by his side sounded a little impatient, as though she wasn't used to being ignored. He thrust the thought of Aila from his mind. At least he tried to. It was as if she'd dug obstinate hooks into his brain and refused to be dislodged so easily.

He focused on Elise. She may have sounded irritated, but she didn't look it. She was married, her husband was absent, and she was, quite clearly, interested.

And all he could think about was whether he'd hurt Aila more than he'd realized.

"Aye?" Hell, what had she asked him? What had they been talking about? If he wanted any chance of securing this woman's favor tonight, he had to concentrate. Except it had been years since he'd flirted with a woman for the sole purpose of parting her thighs. He'd obviously lost his touch. Become too used to having Maeve.

Elise smiled, as though his distractedness bothered her not at all. "You were about to tell me why you are here, oh savage Scot."

He might not recall what they'd been talking about, but he knew it hadn't anything to do with his king's command.

"Much as it grieves me to disappoint a lady, my words are for your king only." He offered her his most disarming smile. The one Maeve told him possessed the power to melt even the iciest of female heart.

Elise pouted and feathered the tips of her fingers over his hand. But before he could fully enjoy the sensation, once again the inexplicable certainty of being watched shuddered along his spine.

"That's a pity," Elise said, abandoning his hand in favor of toying with the stem of her goblet. "I dearly love gossip."

Her comment, so apparently artless, caused an unintentional laugh to escape him. And once more he fought to banish the feeling of being spied upon. Perhaps he was. But if the Pictish queen hoped to catch him or his men unawares, she was destined to be disappointed.

"Speaking of gossip, I've met with the younger Princess Devorgilla of Ce, but not yet with the elder. Is she at the high table?" He watched the slaves clear the high table in order to display the following course's centerpiece—a magnificent stuffed peacock, replete with vibrant feathers.

When Elise didn't immediately respond, he turned to look at her. She had an odd expression on her face but as soon as she realized his scrutiny, she recovered instantly and bestowed a blinding smile in his direction.

"The eldest Princess Devorgilla?" She raised her eyebrows and made a great pretense of peering up at the high table. "Why, no. I don't believe she is. What is your interest in her?"

"No interest." It wasn't precisely a lie. Even if she was the reason he was in Ce, he personally didn't give a shit where the eldest princess was. It was merely a tactic to discover why not every noblewoman attended this feast. "Mere curiosity, that's all."

"Curiosity is meant to be the preserve of the female of the species."

Amusement flared. "Perhaps we Scots possess more curiosity than you Picts."

"Doubtful."

"So tell me." He angled toward her. "Does your princess insist on her ladies not attending a feast if she doesn't?"

Elise blinked in apparent confusion. "Why should you ask such a thing?"

"I've noticed not all the ladies I saw earlier are in attendance tonight." One in particular. Damned if he knew whether any others were missing.

He watched Elise glance around the table, a faint frown marring her forehead. Finally she looked back at him. "No. I believe everyone who should be here, is." She picked up her goblet, pressed the rim to her lips then hesitated. "Which ladies do you mean?"

Belatedly it occurred to him that mentioning Aila's name would likely do him no favor with Elise. But she was staring at him with an enquiring look on her face and clearly had no intention of allowing him to bypass the issue.

From the corner of his eye, he saw Ewan kiss the fingers of one of the young women he'd disappeared with earlier that day. Obviously, Ewan would not be lacking for bed partners during their stay in Ce.

"I recall only one name." He helped himself to another serving of beef. To show his apparent nonchalance. "I believe she is called Aila."

Elise choked on her wine, but when he turned to her to see if she required assistance, she had already composed herself.

"Are you well?" he said.

"Indeed." She flashed him a smile, but it didn't reach her eyes. They no longer sparkled with mirth. Instead it seemed a dark shadow had touched her soul and as if to reinforce the notion a delicate shudder rippled over her.

Intrigued as to why Aila's name should cause such reaction, he waited for her to continue. But she didn't. She merely played with the stem of her goblet and remained silent, as though her previous exuberant flirting had all been a flimsy facade.

He should change the subject. Focus on Elise. He didn't want to spend yet another night alone and that was exactly his fate if he didn't recall the basic rules of seduction.

Elise was beautiful. Most certainly desirable. But he couldn't rid his mind of Aila.

"Are you acquainted with Lady Aila?"

Elise offered him a restrained smile. Aye, he'd ruined his chances with her. Ewan would find it highly amusing in the morning.

"I'm acquainted with all the queen's ladies."

So she was one of the queen's ladies. How then could she teach in the monastery?

"Is she unwell?" She had worn a cloak despite the mildness of the day. Although why it should concern him, he couldn't fathom.

He wasn't concerned for her health. Merely wanted reassurance she wasn't hiding this night because of him. It was scarcely likely. And yet he couldn't forget the mortified blush that had stained her cheeks. Or erase the insidious feeling that he'd crushed something infinitely precious and fragile.

"Lady Aila is... quite well." Elise's voice was oddly contained, giving the impression her words conveyed their opposite meaning. "Forgive me, Connor." Once again, she brushed her fingertips across his. "I have a fearsome headache. I'll return shortly."

As Elise left the hall, he caught Ewan's knowing grin. Clearly his friend thought an illicit assignation was in process. Unheeding of the orders he'd given his men, Connor drained his tankard, but it did nothing for the rising irritation heating his blood.

In the course of less than half a day, he had managed to grievously insult two young women. For a moment, he contemplated finding a willing serving girl. Perhaps if his cock gained satisfaction it would allow his brain to once again function.

With a smothered curse he stood. He would find Elise and apologize for his behavior. Explain he was merely concerned that he'd offended Aila earlier that day, nothing more. If he was lucky, Elise would forgive him and instead of another night of solitary gratification, he could lose himself in her scented embrace.

WITH A SENSE OF DETACHED INEVITABILITY, Aila watched Connor stride after Elise. She should have stayed in her chambers. At least that way she wouldn't have had to witness, firsthand, Connor succeed in seducing one of her closest friends.

She turned from the spyhole and caught sight of her mother's appointed bodyguard. The thought of returning to Floradh so soon, of having to pretend nothing was wrong, was too much. She didn't want the stuffy, heated confines of her bedchamber. She needed fresh air to clear her head. To scour these foolish emotions that slithered through her chest like poisoned serpents.

What she really needed was for the Scots to leave Ce.

"Come, Drun." She continued down the worn, stone steps, no longer trying to smother her bubbling resentment. Connor's arrival had shattered her equilibrium, scattered her fragile sense of peace. And she didn't like what lurked beneath.

She left the hidden staircase and entered the outer hall of the palace. But before she reached the door, Elise was by her side.

"Aila. I was coming to see you." Elise looked strangely flushed. All Aila could think about was Connor holding Elise in his powerful arms. Crushing his body to hers. Claiming her lips with his.

"I must speak with you." Elise glanced over her shoulder, as if searching for her impatient lover. Aila had no doubt he'd be wonderful. Inventive. Mindful of his lover's pleasure.

God knew, Elise could do with such a man.

But so could she.

She gave a heavy sigh and took Elise's hand. It was chilled. The realization stabbed through her, incomprehensible.

It had been years since she'd experienced such a thing. *She* was the one whose hands were always icy. She only just prevented herself from lifting Elise's hand to stare at it.

"One of the Scots, Connor MacKenzie." Elise's voice was hushed. For the first time Aila noticed the shadows in her cousin's eyes, and presentiment trickled along her arms. "He's been asking about you."

The sensation vaporized and foolish pleasure raced through her. "What did he ask?" Not that she cared. *Much.*

"He wanted to know about the eldest Princess Devorgilla of Ce."

And the pleasure died. He hadn't been asking after her at all. "And what did you tell him?" After the Scots returned to Dal Riada, she would confide in Elise and they could comfort each other as to the cruelty of men. But not yet. Not tonight, when her pride was so wounded.

"Nothing." Elise widened her eyes and looked shocked by the question. "But Aila, that's not all." Again she glanced over her shoulder, and Aila followed her gaze. But the only others in the outer hall besides themselves were countless servants and slaves who were attending to the needs of the feast.

And the needs of the warriors. Her glance slid over to a darkened corner where a slave girl was on her knees before one of the Scots. At least it wasn't Connor.

"He also asked after you. *Aila.*" Elise gripped her fingers. "He thought you were two individual women. And, my love." She cupped Aila's jaw, as though she were the elder cousin instead of five years Aila's junior. "He wants you."

Aila ignored the way her heart knocked in response to Elise's words. "No. He doesn't." She attempted to laugh, failed dismally, so shook her head instead. Even she had limits when it came to maintaining her facade to the outside world. "I do believe it's you he wants, Elise."

Elise's hand slid from Aila's face and gripped her shoulder. "I know you don't believe in our ways anymore. But trust me on this. I know he wants you. And I know a terrible darkness is descending."

Aila recalled the blood-drenched memory—*not vision*—that had assailed her the morning before the Scots' arrival.

"That doesn't mean anything." Not the fantasy that Connor wanted her, or the devastation Elise was so sure was approaching. "There are always wars, Elise."

Bloodshed was a way of life. But since the brutalizing battles against the Vikings four years ago, there had been tentative peace between Pict and Scot. Yet much as she distrusted the Scots, since her disastrous encounter with Connor she had been unable to believe they were here with malicious intention.

As if summoned by their whispered conversation, Connor appeared through the throng. Tall and muscular, his hair no longer a wild black mass, his foreign presence commanded attention. And in that brief, unguarded moment, Aila saw dark, unbridled lust glowing in his eyes.

CHAPTER 5

"*L*adies." Connor's deep voice sent steamy tremors vibrating through her blood, pooling into liquid heat between her thighs. She gripped her cloak as if it were her savior, when all she really wanted to do was let it drop to her feet and allow a cooling breeze to soothe her burning flesh.

She hoped the flames from her torch didn't allow him to witness her blush of mortification. Would this man always catch her off guard?

"Connor." Elise tilted her head to one side and even though Aila couldn't see her face, she knew her cousin would be giving him that sultry glance beneath her lashes that had men begging for more.

"I trust your headache isn't causing you too much pain?" Connor spoke to Elise in Pictish, but for a fleeting second glanced in Aila's direction. Or had she imagined it? The flames so easily distorted vision.

Elise pressed the back of her hand against her forehead. "I'm sure I will survive." She moved toward the Scot. "Now, shall we return to the feasting?"

Connor offered her a half-bow but instead of taking her arm, he turned back to Aila. Her fingers tightened around the torch. What now? Hadn't he covered every topic of polite conversation on their walk back to the palace this afternoon?

"Lady Aila."

She inclined her head. He hadn't been so formal earlier. She almost told him who she really was, simply to see the shock on his face. But what was the point?

It wouldn't change anything.

"Connor." Damned if she would address him any other way. Elise hadn't. And the childishness of her thought caused fresh irritation at how this man managed to unbalance her so completely. Apparently without him even trying, and somehow that made it worse.

"May I escort you and Lady Elise back to the feast?"

From the corner of her eye, she caught the sharp look Elise shot her. *I told you.* Her cousin's thought was as clear as if she had said it aloud.

But Elise had no inkling of what had passed between her and Connor earlier. She knew it wasn't the Scot's fault she'd misinterpreted his attention. But it didn't make her feel any better. He was the first stranger she had willingly engaged in inconsequential banter with since her husband had died. And he had pulled back.

"I've already dined." Could she sound haughtier if she tried? "I was merely going to… take some air."

Their eyes locked. They might have been the only two people in the hall. But even though she was aware of her cousin, even though she knew that two dozen or more people passed through the hall, she couldn't drag her gaze away. The rest of the world faded, muted their incessant noise, leaving her and Connor in a strange, untouched sphere.

"Perhaps," Elise said, shattering the ethereal moment into splinters of stark reality, "we should all take some air. It would greatly relieve my headache and I'm sure Connor won't mind offering us his protection against the night."

Aila shot her cousin a glare that Elise ignored as she turned toward Connor. Who was still staring at Aila. Why did he continue to stare at her?

If she didn't know better, she'd imagine he lusted after her. As Elise imagined.

"It would be my honor." Finally, he looked at Elise and rejection scuttled through Aila's bones.

For God's sake. Disgusted by her reaction to every slightest thing Connor MacKenzie said or did, she thrust the torch toward her bodyguard who took it without a word. If she refused to join them outside, Connor might read more into it than a simple rejection of his company. He might imagine he'd wounded her earlier that day. Might assume she wished to avoid him at all costs.

The last thing she wanted to do was spend any more time with him than absolutely necessary. And it was, of course, absolutely necessary that she accompany him outside with Elise.

Since she couldn't quite justify her logic, she ignored it.

Elise took his arm. With a stab of alarm—*certainly not anticipation*—Aila watched him extend his other arm to her.

Her heart thundered, sending tremors of excitement skittering through her blood. How tragic that she found the notion of holding his arm so intoxicating.

FOR A MOMENT, Connor thought Aila was going to refuse, but then she gave a barely discernible sigh before she rested her hand on his forearm.

Awareness sizzled through his skin where her hand rested against his naked arm. Unbidden, images of them both entirely naked, entirely alone, flashed through his overheated brain. A sideways glance proved Aila looked as coolly remote as ever.

So cool, so remote. Had he imagined her interest earlier this day? Surely a woman couldn't so completely hide her true feelings?

As they approached the doors and Elise chattered inanely, he risked shooting Aila another glance. Did she never remove her cloak? If he hadn't glimpsed her slender figure by the stream, he'd be inclined to believe her quite shapeless.

His cock stirred, reminding him that Aila was anything but shapeless.

The chill of the night was a welcome relief, except it did nothing to relieve the escalating fire in his groin. He tried to focus on Elise, maintain a semblance of sane conversation, but all he could think of was the silent Aila.

Torches blazed outside. It was almost as bright as inside the feasting hall. Pictish warriors stood guard and instead of strolling to a more secluded location, Elise drew them to a halt at the perimeter of the fiery glow.

"It's quite an occasion, isn't it, Aila?" Elise said from his right. "Having so many fierce Scots as our guests?"

Aila's fingers stirred against his arm. He thought she was going to sever their tenuous contact and the insane notion stabbed through his pounding brain to slide his fingers through hers. Trapping her so she had no choice but to remain by his side.

But she didn't remove her hand. She merely caressed his skin, causing the hairs on his arm to stand on end. And damn it, that wasn't all that was standing at attention. If any more blood descended to his groin, he'd likely pass out.

"Are you a fierce Scot, Connor?' Like Elise, Aila spoke in Gaelic, but she sounded only marginally interested in his response. And she remained gazing out into the dark night, apparently fascinated by the view of shadows.

"If the occasion warrants it." He had to stop staring at her. But in the flickering glow from the countless torches, her hair looked more magical. Her profile more delicate.

And the reason for her forbidden status receded even farther into the depths of his conscience.

"If your king commands it." She didn't sound censorious. Merely as though she stated a fact.

And, of course, it was a fact. For any warrior, no matter their nationality.

"My king desires nothing but peace between our people." He couldn't tell her the true reason he was in Ce, but his comment was the truth, nevertheless. Strong political marriages would eliminate, for the most part, the constant need for war.

Finally, she turned to him. The flames obscured the true color of her eyes, but they were no less mysterious for that.

"Peace." There was a wistful note in her voice. "I desire that too. More than anything."

No longer were only the tips of her fingers grazing his flesh. Her entire arm, from wrist to elbow, melded against his, her skin smooth and soft and warm.

How easy it would be to pull her into his embrace. To feel her lips beneath his. To plunge his fingers into her glorious, silken hair. Good sense incinerated and primal desire that had nothing to do with peace between kingdoms blazed through him.

She suddenly stiffened and drew back. And only then did he realize his free hand had reached for her. That he had been a hairsbreadth from stroking his fingers along her face, indulging his fantasy of drawing her into his arms.

Not until her gaze slid from his did it even register that Elise was no longer with them.

Aila pulled her cloak more securely about her. And despite the inferno scorching his reason, an involuntary shiver crawled over his arm at her withdrawal.

"I'll keep you no longer." Her tone was formal, her stance unmistakably aloof. "Goodnight, Connor." Without waiting for his response—but God, what response could he give when what he wanted was the last thing he could take?—she turned and walked regally back to the doors, her dog a faithful shadow.

~

AILA KEPT her temper in check until she entered the palace and caught sight of Elise hovering by the doors to the feasting hall. Her cousin, after ensuring Connor wasn't following, hastened to her side.

"Why are you back so soon?" Elise whispered, sounding put out. Aila swung on her heel and marched toward the concealed stairway, irrationally infuriated by Elise's question. Elise followed her. "Aila, isn't it plain to you? Connor desires you. He can't take his eyes from you."

Aila stamped up the stairs, for once unthinking of Drun's inability to navigate steps without great discomfort. But Elise didn't take the hint and continued to follow her. Only when they reached the door to Aila's chambers and the guard resumed his place along the corridor did she turn, grip Elise's wrist, and pull her into the room.

Floradh glanced up at their entry and after a calculating glance at Aila she retired to the antechamber, leaving them alone in the bedchamber.

"Well?" Elise demanded.

Aila rounded on her. "What possessed you to leave us out there alone?" But the real question was why hadn't she noticed Elise leaving? Was she truly so besotted by the cursed Scot that he blinded her to what happened before her very eyes?

Elise gripped Aila's hands and appeared not to notice when she tried to pull back.

"He was the Scot you were seen walking with earlier today, wasn't he?" Elise appeared thrilled by her deduction and Aila glowered. Obviously that nonevent was now common knowledge. "Why didn't you tell me, Aila? I thought Connor had seen you from afar and wanted to make your closer acquaintance."

Finally, Aila succeeded in wrenching herself free. She flung her cloak onto the oak chest, began to make her way to the fire to warm her hands and then realized there was no need. Her fingers were far from chilled. In fact, she was so irate her skin burned.

"Connor most certainly does not wish to make my closer acquaintance." Just because he kept looking at her, just because he had ignored Elise in favor of addressing *her*—didn't mean anything.

Elise wrapped her arms around her waist and danced across the floor. "I might not have existed for all the notice he took of me." She spun to a halt in front of Aila, amusement bubbling in her voice and glittering in her eyes. "And you can deny it all you wish, but I know you find his appearance pleasing."

Ravishing was how she found Connor, but she could scarcely admit that to herself, never mind her dearest friend. "Elise, it doesn't matter what I may or may not feel toward him. Now will you kindly—"

"Oh, Aila." The gaiety vanished from Elise's voice as she once again gripped Aila's hands.

With a smothered sigh she let her. There was no help for it. She would have to confide, otherwise Elise would keep on and on, convinced she was right about the direction of Connor's regard.

"I would never suggest you could love another. I know how your heart is forever entwined with Onuist." Elise lowered her head as a mark of respect for Aila's young husband, a man she had met only a handful of times while still a child. A man she knew only through songs of the bards and his last magnificent act of heroism that had cost him his life.

Corrosive guilt twisted deep inside Aila. She knew she could never love again. But why did everyone believe that was her fate?

Heat flared through her although she was far from the fire.

Why was she thinking of love? It was lust she felt for Connor. She could admit to that, if nothing else. Yet even that went against the teachings of the church.

The new church.

The church she had embraced after rejecting Bride.

"But, Aila." Elise tugged on her hands to regain her attention. "A little flirtation— what's wrong with that? Connor is beautiful and strong. He would make a wonderful distraction, don't you think?"

He was already a distraction. One she feared would linger long after the Scots had returned to Dal Riada.

"Yes." It was an admission of more than Elise imagined. More than Aila was willing to examine. An admission that, after so many years of welcomed celibacy, primal desire once again stirred deep in her soul. And not for a safe, dream-lover.

Elise smiled in clear triumph. "Then return with me to the feasting hall. Take my place next to Connor. And if—"

"Elise. I offered my friendship earlier this day. I mistook his kindness for something more." Even now, hours later, that admission still possessed the power to make her cringe. "He may not loathe my company, but he most certainly doesn't want what you're suggesting." But why had he followed her if he hadn't been interested?

"But that can't be." Elise frowned, clearly confused. "I know he deeply regards you, Aila. You must be mistaken."

"You also *know* dark devastation is coming." Her voice was scathing, despite the stubborn shard in her soul that refused to entirely disbelieve. "What of that, Elise? How do you reconcile Connor's alleged regard for me with *that?*"

Regret seared her at the stricken look on Elise's face. She had no right to mock Elise's beliefs. Not when for almost two-thirds of her own life she had believed in them also. When she had imagined her destiny lay in becoming a priestess dedicated to the ancient ways.

"I don't know." Elise released her hands and twisted her fingers together, a clear sign of her agitation, and shame clawed through Aila's heart. "The two are connected and yet not. It was so fleeting, Aila. I'll give sacrifice and beg for the goddess' advice."

"I don't want your heathen goddess' advice." The words were out before she could prevent them, poisonous and jagged, suspended between them.

"Do you no longer believe at all, Aila?" Elise sounded wistful.

Aila clenched her fists and fought against the rising turmoil that twisted through her breast and constricted her breathing. "No."

A gust of wind, from seemingly nowhere, whipped the heat from her body. She snatched up her cloak and slung it around her shoulders.

Her impenetrable defense against the outside world.

CHAPTER 6

*E*arly the following morning, Connor was halfway to the copse where he'd encountered Aila before he realized the direction he was heading. With a curse he halted. Why couldn't he get her green eyes and oddly sorrowful expression out of his head?

"Connor," Ewan called, and Connor exhaled a resigned breath as he waited for his friend to reach his side. The gleam in Ewan's eyes left no doubt as to what topic of conversation was on his mind. "I didn't expect to see you up and about so early."

"Nor you." Connor turned so they were no longer facing the direction of the copse. If Aila was, indeed, by the stream he didn't want to come upon her with Ewan although he wasn't entirely sure why.

"I needed a respite." Ewan grinned and slapped Connor on the back. "Why did no one ever tell us how insatiable Pictish noble-women are?"

Was Aila insatiable? Why did he keep thinking of her in that way? He managed a disagreeable grunt in response and scowled at the panorama of mountains and glens.

Last night, his dreams had been filled with erotic images of

Aila in his bed, her unbound hair caressing his burning flesh, and her mouth tormenting his rigid cock. The fantasy had consumed him, splintered his mind, but despite the raw pleasure of his solitary release, a cloud of dissatisfaction lingered. He feared it would linger no matter how often he tried to slake his forbidden desire for Aila.

"And how was the golden-haired beauty you snared?" Ewan rolled his shoulders and massaged the back of his neck. "She looked delectable."

When had Ewan seen him with Aila? He clawed through the rising irritation clouding his reason but still couldn't fathom it. Aila had never entered the feasting hall last night.

"She is doubtless delectable." He sounded as frustrated as he felt. Shit. "But since she is also a widow, you would also know she doesn't interest me in that way." But even saying the words aloud didn't make any difference. They were hollow, meaningless, mocking his previously held convictions.

"Widowed?" Ewan stopped leering and frowned. "Is that what she told you? Then I fear she's leading you astray, Connor." The frown vanished and Ewan grinned. "God, you didn't turn her down because of that, did you? No wonder you're in such a foul temper."

Not a widow? Something dark and malignant coiled deep in his gut. Why had she lied to him?

"Lady Aila has no interest in such intrigues." Not anymore she didn't. And he was starting to wonder if she ever had. Had he mistaken the look in her eyes yesterday? Had she been offering nothing more than polite conversation and it was his own over-heated lust seeing encouragement where there was none?

"Lady Aila?" Ewan slung him another frown. "I've not met Lady Aila. I was referring to the vision of loveliness who appeared to hang on your every word at the feast last night. I believe her name is Lady Elise."

The tight knot in the pit of his stomach eased. Aila hadn't lied to him. Not that it mattered. She was still forbidden to him for a brief affair. Even if she was willing—and he was no longer convinced she ever had been.

"Lady Elise is certainly most desirable." Unfortunately, by the time he'd cooled his blood sufficiently to return to the hall, Elise was nowhere in sight. Neither, naturally, was Aila.

"Yet you didn't take her." Ewan sounded resigned. "Connor, do you intend to wed Maeve?"

"Maeve?" Connor turned to stare at Ewan in disbelief. "No. Why would you think such a thing?"

Ewan shrugged, and glared at the distant mountains as if he wished he'd not brought the subject up. "You like stability in your bedchamber." Ewan tossed him a dark glance. "You always have. I wondered if, now Maeve is free of that bastard, whether you intended to make her your wife."

How had he and Ewan got onto the subject of matrimony? It was one thing to talk about feminine conquests. Quite another to speak of something as serious as wedlock.

"The thought of remarriage has never crossed my mind." He focused on some indeterminate point in the distance. "Maeve and I are no longer together."

Ewan made a gruff noise in the back of his throat and for a few seconds there was a strained silence. Finally, Ewan glanced in his direction once again.

"In that case, it's my duty as your friend and blood brother to ensure that tonight you are well and truly serviced." There was no trace of the fierce awkwardness of a moment ago.

"I don't need your assistance for that." Although he could likely do with some of Ewan's easy charm when it came to seduction, since his own technique was sadly lacking.

Ewan snorted with derisive laughter. "As last night testifies. You'll be doing me a favor. The ladies I entertained would, I believe, be more than eager to join a small party tonight. What do you say? Are you up for it?"

He imagined the two nubile young women Ewan had been with the previous day. Imagined their lithe, naked bodies sliding against his, warm and willing and uninhibited. Why the hell not? He wasn't beholden to any woman and it had been seven years since he'd enjoyed such multiple bed sport.

"I'll think about it." From the corner of his eye, he saw the stone monastery. And as swiftly as that, the frolicking females in his mind transformed into Aila, her mesmeric eyes condemning his fantasies even as her naked body wrapped around him.

"Good." Ewan slung his arm around his shoulder. "We can imagine, for one night, we're both nineteen and carefree once more."

A futile dream. He pulled from Ewan's embrace and gripped his biceps. "I'll meet with you later. There's something I need to do." He strode toward the monastery, even though common sense warned him to retreat, to remain with Ewan, to make unbreakable plans with the noblewomen for that night.

"What?" Ewan sounded astonished. "You're going to the monastery? Do you pray for forgiveness for your sins before you even commit them now?"

Heart thudding, Connor opened the arched timber door. The stone interior was cool, dim, and tranquil and the inexorable passage of the ages clung to the ancient walls and permeated the faintly incense-scented air.

It was like stepping into any one of the centers of learning in Dal Riada. And yet, somehow, entirely different.

Slowly he advanced toward the chancel, where the altar stood. He wondered what heathen sacrifices the Picts used it for before thrusting the images from his mind. It was hard to reconcile the stories he'd learned of the Picts with the reality facing him. Until yesterday he'd thought them a savage race without any finer accomplishments, thirsting only for war.

Movement in the doorway ahead caught his eye and he paused as a man entered from the room beyond. Only the large cross hanging from a chain around his neck gave Connor a clue that he was a monk. There was nothing in the brightly colored tunic that fell to his ankles nor his deep-red hair that flowed well below his shoulders to indicate he was a man dedicated to God.

"Good morning, my son." As had everyone he'd met in Ce, the man spoke his language perfectly. Connor dipped his head in respect. "Your eagerness does you credit."

Connor jerked upward. He'd entered this sacred place with only one thought in his head. To see if Aila was here. And that wasn't the kind of eagerness a monk—even a Pictish monk— would appreciate.

Or even understand.

"Who is it, Uuen?" Summoned from the fevered pit of his imagination, Aila's voice floated from behind the monk. Uuen strolled into the chancel and Connor received the distinct impression that avid curiosity gleamed in the monk's eyes.

He didn't care what glowed in the monk's eyes. Because Aila now appeared in the doorway, her cloak slipped to her waist and draped across her forearms, displaying a captivating hint of cleavage above the exquisitely embroidered bodice of her sky-blue gown. And his previous night's fantasy thundered through his mind in glorious, graphic detail.

AILA STARED at Connor and tried to ignore the way her heart galloped. What was he doing here? At this hour? Hadn't he found more earthly pursuits to enjoy after she'd left him last night? And if so, why wasn't he still enjoying them?

"Lady Aila." He offered her a formal bow, as foreign and exotic as the way he wore his plaid. He sounded entirely unmoved by her appearance and yet despite his indifference his voice curled around her, deep and dark and dangerous.

"Ah. *Lady Aila.*" Uuen's whisper vibrated with a hint of

intrigue. Aila hoped he wouldn't reprimand Connor on his incorrect use of title. She didn't feel up to explaining why she'd deliberately misled him yesterday. Considering the outcome, her reasons now seemed excruciatingly pathetic.

"Connor MacKenzie." Thankfully, her voice sounded as uninterested as his. She hoped. "Are you here to pray for your sins?"

His lips twitched, as if he found her comment amusing. Not that she had intended it to be.

Perhaps she had.

"I wouldn't burden your monks with the list of my transgressions."

"Oh." Uuen stirred against the altar. "It would be a pleasure to hear your confession, Connor MacKenzie. I hear the Scots are veritable propagators of sin."

Illicit tremors of desire curled through her core. Connor was built for sin. She had half expected her shameless imagination to use his face for her dream-lover last night, but if she had dreamed at all, she remembered nothing.

"A weighty charge." Connor didn't appear in the least offended by Uuen's remark. "I trust a longer acquaintance will prove you wrong."

Uuen leaned over the altar, clearly prepared for a lengthy conversation. And of course he was. He loved meeting new people, baiting them, testing their limits. Sometimes she wondered why he'd entered the church when he could have indulged his passion for gossip by becoming a traveling bard.

"What can we assist you with, Connor?" Aila injected a polite note in her voice as she responded in Gaelic, and hoped her expression was merely neutral and not covetous. She studiously avoided glancing at Uuen. He could be annoyingly perceptive at the most awkward of moments.

Connor returned his attention to her. Damn him for invading this private sanctuary. Now, when he left, she would even be reminded of his presence during the hours she devoted to her work.

She ignored the probability that she would have thought of him regardless.

Perhaps something of her feelings did show on her face, after all. His half-smile faded, and his eyes clouded. She told herself she hadn't noticed. That it was a trick of the light. Her fingers clenched in the folds of her cloak. The cloak that was stifling her even though it had slipped to the small of her back and scarcely covered her.

"Forgive me. I didn't mean to intrude."

How could he do anything but intrude? He was a stranger, a foreigner, and his very nationality ensured he couldn't be trusted. And yet even now, deep in a long-buried corner of her being, her lonely heart cried out to trust him.

It made no sense.

"Of course you're not intruding, Connor MacKenzie." Uuen sounded as though he was thoroughly enjoying himself. "If you have no wish to avail my services and unburden your sinful conscience, then perhaps Lady Aila will condescend to give you a tour of our humble establishment?" His emphasis on her personal name was slight but meaningful as he shot her a sideways glance. She hoped Conner had noticed neither.

Aila glared at the monk, who was now smiling at Connor in a bland and unassuming manner. How false. Uuen was many things, but bland and unassuming were not among them.

"I'd like that." Connor sounded sincere but he probably didn't want to offend Uuen by refusing. She couldn't imagine why looking round an old monastery should interest him in the slightest.

It isn't the monastery that interests him.

She lingered on the seductive thought before discarding it in disgust. She had no intention of showing him around. Last night's enforced intimacy had been bad enough and she had no desire to repeat it.

Fully resolved, she looked back at Connor. And the words turned to ashes on her tongue.

Everything about him, from his black hair down to his plain leather boots, enticed her. It wasn't a comfortable realization but that didn't make it any less true. And the truth was—she wanted to spend time with him, no matter how agitating she found him.

He would be gone from Ce soon enough. And then she would never have to endure his intoxicating presence again.

With a long-suffering sigh designed for both men to hear, she turned on her heel.

"Very well." Absently she brushed her fingers across Drun's head as she reentered the hall of learning. Their monastery, although not large, was renowned in Pictland for its incomparable library.

She heard his sharp intake of breath as he followed her, and turned to see him staring, spellbound, at the stone-and-timber shelves full of books.

"Did you think us illiterate savages, Connor?"

"No, of course not." He dragged his gaze from the library to focus on her and she saw the truth in his eyes.

"No matter." She struggled to keep the smile from her lips because what was there to smile about? And yet she couldn't quite succeed. "I was taught Scots were illiterate savages but I'm willing to accept you can read as well as I."

"I believe there's a great deal we can learn from each other, Aila."

Her mouth dried at the bone-melting smile he directed her way. Before her marriage—ah, why did she lie? Even after her marriage she had adored flirting. Adored the doublespeak, the look in a man's eyes when he admired a woman. But she hadn't indulged in such pastimes for years. Hadn't wanted to.

Until yesterday by the stream when she had made a humiliating error in judgment. And she was on the verge of making another now.

Connor meant exactly what he said. There was no secret code to decipher. Any other, more personal, impression she gained from his words existed entirely in her own ripe imagination.

"I'm sure that's true." *Break eye contact.* Yet she couldn't. But if she didn't, he would see she meant more, wanted more, than he offered.

She wrenched her gaze from his and focused on the rows of antiquated books. Without success, she tried to smother the thoughts that now seethed in the dark recesses of her mind. Yesterday all she'd wanted was a dangerous flirtation. But now she couldn't hide the truth from herself. She wanted an illicit liaison.

"We have a glorious history." Her voice was breathless as erotic images, far more potent than her heathen dreams, flooded her mind. She would surely go to hell. "Our records go back centuries."

She was aware he moved to her side. Far too close for propriety or comfort. Despite her good resolve, she shot him a glance and saw the look of awe on his face as he stared at the repository of the entire heritage of her people.

"We have nothing to equal this in Dal Riada." His voice was hushed. It was clear that, far from dismissing the learning of ages as some warriors did, he understood the magnificence of what she showed him.

"Perhaps when you've lived in the Highlands for more than a thousand years your people too will have something worth preserving."

He caught her eye. Amusement glinted "Is that a veiled insult, my lady?"

She hadn't intended it as such but now saw how it could have been received. And yet Connor had chosen not to take offense. A silent sigh quivered through her heart. He was pleasant to talk with. He made it so easy to forget this was simply his natural charm and had nothing to do with him finding her desirable.

How tragic she still harbored the wish that he found her desirable.

"No. Only the truth. My people have been a part of this land forever."

For a moment there was silence, but it wasn't strained. He appeared to genuinely contemplate her words.

"Isn't this land able to embrace the cultures of two different peoples, Aila?"

She wouldn't look at him even though he turned toward her. Even though every fiber of her being screamed at her to look his way.

She looked at him. How could she not? His stormy-gray eyes captivated her, as if they pierced her fragile facade of nonchalance and saw into the heart of her soul.

"I believe this land could embrace anything. But can a Scot embrace a Pict?"

His eyes darkened, as though her words held hidden meaning. But they didn't. She meant them politically, not personally.

Except that was a lie. Even as the words formed on her tongue they had taken on an entirely intimate implication. And still she had voiced them.

"Perhaps," his voice had a husky timbre. "That's the only way two peoples can ever live in peace together."

It was hard to draw breath into her lungs. Her heart skittered, pulse raced, and liquid heat swirled between her thighs. Every word, every glance indicated this conversation seethed with heated undercurrents. But suppose she was wrong? Suppose it all existed in the confines of her mind?

"I would do a great deal to ensure peace in this land." She caught a seductive trace of Connor's exotic, masculine scent and for a moment coherent words fled. "And anything within my power to vanquish the Vikings' insidious advance."

"The Vikings," he said. God help her. He spoke of her deadliest enemies and yet his words were a smoky caress along her jagged nerves. "I too would do anything to vanquish them from our land."

He was no longer smiling. His face was tense, watchful, his eyes never leaving hers.

"Would you?" It was a husky whisper and she scarcely knew what she asked. Only knew she never wanted this moment to end, when Connor looked at her as if she was the only woman in the world.

"Aye." His gaze flicked over her face and hesitated on her parted lips. "They killed my father in the battle of '39."

"I'm sorry." Her fingers tightened on the folds of her cloak to prevent her from reaching out and offering comfort. "We also suffered heavy losses in '39."

Heavy losses? They'd suffered a brutalizing defeat four years ago. As had the Scots.

Connor's gaze meshed with hers. Lightning coursed through her, prickling across her skin, and coiling around her aching nipples. "It would appear to me there's only one enemy in Pictland. And they aren't standing in this room."

Connor stared into Aila's wide eyes and battled the overwhelming urge to fling caution to the wind and drag her into his arms. What if she were a widow? What if by desiring her he was going against every conviction he'd lived by for the last few years?

What if they were in the house of God?

The last thought slithered like a serpent across his mind. He'd forgotten where they were. But whenever he was with Aila he forgot where he damn well was.

"Pict and Scot." Her words were low, breathless. Was she as

affected by their closeness as he? "Allies?" There was a questioning wonderment in her tone, as if such a thing had never seriously occurred to her before.

And why should it? Until six days ago, such a thing had never occurred to him either.

"It has merit." Her head was bare again and as the sun streamed in through the surprisingly large arched windows, the light bathed her in a golden glow. He ached to take her. And not just into his arms.

"Is that why you're here? To negotiate terms of lasting peace?"

While he could think of nothing but seducing Aila, she clearly thought nothing of the kind. With difficulty he shoved his licentious thoughts aside.

"My king would have my head on a spike if he discovered I broke my oath of discretion." He offered her his disarming smile, the one that hadn't affected Elise last night. But last night he hadn't especially wanted it to.

Aila's smile slid from her lips and although she didn't move a muscle, he could feel her retreat with every sense he possessed. Christ. He'd never had that reaction before.

"I certainly don't want that on my conscience." She attempted to smile at him, but it didn't reach her eyes, didn't fool him for a second that something had badly shaken her.

"My lady, are you unwell?" He extended his hand as a gesture of assistance, taking care not to touch her. "You've gone—pale." He could hardly tell her she looked as if she was about to faint.

She flicked her hand at him, dismissing his concern. "I'm quite well. I'm sorry. It's nothing." She turned from him and stared at the astonishing library, offering him an unhindered view of her delicate profile.

Tension vibrated in the air surrounding them. He could tell she was a hairsbreadth from fleeing. He scoured his mind for the reason why she had suddenly withdrawn from him. Why she looked as if she had just pulled back from the grasping jaws of hell.

Something flickered. Had he, by his careless words, given her the impression his king was a barbarous heathen?

"Aila, forgive my depraved humor. I meant only to jest, not offend."

Again, she gave that dismissive gesture. "I know. It's just..." she hesitated and bit her lip and a sense of dread uncoiled in his gut.

"Just what?" Without thinking he gently touched her shoulder and felt the heat of her flesh through the soft fabric, but the sensation registered in only a corner of his mind.

There was something wrong with Aila, something that he'd caused, and he had to discover what.

She expelled a sigh that vibrated through her bones and echoed along his fingers. He could feel the effort she made to remain calm. In control.

"My husband was murdered by Vikings." Her voice was low, but steady. The dread in his gut seeped into his blood as a horrific suspicion formed. "They impaled his head on a spike. It's —it's the last image I have of him."

CHAPTER 7

Revulsion clenched deep in Connor's gut. It was hard enough for a warrior to watch one of his own cut down and mutilated by the Norse barbarians. He couldn't even begin to fathom how a young girl like Aila had coped with such trauma.

He took her hand, and her cloak slid to the worn stone floor. She stared at him but didn't protest at his action and he had the uncomfortable sensation she had tumbled back in time to that horrifying moment.

The recollection that he, through his own clumsy attempts at humor, had inflicted upon her.

He led her to a carved timber chair by one of the windows and continued to hold her hand as she gracefully sat. "Is there anything I can get you?" His voice was gruff. "Shall I call the monk, Uuen?"

She blinked, as though awakening from a dream. A nightmare.

"No." She sounded surprised by his question. Her fingers slid from his. "I'm sorry, Connor. I know it happened long ago but… it still has the power to affect me."

"Of course." Shame burned his throat. "It's not something you could ever forget."

Her dog laid his great head across her lap and she wrapped her arm around his neck. "Yet people have been telling me for years that's exactly what I should do."

He snatched her cloak from the floor and shook it, silently cursing his tactlessness. "An easy command to give." He carefully draped her heavy woolen cloak across her shoulders. A golden chain glittered across her nape and disappeared into the depths of her cleavage. Feeling that he somehow soiled her by such liberty, he jerked his gaze away from the tempting curves of creamy flesh. "You must have been very young."

"Not really." Her free hand went to her breast, and her fingers traced the chain as if reassuring herself it was still there. "I was seventeen." And then she frowned. "Yes. I was young." She sounded surprised. "A bride of two years."

She was the same age as he. And while he had been claiming first blood on the battlefield, she had seen her husband murdered. By their common enemy.

If he hadn't agreed with MacAlpin's plans before, Aila's revelation would have been enough to convince him. He hoped her king returned soon so he no longer had to keep his plans confidential.

He knew Aila would approve. Somehow it was important she agreed although he couldn't fathom why. It was small recompense for the loss of her husband.

It was obvious she'd cared for him. Even if he hadn't been a husband to her in the fullest sense of the word.

And there was his other reason why Aila was so completely off limits. But it made no difference. The longer he was in her company, the tighter she ensnared him. Without even trying.

Last night her face and body had haunted his dreams. But even when he was awake, he couldn't escape her mystical enchantment. No, because he had to deliberately seek her out as if her presence was somehow necessary for his peace of mind.

Except peace of mind was the last thing she gave him.

"So you returned home to Ce and continued your husband's calling." It wasn't a question. The facts were plain. But she gave him a strange look, as if she didn't understand his meaning.

For a moment there was a silence. Then the tip of her tongue flicked over her lips, and his good intentions not to think about her in a base, lustful fashion evaporated as swiftly as dew on a summer morn.

"Would you like to see some of my work?" Her voice was diffident, and her glance slid from his as though she expected him to decline.

His fleeting resolve to make his excuses and leave vanished with insulting ease. Obviously, his body enjoyed the sweet torture it endured while in her company. "I'd be honored."

Her glance met his. Did she doubt his sincerity? But without a word she inclined her head and rose, leaving her cloak draped over the chair.

He watched her open a heavily carved chest. She turned and spread the vellum onto the table and his gaze riveted on the exquisite hunting scene depicted.

Fascinated, he braced his palms on the table, on either side of the vellum. The scene was just over half finished and the brilliant colors and vivid detail rendered him speechless.

This was Aila's work? It had the touch of a master.

"It shows the beginning of time in Pictland."

He shot her a glance then looked back at the illumination. "Not a hunting scene?" There were noblemen and horses in a forest setting, with a waterfall glinting in the distance.

"It's not finished, obviously." Her fingers fluttered over the untouched side of the vellum. "But this is our great High King Cruithne and his seven sons." Her arm grazed his and her silken hair was mere inches from his jaw. He kept his gaze on the vellum. But every sense he possessed vibrated in acute, agonizing awareness of her gentle touch and evocative womanly scent.

Connor was certain she was unaware of the effect she had on him. She pressed more firmly against him as she focused on her art. He held his breath and tensed his muscles, but it didn't ease the pounding need in his blood.

"The seven princes who named our seven provinces." She turned and smiled at him and with a jolt, he realized that shadow of sadness was no longer present in her eyes. Instead they sparkled with life, as they had done down by the stream.

Before he'd rebuffed her.

"Here is Ce." As she reached across him, the curve of her breast brushed his biceps and every muscle clenched with involuntary reaction. For one torturous second, he thought she was offering herself to him, until his lust-fueled senses realized she was only pointing out one of the finished figures, who sat astride a magnificent stallion. "And this is Fidach—prince of our northwestern kin."

"This is..." He struggled to find the right word. Failed. "Remarkable." Part of him wanted to move away from Aila so he could regain full possession of his senses. But the other part—the greater part—rebelled from retreat. He could enjoy her innocent touch and respond intelligently to her conversation. It would simply take—concentration.

"Don't you have anything like this?" She straightened, severing the excruciating featherlike touch, but didn't appear to notice how close they were.

He clawed through the fog in his brain and trampled the lust stampeding through his blood. With every second that passed he became more convinced he'd misread the signs yesterday afternoon.

Aila did not flirt. She just *did*. And it was his misfortune that everything she did he found hopelessly arousing.

"Mostly our illuminations are in texts." He sounded as if a toad were lodged in his throat.

"I teach the texts." She sounded matter of fact, as though it was no great skill. "This," she nodded to the work before them, "is to update our histories. They're starting to disintegrate."

~

AILA WATCHED Connor as he struggled to regain his equilibrium. A bright frisson of triumph streaked through her. He wasn't as immune to her touch as he liked to pretend.

On the heels of that thought slithered the inevitable serpent of guilt. How could she think of such things here, of all places? When only minutes ago they had been talking about Onuist's horrific death?

He had died nine years ago.

And in many ways, so had she. But her heart had continued beating. Her lungs had continued to draw breath. Her old goddess turned deaf ears to her pleas to join Onuist, intent on punishing her by keeping her alive against all rational odds.

In defiance, she'd turned to the new God. And found purpose once more for existing.

Connor turned to her. Admiration glowed in his eyes but was that for her skill with the paint or for herself as a woman?

"I believe the Scots could learn much from the Picts." His voice cocooned her like sun-warmed honey.

"And I believe we could learn much from you, also." Her words sounded husky, but she didn't care. She didn't understand what had happened yesterday by the stream and it no longer even mattered.

The moment shimmered between them and beneath the veneer of civility a wild, primitive desire simmered. She was standing so close to him, she could admire the thick lashes framing his eyes, see the faint scar that slashed along the length of his jaw and inhale his unique male scent of woods and spices and danger.

"Aila." Almost a whisper, his voice caressed her senses as evocatively as if he'd trailed his fingers along her naked arm. He leaned closer to her, his eyes dark, his gaze intent and her breath tangled in delicious anticipation. He was going to kiss her.

"My deepest apologies." Uuen's unapologetic voice sliced through her foolish daydreams as effectively as a newly forged broadsword. It took all her willpower to remain exactly where she was and not leap back, as though he had caught her doing something untoward.

Instead she slowly turned to him and Connor jerked back, suddenly appearing to realize the inappropriateness of their close communion.

She smothered the insane urge to giggle at his obvious discomfort. Because with every second that passed, she became more convinced Connor MacKenzie saw more than an aloof, impenetrable ice maiden whenever he looked at her.

"Yes, Uuen?" Her voice sounded in perfect control, despite her breathlessness. Uuen was too far away to notice any physical signs of her attraction toward Connor and would never guess her true thoughts.

Unfortunately, Uuen's lips twitched. It was obvious he guessed far too accurately. She ignored his pointed pause and refused to break eye contact. Eventually the monk flashed her a knowing grin and gave a half-bow. "Your students await, my lady."

Disbelief trickled along her spine. She'd forgotten about her students. How had she managed to forget something like that? Thank God Uuen had been able to prevent them from entering the library and witness her shamelessly flirting with the Scot.

I wasn't doing anything wrong.

The voice of defiance was surprisingly strong, effectively smothering the coils of guilt that threatened to engulf her. She probed that flare of rebellion, but it didn't waver, didn't back down. With a sense of disbelief, she felt the guilt retreat, fade, *vanish*.

"Lady Aila." Connor's low voice penetrated her bemusement and she looked up at him as he gazed with fierce intent at her. "Would you do me the honor of sitting with me at the feast tonight?"

Her thoughts tumbled, incoherent. But one thing glittered with absolute clarity. Connor wanted to continue their acquaintance. For an abandoned, glorious moment, she almost acquiesced to his request. And then reality returned.

If she dined in the hall this night, there was no chance Connor would remain in ignorance of her true status. It was possible her royal blood would make no difference to him. No. She was convinced it wouldn't.

And yet it would change things. How could it not? She was the eldest Princess Devorgilla of Ce. But with Connor, she was Aila.

She knew she was making absurd distinctions. That Connor's attitude would remain the same toward her. But the possibility of prolonging this intrigue, of snaring this Scot's continued interest without the complication of her lineage coming between them, beckoned like an illicit flame.

She would go to hell for her sins. *Haven't I been to hell already?*

The instant rebuttal shocked, yet excitement sizzled through her at her daring. And still Connor awaited her reply.

"I won't be attending the feast tonight." Yet for the first time since returning to Ce after the death of Onuist, the thought of participating didn't send shivers of terror along her spine.

She thought he was going to ask her why. She could see the question in his eyes and braced herself. But then he appeared to reconsider.

"I'd like to speak with you again, Aila."

From the corner of her eye, she saw Uuen standing in the

doorway, blocking her students from entry. As if he wished to give her additional time alone with the Scot.

Madness, of course. Despite his love of gossip, Uuen would want no such thing for her.

But Connor wanted to see her again.

Her fingers went to grasp her cloak in a gesture of comforting familiarity. Except her cloak remained on her chair. For a second the realization disoriented her. "Perhaps I may venture to the stream this afternoon."

Her words vibrated in the air between them. An invitation? Or merely a statement? The choice was his.

The tension etching his face eased into an irresistible smile. Her breath caught in her lungs and her stomach fluttered as though she were a young maid. It was only a smile, but its power slid into her blood like a potent aphrodisiac from the far-flung, exotic, Eastern Empire.

"Then perhaps," his husky whisper entwined with the lingering magic of his smile, "I also may venture to the stream once again."

She wasn't sure she could reply without him discovering how deeply he affected her. And so she inclined her head and offered him her hand.

His warrior hard fingers slid beneath hers. Such a gentle touch from one accustomed to battle. He bowed before her, his dark head so close as he bent over her hand, she had to hold her breath to prevent herself from burying her face in his wild, Scots hair.

Lips brushed her knuckles. So fleeting she could scarcely feel them at all, yet so profound she felt his touch imprint upon her soul.

He straightened and their gazes locked. Slowly his fingers slid from hers, flesh against flesh. Every second stretched into a golden infinity, focused on the sensitized tips of their fingers as they clung together, as though a force beyond anything she had previously encountered enchained them.

Finally, they separated. Her skin tingled from their contact, as if they had just enjoyed a far more intimate exploration of the flesh than an innocent, everyday farewell.

There had been nothing innocent about that touch. And as she watched Connor stride across the room, a ragged cry of caution echoed through her heart.

If she met Connor by the stream today, she would irrevocably alter the predestined course of her life.

CHAPTER 8

Connor reined in his mount, crossed his forearms across the pommel of his saddle and surveyed the glens below.

"Impressive," Ewan commented as he pulled up alongside. "And the stronghold of Ce-eviot still towers above this mountain."

Connor glanced across the glen toward Ce-eviot. They'd left the formidable ramparts surrounding the lands of the King of Ce for an uninhibited gallop across the countryside. Yet still the Pictish palace dominated the landscape.

No wonder MacAlpin was eager to negotiate. Eager to lay claim to this wealthy northern province through a strategic political marriage.

He glanced back at the two Ce warriors who'd accompanied them and remained on guard some distance off. The excuse had been so no other Ce tribe would attack the lone Scots, but Connor wasn't fooled. The Ce queen trusted them no further than she could see them. Probably not even that.

"Still no sign of the princess?"

Ewan shrugged. "I begin to doubt her existence. I hope to God MacAlpin is certain there's an elder one. I don't want to bear any responsibility in tethering that bonny wee Devorgilla to your brother."

Connor narrowed his eyes against the sun that glinted on distant rivers in the glens. "There's an elder princess. And MacAlpin wasn't exaggerating as to her being a recluse." Which likely meant the rest of his description also rang true. Hard to fathom when the younger princess was such a friendly, mischievous child. "And we can hardly demand to see her when we can't explain our purpose here until their king returns."

Ewan flung him an amused look. "Maybe it's the queen herself who keeps the princess locked away. Maybe she's mad as well as a hag."

"So long as she's capable of bearing an heir. That's all that's required of her."

"I almost feel sorry for your brother." The grin on Ewan's face belied his words. He obviously believed Fergus more than deserved the unappealing, widowed princess.

"Fergus will do his duty." Whether he liked it or not.

"I just hope she's malleable. I don't relish the notion of accompanying a fractious female back to Dal Riada."

Connor shot the glowering Ce horsemen a glance. They were too far away to overhear the conversation but clearly resented the fact they were here at all. "I doubt we'll have much to do with her. Let her entourage deal with her tantrums."

Ewan grunted. "Speaking of tantrums. That damn hotheaded MacNeil started a fight this morning. Can't get it through his thick skull we're trying to ally ourselves with the Picts, not assassinate them one by one."

"I'll talk to him. He can't jeopardize our mission because of his personal feelings." Hell, they all had personal feelings when it came to the Picts. But sometimes a warrior had to follow orders that went against his natural inclinations. And Cameron MacNeil had sworn, back in Dal Riada, that his undying loyalty was Connor's.

A certainty that went beyond fealty to his king and duty to his people coalesced deep in Connor's gut. They couldn't afford to fail in this mission.

~

AFTER THE LAST of her students left the library, Aila took out her vellum and prepared to continue working on the histories of her people. It was an endless task, but she enjoyed it because it absorbed her mind and soothed her soul.

Gave her purpose.

Uuen strolled over and perched on the edge of her desk. After a few moments when it became clear he wasn't going to take her continued silence and refusal to look up at him as blatant signs she didn't want to talk, she gave a loud sigh. "Yes, Uuen?"

"My lady." She could tell by the tone of his voice he was in the mood for gossip. "Your confession yesterday made no mention of a certain Scot warrior."

"That was because I had nothing to confess." She kept her eyes on her work. Her thoughts concerning Connor had been far from pure and most assuredly required absolution. Yet, like her erotic dreams, she had no intention of confessing such things to Uuen.

He settled more comfortably on the edge of her desk and finally she glared up at him. He grinned back. "Excellent. That means we can converse about him in comfort."

"I have no wish to converse about him."

"I have rarely," Uuen said, "seen you so animated in the presence of a stranger. It fills my heart with joy and felicitation."

Aila deepened her glare then gave up. It wasn't worth remaining angry with Uuen because he simply failed to react.

"I'm merely extending hospitality to our guests." Just because she never had before, was quite beside the point.

Uuen raised one eyebrow in clear disbelief. Then he leaned

85

toward her. "And has our handsome Scot confided what brings his savage band to our palace?"

"Why would he confide in me if he hasn't in our queen?"

The monk gave a theatrical sigh, not hiding his disappointment that she had no gossip to share on that subject. "I believe they come in peace."

She was sure they did. "It would be a wonderful thing if Pict and Scot could become allies. Surely then, together, we could eliminate the Viking threat?"

Something flared in his eyes, compassion—regret. But she didn't want his compassion. And she had lived with regret for too long.

Somehow, she knew the coming of the Scots heralded a new beginning. It wasn't simply the attraction she felt for Connor—it was more than that. A bone-deep conviction she didn't understand but couldn't ignore.

"What do the Scots have that we Picts covet?" Uuen appeared to consider the matter. "They live on our lands, are subject to our laws. Even if they break them with every breath they take."

"Yes." She knew all that was true. "But they have strength of numbers. If our warriors united, imagine how formidable we would be."

"Hm." A thoughtful expression creased his face. "That would be worth considering. Of course, it depends what price the Scots demand for such allegiance."

There was no doubt in Aila's mind. "As long as they don't crave human sacrifice to pagan gods, any price would be worth paying."

AILA FOUND HER GRANDMOTHER, Brilicie, dowager queen Eilidh of Ce, in her favored eastern-facing garden. Grandmamma said if the wind was right, she could smell the sea, and it reminded her of her girlhood in the neighboring Kingdom of Circinn.

"Aila." Her grandmother smiled in welcome and patted the stone bench on which she sat. She might have been approaching her sixty-fifth summer but her back was straight, her eyesight clear and mind as sharp as ever.

Aila sat and her cloak slid unhindered to pool onto the bench.

"Not cold?" Her grandmother gave her a searching look. The kind of look she hadn't given her for years. Not since Aila had embraced the new religion to the exclusion of their old.

She decided to ignore *the look*. "It's uncommonly warm today."

"For spring." She couldn't tell whether her grandmother's remark was expressing agreement or not, but it scarcely mattered. The temperature had risen quite astonishingly. "Have you had any further interaction with your mystery Scot, Aila?"

Aila smothered a sigh. It appeared her entire family knew of her conversation with Connor the previous day. As long as that was all they knew. She didn't feel up to explaining the other times they had conversed.

Or touched.

Her fingers curled against her gown and she attempted to push the memory aside. Her grandmother, unfortunately, possessed pagan gifts and she didn't want her innermost secrets exposed.

"Only in passing." She shot her grandmother a glance and saw her lips give a twitch of amusement. "And he isn't my Scot." Belatedly realization dawned. Perhaps she should have said that first?

Their conversation was interrupted by the arrival of her mother who flounced into the garden accompanied by two of her ladies and her personal bodyguard.

"Goddess." Her mamma sounded irritated as she swept her glance around the courtyard at the half dozen servants who tended the garden. "Can I believe my eyes? Are there truly no foul Scots polluting this corner of my kingdom?"

"Calm yourself, Devorgilla," her grandmother said. "They'll be gone soon enough."

Aila tried to ignore the odd pain that twisted through her heart at those words. The Scots would be gone soon. And so would Connor.

"Indeed." Her mamma glowered at her mother. "And if they had the manners to convey to me the purpose of this imposition, they could leave this very day."

"I fear," her grandmother said, "their presence is required for longer than one day. Although not for the purposes they imagine."

Her mamma frowned, trying to make sense of the words, and Aila stifled a resigned sigh. When her grandmother spoke in riddles, people assumed she was channeling a god.

"What do you—" Her mamma glanced at Aila and her eyes widened in apparent astonishment. Then she returned her attention to her mother and Aila saw a meaningful look pass between them.

"No." Aila accompanied her denial by standing up for added emphasis. "I'm not returning to the fold as you so quaintly phrase it. I have no use for your old beliefs so please stop trying to persuade me otherwise."

The two women stared at her, but it was her mamma who finally responded. "I know that, my love. And although it grieves me you chose to discard your gifts— gifts I would sacrifice a great deal to possess as you know—I wasn't thinking of that."

"What were you thinking of, then?" She knew she was overreacting, but she couldn't help it. Why couldn't her kin accept her decision? Even after all these years, she knew they still harbored the illogical belief she would one day reopen her heart to Bride.

So many of their people now worshipped the new God without it affecting their devotion for the ancient ways. But she couldn't stomach the thought of allowing Bride back into her life. Before Onuist died, she'd had no time for the new religion. And now she had no patience for the old.

Her mamma glanced pointedly at the bench. Aila followed her gaze and stared at her discarded cloak.

"This is the first time since you returned from the veil of the Otherworld that I've seen you outside not wearing your cloak."

Despite the heat of the day—and it truly was a hot day—a shiver chased along her arms. Even in the height of summer she would wear a thick shawl. She flexed her fingers, fingers that were not chilled at their tips.

"And is this a sin?" Her voice sounded oddly hushed, mocking her effort not to allow her mamma's awe to affect her.

"No." Again her mamma glanced at her mother. "It's a miracle."

~

IN HER BEDCHAMBER Aila secured her blue silk veil with a gold circlet embedded with three sapphires. The precious circlet had been a wedding present from Onuist, procured at great expense from pirates masquerading, at the time, as merchants. She shook her head, but the veil remained in place.

As it should have remained in place since her wedding day.

What was she thinking, to even consider meeting Connor by the stream? It felt like an assignation, an illicit rendezvous. But what it really felt like was a betrayal of Onuist.

Desperately she clawed through her memories, seeking reassurance in Onuist's familiar features. But all she could recall with clarity was his deep-chestnut hair, his infectious laugh, and the way they had run, as children, hand in hand through sun-filled glens.

With every passing year his face became harder to recollect in detail. And the details she could remember were of the boy he had once been, not the man he had become.

Guilt flared and indecision snaked through her soul. It didn't matter how much she desired Connor, she had no intention of succumbing to an affair. And instantly fevered visions of her lust-fueled dreams filled her mind and fired her blood.

Would it really be so wrong?

Silence condemned her. Her fingers curled around the chain at her throat and she pulled the heavy cross up from where it nestled beneath her bodice. She stared at it in her mirror and the familiar, distressing maelstrom of love and loathing tangled her thoughts and constricted her breath.

This cross, another gift from her seventeen-year-old bridegroom. He had given it to her not because of its religious significance but because of its remarkable heritage.

And nine years ago it, like she, had been wrenched from its moorings.

She shoved the thought aside. She wouldn't think of that time, not now. Not when she was going to meet Connor. If he showed.

Somehow, she knew he would. Just as she knew that if she met with him today, she risked losing forever the fragile peace of mind it had taken her so long to attain.

SHE WASN'T COMING. Connor glanced up at the ridge as if he could make her appear by sheer force of will. But the grassy slope remained void of an enchanting Pictish lady.

Damn it, did she expect him to wait for her all afternoon? His irritation only increased when he realized that, most likely, he *would* wait here all afternoon. Just in case she changed her mind and condescended to meet with him.

He kicked a stone into the stream and tried to recall the last time he had been kept waiting by a woman. And couldn't.

Because Maeve never had, his mistress before her never had and before then—

Before then he had been married. And his wife, God keep her, had never had occasion to keep him waiting.

Aila wasn't going to meet with him. She had never intended to meet with him. It was the sign he needed to reinforce his certainty that by continuing to see her he was in serious danger of compromising his convictions.

So what was he still doing here? In fact, why had he ventured this way at all? It wasn't as though seduction was on either of their minds.

Damn lies.

The notion of seduction haunted his mind and tortured his body. But even knowing this encounter wasn't a prelude to a sexual liaison, he'd looked forward to seeing her again. As if he was a star struck fifteen-year-old boy instead of a warrior of twenty-six whose stars had been seared from his eyes long ago.

No sound alerted him, but a strange awareness prickled the back of his neck. Slowly he turned and Aila stood on the ridge, looking down at him.

CHAPTER 9

He stared at her, spellbound. The afternoon sun cast a halo around the delicate fabric of her sapphire veil, illuminating the gold and auburn of her hair. A light summer shawl caressed her shoulders, allowing him an unhindered view of the blue gown that clung to her breasts and waist and hips.

Only after he'd approached and offered her his hand did he notice the heavy Gaelic-inspired cross. And although it reinforced the twin reasons why he and Aila could never enjoy a brief affair, the warning was distant in his mind.

"My lady." He smiled up at her, because how could he not? With one glance his irritation had dissolved. "Take care."

She smiled back and allowed him to take her hand. "I'm familiar with this land, Connor. I know quite well how to take care."

He clasped her fingers and assisted her down the slope although it was plain she required no such help. "Do you wish to sit by the stream? Or shall we walk for a while?"

Her fingers slid from his and for a second he felt oddly bereft. Yet she didn't turn away. Didn't rebuff him by word or glance. She simply held the folds of her shawl to keep it in place.

"We can walk if you wish." She glanced at the dog by her side. "But not too far. Drun's days of tramping the mountains for hours on end are long past."

Connor followed her glance. "He did well to recover from such an injury. What happened? Did a stag fall on him during a hunt?"

Aila, face averted, ruffled her dog's head. "Not exactly. Although," she hesitated, obviously uncertain whether to continue. "It was a hunt, of sorts."

He couldn't imagine what she meant. "His devotion to you is clear."

This time she did look at him. For a moment, he thought he saw an icy bleakness in her eyes but then she blinked, and it vanished.

"Oh." She offered him a small smile. "The devotion is mutual I can assure you."

Lucky dog. The thought chased through his mind and dark amusement unfurled at the realization he envied a dog Aila's regard. "Then we will walk until the noble Drun wishes to rest."

This time her smile reached her eyes and they sparkled with mirth as they had yesterday. Before his blunder. And the oddest sensation assailed him.

She was made for laughter. And yet an aura of sadness clung to her, as if the loss of her husband was a recent tragedy, still raw.

The dog limped between them, a four-legged chaperone. They followed upstream, leaving the copse and entering untamed woodland, where seclusion beckoned.

Except he wasn't searching for a secluded hollow in which to take Aila. Much as the notion enticed.

"So, Connor." Aila glanced at him as she detoured from the stream. And because he didn't care where she led him, he followed. "What do you think of our Highlands? Isn't it the most beautiful country you've ever seen?"

"Aye." He grinned back at her. "It's beautiful, Aila. But Dal Riada is also beautiful in her own way."

Aila lifted her face to the sun that penetrated the sparse, leafy canopy and her exquisite golden circlet tumbled from her head. As he bent to retrieve it, never taking his eyes from her, the blue veil slid to her shoulders.

She appeared not to notice.

"Dal Riada could never compare." She turned and looked surprised to see him on his knees grasping her circlet. "This land is in my blood."

He rose and offered her the circlet. She took it and then appeared unsure what to do with it.

"And Dal Riada is in mine."

She slid the gold circlet through her fingers and finally placed it back on her head, although she forgot to secure her veil first. He didn't remind her. Wasn't sure why.

"Well," she said. Her circlet was a little off-center, giving her an oddly endearing look. He battled the urge to straighten it before it slid off her hair once again. "We have that in common, at least. A love for our country."

"It's a good start." The words were out before he could prevent them, before he could analyze what, exactly, he meant by them.

"Yes." She didn't appear to think there was anything strange about his remark. And why should she? It could easily refer to a long-term peace between their two peoples.

Wasn't that what he'd intended to convey? Yet even as he tried to convince himself he knew, deep inside, he'd meant something more. Something personal.

"It's a good start." She repeated his comment and he caught her eye, and a flash of awareness seared through his chest. Perhaps she, also, infused the words with intimate possibilities.

Then she looked away, but the connection remained, sizzling in the air between them. He followed her deeper into the woods, where the trees grew closer together and the sunlight faded to green.

And then she paused.

"Perhaps we could rest awhile." She indicated a fallen tree, its mossy trunk a more than serviceable bench. "I don't like to overtax Drun."

"Of course." Hell, he didn't care whether they walked or sat or paddled their feet in a freezing loch in a nearby glen.

She sat, as regally as a queen, and then bent toward Drun and her circlet once again slipped. He caught it at the same instant she did, and their fingers tangled against the slender gold band.

She gave a breathless laugh and he was enchanted to see the blush stain her pale cheeks. "I keep forgetting I'm wearing it."

"It's exquisite." He took the circlet from her limp fingers and examined it. The workmanship was superb. The sapphires genuine. "A family heirloom?" If so, her family was grand indeed. And again, he wondered why her father hadn't insisted on her remarriage. One worthy of her status.

"No. My husband gave it to me on our wedding day. It's quite unconnected to any of our kin."

Her husband. Suddenly he lost interest in discussing the masterful craftsmanship of the circlet. Except if her husband had been able to afford such riches, he had likely been of the nobility. And because he didn't know what else he could say, he handed the band back to her. She took it, traced her fingers over the sapphires and then placed it on her lap.

Carefully he sat next to her. Closer than decorum decreed but not as close as he wished. She didn't appear to mind, unless the way she toyed with her cross was an indication of distress.

His glance snagged on that cross. In Dal Riada many women possessed such items of jewelry although he'd never seen one this elaborate outside of a church.

Realization dawned and it wasn't particularly welcomed. "Another gift from your husband?" He nodded at the item although he couldn't fathom why the damn object offended him. Just knew that it did.

Aila snatched her hand from the cross. "What?" She appeared distracted. "Oh, yes." Her fingers fluttered over the intricate carvings before dropping once more to her lap. "This was a family heirloom. Rumored to have once belonged to Columba himself."

Connor frowned and leaned in to get a closer look at the artifact. If it was a relic from Columba's time, it would make the cross almost three hundred years old.

And it certainly looked it. He'd wondered at its Gaelic influence. Was it possible the Christian saint, who originated from his own ancestors' land across the water, had lived among the Picts long enough to bestow upon them personal items?

Connor had always believed the saint's relics remained on the sacred Isle of Iona. It was one of the reasons the cursed Norsemen kept raiding. For the treasures left there over the centuries.

"A precious heirloom, for sure." No wonder she kept it close to her heart. Not only was it a gift from her dead husband. It had also belonged to the man who'd brought the light to a pagan land.

He knew, now, the Picts weren't the savage heathens he'd first thought. But neither were they truly Christian. The queen and her kin made no secret of the fact they continued to worship the old gods. So why then would a noble-born lady like Aila not follow the conventions of the royal house of Ce?

"It is precious." Aila's voice penetrated his thoughts. She traced one finger over the cross then looked over at him. "It was crafted with a matching casket. The cross fits into the lid. It's a kind of key—lift out the cross and twist the mechanism beneath to open the casket."

"It sounds ingenious." More than precious. Priceless. "A treasured keepsake." From a husband who had clearly loved his bride. Would such a love have transcended the physical? He was beginning to doubt his earlier assumptions. Just because men of the church in Dal Riada followed orders of chastity from Rome didn't necessarily mean the Picts did.

"Yes." Her hand dropped to her lap. "I would have treasured it forever. Not because of its heritage. But because Onuist gave it to me." She hesitated. "But the Vikings stole it nine years ago."

The same time they had murdered her husband. He ached to take her hand in his. To offer comfort. And yet despite how close he sat to her she remained aloof, strangely untouchable, as if his acknowledgement of her deeply held grief would somehow diminish her.

"The Norse have a lot to answer for."

She shot him a glance and in the second their eyes met, he saw surprise and gratitude merge. It was clear she had steeled herself for his pity and his lack warmed her.

But she didn't answer straightaway, as if allowing the memories to fade. The silence soaked into him, oddly companionable, as though they had known each other for a long time and words were not needed to shatter a pause.

Finally, she stirred. And he realized he had been staring at her as she gazed into the woods; staring and not realizing because to look at her was as necessary to him as breathing.

"You know many of my secrets now." She offered him a smile that told him there were many other secrets she kept and had no intention of ever revealing. "Yet I know nothing of you, save you're a savage Scots warrior."

"What else is there to know?" Did she really still think his race savage? "I serve my king. There's nothing else."

"Nothing?"

A sad reflection on his life, yet nonetheless true. "What do you want to know?" Perhaps he could persuade her Scots were as refined as her Picts. Even if their monasteries didn't hold as many books, or their people weren't given a choice in the god they worshipped.

A small smile tugged at her lips. "Are you married, Connor?"

Dull pain twisted his heart. It was his own fault. He should have known her question would be personal because she was a woman, and personal was what women did.

With anyone else, woman or otherwise, he'd turn the subject. He didn't like talking about that time in his past.

But Aila was different. She had told him so much. How could he dishonor her by refusing to share his pain when she had shared hers?

~

AILA SAW the way Connor stiffened at her question. She'd obviously touched a raw nerve, something he never spoke of. And although it made no difference whether he possessed a wife or not, she knew that it did.

It made all the difference.

She rubbed her thumb over the sapphires on her circlet. So few members of the aristocracy married for love. She and Onuist had been an exception and she would rather have cut her own throat than been unfaithful to him.

But that wasn't the norm for most of society. Both husband and wife thought little of taking lovers. Discretion was expected, the occasional bastard was accepted. Marriage was for strengthening allegiances. Love was for pleasure.

Were the Scots any different?

"I was married." There was a strained note in his voice and her fingers tightened on her circlet as his words penetrated. *Was.* Dear God. She hadn't meant to cause him pain by her question, but it was obvious she had. "She died four years ago."

"I'm sorry." She struggled against the urge to reach out to him. Offer him comfort. Instead she stared at her fingers as they gripped her circlet, the gold cutting into her flesh.

"I was at war. As always." Bitterness tinged the last two words, or was that her imagination? Warriors thrived on battle. It was their life. "While I fought the Norse and secured a trophy envied by all, Fearchara fought for survival. But she perished in childbirth."

He had a child.

Her heart wrenched, a physical pain that obliterated the empathy she'd felt for the loss of his wife. Because...

He had a child.

What wouldn't she have done to own the right to say *she* had a child? A living reminder of Onuist. A manifestation of the young, carefree love they had shared. Before the ugly darkness had descended.

Foolishly she thought she'd resigned herself to the fact she would never know the joy of feeling a babe growing within her womb. Never hold her own child in her arms. But the anguish was as raw as ever. The resentment in her heart as fierce.

Yet another reason why she had turned from Bride, the goddess she'd adored as a young girl. The goddess who, on so many occasions during those early years, had teased her with fleeting glimpses of children Bride knew Aila would never have.

"Connor." Her voice was husky, a combination of sorrow for his loss and sorrow for something that could never be hers. "At least you have your child. That's more than some are blessed with."

He looked at her. Stormy-gray eyes glazed with pain-filled memories. For one incomprehensible moment she wondered if he resented the child, could not bear to look upon it because it was the reason for his wife's death. And rejected it, for how could he think such a thing? How could he not rejoice that, even in the midst of death, he'd been given the most precious of gifts?

"No." The word was hollow, and a shiver trickled along Aila's spine as her certainties suddenly shifted. "They tried to save him, but he was already dead before they sliced open her womb."

CHAPTER 10

There were no words of comfort. In silence she curved her hand around his where it lay clenched against his thigh. He didn't jerk away. Instead he curled his fingers around hers and pressed her palm securely against his plaid.

The woodland birds' haunting melodies vibrated in the air and drifted on the breeze. Leaves rustled, Drun sighed. And Connor continued holding her hand.

Eternal moments shimmered with every magnified beat of her heart. His hand imprisoned her and beneath her fingers, even through the thickness of his plaid, she could feel the coiled strength of hard muscle. Yet she knew if she so much as gave the slightest murmur of dissent, he would release her instantly.

She remained silent. And still.

And waited.

Finally, he stirred, but instead of untangling their fingers his grip tightened.

"We were married for barely a year and a half." He looked at her and his smile tore her heart. "All she ever wanted was a child."

"Then you gave her what her heart most desired."

His smile slipped and a frown etched his brow. "I did what?"

He sounded as though he thought she mocked him, yet he didn't loosen his grip on her.

Could he really not see? "Connor, she wanted your babe more than anything. And you gave her that joy. How happy she must have been, knowing your child grew within her."

He stared at her as if she spoke in riddles. "I killed her, Aila. I wasn't even there to offer comfort at the end."

"No." She leaped to her feet, unmindful of her circlet, and grasped his free hand. "God, Connor. Is that what you think?" How could he have thought that? "It was no more your fault than it was hers. It wasn't fair, but life isn't about *fair*. It just *is*. And at least for nine months your wife was, I'm sure, the happiest woman alive."

He stared at her as though her words made no sense. "I would rather her have been barren than to have suffered such agony on my account."

Fragile barriers collapsed and ancient anger, repressed regret and a bleak, bottomless despair streamed through her blood. *Barren.* The word that had haunted her brief marriage to Onuist, despite his laughing assurances they had all the time in the world to make babies.

"Connor, I don't doubt your wife would have suffered any agony on your account. But don't dismiss women so easily. We're more than capable of suffering childbirth entirely for our own purposes." Not that she would know. But she'd spent many hours imagining such things. "Men suppose we live only to give them the heirs they so desire. But we have equal desires also."

His frown intensified. "Aila, I didn't mean to offend by my comments." He sounded as confused as he looked. He clearly had no idea where her outburst had come from and even less as to how he'd caused it.

What had she just done? Horrified by her behavior she broke eye contact and focused on their entwined hands. Oh, dear God. They were holding hands. And she had just verbally attacked him. After he had confessed in a clumsy, masculine manner how much he had loved his wife.

It wasn't Connor's fault that she had been unable to conceive Onuist's child. It wasn't Connor's fault Onuist had died. And he certainly didn't deserve her anger over the long-ago events that had shaped her life.

Mortification at her lack of manners collided with shame at how she had lost control. She hadn't allowed her deepest, most fragile of secrets to surface for years. Somehow, she'd lulled herself into believing she no longer cared about it.

Such tragic self-delusion. Only now could she see that by burying it, far from healing, the wound had continued to fester.

And she had flung the bitter recrimination in Connor's face.

Dear God. *Please let the earth swallow me.*

CONNOR WATCHED the blood ebb from Aila's flushed cheeks and alarm spiked. She looked on the point of fainting and he stood, still clasping her hands.

"Aila, sit down." He tried to maneuver her around but despite her diminutive figure and brittle appearance, she resisted his gentle efforts to have her sit. "Forgive me." Obviously, his thoughtless words had distressed her. What had possessed him to speak of such things? "I should never have spoken so freely." He should not have spoken at all. He rarely mentioned Fearchara. And never had he admitted aloud the acidic guilt that ate through his conscience at the manner of her death.

So why had he broken his golden rule?

Probably because, since meeting Aila, he was breaking every rule he'd ever made?

"No." Her voice was unnaturally high, and she pulled her hands free and clutched the edges of her shawl. "It's I who—truly,

I'm ashamed of my callous words. I'm not usually so… unguarded."

He stood before her, hands at his sides, and didn't have the first idea what he should do.

He wanted to take her in his arms. He wanted to kiss away her tortured words. But although only inches separated them, it was a gulf so vast he feared a wrong step would cause Aila to slip from his grasp forever.

The thought made no sense. Aila wasn't his to lose. Yet still he couldn't reach out to her. Still he couldn't find the words to comfort her.

He cleared his throat. "Nor am I." His voice was gruff. "It was inconsiderate of me to burden you with such things." And again, he could scarcely believe he had. He didn't even speak of Fearchara to Maeve and the two women had been good friends. And it certainly wasn't something he would ever discuss with Ewan.

So why Aila?

"Please don't." Her hand fluttered as if to reinforce her denial. "I only wished to ease your distress. Truly I didn't mean to suggest you were insensible to your wife's innermost feelings."

Was that what she had done? If so, he'd been insensible to *that*.

"Such a thought never crossed my mind."

She looked at him and he imagined he could see tension seeping from her. As though his words reassured. He clawed through his mind for other such words.

"It would never occur to me," he said, "that you would ever intentionally cause distress by word or action."

"I certainly would never wish to cause you any distress, Connor." And then she smiled, a small, tentative smile as though unsure of his reaction.

His chest tightened, the pain jagged yet not wholly unpleasant. Strange. And as he focused on the slight tremble of her lower lip, raw protectiveness seared through him, a primitive urge to pull her close and claim her as his own to the world.

Unnerved by the power of the image, the suddenness of its overwhelming demand, his first reaction was to recoil. But instead he remained rooted to the spot, unable to tear his gaze from her, unable to sever the tenuous connection that shimmered, beyond mortal sight, in the air between them.

The fanciful notion shattered the moment of paralysis, but not the sense of protectiveness that, if anything, gathered momentum by the second. And although a distant sliver of sanity urged caution, he held out his hand.

With only a moment's hesitation Aila placed her hand in his, and he curled his fingers around her. Such a small gesture. Yet somehow, incomprehensibly, significant.

He picked up her abandoned circlet and they began the long walk back to Ce-eviot.

AILA SAT on the bench next to her grandmother in the secluded garden and watched as Finella played with three young kittens at the base of the ancient sundial. The sun was shining. The sky was blue. A riot of purples and pinks and white spring flowers bloomed. Had the grass always been this vivid emerald hue? Had she ever before been able to smell so acutely the sharp tang of the sea in the breeze?

"…of great changes."

Her grandmother paused and stared at her in a pointed manner. Aila stifled a sigh and attempted to concentrate. But since that afternoon with Connor four days ago, when they had both opened locked sections of their souls, she'd found it progressively harder to concentrate on anything that didn't involve a certain black-haired Scot.

"Great changes always occur at this time of year," Aila said. It was safe to assume her grandmother was speaking of some imagined sign from a goddess. Spring was Bride's season, but Aila had no use for any message she might deign to deliver.

"Hm." Her grandmother didn't sound impressed by her deduction. "Since you clearly haven't heard a word I've said, then allow me to change the subject."

Aila smiled indulgently. Shortly she would leave and meet Connor. As they had met every afternoon this week. It was hard to recall what she had once done with her afternoons before his arrival.

"Very well," she said, watching Finella yet not seeing her at all.

She still hadn't told Connor who she really was. Somehow the moment never seemed right. It wasn't the sort of information she could casually throw into the conversation and yet the longer she knew him, the harder such confession became.

Ah, why was she concerning herself with such a detail? She'd tell him soon enough and he wouldn't care for her heritage.

"Although," her grandmother said, "you won't like it."

That finally got her attention. "What won't I like?"

Her grandmother smiled. On anyone else Aila would have considered it a smirk. "I've watched you this last week, my love, and you can deny it all you wish but the truth is plain. The goddess has returned and reentered your heart."

A week ago, had her grandmother suggested such a thing, Aila would have bristled with affront. But today she had to stifle the urge to laugh.

She didn't quite succeed and coughed to cover her indiscretion.

"I can assure you she hasn't." Only one thing had changed during the last week and that was her meeting with Connor. The goddess, such as she existed, certainly had nothing to do with *that*.

"I believe," her grandmother continued, as if Aila hadn't replied, "that young Scot warrior who leads the savages has more on his mind than battle maneuvers."

Aila's amusement faltered. The only ones who knew of her assignations with Connor were Elise and Floradh. Because of course she had to confide in her dearest friend, otherwise she would have burst from contained excitement. And Floradh, her faithful servant, had soon guessed the reason for Aila's change in habits.

But they would tell no one. So how then did her grandmother suspect anything?

"Does he?" She decided to play ignorance. "I wouldn't know."

She knew this strange, magical week couldn't last. Knew that sooner or later Connor would return to Dal Riada and the chance of them ever meeting again was remote.

Knew also that her kin would violently disapprove if they knew of her clandestine meetings with him. Even if the meetings were chaste in action—if certainly not thought.

"And I," her grandmother said, "obviously know a great deal more than you give me credit for."

Was her grandmother telling her that not only did she know Aila was meeting Connor, but she believed the Scot responsible for the changes in Aila this week? She felt the blood heating her cheeks, saw her grandmother's self-satisfied smile and couldn't reconcile the facts in her head.

If her grandmother knew about her secret rendezvous, then why would she smile? And what on earth did any of that have to do with her assertion that the goddess had returned?

She turned toward her, curiosity burning. But before the question could form, her mamma entered the royal garden with her small entourage.

"Good news." She beckoned Finella over before taking her place on the bench beside her mother. "The messenger has returned. Your father, brother and our nobles will arrive first thing in the morning." She wrapped her arm around Finella's shoulders and shot Aila a triumphant smile. "And then those cursed Scots can be on their way."

CHAPTER 11

Connor frowned into his tankard of mead as beside him Ewan extolled the virtues of his latest conquest. The tavern was small, dark, and noisy and, far from the off-duty activity relaxing his mind, it only succeeded in tightening the tension pounding through his brain.

Ewan slammed his tankard onto the timber table, clearly irked by Connor's lack of interest in his exploits. "Do you ever intend to bed this elusive Lady Aila or not?"

Connor's frown slid into a glower. "Watch your mouth." Aila wasn't a woman about whom he would talk in taverns.

Ewan leaned back against the stone wall and eyed him. "So that's how it is."

Connor drained his mead, but it didn't help the throbbing pain inside his skull. "No." Thinking of Aila wasn't like anything he'd experienced before, and he was damn sure it was nothing like Ewan had. So how could his friend say that was how it was when neither of them knew what the devil *it* was?

"No?" Ewan sounded caustic. "Then let me enlighten you. First, you refuse to introduce this lady to me. I can only assume it's because you fear my natural charm will blind her to yours."

Connor snorted. Ewan ignored him.

"Second, you swear me to silence. God, man. I could've discovered her entire history by now. These ladies love nothing more than to gossip about their fellow nobles."

"I know her history." They had spoken of many things over the last few days. She'd told him of her younger brother and sister. In turn, he'd shared a few anecdotes about his childhood with Fergus. And while he didn't know the precise details of her kin, he knew her father was away with the king, and her mother was close to the queen. Within the royal circle, had been her exact words.

"Third," Ewan said, pushing off from the wall and resting his forearm along the table. "And most interestingly if you ask me, not only have you yet to bed the lady but you refuse to take any other in the meantime."

Connor glared into his tankard, but it was empty. Ewan had presented him with ample opportunity to slake his lust over the last few nights and while all the ladies had been enchanting in their own ways, they hadn't been Aila.

Aila was the one he wanted. And the one woman in Ce, it would appear, who had no intention of taking a Scot as her lover.

"Any other," he growled, wondering if the tankard connecting to Ewan's thick skull would manage to shut his friend's mouth, "would fail to satisfy me."

"And there's your problem."

With difficulty Connor unclenched his fingers from the tankard's handle. Smashing it against Ewan's head might give him temporary satisfaction but wouldn't touch the root cause of his current frustration.

He gave his friend another dark glower. "The problem is I'm a Scot and she's a Pict."

To his intense irritation, Ewan smirked. Perhaps he'd use the tankard after all.

"Trust me, Connor. There's no problem at all between a Scot and a Pict in the bedchamber."

"That," Connor said, "is not the problem."

The silence hung between them, heavy with meaning. Finally, Ewan frowned.

"Do you want to take her back to Dal Riada as your mistress?" He sounded torn between astonishment and disbelief. "A woman you haven't even tasted?"

Hell, aye. But reason blocked his want. A hard, relentless reason wrapped in the fragile figure of Aila herself. "She would never leave Ce."

"How do you know? Have you asked her?"

There was no need to ask. He already knew. "And her status is such that she would never consider becoming any man's mistress."

"Goddamn." Ewan sounded shaken. "Are you saying you wish to wed the lady?"

Was that what he was saying? Was that what he wanted? Marriage?

He dragged a hand through his hair, gripped the nape of his neck and leaned back against the wall. Since Fearchara's death, he'd never seriously considered the thought of taking another wife. A welcoming mistress for whenever he required a woman's soft touch had been enough.

But the thought of Aila becoming his mistress didn't, for an obscure reason he couldn't fathom, entirely appeal. Yet what did it matter? She would never leave her beloved Highlands.

And his place was with his king, in Dal Riada.

He heaved himself upright as Cameron MacNeil headed toward their table. Since talking to the younger man the other day, MacNeil had buried his loathing of the Picts and curbed his tendency to respond to taunts with his fists instead of his wit. But he still gave the impression of tethered fury.

Today, that fury looked somewhat appeased.

He pulled out a stool and sat. "Have you heard?"

"Heard what?" Ewan said.

"The Pictish king returns in the morn." Satisfaction gleamed in Cam's eyes. "Then we can leave this pagan place and return to civilization."

"There's still the small matter of negotiations." Ewan flicked his forefinger against the side of his tankard. "I confess I'll miss the sweet comfort of these Pictish ladies."

Cam made a sound of disgust in his throat. Ewan shot him a glance. "Come on, Cam," Ewan said. "Don't try telling us none of them have caught your eye. When you're not scowling, you're not so very ugly. I've seen the way some of the Pictish ladies bat their lashes at you."

Connor knew their time in Ce had always been short. But now the end was in sight. And instead of thinking with pleasure of returning to his home, all he could think was he might never see Aila again.

"I'd rather go blind," Cameron MacNeil said between gritted teeth, "than bed a heathen Pict."

Connor reared to his feet, pushed Cam from his path and shoved his way through the crowded tavern. He needed air. And to get away from MacNeil before he slammed his fist in his face.

He didn't want to leave Aila behind when he returned to Dal Riada. Would she consider leaving Ce for him? He knew how much she loved her homeland. But if he gave her the choice—would she choose to stay?

Or would she choose to embrace a new life?

As his wife?

CONNOR WAS WAITING for her by the stream, as he'd waited for her every afternoon. Her heart lurched in her breast, a painful reminder that soon he would no longer be here waiting for her.

Because soon he would return to Dal Riada. And she, once again, would embrace her solitary existence, despite how the love of her kin encircled her.

He took her hands, as he always took her hands, but this time he pulled her close. The heat of his body sank into her soul and his masculine scent tantalized her senses. He rested his forehead against hers and his uneven breath drifted across her face.

Her lips parted to ease her breathing. He had never held her so before. Had he heard of her father's return? Did he feel, as she did, that this might be the last time they ever met this way?

Tomorrow she would have to tell him who she truly was. And while it would change nothing between them, in the end that didn't even matter. Because once Connor's business with her father was concluded, he would leave Ce-eviot.

"Each afternoon," he said, and his words whispered against her lips, "I fear you may not come to me."

"I promised I would." Their lips were so close. Did she dare steal a kiss? "I never break my word, Connor."

"I cherish your loyalty, Aila."

He had so much more than her loyalty. In the silence of the night, during the quiet moments of the day and whenever she was with him, she faced the truth of her feelings. He filled her heart with joy, her soul with sunshine. She no longer woke each morning with a sense of resignation. Instead she couldn't wait to arise, couldn't wait for her students' lessons to finish. Couldn't wait until the moment when it was time to meet by the stream.

She lifted her head and Connor's lips brushed hers. A fleeting, tantalizing touch. A touch that seared her with a wild, reckless longing.

"I've wanted to kiss you since the first moment I saw you."

His ragged whisper scorched her parted lips. She hadn't been mistaken. "I thought you far from interested that first day. You surely didn't give any indication of your thoughts."

He moved closer. The breadth of his shoulders blocked out

the rest of the world, and his white linen shirt sculpted his impressive chest. And the weave of his plaid branded her through the softness of her gown.

"How could I? You were an aloof Pictish lady and I a mere savage Scot."

She leaned into him, soaking up the hard ridges of his chest, the fresh scent of his hair, the faint sweetness of mead on his breath. "So what has changed?"

"Nothing." His fingers tightened around hers and his eyes enslaved her. "Yet everything."

His words curled through her heart, shimmered in her blood. Nothing. Yet everything. The chance of them having a future together was remote. And yet she had been given this time with him. Moments to savor, to cherish. To remember for the rest of her life.

She wouldn't hold back through fear of ridicule or the possibility he did not feel as strongly as she.

"I never imagined I would ever feel this way again, Connor," she whispered, superstitiously afraid her words might be overheard by a vengeful goddess. "You've shown me the way back into the world I once knew."

He swallowed, as if words lodged in his throat. But that was all right. She hadn't expected him to feel the same. It was enough to know her words affected him sufficiently for such a reaction at all.

"Aila." His voice rasped and his grip on her fingers became painful. "God, there's something I—"

Drun, lying at their feet, lifted his head and growled softly. Connor hesitated and at the same moment, she became aware of movement on the ridge.

Instinctively she pulled back and Connor didn't attempt to restrain her. Turning, she saw another Scot bearing down upon them and stiffened at the cold glance he shot her way.

"Connor." After that one look, he behaved as if she wasn't

even there.

"What is it, Cam?" Connor sounded as though he was struggling not to throttle the other man. Aila wrapped her arm around Drun's neck. Fighting was second nature among men, especially warriors, and rarely meant anything. But she hoped they would settle whatever differences they had without resorting to fists or swords. Violence tarnished and she didn't want anything to tarnish this moment.

"Devorgilla, Queen Brilicie of Ce, commands your presence." There was unmistakable derision in his tone and Aila bristled in affront. How dare he speak her mother's name in such a manner?

Connor looked on the point of declining. Then he exhaled an impatient breath. "I'll come directly." But he didn't move a muscle. Neither did the other Scot. Connor glared. "Thank you for delivering the message, MacNeil."

MacNeil jerked his head at Connor and without so much as a glance in Aila's direction marched back up the ridge.

"Your queen has excellent timing," Connor said and there was a trace of the same derision in his tone as the other Scot had used when speaking of her mother.

"I love my queen." She traced her fingertips over the corded muscle of his chest, and imagined no linen lay between them. *Naked.* How strange that, since meeting Connor, no fevered dreams had enslaved her nights. He covered her fingers with his, pressing her hand against his heart. She dragged her mind back to the present, but only partly succeeded as she realized how much she missed those heated encounters. Especially when now she could imagine her shadowy lover possessed Connor's face. "You can't blame her for not trusting the Scots."

He smiled and shook his head. "It's not your queen I care about." He hesitated. "I haven't pressed you before, Aila, but I would like to know. Is it the eldest Princess Devorgilla who prevents you from attending the nighttime feasts?"

Her heart, already galloping at the way he'd so casually intimated that he cared about her, slammed against her ribs. Now was, perhaps, the perfect time to tell him of her true identity. But the faintest whisper of an idea, an outrageous, scandalous idea, flickered on the edges of her consciousness.

An idea that depended on her concealing her true heritage for just one more night.

"Yes." The word was breathless. And it was the truth. She hoped he wouldn't press further.

"I should like to have words with this elusive princess." He sounded irritated and she had to smother a nervous giggle.

"I'm sure you'll be given the opportunity to tell her exactly what you think of her."

"I'm sure I will." He raised her hand and brushed his lips across her knuckles. His eyes never left hers. "But I doubt I'll waste my breath."

Illicit excitement surged. She now knew exactly when she was going to tell him her true name, and if all went well, he wouldn't possess the breath to speak, let alone condemn her for her mild subterfuge.

"I believe I may cancel my lessons in the morning." He had no idea how rarely she canceled lessons, but that wasn't important. Tomorrow might be the last time they would ever see each other. "I believe I may spend the entire day here, by the stream."

Even though her father was returning in the morning, it would be hours before he was ready to greet his daughters. And he certainly wouldn't grant an audience with the Scots straightaway.

Connor smiled. It was a smile that reached deep into her heart, warming her, reassuring her that her half-formed plans of intrigue for tonight would be more than welcomed.

"I believe so shall I." His smoky whisper stoked her senses, igniting a slow burn that curled deliciously between her thighs.

CHAPTER 12

As Aila peered through the spy hole onto the feast below, her stomach twisted, as if giant fingers clenched her insides. Elise, sitting next to Connor, made her excuses and as she left the table, she pulled a heavy cloak over her head, hiding her face and gown.

Aila straightened and in her haste to meet her cousin, she stumbled over Drun. She grimaced and only just managed not to glance over her shoulder at her bodyguard. It was imperative she give him no cause for suspicion. And rushing down the stairs, falling over Drun, would alert him that his princess was anything but her normal, calm self.

Slowly she descended the curved steps, breathing through her mouth. She had to regain control. If she was this nervous now, how would she fare later?

Fortunately, her mind had no time to dwell on the enticing vision of *later* as Elise appeared. Her face was entirely obscured by the woolen cloak.

"Aila." Elise's voice was strangled. One hand clutched her face through the folds of the cloak. "I have the toothache. I can scarcely speak for pain."

"Oh, I'm sorry to hear that." Aila hoped she sounded more sincere to her bodyguard than she did to herself. "Come, I'll—I'll soothe your pain."

In the flickering glow from the torches, she saw Elise hook a finger into the folds of the cloak and pull it from her face. She appeared on the verge of giggling. Aila glared. Just because she was hiding Elise from her bodyguard's sight didn't mean he might not suddenly approach.

"Please do." Elise, still grinning, emitted a mournful moan that echoed off the stone walls.

Aila closed her eyes and attempted to stifle the bubbles of laughter that tangled with the nerves twisting through her stomach. She had to control herself. Hastily she adjusted Elise's disguise, slung her cousin a stern glare, turned and led the way upstairs.

Once inside her antechamber Aila leaned back against the door and pressed her hand to her mouth. Floradh stood by the door to the bedchamber, clearly ill at ease with Aila's plans. But she had raised no objection and Aila knew she could trust her to remain silent forever on the events of this night.

Elise slung the cloak onto the bed and began to unfasten her gown.

"Hurry, Aila." Her whisper was urgent, but her eyes sparkled with mirth. "I gave strict instructions to Berthe on how long to wait before passing my message onto Connor, but you know how dreamy she is." Elise stepped from her gown. "You don't want him to reach his bedchamber before you."

Aila fumbled with her bodice but her fingers refused to work. In silence Floradh brushed her fingers aside and began to unfasten the ties.

Shouldn't she be feeling guilty? She was about to seduce a Scot. This was no heat-of-the-moment indiscretion. This was a carefully executed plan.

And yet guilt was the last emotion tumbling through her

breast. What she was about to do wasn't wrong. She wasn't betraying Onuist. And even if her church frowned on such things, it was only for tonight.

She deserved one night with Connor. One night to cherish close within her heart, forever, after he had left Ce.

"My lady." Floradh's ancient, beloved face was creased with concern. "You have made suitable preparations for this night, haven't you?"

"Yes." Aila avoided eye contact. Floradh had accompanied her to Fidach when Aila had wed. She loved her servant but there was one thing she had not confided.

Aila's childlessness was put down to the fact her marriage had been so brief. Nobody knew how desperately she had tried to conceive during those two years. Nobody ever would.

Let them all imagine she had taken feminine precautions. As she would allow Floradh and Elise to believe she had done this night.

Elise let out a relieved breath. "The Scots are good company, but it would be disastrous to bear their bastards." She took Aila's gown. "Although doubtless in nine months there will be several half-blood slaves born." Resignation tinged her voice.

Aila took Elise's discarded gown. While she sympathized with the female slaves' lack of choice when it came to servicing visiting warriors—God, she sympathized more than any of them would ever imagine—a shard of envy sliced through her. Bastard or not, she'd do anything to conceive Connor's babe this night.

For a moment she hesitated, her hand clasped around her cross. And then, before she could change her mind, she pulled the chain over her head and slid the cross beneath her pillow.

She wasn't betraying Onuist by going to Connor. Yet removing the cross somehow felt like the right thing to do. The right thing for Connor.

Elise quickly wrapped her cloak around Aila, hiding her hair and pulling the fabric across her face. "Make haste." She kissed her cheek and then wrapped her arms around Drun to prevent him from following her. "I'll see you later."

"Take care, my lady," Floradh said and Aila thought she heard approval in her servant's voice.

But that was probably just her own conscience seeking reassurance. She took a deep breath to calm her fluttering nerves, but it didn't help. She pulled open the door, lowered her head and walked past her bodyguard, who gave her only a fleeting glance.

It had worked. She could scarcely believe it had been so simple to deceive him with her cousin's disguise. Now all she had to do was enter Connor's chamber and wait for his arrival.

CONNOR EYED THE HIGH TABLE, where the queen held court with her intimate circle of ladies. Despite her command that afternoon, she'd kept him waiting for hours before deigning to see him. And then it had been only to inform him of the Pict king's expected arrival.

But during those enforced hours of inactivity, when he'd been required to remain within her antechamber, a thought had formed.

The truculent eldest Princess Devorgilla of Ce clearly kept a tight rein on her ladies. The fact Aila wasn't permitted to attend the feasts attested to that—although at least the princess allowed her more freedom during the day to do as she wished.

When the princess left for Dal Riada, she would certainly insist upon her ladies accompanying her. Aila could well have little choice in the matter. It wasn't particularly noble that he gained a sense of satisfaction from that possibility, but it was the plain truth.

If Aila moved to Dal Riada, the biggest obstacle between them forging a future together was removed.

"Connor MacKenzie." The breathy whisper at his ear jerked

him forcibly back to the present. He turned to see a young noble-woman sliding into Lady Elise's vacant place.

"Aye." He shot Ewan a feral glare, but his friend was otherwise occupied. Perhaps he hadn't sent this lady to him. It would, after all, be in poor taste after he'd all but admitted he wanted a more permanent arrangement with Aila earlier that day.

The lady blinked and shifted on the bench, clearly unnerved by his countenance. "I have a message for you." Her voice was so low he had to bend toward her to catch each word.

"A message?" he prompted when it appeared she had nothing further to say.

"Yes." She drew in a deep breath. "The one you desire above all others is waiting in your bedchamber." The words rushed out, as though she had memorized them.

Lust punched through his groin and his damn cock, already at half-mast through thinking of Aila, hardened with shocking alacrity. His fist clenched on the table and erotic images thudded across his mind.

The one he desired above all others was most certainly *not* waiting in his bedchamber.

"And who is that?" He strove to make his voice nonchalant. Let her imagine he was used to strange ladies approaching him and delivering such messages.

Her eyes widened in astonishment. "But I have no idea." She sounded scandalized which, given the nature of her message, struck him as darkly amusing. "Don't you know which lady you desire above all others?"

"I trust this isn't a jest that Lady Elise is playing." He liked Elise. She was charming and fun. After that first night, she'd dropped her seductive facade and became an enjoyable feast companion.

"Why no. Lady Elise was quite adamant."

So the message did originate from Elise. Could Aila be

waiting in his chambers? Now that the thought had been planted, he couldn't dislodge it. No matter how unlikely he found it.

And yet Elise was Aila's dearest friend. Would she have passed on such a message if it wasn't true?

In the end, it didn't matter. He could no sooner ignore the possibility than he could the reality that tomorrow he faced the Pict king.

He scarcely noticed when his unlikely messenger heaved a sigh and left. But as soon as she was safely back in her seat, he rose and left the hall.

WITH SHAKING FINGERS, Aila plucked a torch from its sconce and, after swiftly ensuring she was alone in this part of the palace, she entered Connor's chamber.

She knew it was the right chamber. Her mother had complained bitterly about giving the Scot leader her best lodging, although pride had decreed she offer him nothing less.

A subdued fire glowed in the fireplace, casting a muted glow and dispelling the chill. It wasn't as richly furnished as her own. But as she approached the recess in the far wall, she saw the quality of the furs and fineness of the linen. Doubtless his mattress was newly stuffed also.

Although why she was thinking of the state of his bed when shortly she would be lying there, she couldn't imagine.

Except she could. It kept her mind occupied. It had been nine years since she had been with a man. For one terrifying moment, her vision blurred, and her heart thundered, as she recalled that last time. The last time she had seen Onuist.

Her fingers clenched around the torch and she dragged herself back to the present. Tonight, with Connor, she would finally destroy the lingering remnants of nightmares that haunted her memories. She would conquer her fear of intimacy with a man who was not Onuist.

She secured the torch into a wall sconce some distance from the bed. Shadows reached out to her, as she stood within the halo of light, swallowing all signs of the fur swathed bed in the recess. But its image was burned into her mind. As too were the images of what she would soon be doing beneath those furs.

The heavy timber door opened, and flickering light spilled through the widening gap. She gripped her fingers together and tremors of anticipation raced over her arms. For the first time in her life she was initiating an illicit liaison and not even a faint echo of guilt haunted her soul.

Connor entered, torch aloft, and then froze as though he saw not her but a dreadful apparition.

Her mouth dried, and her fingers became clammy. This wasn't the reaction she had imagined. Had she made a terrible mistake? She'd thought the second he saw her he would smile, that lust would gleam in his eyes, that he would tug her into his welcoming embrace.

But instead he remained immobile by the door. Should she say something? Go to him? Or wait until he came to her?

CHAPTER 13

"*A*ila?" His voice was low. "Is that you?"

She licked her lips and prayed her voice wouldn't tremble. "Yes."

The door closed behind him. He stepped farther into the chamber and now she could see the way his gaze swept over her. "You're dressed as Lady Elise." Was that a hint of amusement?

Her tension eased and relief flooded through her, leaving her strangely lightheaded. That was why he'd hesitated by the door. Because he had thought she was Elise—and he hadn't wanted Elise.

"It was the only way." To lose her bodyguard. But she didn't want to go into details.

He came to stand before her. "I never thought to see you in my bedchamber."

"Should I leave?" She tilted her head, and her heart melted at the smile he offered her. She doubted she could leave, voluntarily, if her father the king commanded it.

He took her hand and led her toward the bed. Once again nerves danced low in her stomach, nerves but something else as well.

Desire.

Yes, she desired him. Wanted him. It was the reason she had gone to such lengths to be with him tonight. But she wasn't quite *ready* for him. Would he understand? Could she find the words?

He slid the torch into a sconce by the side of the bed. Instantly the shadows vanished. Was that a good thing? Wouldn't it be easier, in the dark?

He turned to her and cradled her face between his calloused hands. For a second, she was transported back to her nighttime fantasies. But her dream-lover was nothing but a figment of her imagination. And Connor was not. His hard fingers holding her so gently was infinitely arousing.

"If you leave, I would have no choice but to follow."

"And drag me back?"

His thumbs grazed her cheeks. "Would I need to drag you back? Would you not come of your own free will?"

A strange thought teased her mind. She would go through hell for him. But she couldn't say that aloud.

"I came here of my own free will. And, as you can see, it took some planning on my part."

As if they had all the time in the world, he slowly slid the cloak from her head and shoulders and carefully draped it at the end of the bed. Then he turned back to her and slipped his hands around her waist.

A light touch. It would take no effort for her to pull away and sever their contact. And yet the heat of his fingers branded her through the fine linen of her gown.

"Are you certain this is what you want?" His forehead rested against hers, reminding her of the moment earlier this day by the stream. "Tell me now if all you intended was to… converse."

A breathy laugh escaped, and she leaned into him, embraced his heat, and flattened her hands against his warrior-hard chest. "There's nothing to stop us from conversing as well."

"Pillow talk?" Amusement heated his tone. Amusement—and rising desire. "You continue to surprise me."

"I trust I always shall." She trailed her fingers over the length of plaid that swept over his shoulder and across his chest. "It would prevent boredom from intruding."

He began to untie one of her plaits, dropping the strip of blue linen onto the floor and teasing free each bound segment. "I'd never be bored with you." He transferred his attention to her other plait as her fingers tightened on his plaid.

He had scarcely touched her yet already desire licked at the apex of her thighs, a molten tongue promising abandoned delights. "Nor I with you."

His fingers speared through her hair, before he clasped her head. "It appears we agree on the fundamentals of a satisfactory life together."

He smiled that devastating smile. The smile that reached into her soul and bathed her in summer sunshine.

It didn't matter whether he meant the words or not. All that mattered was he had said them, and she would be able to savor them in the years ahead. Relive them in her mind, like glittering emeralds in an arid landscape.

His roughened fingertips trailed the length of her throat and across the tops of her shoulders. There he paused, his eyes never leaving hers. "I want you, Aila of Ce. You've haunted my dreams since the moment I first saw you." He traced the edge of her bodice, skimming her flesh, yet he branded her with flame. "I want this night to last forever but, God help me, it's been awhile since—" He cut his words off, inhaled a sharp breath. "I don't want to disappoint you, that's all."

"I don't believe it's possible that you could disappoint me," she whispered. She traced the outline of his lips with her finger. His uneven breath seared her skin. "It's been nine years for me. I have all but forgotten what to do."

He kissed her fingertip, sucked it into his warm mouth, and

nibbled. Entranced, she watched, as though she had never witnessed such foreplay before in her life.

Finally, he released her. "I believe our first course of action should be to remove this exquisite gown." He began to loosen her ties, his knuckles skimming the tops of her breasts as he parted her bodice. "I ache to see your naked body."

Her nipples hardened at his words even though they were still hidden from his scorching gaze. "I trust you won't be disappointed." The words were uneven and as he urged the linen over her breasts, he shot her a bone-melting smile.

"I'll let you know."

She laughed at his unexpected response, and his warm hands slid beneath the fabric and cupped her breasts. The laugh evaporated in her throat. This felt so good. His hands holding her. His thumbs nudging against her erect nipples. His intense gaze never flickering from hers.

"What is your verdict so far?" Her voice was husky. She wanted to touch him, needed to touch him, but her disheveled gown prevented unrestricted movement.

"Favorable." The smoky word wrapped around her. "But I can't make a final judgment on so fleeting an examination."

"Then may I suggest you proceed with all haste?" Amusement mingled with desire. Such a combination she had never imagined feeling tonight. But his teasing words eased her unspoken fears. As if he knew how nervous she was. No matter how much she wanted this. No matter that she was the instigator of this assignation.

"My lady Aila." His hands slid from her flesh and she ached at his withdrawal. "I didn't imagine, from our previous acquaintance, that you possessed so impatient a nature." As he spoke, he tugged at her gown, exposing her breasts, and then he eased the gown over her hips before allowing it to slide down her legs.

The room wasn't chilled and yet she began to shiver. She

clenched her fists against her thighs in an effort not to wrap her arms around her body. To hide from him.

Because, deep in her heart, she didn't want to hide from him. And yet the urge to do just that was great.

"Aila." His tone no longer held a bantering note. "Don't tremble." He cradled her face within his palms and held her gaze as if she wasn't naked and vulnerable before him. "I swear I won't do anything until you're ready. You believe me, don't you?"

She wrapped her hands around his wrists. "It's not that." And it wasn't. No matter how desperate he might be for satisfaction, she wasn't afraid he would hurt her with his passion. "It's—you're the only man I've stood naked before, aside from my husband Onuist."

His tense expression relaxed. "Then climb in the bed and cover yourself. I have no wish to cause you any distress."

For a moment she was tempted. It would be so easy to hide in the bed and wait until he joined her under the furs. But the very fact he had suggested such a thing, when she knew how much he wanted to look at her body, made her pause.

Tonight was all they had. Did she really want to hide under the furs?

"No. This doesn't distress me. It's just very new for me." She slid her hands along his muscled forearms and another tremor entirely unconnected to modesty assailed her. "That's why I tremble."

He swallowed, affected in a way she hadn't intended. "Then I also hope I don't disappoint."

She tightened her grip around his magnificent biceps. Such potent strength flexed beneath her fingers. There was no doubt in her mind that he would never be a disappointment. "I'll let you know."

As she had hoped, he laughed, and the strange tension her confession had created vanished. "I'm under no pressure, then?"

"None." She could scarcely believe they were having this

conversation while she stood naked before him, when seduction scented the air, when only moments ago she'd been seething with nerves. For one glorious second she imagined a lifetime ahead when they could share such moments. And instantly, but not quickly enough, pushed the enticing image from her mind.

She would enjoy tonight. And not think of tomorrow when reality would once again intrude.

CHAPTER 14

He unclasped the brooch on his left shoulder and placed it on top of the chest against the wall. Although he'd told her he ached to see her naked body, so far his gaze hadn't slipped from hers.

It was oddly endearing. As if he understood that the years of abstinence had inevitably weaved unwanted modesty throughout the fabric of her being.

When his hands fell to his leather belt, her glance followed. Fascinated, she watched him drop the belt to the floor before he began to unwind the great length of plaid.

"Do you require any assistance?" She scarcely recognized the smoky voice as her own.

He tossed the plaid from his shoulder and the rest of the material fell to the floor, leaving him clad in only his knee-length linen shirt and boots. "Aye."

She tugged at the fastenings and he bent toward her, allowing her access to pull the shirt over his head. She felt clumsy, like an untried maid, but it didn't prevent her from flinging his shirt across the floor or gazing at his sculpted chest in reverent wonder.

"What is your verdict?" His voice throbbed with need.

She flicked the tip of her tongue over her lips. A dusting of dark hair shadowed his chest and scars of battle scored his hard warrior body. So utterly different from anything she had previously experienced. "Favorable."

A laugh rumbled. "Then we are even."

Even as he reached out to her, her glance slid down. The flickering torches cast darkness and light across his groin but couldn't disguise the extent of his arousal. His cock, fully erect, thrust upward, his length impressive, his girth surely impossible.

Had she forgotten so much?

"Aila." His heated whisper ignited her senses as he pulled her into his arms, and his rigid length scorched her belly. "My sweet Pictish lady." His hands slid along the length of her back, sculpting the lines of her body, tantalizing and tender.

She mirrored his movements, molding her palms over the hard planes of his shoulders and back, before gliding over the taut muscles of his buttocks. He jerked against her, his hot shaft searing her flesh, and molten need spiraled through her.

Without a word, he lifted her in his arms, and she clung on to his shoulders although she knew he would never drop her. With infinite tenderness, he lowered her onto the furs and sat beside her.

"Come into the bed." She wanted to wrap herself around him. Feel his hard body meld with hers. Hold him close in her arms this night and within her heart forever more.

He grinned and pulled off one boot. "I intend to." He discarded his second boot and turned so he was lying beside her, looking at her. "Your hair is like the finest of spun silk." He slid a long curl between his fingers. "I've never seen such beautiful hair."

"You can thank my grandmother. I have her coloring." She flattened her palm over his heart, feeling the beat echo through her blood. "I like your chest." The words were out before she could prevent them. God! He would think her infantile. Yet the truth remained.

She liked his chest. It was scarred, sprinkled with hair and so enticingly broad.

The chest of a man. A warrior. But why had she allowed such a thought to spill from her lips?

Even as she cursed her tongue he laughed, a deep, rumbling laugh that vibrated through her body. His hand left her hair and trailed across her breasts, thumb dragging across her sensitized nipples.

"And I like your chest." Before she could draw breath, he stole a fleeting kiss. "Very much." His words grazed her lips, as his hand cupped her breast.

"So once again," her voice was breathless in his mouth, "we are even."

His tongue stroked the inside of her lip, an intimate caress that sent tremors cascading along her exposed flesh. Involuntarily her fingers clenched over his heart, and his unyielding muscles thrilled her soul.

"It appears we are in perfect agreement." His husky words mingled with her breath, and she slid her hand around his neck and tangled her fingers in his wonderful hair. He deepened their kiss, his tongue invading, exploring. Teasing the roof of her mouth, discovering sensitive nerves she had never imagined existed before.

He half rolled onto her, pushing her back into the soft furs, his thigh between hers. Lightning spiked low in her womb, pleasurably painful, and warmth flooded her trembling sheath.

His hand cradled her breast, tweaking her nipple, rolling it between his thumb and forefinger. Pleasure streaked with pain quivered from the tip of her breast to her sensitized core, a fiery internal caress. Her dream-lover had never delighted her so. She arched into his touch, as much as she could, but his body was heavy, pinning her to the furs. She froze, black memories screeching through her mind, but instantly he rose on his elbow, releasing the pressure, and stared intently into her face.

"Did I hurt you?" His concern was evident, and the memories faded back into the pit where nightmares lurked.

"No." This was Connor. And she wanted Connor tonight, more than she had ever wanted anything for the last nine years. "You won't hurt me." She was no virgin, after all. "Just don't stop, that's all I ask."

Tenderly he brushed tendrils of hair from her face. "You're a hard mistress, Aila. But I will do my best to obey your command."

A breathless laugh escaped. His mistress. Is that what she would be, after tonight? Even if they only ever had this one night?

It was a scandalous notion. A Princess of Ce contemplating such a thing. But the thought entranced, nevertheless. It would, after all, exist only in her imagination.

She speared her fingers through his luxuriant hair as he nibbled kisses along the column of her throat. Once again, he rolled onto her, his heavy body pinning her into the furs. But this time she savored the sensation of his shoulder against hers, the rigid planes of his chest crushing her breasts. And the way his thigh angled over hers, brushing so close to her damp sex.

His hand clasped her other shoulder and his teasing lips followed. His roughened jaw scraped the swell of her breast and she stirred restlessly, fingers digging ruthlessly into his scalp.

He gave a silent laugh and his hot breath caressed her tender flesh. "I'm trying to slow things down. Do you wish me to ravish you like a beast?"

"No." She raked her fingernails across the back of his shoulders, and he reared above her, his black hair disheveled, his eyes glinting in the flickering glow of the torches. Awareness tingled across her skin as she gazed up at him, and slowly she dragged her nails along his straining biceps.

Such leashed power.

The knowledge thrilled her. Connor MacKenzie, savage Scot from Dal Riada, was naked in her arms and battling his desire to take her like a primitive barbarian.

"Then I suggest," he said between gritted teeth, and she had to stifle the urge to giggle, "that you unhook your claws from my flesh."

"Forgive me," she whispered, but before he could respond she slid her hand between their bodies, delighting in the way his hair tickled her palm. "I'll use my claws for more pleasurable pursuits."

"I didn't say it wasn't—*Aila*."

Her name emerged as an agonized groan as her searching fingers found their target. For an eternal moment she forgot how to breathe as his cock jerked against her palm. So hard. So hot. Tentatively she moved her hand, feeling his length, and he angled forward to accommodate her exploration.

"Pleasurable?" The word was a gasp as his heavy balls filled her hand. Stunned by her discovery, even though she was no stranger to a man's body, her fingers twitched uncertainly around their prize.

"On the edge of agony." Without moving the lower half of his body, he crushed her breasts beneath his weight. "I fear my self-control is sadly lacking this night, my lady."

Her fingers closed around his tight sac. She had him in the palm of her hand. The knowledge thrilled and an exhilarating sense of power thundered through her. Restlessly she stirred beneath him and once again her other hand tangled in his hair.

His body tensed, muscles straining and roughly he kneed her thighs apart. She lost her grip as he moved over her, spreading her further, his gaze intent.

"Connor." His name was a whisper and she didn't know what she wanted to ask him. To make haste? Or to wait until the last thread of anxiety in her soul had diminished?

"My Aila." The words were a caress, as erotic as the way he

speared his fingers through her hair, as the way he looked at her with such infinite desire. "For all time."

She slid her arm around him, held him close, delighting in the feel of his warm flesh, hard muscles and the restrained strength that flexed beneath her questing fingers.

For all time. Did he know how seductive she found that promise? A promise made in the heat of night, the throes of passion. A promise that meant nothing, yet she would hold the words close in her heart—*for all time*.

He bowed his head and his lips seared her in a trail of scorching kisses across her breasts. And then his mouth closed over her nipple and she gasped in shock. Raising her head, she watched him, his dark head nestled against her as he teased her throbbing nipple with his tongue and teeth and lips.

Such sweet ecstasy. His hand traced the curve of her waist, the flare of her hip, sending tingles skittering over her skin. He slipped between her thighs and the breath caught in her throat as he explored the tender flesh of her belly. *Lower*.

And then he looked up at her, to watch her reaction to his touch. But as his searching finger trailed over her sensitive clitoris, the strength rushed from her and she fell back on the bed, her breath erratic.

His face pressed against her stomach, his mouth moved against her burning skin. She caught a strangled curse but then he rose over her, hair tumbling over his shoulders, eyes wild with passion.

"I need to be inside you." It was a demand and a request. The head of his cock nudged her, but he didn't penetrate. Just continued to rub his shaft along her cleft, up and down, caressing and teasing her quivering sex.

"Yes." It was permission, an entreaty. She had never been touched this way before. Lust and need collided and she hooked her ankles around the small of his back.

Forearms on either side of her shoulders, he cradled her head. And then he thrust with a suddenness that seared the breath from her lungs. Shock speared through her heart, and her muscles tensed as she dug her nails into his back, her mind a vortex of black.

His agonized groan dragged her back to the moment, to the realization she was with Connor. That he was inside her, that everything was all right. "You weren't ready." His fingers tightened in her hair. "I'm sorry. I wanted to prove to you that I'm no savage Scot, but my actions betray me."

Although his cock stretched her beyond anything she had been subjected to before, she gave a breathless laugh. "You are a savage Scot," she managed to say over the violent hammering of her heart. "And I am more than ready."

His uneven breath fanned her face. "I wanted to make this first time last. But, God. You're so tight around me. I can scarcely see straight, never mind think."

She knew he didn't mean to arouse by his words. But renewed desire rippled through her, soothing the raw ache of his swift intrusion. Instinctively she tightened her thighs around him and raked her fingers through his hair.

"Now is not the time to think," she whispered.

Now was a time to feel. And she could feel his arms embrace her. Feel his hard body above her. And, most glorious of all, she could feel his cock inside her, pushing to her limits. Filling the void she'd nurtured for too many empty years.

Slowly he withdrew, until only the tip of his shaft remained embedded within her. For one long moment, she saw eternity in his eyes and then he sank into her, so deep she stifled a gasp. His mouth claimed hers, claimed her gasp, her breath, her very soul. His tongue invaded, withdrew, invaded again and her rigid muscles relaxed.

His thrusts became less gentle, more frenzied. The friction sizzled along her nerve endings, an exhilarating ride, and she slid her tongue into his mouth, connecting them ever more intimately.

He shifted his angle and as he pulled back the length of his cock dragged against her swollen clitoris. Lightning speared, shattered, and she reared against him, as her choked cries spilled into his willing mouth.

He rammed into her, hard and fast, and without conscious thought she matched his rhythm. Every stroke caressed her core, stoking the inferno, sending spirals of molten need spinning through her.

Nothing existed but this man, this moment, and as her vision faded, she convulsed around his thrusting cock. Again and again. Hugging him within her, squeezing his shaft. Indescribable pleasure cascaded through her sheath and tremors claimed her weakened limbs.

Dazed, she stared up into Connor's face. He was looking at her as though she were a wondrous fantasy and even as the absurd thought whispered through her mind, a tortured grin twisted his mouth.

"You came for me." He sounded on the verge of insanity. "Never felt like that before." And then he gritted his teeth and hammered into her with such force she couldn't breathe. But it didn't matter because, as she clung on to him as if her life depended on it, he violently pumped his hot seed deep into her waiting womb.

CHAPTER 15

For a few exquisite seconds Connor crushed her beneath his weight. His hard, battle-toned body melded with hers, still joined, and although her exhausted limbs wanted to slide onto the bed, she tightened her grip around him.

Hers. Physically perhaps for only tonight. But in her heart *for all time.*

He stirred, raising his head from her shoulder, and stared at her intently, as if memorizing her face. His tangled hair fell over his shoulders and she longed to drag her fingers through its untamed beauty.

Languidly she drifted her fingers up his back. She saw the glazed aftereffects of passion fade from his eyes to be replaced with something akin to horror.

"Aila." It was a strangled groan and her fingers froze. Why did he look at her as though he regretted making love? Did he regret it? But how could he? "Aila, I'm sorry."

Ice invaded where just a moment ago heated contentment had bathed her soul. And when he gently withdrew from her, she didn't try to prevent him.

As he left her body exposed to the night she shivered, and this time through shame, not desire. Did he expect her to get up instantly and get dressed? Leave?

She had never intended to stay all night. That was impossible for many reasons. But not once had she imagined he would expect her to leave the moment he had gained satisfaction.

It made no difference what he expected. She was incapable of moving. She was incapable of even speaking. All she could manage was to stare at him and God help her, she knew the pain in her heart was plain in her eyes.

A tortured expression flickered over his face and a possible reason surfaced. Did he imagine she would demand more from him because of this one shared encounter?

Was that his concern? That she would demand marriage?

Perhaps she should reassure him. But how could she when reassurance was the one thing *she* needed above all else in this moment?

As the jagged thoughts tumbled through her mind, he tenderly wrapped a fur around her chilled body. An odd gesture if he truly wanted her out of his sight as quickly as possible. She huddled into the furs and willed the prickling behind her eyes to remain out of sight. She was a Princess of Ce and even if Connor had broken her heart, he would never see her tears.

"Aila." His whisper tore at her as his fingers brushed tangled tendrils of hair from her cheek. He was lying on his side looking down at her. "I've no right to beg for your forgiveness, yet I must. Please believe me when I say I didn't mean to come inside you."

The chill that had claimed her body vanished as her blood heated at his words. She knew her face was flaming, knew he couldn't fail to notice since his fingers traced the curve of her cheek.

But what did he mean?

"I'm sorry." The words sounded as though he ripped them from the deepest pit of hell. Anguish carved his features and yet still he touched her. She couldn't fathom what had changed his mood so radically.

His words suggested he regretted their liaison. His touch suggested anything but.

"Why?" It hurt to speak. Her throat was raw from tears unshed. And yet she had to know. She deserved that at least. "I'm not sorry for what we did."

He frowned in clear confusion. And then, as if a torch had suddenly ignited inside his brain, comprehension appeared to dawn.

"Aila, no." He brushed a featherlight kiss across her lips. "I'll cherish this night forever." His eyes darkened, as if demons plagued his soul. "I lost control." He made it sound a shocking admission, as though he never lost control even in the throes of passion.

But wasn't that the purpose of passion? To abandon all control in the glorious heat of completion?

She wondered how best to reassure him. "So did I. I believe in that, also, we are equal."

Had she imagined the way his fingers shook as he played with her hair?

"I didn't mean to spill my seed inside you." If it wasn't such an outrageous notion, she would imagine he sounded shamed. "I didn't mean to risk your—" He swallowed, clearly unable to continue, but he didn't need to because suddenly she understood.

He had been thinking of her reputation should she conceive his child. Warmth flooded her heart and spilled into her veins, obliterating the torturous scald of humiliation.

She pushed the furs aside so she could cradle his jaw between her hands. She longed to tell him her reputation meant nothing to her if by losing that she gained his child.

But of course, she could say no such thing. Couldn't tell him that if she became pregnant, she would quietly be wedded to a man who would accept another's child in return for the royal status she brought.

Because she wouldn't conceive. Not tonight, not ever.

Yet she would give anything for such a miracle to occur.

For a moment, as she gazed into Connor's troubled eyes, as his fingers gently caressed her face, the image of Bride fluttered through her mind.

Bride. Goddess of fertility. Of the spring and new life. And before she could stop herself the deep longing spilled from the secret places in her heart. Bride turned and looked at her.

Smiled the unmistakable smile of victory. As though she imagined Aila had once more embraced the goddess of her youth.

With a shiver, Aila blinked the image away. Bride belonged to her old life. She would never again worship the pagan ways.

"Aila." Connor's whisper was tortured, and she realized he might take her shiver as a personal reaction against his confession.

She pulled his head closer until their lips all but touched. "I won't conceive this night." How she longed for it be otherwise. "There's no need to concern yourself with such matters. Trust me on this."

Wariness carved his features. "I would never knowingly cause you pain. Yet I behaved like a raw boy with you tonight."

"A boy? I beg to differ. In my arms you were all man, Connor. My man." As a disbelieving grin tugged his lips, she wriggled beneath the furs until they slipped from her body. "I might even say you were my very own savage Scot this night."

"A savage, am I?" The last vestige of worry vanished from his eyes. "And do you intend to tame me, my noble Pictish lady?"

Suddenly daring, although it also seemed the most natural thing in the world, she flattened her hands against his shoulders and pushed him back onto the bed. He lay there, deceptively submissive, as she straddled his hips and offered him a triumphant smile.

"I don't think I want to tame you." Her hands were still flattened against his shoulders, bracing her weight as she hung over him. "Your savage ways excite me."

"You compliment and insult me in the same breath." His hands cradled her hips, warm and comforting and desire curled through her. "A remarkable achievement."

Experimentally she lowered herself onto him. His cock, gratifyingly erect already, jerked as she slid her damp sex along his rigid length.

"Tonight has been remarkable altogether." She flashed him a smile, loving how her long-unused methods of seduction affected him. He had a sardonic grin on his face, yet tension clearly etched around his eyes and mouth. It obviously took great willpower for him to remain motionless and compliant beneath her teasing touch.

Slowly she slid back up his glorious erection, every inch of him gliding against her swollen clitoris. She'd intended to play with him for some time, but now all she could think was how he felt when he entered her body.

When he emptied his seed within her.

She leaned forward a little more, gave herself more leverage and brushed her aching core over his sensitized glans.

His grin evaporated and his grip on her hips tightened. Encouraged, she repeated her action, her erratic breaths mingling with his.

"Do you intend to torture me for the rest of the night?"

"I might." But much as she enjoyed it, she had no intention of doing any such thing. Her need for completion was too demanding, too intense. "It depends on how well you behave yourself."

His hands slid from her hips. He palmed her bottom, his fingers perilously close to her immodestly exposed crevice.

Even that thought inflamed her.

"I can't promise to behave myself when your sweet clit teases me without mercy." His fingers grazed the tops of her inner thighs, skimmed deliciously between her heated lips. "Your savage Scot aches for you."

Desire coiled tighter at his seductive admission. She angled herself over him. "I'm too soft-hearted to watch you suffer." She shifted, felt him nudge against her swollen lips and her teasing words fled her mind. "Connor, I need you inside me." It was a plea and instantly his strong hands cupped her buttocks, positioning her for his imminent penetration.

Except he didn't penetrate. "Take me, Aila." It was an erotic command, one she had never imagined Connor would make.

Slowly she sank onto him, savoring every moment as he stretched her once again. She clenched her internal muscles, hugged him tight, felt his groan vibrate throughout her blood.

Still cupping her bottom with one hand, his other hand trailed over her trembling flesh to capture her breast. She gasped, arched into him, quivered as his finger and thumb pinched her hard nipple.

She returned the favor and he reared beneath her. Panting, she gazed down at him. Saw the same raw need reflected in his passion glazed eyes. Abandoning his nipple, she gripped his shoulders. "Are you ready?" The words were scarcely coherent, but he appeared to understand.

"For what?" His smoky voice enflamed her and his fingers exploring her breast and buttock drove her to the edge of sanity.

"For this." She braced her weight on hands and knees, lifting her hips until their bodies all but separated. And then she slid down his length, his size filling her, and it felt so right, so perfect.

Breath scraping her lungs, she pulled up, plunged down, meeting his thrust halfway and the exquisite friction unraveled her tenuous restraint.

"Aila." His voice was rough, as primal as the way he rammed into her, as primitive as the way he gripped her bottom for added leverage. *"Is it safe?"*

She understood his agonized question and a wave of heat,

separate yet inextricably entwined with the lust consuming her, flooded her senses. Even now he thought only of her.

"Yes." The ragged whisper tore from the depths of her being. "Come inside me, Connor." She saw how her words aroused him by the way his breath rasped between gritted teeth, the way his eyes glittered on the verge of madness. As the first delirious wave of orgasm swept toward her, she gasped with her last coherent breath. "I want to feel you pump your seed deep inside me."

He roared her name, thrust so hard he surely touched her soul. As she convulsed around his rigid length, she could feel his hot seed filling her, could feel her body grasping and embracing, could hear her choked scream echo around the bedchamber.

Connor. *Her love.*

CHAPTER 16

Propped up on one elbow, Connor stared into the sleeping face of the woman by his side. The torches had burned out long ago, but when he'd awoken just now, he'd opened the timber shutters.

In order to look at this fascinating, incredible woman.

With her gold-auburn hair spread across the pillows, she looked like an angel. Yet her passion owed nothing to such sexless beings.

Her passion had astounded him. Even now, the memory of how she'd responded to his touch, how she had teased and taken and most of all given, caused the blood to thicken his shaft and quicken his heart.

His Pictish lady, so reserved in public, revealed a fiery demand for sex in the privacy of the bedchamber.

Unable to help himself, he gently tugged the furs he'd wrapped around her after their last lovemaking. Her small breasts, so perfectly formed, boasted rosy nipples already hardening as the air caressed her naked flesh.

He cradled her breast, delighting in how she fit so snugly into his palms. So warm and silky-soft. His heated gaze traveled the length of her body. She was so fragile. So small.

For a moment black fear gripped his chest and curdled his stomach. Last night his passion had overcome his iron-clad control.

God. How could he have put her life in such danger? She wasn't big enough for childbearing. He never wanted to bear responsibility for killing another woman through the consequences of his lust. That the woman might be Aila didn't bear contemplation.

Yet she assured him all was well, and he shoved the doubts aside. A woman knew her own body. Perhaps, in time, he would relax enough to enjoy other nights like this one. Nights when he didn't need to withdraw before completion, a practice he'd remained faithful to for the last four years.

She stirred, a soft sigh whispering from her lips, as he stroked her nipple with his thumb. Later this morning, when they met by the stream, he would ask for her hand. He'd ask her now, but he needed time to work on his strategy. Consider any objection she might have and come up with solutions that would lighten her heart. Present his heritage in its most positive light. He was, after all, related to royalty through his half-brother Fergus.

And then, when Princess Devorgilla of Ce demanded her presence in Dal Riada, as he was sure she would, Aila would already know a new life waited.

With him.

His chest tightened and he lowered his head and trailed kisses over her pale, luscious globe. His tongue flicked over her nipple, sucked her into his mouth, her erect nub sending arrows of raw lust streaking directly to his rigid cock.

There was plenty of time for another leisurely joining before they needed to face the day.

Her fingers tangled in his hair and she stretched, angling her breast more securely against his greedy mouth. God, she tasted good. He would taste her all over before he allowed her to leave this bed.

And then she stiffened. "How late is it?" There was an unmistakable thread of panic in her voice.

With reluctance, he relinquished her irresistible flesh.

"Don't distress yourself. Dawn has only just broken." He grinned up at her over her wet, erect nipple. "Good morning, my Pictish lady. I trust you slept well."

Instead of a teasing response, her eyes widened in growing alarm. "I have to leave." She scrambled to sit up and because he knew he could persuade her to stay a little longer, he allowed her to. "I have to return to my chamber before anyone is about—I didn't mean to fall asleep." She sounded as though her world was crashing around her ears.

Damn the importance men placed on a woman's reputation. And yet he would not do anything to besmirch the reputation of this woman.

"It's still early." Aye, and he was as hard as a rock and despite the early hour he was destined to remain so until tonight. Surely Aila would visit him tonight. They could celebrate their betrothal. "No one will be about yet."

Her fingers clutched at the furs. She looked anything but reassured by his words.

"There was something I—but never mind." She gave him an oddly furtive look. "You will still meet with me later this morning?" Was that a hint of uncertainty he detected in her tone?

He covered her hands and pressed her palms against his heart. "My king himself couldn't keep me from you."

She smiled, as if she doubted his word. But at least she smiled.

"There are things we need to discuss. But I don't have time now." She glanced around, obviously searching for her discarded clothing.

He put his own needs aside and dutifully brought her gown to her. "Aye. There are things we need to discuss. I'll be at the stream at the fourth hour."

She relaxed. "We'll have a beautiful day today, Connor. I promise you."

WITH A SENSE OF SATISFACTION, Connor emerged from the Pictish king's inner sanctum, Ewan by his side. He hadn't expected the early morning summons, but it was obvious the king didn't want to waste any time before discovering why the Scots had descended upon his kingdom.

"That didn't go as badly as I feared." Ewan's remark mirrored his thoughts on the matter. "Although I was sorely tempted to give a more realistic impression of the noble and honorable Lord Fergus when mac Lutin asked after his character."

"What did you expect me to say?" Connor rolled his shoulders, attempting to dislodge the knotted tension. "We wanted him to agree to the match, not sling us out on our arses."

As they crossed the feasting hall, its long tables now stacked against one side of the room, Ewan grunted. "He did seem overly interested in Fergus on a personal level though, didn't he? As if that mattered more to him than the royal connection."

It had been odd. Connor had expected a great many questions and demands from the Pictish king, but he hadn't been prepared to give personal recommendations on the proposed bridegroom. "It appears he might be fonder of his eldest daughter than we believed." A twinge of guilt assailed him. But what could he do? This was politics. He was only following the orders of his king. If the Pictish king decided to give his own daughter in marriage to secure an alliance, it was nothing to do with Connor.

He hadn't lied about his half-brother's qualities. He'd just been economical with the truth.

Just before they left the hall, he caught sight of a time-keeping candle in a recess and cursed violently. The flame was already halfway between the fourth and fifth hours of the morning.

He was late for Aila.

THE MOMENT he crested the ridge and saw the woman by the stream, tension knotted in his gut. Where was Aila?

Lady Elise turned at his approach and he offered her a bow. "My lady."

"Connor." She inclined her head. "I have a message from my lady Aila."

"Is she quite well?" He recalled asking Elise a similar question days ago. How much had changed since then.

"Yes." Elise's fingers clenched on her shawl and instantly his sense of unease heightened. "She asked me to convey her apologies but her—her father is returned and commanded she wait at the palace to receive him later this morning."

His tension dissolved. The delay was nothing to concern himself with. Not that he'd been concerned. Why wouldn't Aila wish to see him again today?

She herself had made the arrangements. But a single, or widowed, woman could no sooner disobey her father than she could her husband. Or than a husband could disobey his king.

"Thank you. And I'm sorry I kept you waiting. I also was unavoidably detained this morning."

She waved her hand in a gesture that reminded him of Aila. "Of course. I understand." She hesitated as if there was more she wanted to say and yet couldn't decide whether she should. "Connor."

"What is it, my lady?" Now he was no longer concerned that Aila had changed her mind about seeing him, he noticed the tension etched on Elise's face. If he could help her, he would.

Although he couldn't imagine how a Scot could help a woman with Elise's fine pedigree.

"Aila—my beloved cousin—thinks very highly of you."

He couldn't help the satisfied grin. And then Elise's words fully penetrated.

Her cousin. And Elise was a minor princess from the neighboring Kingdom of Circinn.

Far from trying to impress Aila and her unknown father with his own connection to royalty through Fergus, it appeared royal blood flowed through her own veins.

"I think very highly of Lady Aila also."

"It's just…" Again, Elise hesitated. "She does not indulge in such romantic intrigues as many ladies do." A blush stained her cheeks. "Goddess, I shouldn't be speaking so to you."

"What are you trying to tell me, my lady?"

Elise took a deep breath. "There's something she wishes to confide in you. I don't know how you will react but please, don't be angry at her." Before he could demand to know what the hell she was talking about, she continued, "And promise me upon your word of honor that you won't tell her I warned you in advance."

Warned him about what?

"I'll keep your counsel, my lady." His voice was hard, and Elise flinched. Another time he might have queried such an odd reaction. But now only one thought thundered through his brain. A foul, distorted thought. And as Elise turned to leave, he asked the question that now haunted his mind. "Is she married?"

Elise swung back and stared at him in obvious surprise. Whatever Aila's great secret was, it clearly had never occurred to Elise he would imagine it to be that.

"Of course not. My lord Onuist died a hero's death, nine years ago. While saving Aila from certain capture and slavery at the hands of the Vikings."

~

FOR THE THIRD time Aila checked the shadows on the sundial. She was already half an hour late for her liaison with Connor and despite her father's command that she wait for him, he had yet to send for her.

Of course she longed to see her father again. But why did he want to see her so urgently? He had only been gone for two weeks, after all.

"Aila." Her grandmother's voice pulled her back to the present and she turned to where she sat on her favorite stone bench in the secluded royal garden. "What is your obsession with the time this morning?"

Aila gave a dismissive flick of her hand and forced herself to sit beside her grandmother. "I'm anxious to see my father." It wasn't a lie. She loved her father and *was* anxious to see him.

She simply wanted to see Connor first.

Her grandmother glanced to the far side of the garden, where the queen was addressing a couple of servants.

"Your mother might believe that, but whether you choose to ignore it or not, you and I are too similar in character. It most certainly isn't your father who occupies your thoughts at this moment."

Blood heated her cheeks. Curse her grandmother's perception. And then another, far more shocking thought intruded. Suppose her grandmother guessed—or knew— what she and Connor had done last night?

"Really, Grandmamma, I'm sure I don't know what you mean." She avoided eye contact because she knew, in her heart, just how similar they were. It wasn't only her grandmother's hair and eye color she had inherited.

But they were the only gifts she chose not to ignore.

Her grandmother gave an impatient sigh, as if she still hadn't given up hope of Aila one day embracing all she had once rejected.

"Then allow me to tell you this."

Against her better judgment, Aila looked back at the dowager queen. For a fleeting second, she had the uncanny sensation of looking at an image of herself from the far future.

In forty years' time perhaps she would look like her grandmother. But unlike the dowager queen, Aila would never be surrounded by the love of her direct blood descendants.

"Tell me what?" It was a whisper, and she didn't know why she had asked. Why she was encouraging her grandmother. Aila had no interest in whatever message the old gods might wish to convey.

Her grandmother covered Aila's hands that were clenched on her lap. "The Scots' true purpose here is concealed, obscured by dark fog. Even they themselves are unaware of what lurks in the deep."

She wanted to pull her hands free. To laugh in derision at her grandmother's dramatic declaration. But against her will, in the fundamental core of her being she understood the truth of the cryptic words.

"We'll know of their true purpose soon enough. My father will tell us." And yet even as she spoke the words, she knew she didn't believe them.

No matter how much she wanted to. No matter how hard she fought against the insidious, intangible sense of *knowing* that had once, long ago, been an integral element of her existence.

Her grandmother didn't look convinced, which served only to increase her own disquiet.

"The darkness swirls about you, Aila. And yet you're protected from its worst destruction."

This time she succeeded in snatching her hands free. "Grandmamma, I'm not interested. You can believe the malevolent whispers in the night if you wish, but I choose not to."

"Because," her grandmother said, as if there had been no interruption, "you are the founding stone. For the bridge that will one day unite all our kingdoms."

Aila stood and marched toward the sundial, unable to remain still for a moment longer. She had no desire to be a founding stone. All she wanted was Connor and that was impossible.

Her fingers clutched the stone edge of the sundial as the impossible wavered before her eyes.

Was that what her grandmother was telling her? That her dreams weren't impossible? That it was acceptable to love again —to hope for a future where nightmares no longer haunted the darkest hours?

Were the old gods telling her, through her grandmother, that her penance was paid, her guilt absolved, and freedom beckoned?

She dug her fingers into the stone, scraping her flesh. She no longer believed in the old gods.

But would she believe once again, if this was the pathway for a lifetime with Connor?

Slowly she turned, heart hammering. Her grandmother stared back at her, concern clouding her normally clear green eyes.

"What should I do?' She didn't know of whom she asked the question. God? Her grandmother?

Or the deities of her ancestors?

"Never lose faith in him." Her grandmother's voice held a strange, otherworldly note. "Do what you know in your heart is right."

CHAPTER 17

*H*er father received her in his inner sanctum, but Aila knew even before she entered the chamber something was amiss. Why else would he choose this chamber? And why had her mother and grandmother been summoned but not Finella?

"Aila." He embraced her, a huge hulk of a man, his long red hair tied back into a thick braid. "We have a grave situation to discuss, daughter."

She inclined her head and attempted to push Connor from her mind. It didn't feel right, to be dreaming of her wild Scot lover while in the presence of her father. But no matter how she tried, she couldn't stop thinking of her grandmother's last intriguing words.

Never lose faith in him.

She had to mean Connor. Who else could *he* possibly be?

But she still couldn't imagine what the cryptic comment was meant to convey.

"Bredei." Her mother sounded scandalized. "You told me this morning you had little intention of pursuing that matter further."

Instantly her attention snapped back to the present. Her

mother had taken her place beside the king, where he now sat on his carved throne. Her younger brother Talargan stood with his back to the window, arms folded, a dark scowl distorting his features.

"Circumstances have changed since we last spoke, my queen."

The formality of his address sent skitters of alarm along Aila's spine. She glanced at her grandmother, seated on the queen's left, and the dowager gave a barely discernible shrug. It was clear she did not know to what the king referred.

"Circumstances," her mother said and Aila could almost see the icicles forming in the air around her, "most certainly have not changed, my lord."

"Devorgilla, the Scots' proposals change everything."

"Then perhaps you could enlighten us." The queen's tone suggested there was nothing on this earth the Scots could propose that would change her mind on the matter.

Whatever *the matter* was.

Her father beckoned her forward and she gave him her hand. She loved both parents dearly and it hurt to know they had never shared the kind of love she and Onuist had.

The love she bore for Connor.

"The High King Wrad's death has left potential disarray in the kingdoms," he said. "But you know this, of course."

"Yes." It was the reason her father and brother and many of their warriors had traveled to Fortriu, Supreme Kingdom of Pictland. "Who was chosen to succeed?"

"The lineage is fractured." Her father tightened his grip on her hand before releasing her and casting a swift glance at Talargan's stony countenance. "There is only one living Princess of Fortriu and she remains childless. Until such time as she produces an heir—an uncontested direct descendant of the crown—there are eight nobles besides me who claim matrilineal rights."

"Not including that bastard upstart, MacAlpin," Talargan said, the fury clear in his voice.

Aila stared at her brother. "The Scot? How can a Scot claim such a blood tie?"

"His mother was the previous High King's youngest daughter," Talargan said.

She had never heard of this youngest daughter. This, then, was the news Connor had delivered from Dal Riada.

"Ah, Clodrah." Aila's grandmother sounded oddly sentimental. "Your sister, Devorgilla, is named after my dear childhood friend, Clodrah."

"I know nothing of this other Clodrah, Mamma." An irritated frown creased the queen's forehead. "So it's true? The Scot's claim is valid?"

"Oh, it's true. Clodrah was always headstrong and when she decided she wanted to wed the barbaric Scot Alpin, there was no talking sense into her."

Talargan finally joined them. Rage emanated from him in an almost palpable fog. "If Mairi had wed a warrior who could have filled her womb instead of that feeble old man she was forced to accept, the lineage would be secure."

Sympathy streaked through Aila. Even after all these years her brother still loved Mairi, the Princess of Fortriu. She reached out and took his hand and, great warrior or not, he allowed her to. There were only eighteen months between them, and their bond of blood went deep.

"I'm surprised," the queen said, after a soft glance in her son's direction, "her father didn't marry her to a suitable Pictish prince. Didn't he know of her infatuation?"

"It was during the summer of '95, Devorgilla." The dowager sighed and appeared lost in her memories. "The Vikings raided the west coast for the first time. The balance was unsettled. Clodrah, scarcely fourteen years old, took advantage and eloped with her handsome Scot."

Aila imagined abandoning all responsibility and eloping with *her* handsome Scot. But of course, she never would. Not only was she not a rebellious maid of fourteen, but Connor had never suggested he wanted anything more than a fleeting liaison with her.

But how dearly that long-ago Clodrah must have loved her foreign prince. To give up everything she had ever known in order to follow him into his strange land. Without the blessing of her kin.

"When the High King, her father, discovered Clodrah's betrayal he cast her from his heart. Erased her name from the annals of Fortriu. Forbade any to speak of her again." Her grandmother sighed. "Yet her impetuous nature comes back to haunt us forty-three years after her death."

Poor, reckless Clodrah. She had enjoyed only five years with her Scot. Yet long enough to bear the son who now claimed his mother's heritage as his own.

"If this knowledge hadn't been suppressed so effectively," her father said, "the Scot's claim could have been deflected years ago with strategic alliances."

"How?" the dowager said. "Clodrah's elder sister inherited, but produced only one frail daughter who, in turn, produced the equally fragile Lady Mairi. It grieves me to admit, but the female line of Fortriu is fundamentally flawed."

"Nevertheless," the king said, an edge in his tone, "when the Scots presented MacAlpin's credentials we were disadvantaged in our own kingdom by such ignorance."

"Indeed you were not." The queen briefly covered his hand with hers. "I know you wouldn't have given them the satisfaction of showing your true feelings."

The king was silent for a moment. Then he looked directly at Aila. "During the council meetings at Fortriu, there was much discussion as to the future of Pictland."

Now they were coming to the matter her mother so vehemently opposed. The matter that MacAlpin's disclosure had somehow managed to change.

"Yes, my lord." Dread coiled in the pit of her belly and she knew her future hung in the balance. She tried to ignore it, brush it aside, but still it lingered.

Because if it wasn't her future at stake here, then why had her father summoned her to his war chamber? Why did he have that look on his face, as though he were about to betray her in the worst possible fashion?

"Bredei." Her mother went unacknowledged. Her father continued to stare at her, as if she were the only one in the chamber.

"The battle of '39 decimated our ranks of strong, noble warriors. Our young noblewomen are, from necessity, wedded to men who are one if not more generations their senior."

Why was he telling her this? She knew how difficult it was for a young woman of noble birth to wed a man similar in age, who was not also a blood relation. Many of her friends, like Elise, were shackled to aged husbands simply because the choice was so limited.

"You know," he said, "how intimately all seven royal families of Pictland are related."

"It has always been so." How else could alliances be made except by intermarriage? She had first and second cousins in all the royal clans.

But with the steady advance of the Viking devils, and the bloody massacres of '34 and '39, the available pool of strong, suitable warriors had dried to a trickle.

What they needed was fresh blood. But until the next generation matured, and assuming many males survived into adulthood, how could they—

An unformed thought teased the edges of her mind. *Fresh blood.*

"My daughter, I say this not to distress you but because I know your strength of mind." Her father drew in a deep breath and Aila held hers as sudden panic gripped her. "If the Vikings attack us in such force as they did before—and should the Scots decide to back them—Pictland will be annihilated in rivers of blood."

Talargan tightened his hold on her hand, silently offering her the strength she had so recently offered him.

"And what did the council decide?" Her voice didn't betray the fear knotting her stomach at the vision of Vikings ravaging her beloved homeland the way they had ravaged the northern border of Fidach.

"It was propositioned that we approach the Scots and offer an alliance against our common enemy."

The dread seeped into her blood, chilling her from the inside out. "Political marriages."

It was no revelation. For centuries such strategy had been used. But until now only between the seven royal clans of Pictland, to prevent the otherwise incessant battles that raged between one kingdom and the next, without such bonds of blood.

"The council was divided. To approach the Scots would give them the bargaining advantage. Something I and my fellow supporters find abhorrent."

The fear compressing her lungs and suffocating her chest eased. Perhaps, after all, her father wasn't intimating her name had been mentioned as the sacrificial bride. Even if her mother's previous reaction suggested otherwise.

"Were no other strategies put forward?"

"Aila." Her father's gaze bored into her and her fear expanded, consuming the tenuous threads of relief. "Fidach has never recovered from the raids of nine years ago. The Vikings press farther across the border with every passing year. If they realized, even for one moment, the true extent of our vulnerability, they would swarm into our lands without a second's hesitation." His hand fisted on the carved armrest of his throne. "It sickens me to confess, but we need the Scots if we want to defeat the Vikings."

"Bredei, there are other princesses of Pictland." There was an undercurrent of pleading in her mother's tone. Her mother, who never begged, whose pride forbade such base emotion to ever blight her existence.

But even as the words lingered in the air, Aila knew her mother realized their futility. There were, of course, many princesses of Pictland. But most of them were married, except for those too young for the marriage bed.

"Yes." Her father's voice was heavy, and he spared his queen a compassionate glance. "But we are no longer contemplating long betrothals, Devorgilla. And would it be less cruel to offer Finella?"

"No." The denial sprang from Aila, repugnance shredding her heart at the thought of her little sister being sent from Pictland. "Not Finella."

"Nor Aila." The queen rose and glared down at her king. "You told me this morning you had informed the council you wouldn't countenance our daughter being offered to the Scots. What happened to the suggestion of holding a lottery of all suitable noblewomen? It's unfortunate for whomever loses but at least there is a semblance of fairness to the matter."

"Because," the king said, "the Scots came to Ce with not only the revelation that MacAlpin intends to contest the kingship of Fortriu. He also proposes a royal marriage to seal our two peoples into an allegiance against our common foe. He offers the son of his first cousin for our eldest Princess Devorgilla."

Her father's words hammered into her brain, battered against her heart. Her brother's grip on her hand tightened, anchoring her to the moment, to the nightmare scenario pounding through her numb mind.

Marriage to an unknown Scot. In return for an allegiance against her bitterest of enemies.

"I forbid such marriage." Her mother hissed the words at the king before turning to look at Aila. "Tell the Scots the eldest

Princess Devorgilla is an invalid, unable to travel and most assuredly unable to consummate such a union. Tell them we will present them with alternatives in due course."

"Is that true, Aila?" her father said, never taking his steady gaze from her. "Do you consider yourself unable to consummate such a union?"

She wanted to scream *yes*. Yes, she was unable. Because that would negate any form of marriage contract. A week ago, there would have been no doubt in her mind that she could never take another man. But now—oh God. Now she knew better.

There was nothing physically preventing her from consummating such a marriage.

The knowledge seared her soul. She had fallen in love with Connor, enjoyed one night of exquisite pleasure in his bed. And for that, she had proved beyond doubt she was ready to resume the duties required of a royal wife.

Except she was barren.

No prince wanted a barren princess. It was a more than adequate excuse to relinquish her place in this alliance. Another would be found and because of the circumstances without causing insult to the Scots.

Nobody moved. Nobody spoke. Her brother glared as though her pain was his own. The king's expression remained grim, the queen outraged. And her grandmother aged twenty years between one breath and the next.

Nine years ago, her world had shattered. When she had recovered, when she realized Bride had ignored her desperate pleas to join Onuist in the Otherworld, she had pledged vengeance. In reality she had always known there was little she could do. But always, in her heart, the flame had slumbered. The flame that promised she would do anything within her power to prevent further bloodshed and devastation at the hands of the Viking invaders.

Here was her opportunity. How could she even think of

trying to escape this fate, even if her barrenness gave her the perfect opportunity to do so? It was cowardly. She wasn't a coward. She was a Princess of Ce, of Pictland, and it was her duty to do whatever she could to protect her people—to protect her sister.

To honor the memory of Onuist.

His name tore through her mind, shredding her fragile veneer of calm. For one terrifying moment she thought she would fall, and allow the agony crushing her heart to consume her.

She had thought, for a few wild, exhilarating days, she had paid her penance. That it wasn't a sin to love another man. To envision a future with him, even though she'd always known such a life was only a dream.

But she had been wrong.

Her penance was not paid. She'd had no right to fall in love again. And now she was faced with duty the prospect of a life-time locked in a loveless political marriage, she dared to even consider trying to evade her destiny?

Connor had been an interlude. It wasn't his fault she had fallen in love with him or harbored foolish hopes of a life together. He'd never suggested anything more, had never attempted to coax promises or an oath of fidelity from her.

She would bury the memory of his touch, of his voice, of the look on his face as he held her in his arms, deep in her soul. Her beloved savage Scot. The man who owned her heart even though she gave her body to another for political stability.

Her father was giving her a choice. Yet there was no choice.

She stiffened her spine, gripped Talargan's hand, and sealed her fate. "I am able to consummate the union. I accept MacAlpin's proposal."

With unconcealed impatience, Connor squinted at the sun. It was directly overhead.

Where the hell was Aila? How long did it take for a father to greet his daughter, even a dearly beloved daughter? And yet he couldn't leave in case she arrived while he searched elsewhere.

This was madness. The longer he waited for her to appear, the less confident he became of her response to his proposal. Yet surely she must have some inkling of his feelings? He'd given her enough clues during the night.

He resumed pacing along the bank of the stream, methodically recounting his arguments as to why they should wed. There was only one matter he had failed to address and that was the issue Lady Elise had mentioned earlier.

To what she referred, he couldn't imagine. Marriage was the only insurmountable obstacle he could foresee, and Elise had assured him that wasn't the case.

What could Aila possibly be hiding from him?

He paused and frowned across the stream into the copse. This morning, before she had rushed from his chamber, she'd been agitated. He'd assumed it was because she was afraid of being seen. Of ruining her reputation. But now he thought about it, hadn't she said they needed to talk? Maybe that had been the reason for her flustered air.

"Goddamn it, Connor." Ewan's exasperated yell bit through his skull and he turned to see his friend glaring down at him from the ridge. "Mac Lutin's summoned us and nobody knew where you were."

Connor snorted in disgust. The Pictish king certainly didn't waste any time. This day was turning into a farce.

He marched up the slope toward Ewan and scanned the area, but Aila was nowhere in sight.

"I wonder if we'll have the honor of meeting the eldest princess this time?" Ewan said as they made their way toward the palace.

Connor wasn't interested in the eldest princess. "When a woman holds a secret close, what would it be?"

Ewan brightened considerably. He always enjoyed talking about one of his favorite subjects. Women. "Usually, my friend, they keep their age a close secret. As if revealing it would initiate a great catastrophe."

He already knew how old Aila was. "No. What else?"

Ewan slung his arm around Connor's shoulder. "How many lovers they have entertained over the years. That's always a popular one."

Aila had told him she had known only her husband. He believed her.

"No. Not that."

Ewan shot him a calculating glance. It appeared he was going to make a personal remark, but then he clearly thought better of it. "I've had ladies keep secret the extent of their experience, the true color of their hair—God, that one was a shock." For a second, he appeared lost in salacious memories. "On occasion they omit to reveal their true marital status or even the number of offspring they've birthed. Once—"

Shock stabbed through him. *Offspring.*

Was that the secret Aila kept? That she had a child? But why would she keep that from him?

It was the one thing he hadn't contemplated. But as Ewan continued to divulge the many and varied secrets ladies apparently kept, the idea clung, and refused to be ignored.

It explained her violent reaction when he'd spoken of Fearchara's death. Made sense of how she'd defended a woman's right to choose the pain of childbirth for herself and not simply for producing an heir for her lord.

She had a living reminder of the husband she had lost. For that, he was happy for her. Happy she had a child, that she had traversed the perilous journey and survived.

As they approached the palace, he attempted to batten down the treacherous image that crawled through his mind. An image he had no right conceiving. Because no matter her past, such selfish thoughts still put her future in jeopardy.

Thoughts of Aila nurturing *his* child within her womb.

"You've yet to tell me," Ewan said under his breath as they entered the inner sanctum of the Pictish king, "what you've decided to do about your Lady Aila."

"One way or another she'll return to Dal Riada with me."

There was no time for further conversation. As Connor swept into a bow before the king, prickles of alarm scuttled over the back of his neck. The war chamber wasn't crowded, but in the moment between the doors opening and his show of respect, his brain registered several royal figures seated on either side of the king.

But something was wrong. His senses were on full alert, yet the Pictish warriors who stood guard over the royal presence didn't emanate especial hostility.

Connor straightened. And saw Aila, sitting at mac Lutin's right hand.

He stared, seeing yet not comprehending. What the hell was

Aila doing there? Her face was so white she looked ill but her eyes, her beautiful eyes, locked on him as though he were her only salvation.

Thunder rumbled in the distance, but perhaps it was only in his head. The king was speaking but the words were muffled, outside his comprehension. And then, without warning, clarity speared through his brain.

"My daughter," the king said, taking Aila's hand. "Aila, the eldest Princess Devorgilla of Ce."

No.

Denial pounded against his temples, disbelief hammered against his ribs. Words lodged in his throat, choked his vocal cords. And still he couldn't drag his eyes from Aila.

Silence vibrated throughout the chamber, an ominous, ugly silence, a silence that clamored against the restrictive confines of his skull.

Hands fisted, his fury mounted. There was a mistake. Aila was not the eldest Princess Devorgilla. Aila was not betrothed to his half-brother Fergus.

He heard Ewan respond to mac Lutin, saw the subtle shift in the stance of the Pictish warriors, as if they suspected Connor of some treachery.

Treachery? He'd give them the devil's own treachery.

But he couldn't vocalize his thoughts. Because, Goddamn it, he couldn't understand his thoughts.

Why hadn't she told him?

Aila belonged to him. He'd be damned if he'd allow his brother, of all people, to lay claim to her. The idea was repellent. Curdled his guts. *Fergus.*

As if sensing the insanity twisting Connor's brain, Ewan clamped his hand around Connor's biceps. The Pictish warriors were no longer being subtle and more than one dagger had been drawn.

He shot Aila one last, infuriated glance. *This isn't over.* He saw her eyes widen, knew she understood. Knew that, if she didn't seek him out, he would find her. Demand to know *why*.

The doors slammed behind them. He had no recollection of leaving the chamber. Only knew that Ewan gripped his arm as if he suspected Connor might ram the doors and violate the inner sanctum.

"Keep walking." It was a harsh command and because he needed air, needed to get out of this cursed Pictish palace, he didn't argue. Just marched outside into the mocking spring sunlight.

And all but collided into Cameron MacNeil.

"Damn," Cam said, glancing from him to Ewan. "So mac Lutin turned MacAlpin down after all."

"No." Ewan continued walking, clearly wanting to put as much distance between the palace and them as possible. "He agreed. The betrothal is official."

The hell it was.

"Why are you looking so pissed, Connor?" Cam fell into step beside him. "Did you finally get to see the elusive princess? Is she such an ugly shrew even Fergus won't be able to bed her?"

Connor's fist connected to Cam's face, shoving the other man off balance. "Shut your mouth."

Cam responded and the sensation of knuckles crushing against his jaw sent morbid satisfaction splintering through Connor's jagged nerves.

By the time Ewan and another three warriors had parted him and MacNeil, his fists were raw and his face on fire.

"Feel better?" MacNeil asked, dragging the back of his hand across his mouth and flicking blood onto the ground.

Connor wrenched free, spat blood. "God help me, open your filthy mouth again and I'll break your neck."

The glare on Cam's face slowly faded. "The princess," he said. "She's not—"

"Enough." Ewan said sharply, jerking his head at the other

warriors and crowd of locals who'd gathered in anticipation of an extended round of entertainment. Only when they were once again alone did he turn back to Cam. "This goes no further, do you hear? Whatever you know, or think you know, keep to yourself."

"Christ." Cam sounded shaken. "None of us will crawl out of here alive if mac Lutin discovers you've been with his daughter."

"Worse than that." Ewan sounded grim. "MacKenzie hasn't even bedded the lady."

Erotic images seared Connor's mind of Aila in his bed last night. Her glorious hair caressing him. Her sweet cries of passion enflaming him.

Her tight sheath welcoming him, as though she had been made solely for their joining.

"You haven't?" Cam frowned, clearly lost. "How's that worse?"

His question hung in the air. Cam's frown finally slid into disbelief.

"Aye." Ewan's voice was hard. "So keep your counsel and mouth to yourself. This isn't about a warrior's pride." He was no longer speaking to Cam. Connor gritted his teeth and continued to glare toward the far village. "It's the difference between forging peace and initiating war."

HE RETURNED TO THE STREAM. It was the only place he could think to go. To return to the palace caused his guts to knot and besides he didn't trust himself not to storm the inner sanctum and demand audience with the Pictish king.

Recant the offer of marriage. Discard the offer of allegiance. Risk the fury of mac Lutin and the wrath of MacAlpin.

Initiate war.

He swung around. Aila stood on the ridge, looking down at him, Elise by her side. Slowly she made her way toward him and this time he didn't help her. Didn't trust himself to touch her. Because to touch her would recall the previous night and the early hours of this morning. How could he touch her without embracing her? Kissing her? Demanding to know what she thought she was doing?

"Connor." Her whisper sank into his heart and savaged his soul. Her face was as pale as it was the first day they had met. Her eyes huge, haunted. Her glance flickered over his battered face and it was obvious the knowledge he had been fighting didn't surprise her. "I'm sorry. I meant to tell you who I truly was last night."

"The eldest Princess Devorgilla of Ce." How he had despised that seemingly elusive lady.

How he damn well wanted her.

Her fingers clutched the edges of her shawl. "I didn't mean to deceive you. Although… I did." Briefly she closed her eyes. "I've no excuse. But I never thought you would discover my true identity in such a…" She hesitated, clearly unable to find words adequate to describe the scene he'd just endured. "Manner."

Unable to help himself, he stepped toward her. She gazed up at him, as if he was her world, her lord. God Almighty, surely she would see she couldn't go through with marriage to Fergus?

Only now did he acknowledge the true reason he wanted to marry her. He loved her. He needed her. After she'd left him this morning, during the hours he'd waited for her perfecting his suit for her, the certainty had solidified. It wasn't just because she intrigued him. It wasn't just because he knew she would not contemplate becoming his mistress. It was more than mere lust, more than simple affection.

With Maeve, he felt both. But while the thought of never seeing her again caused regret, the notion of never seeing Aila again ripped holes through his gut. His heart.

A sorry circumstance for a warrior.

"Why did you agree?" His voice was harsh, and he saw the

way her lip trembled as though she battled for calm. Let her battle. It could never match the battle currently tearing his reason to shreds.

"What would you have me do?" The question was soft yet threaded through with regal pride, as if she were a royal princess and he a mere commoner.

The knowledge that that was exactly the situation stoked his simmering temper. He closed the distance between them until he could feel her ragged breath graze his face. Until he could wind his arms around her and drag her into his waiting embrace.

He clenched his fists by his sides.

"What would I do?" Their lips almost brushed. He could see eternity in her eyes, yet it was an eternity hovering just beyond his desperate grasp. "I would have you in my bed every night, Aila. *My* bed." He scarcely kept the rabid need from his voice. Or the revulsion that, unless she revoked her promise, it would be his brother's bed she shared. "I'd have you under me, on top of me, taking me deep inside your body. Night after goddamn night."

"Connor, don't." She looked at him, but she didn't see him. She couldn't see him, otherwise how could she not fall into his arms? Promise to break the betrothal? Tell him that even if she didn't love him the way he loved her she still wanted him? Needed him?

"Why not?" His whisper was feral. He knew Elise watched from the ridge, but it made no difference. If Aila didn't succumb to his will within the next few moments, then God help him. He'd carry her into the forest and seduce her into submission.

"It was just one night." Her voice was low, as though she were afraid of being overheard. But there was only Elise and she was too far away to hear their conversation. "We both knew it meant nothing more than that. How could it? We're from different worlds, Connor. I never expected anything more from you than… warm memories."

Warm memories? Outrage pumped through his blood, igniting with the fury, the frustration, and the ever-present horror at the prospect of Aila becoming his brother's wife. Of knowing she had no choice but to submit to Fergus' every salacious demand within the bedchamber.

"I was just a convenient body to satisfy your long-neglected desires, is that it?" What the hell was he saying? He knew he was more to Aila than that. But the truth was stark. She was of royal blood and he was not.

She had always been a princess, even when he thought them equal. And no matter what she may or may not feel for him, she had always been aware of the difference in their status.

For one torturous moment, all his original reasons as to why he shouldn't embark in a liaison with Aila taunted him. *She was a widow. She may expect more from him than he was willing to give.*

Aye, she was a widow. But not once would she have expected more from him than he was willing to give. An elder princess did not marry a commoner, even if love was part of the equation.

And now, when he wanted to give her everything that he was, everything that he possessed, she wasn't even in the position to reject him. Because she had already accepted the proposition from his king.

"No." She sounded as if tears choked her throat. "You were never only that."

"Then what was I?" He wanted to damn her for concealing her true identity. Damn her for slipping so effortlessly beneath the armor that had shielded his heart for four long years.

But even as his fingers itched to shake sense into her, his arms ached to hold her. To never let her go. To somehow persuade her that despite the great gulf between them, they could find a future together.

Her hand reached toward him then fell back to clutch her shawl.

"You were—"

"Aila." Elise's breathless voice interrupted as she hurried down the slope toward them. Connor clenched his jaw and somehow managed to hang on to the unraveling threads of his temper. "The royal guard approaches."

"Huh." The word was bitter. "So now you have a royal guard to protect your person, Lady Devorgilla. How did I manage to miss them for this last week?"

"A royal guard?" Aila sounded faint, as if this was news to her also.

Elise glanced between them, an agonized look on her face. "Things are different now. You—you're betrothed to a prince of Dal Riada."

When Aila said nothing, only looked more fragile and untouchable than ever, the last thread snapped. He hissed out a breath and glared into her pale, lovely face.

"Aye, a prince of Dal Riada. My half-brother, Fergus."

$\mathcal{A}$ila sat on the edge of her bed, a paralyzing numbness seeping through her limbs. Connor's face, carved into a mask of furious disbelief as he had caught sight of her in the war chamber, haunted her fractured mind. She hadn't expected his reaction to be so… primitive.

She dug her fingernails into her palm and tried to ignore the crushing pain in her heart. Her heart that ached with every ragged beat, every shallow breath, every anguished thought.

When she'd seen him waiting for her by the stream, it had taken every last shred of resolve she possessed to stop from rushing into his arms. He'd been enraged and she'd said—God, she had said the stupidest things. She didn't mean them. Everything had become twisted and instead of improving an impossible situation, she'd made things worse.

But nothing she had said could compare to Connor's brutal parting shot.

Her betrothed was his half-brother.

Connor had mentioned his brother, during one of their many conversations. And while his anecdotes had made her giggle, as she knew had been his intention, she had also been aware of words left unsaid. Of the thread of cruelty in the older brother toward his younger half sibling.

She'd dreaded the marriage before. But now it revolted the fundamental core of her soul, as though by taking Connor's brother as her husband she was somehow committing an act of incest.

"But why does Aila have to move so far away?" Finella's plaintive voice penetrated her thoughts and she dragged her attention back to the present. As Floradh and a couple of other servants went through her clothes and the personal effects she would be taking with her to Dal Riada, her grandmother and Elise sat with her on her bed, while her mother sat on a stool beside Finella, who curled around Drun on the floor.

"Because that is where the Scot prince lives," their mother said, showing no signs of her true feelings on the matter. "Just imagine. Your sister will help civilize their savage ways."

Her grandmother leaned toward her, clearly not wishing Finella to overhear. "This feels wrong, Aila. Something is terribly amiss. But I cannot fathom what."

Aila stared at their entwined hands. She, her grandmother and Elise. "You said yourself I was a founding stone." The words mocked her. What a different meaning she had placed upon them earlier that day. "It seems you were right."

"You are. But this doesn't sit well with me. The goddess —retreats."

Elise also leaned forward. "Grandmamma, I feel this too." She sounded relieved. "I thought it was only because of—of the circumstances." She shot Aila an anxious glance. "But the darkness has returned. It hovers over the Scots and now Aila too—yet doesn't touch any of them."

Eerie shivers prickled over Aila's arms and she snatched her hands free from her cousin and grandmother.

"Of course there is darkness," she hissed, glancing at Finella to ensure she was still occupied with both Drun and arguing with their mother. "A political marriage is the last thing I desire. Mamma is incensed, Father wearied. And Talargan wishes only to murder every Scot in Ce." She glared at her beloved kin. Kin she would soon be leaving. Perhaps, after her marriage, she would never see them again. The knowledge squeezed her heart. "It would be more extraordinary if darkness didn't linger over Ce-eviot this day."

"I look forward to seeing Dal Riada," Finella said, looking at Aila. "But I don't want to leave you there all alone, Aila."

Finella's sweet face faded as an ethereal mist swirled, obscuring her features. And then the chamber darkened, as if storm clouds hugged the sun, and from the shadows loomed bloodied warriors, their presence permeating the air with the stench of battle, the reek of decay.

She hitched in a sharp breath and dug her fingernails into her palms. Instantly the memory vanished. Because that was all it was. A memory from nine years ago.

Except it wasn't a memory from nine years ago.

She knew it, yet refused to face the truth. *She no longer had visions.*

It was her exhausted mind playing tricks with the shadows in her chamber. It meant nothing. Yet despite the logic of her argument, an overpowering conviction gripped her. Without attempting to analyze it, she held out her hand and waited for Finella to come to her.

"No, my love," she said as gently as she could, hoping the irrational panic stampeding through her wasn't evident in her voice. "You must stay here, in Ce-eviot."

"No, I won't." Finella looked outraged. "I will come with you. Mamma said I should."

Another wave of panic flooded her. "No, Mamma will stay here also. I must—"

"Of course I shall accompany you." Her mother sounded as outraged as Finella. "How you can think I would allow you to make such a journey—such a sacrifice— without me by your side—"

"Devorgilla." Her grandmother's voice was low but vibrated with leashed power. "This journey is for Aila alone."

Her mother's lip trembled. She looked from the dowager to Aila and finally Elise. "Is that your opinion also?" Her voice was chilly.

"Yes, madam." Elise sounded as if she wished otherwise.

"How odd," her mother said and now there was a trace of bitterness in her tone. "That finally the three of you are in accordance."

"Mamma, it's not like that." Aila tried to shake free of the sensation of devastation that continued to dig relentless claws into her soul. "I just—I think—" She caught sight of the confusion on Finella's face and desperately searched for a rational explanation for her behavior. "Drun needs you here, Finella. His heart will break if we both leave him." As her heart would break when she left him behind. But Drun was too old for such a journey. Better he stay with those who loved him than face an uncertain future in a strange land simply because his familiar presence would make her feel better.

Her mother gave a mirthless laugh. "Pray do not patronize me in such a manner. For fifteen years until your marriage to Onuist I was privy to your insights. Just as, when I was a girl, I was used to my mother's."

"This is not an insight." Aila fought against the renewed wave of panic that threatened to swamp her. This was not an unwelcome message from an unwanted goddess. It was just a... feeling.

"My sister Clodrah and I both clearly wished the goddess had blessed us so. But not one of our cousins received the gift either. Our entire generation was ignored."

"The world is changing, Devorgilla." Her grandmother sounded wistful. "I remember my own great-grandmother telling me how three of her sisters and two brothers were so blessed, as well as countless cousins. But now..."

Aila's face burned at the unspoken reproach.

"Clodrah was beside herself when it became clear Aila had inherited the gift." Her mother sighed. "She was the elder sister and already had four daughters." Her gaze shifted to Elise. "And then you were born. My eldest and her youngest." She looked back at Aila. "The three of you warn me not to travel to Dal Riada, and you think it has nothing to do with Bride?"

"Aila." Finella's fearful whisper intruded into the taut silence. "Is something bad going to happen at Dal Riada?"

With clear impatience, her mother beckoned over a servant. "Take Lady Finella into the royal garden. I'll join you shortly."

Despite her protests, Finella went. And only then did her mother once more face Aila.

"Well? Is that true?" Her glance swept from the dowager to Elise and back again. "Is that why you don't want your sister or mother to accompany you?"

Unnamed fear clogged her throat. She surged to her feet and then didn't know where she wished to go. Only that Dal Riada, whether she wanted it or not, was her destination.

"I don't know." The admission tore from her against her will. "I just don't want you and Finella to see me joined to a stranger. A man I have never even met before in my life."

But that was a lie. She did want her mother there. And yet a terrible foreboding knotted her stomach at the thought of the queen entering Dal Riada.

Her mother stood and took her hands. The familiar touch did nothing to soothe Aila's jagged nerves. "What else do you see, Aila?" It was a demand, yet so much anguish threaded each word it was a plea for reassurance. But she had no reassurance, for she saw nothing.

Why wouldn't her mother believe her?

"Devorgilla." The dowager queen also stood and curled her

fingers around their joined hands. "There is nothing else, my daughter. Only the knowledge Aila must make this journey alone, despite our personal objections. That from this darkness that clouds our view, a new alliance will be born. But like all births, pain is inevitable."

The Vikings would be defeated. Her heart was a small price to pay. And while she would pledge her loyalty to her unknown husband, she knew it would never stop her longing for what could never be hers.

Uuen swung a casket onto the desk she used to teach her students. He had been uncharacteristically silent since she'd informed him of her imminent departure, and yet she also had the impression he wasn't surprised by the reason that had brought the Scots to Ce.

They packed vellum, her paints, and the unfinished illuminated history of her people. Would Lord Fergus, Prince of Dal Riada, allow her to continue with her artistic passion? The Scots were not Picts. She'd heard the status of a wife in Dal Riada was little above that of a slave.

But then, she had also once thought all Scots were savages. And then she had met Connor. Perhaps her people misjudged the Scots. Perhaps there was not so much difference between them at all.

The possibility didn't make her feel any better.

Finally, Uuen turned to look at her. "I hope that one day I'll have the honor of seeing the finished manuscript, my lady. And that you'll be able to place it in our library with your own hands."

Aila closed the casket and placed her palm on the carved lid. "So do I." And then she couldn't help herself. "Will I ever return to Ce, Uuen?" But why was she asking him? He was a servant of

God, but this God didn't send obscure messages by way of incomprehensible visions to those who worshipped at his feet.

"That's not for me to know." There was no trace of Uuen's usual joviality. "I confess, my lady, I had hoped for a different outcome for you this week. But the ways of God are mysterious and not for us to question." His gaze locked with hers. "Have faith in Him, my child. He'll show you the way."

His words, intended to comfort, stabbed through her heart. *Never lose faith in him.* She'd imagined, foolishly, her grandmother was referring to Connor. But that was before she'd been given the ultimatum of marriage or the possible annihilation of her people. When she had still harbored, in the secret core of her heart, the impossible dream of a future with her Scot.

But her grandmother hadn't been speaking of Connor at all. It had been a timely rebuke from the God she now followed, a reminder she was no longer beholden to the goddesses of old.

Only when one of the royal guards took the casket from her did the incongruity strike her. No matter that she no longer listened to the ancient ones. Her grandmother believed. Her grandmother was still a conduit.

Why would her grandmother urge such a thing?

ila flexed her fingers and dropped her embroidery onto her lap. For three days she and all the noble ladies in Ceeviot had gathered in the queen's private chambers and sewed as if their lives depended on it.

Her mother was determined Aila's gowns would be a source of great envy among the Scots ladies once she arrived in Dal Riada.

Surreptitiously she glanced around the chamber. Every head was bent, every needle busy. It appeared no one wanted the eldest Princess Devorgilla to be outshone in her new home.

Aila knew she should care. She was the first to make such a marriage and there was little doubt in her mind that others would follow. It was her duty to make a good impression. To foster harmony and trust between her people and those of her husband.

But every time she thought of her unknown husband, acrid fear gripped her heart.

It was one thing to know she could make love with a man who was not Onuist. It was another thing entirely when that man wasn't Connor.

Connor.

It had been three days since she had last seen him.

Since the betrothal, she'd been watched as though she were a highly prized hostage. A royal guard of four shadowed her every move. Yet every moment of her waking day was spent with her mother, her grandmother, sister and cousins and various other ladies.

Only now, when her life was about to change so drastically, did she truly appreciate how much freedom she had enjoyed over the last few years.

She'd all the privileges of her rank, but none of the usual responsibilities that went with it. No husband, no household to run, no servants or slaves to supervise. No children to worry about.

She had poured her passion into her art, into her teaching, as if by so doing she was somehow keeping the memory of Onuist alive. But Onuist would never completely die, not as long as he was remembered. And she had ensured, nine years ago, his memory would live on, honored and revered.

Drun gave a heavy sigh, his head across her feet. Ah, Drun. She thought of her true, unspoken hero. But some things could never be shared and Drun would never condemn her for her silence.

CHEST HEAVING, Connor acknowledged his opponent with a jerk of his head. For three hours he'd fought one warrior after another, broadswords clashing in this field so distant from his home, sweat dripping into the ancient Pictish earth.

It had been three days since he'd last spoken to Aila by the stream. And since then she'd been guarded as if she was—

A bitter laugh escaped. As if she was a princess.

Hands braced against his thighs he sucked in air, only half listening to the conversation of a group of warriors behind him.

"How much longer will that damn princess make us stay in this heathen land?" MacGregor said.

"I doubt the princess has anything to do with it," he heard Cam say. If he wasn't so twisted with fury about the entire situation, he might find wry amusement in the notion of Cam, of all people, defending a Pictish princess against slander. "They're still waiting for the messengers to return from the other Pictish kingdoms."

"I'm reliably informed," said a third voice, MacIntosh, "that the princess intends to take with her three wagonloads of personal possessions."

Connor turned and glared. Only Cam looked uncomfortable. Which just proved how well his relationship with Aila had been concealed from his men.

MacGregor slapped his shoulder, oblivious to how his insult against Aila rankled. "You look like shit. How about we find some willing Pictish maids to entertain us this afternoon? The ladies are all otherwise engaged in attempting to make the princess less hideous to her bridegroom but some of the serving wenches are—"

"Shut it, MacGregor," Cam said with his ever-present glower.

"Aye, you could do with one as well, MacNeil," MacGregor said without rancor. "Might loosen some of that aggression."

"I'll wait," Cam said between his teeth, "until I'm back among my own kind."

"Connor," MacIntosh said under his breath. "Is there a problem you've not shared with us? Did mac Lutin stipulate clauses you doubt MacAlpin will consider?"

With an effort, Connor dragged his attention from the other two. From the enticing notion of smashing their skulls together.

"No, mac Lutin agreed to all the major clauses in principle. He intends to finalize the contract in person."

"I heard he had strong views over the bride price."

His views over the bride price had been immovable. Everything Aila took into her marriage remained hers and, should the marriage for any reason be dissolved, returned to her. But since MacAlpin had foreseen such possibility, he and Ewan had been given permission to concede on this point, if it was raised.

Ewan had conceded. Connor had been excluded from the subsequent meetings. But he hadn't been dragged before mac Lutin nor questioned. And surely if they suspected he had so much as touched their princess, let alone had her in his bed for one glorious night, his head would already be impaled on a spike.

"Everything is going to plan, MacIntosh." Bitterness scorched his voice. Already the messengers that mac Lutin had sent to Fidach, Circinn and Fotla had returned. When the last three reported back, there would be no further reason to delay their departure. "We'll be leaving by week's end."

FINALLY, word came. They were to leave Ce the following morning. Twelve days after they had first entered the kingdom.

It had been five days since he'd last spoken to Aila. Five days since he had even seen her. Now, when he knew how false the rumors surrounding her were, she became as elusive as he had ever accused the eldest Princess Devorgilla of being.

Tonight's feast was a great celebration. A farewell. A goddamn travesty. And yet to refuse to attend would be an insult.

Aila would be there. Like a love-struck youth, he ached to see her, even if only from a distance. Even if seeing her stoked the insanity churning his mind and fueled the fury incinerating his heart.

Aware of the furtive glances he drew as they waited for the royal arrival in the feasting hall, his glower intensified. He knew he looked formidable. Days of drinking and fighting to excess and then the inability to fall into oblivion at night did not make a man look his best.

The senior royals entered the hall. His gaze fixed on the slender figure of Aila as she followed the dowager queen. She was dressed in a forest-green gown with matching veil. Her beautiful hair glowed like ethereal flames in the flicker of the lamplights. Even from this distance, he could see jade, or perhaps emeralds, threaded through her plaits at each point of every lock.

She looked every inch a princess. A royal bride-to-be.

The woman he loved.

As the royal party sat, her gaze caught his. Her veil framed her face, sweeping beneath her chin and draping over her shoulder, and the heavy gold band upon her head glittered with precious jewels. A sacrificial innocent, to appease the bloodthirsty greed of men.

The king's speech, on the benefits of an alliance between Ce and Dal Riada, on the marriage of his beloved daughter to a prince of the Scots, seared through his chest like acid.

Only Ewan's remorseless hand on his shoulder forced him to sit when everyone else did. Only Ewan's solid presence by his side forced him to remain seated when every fiber of his being demanded he march up to the high table and claim Aila for his own.

Claim her. And risk her reputation, his head, and another blood-drenched war.

The feast was interminable. One magnificent dish after another and every one tasted of ashes. Slivers of conversation penetrated his black fog.

"Damn, the princess is a beauty," said MacGregor, sounding torn between astonishment and rising lust.

"Fergus will find it no hardship bedding this bride," MacIntosh agreed.

All his men cared about was the fact Aila wasn't a repellent hag. That Fergus would find her desirable. That within a month, two at most, she would be with child.

He stifled the rage that demanded he challenge them. How dare they speak so of her? Yet all the while, bitter knowledge curdled in his mind. For less than two weeks ago, his opinion had been no different from theirs.

When, hours later, the two long tables were pushed back to the walls to allow space for the entertainment to begin, his patience frayed.

He'd go insane listening to bards and their endless songs of true love. He needed air. Deliberately not glancing in Aila's direction, he marched from the hall.

Unlike the last time he'd escaped the confines of the hall, he was alone outside, apart from the requisite Pictish guards. Unable to remain still, he walked on toward the outer edge of the bright glow thrown by the dozens of torches that surrounded the palace.

Haunting fragments of harp music floated on the breeze and with a muttered curse, he walked farther from the source, around the side of the palace, where silence enveloped him like a malignant savior.

This was only a taste of what was to come. When they reached Dal Riada, when the clauses in the marriage contract had been settled to both kings' satisfaction, there would be a formal betrothal. And then the wedding itself.

Not if he had anything to do with it.

As if summoned by his frenzied thoughts he watched her emerge from stone shadows, accompanied by Elise. Somehow, she'd escaped her royal guard, had used a different exit to the main doors that were so heavily guarded. She hesitated in a pool of light, as though unsure of his reaction.

Desperate hope surged. There could be only one reason why

she sought him out, and he marched toward her, scarcely acknowledging how Elise vanished back into the palace.

"Aila." How good it felt to say her name once again. To see her gazing up at him. To touch—

She held out a hand, warning him against such action. "Douse the torches," she whispered. "No one must see us, Connor. It's too dangerous."

CHAPTER 21

$\mathcal{H}$e wrenched a couple of torches from their iron supports and rammed the flames into the ground. It gave them a degree of privacy. From a distance, no one would be able to distinguish she was the princess.

She'd removed the distinctive crown and already her veil slipped over her silken hair. But she didn't appear to notice.

"I can't stay long." Her whisper was so low he had to bend toward her to catch her words. No hardship. He breathed in deep, savoring her fresh, evocative fragrance. "But I had to see you. I had to tell you how wrong you are."

He stilled. "Wrong?"

She shivered. Instinctively he wrapped his arms around her shoulders, trying to transfer his body heat to her. God knew, his blood was hot enough for the both of them.

She sank against him. He brushed his lips across the top of her head, her hair silky soft, and one hand slid the length of her back to curve around her waist.

She had come to him. She intended to sever the contract. And although she would be disgraced, at least she would be free.

Right now, he couldn't think further than that. But so long as she remained free, there was hope for them both.

Then she straightened and a chill invaded where only seconds before her soft body had shared his warmth. Yet he kept his arms around her, despite the way she stiffened as though his touch no longer pleased her.

"I didn't want you to think the night we shared didn't mean everything to me."

"I didn't think that." Everything to her? That was more than he'd hoped. But he'd never truly believed all he had meant to her was warm memories.

In the shadows it was hard to see her clearly, but he saw the way her lip trembled, as if his reply touched her deeply.

"It was…" she hesitated for a moment. "It was truly the most beautiful night of my life."

He rested his forehead against hers. Bone-deep relief streaked through him. Somehow, she would be his, and they could spend a lifetime creating such nights together. "I'm glad." His voice was rough with need.

Inexplicably she pulled back, and his fingers relaxed, allowing her to break free. Because the only thing she was breaking free from was that cursed marriage contract.

Not him.

She stared up at him, as if committing his features to memory. But she had no need because he would always return to her no matter where his king sent him.

Damn the poor light. He wanted to see the mesmeric green of her eyes, the extraordinary glow of her hair. But most of all he wanted to take her in his arms, carry her off to his bedchamber and show her without the need for awkward words everything she meant to him.

"It would break my heart," her voice was soft, "to think you believed I only used you."

"Hell, Aila." He ached to hold her, but something in the way she continued to look at him stayed his hands. But no matter. There would be plenty of time to hold her later. "I only said that because I was angry. Don't dwell on it. My words in the heat of the moment mean nothing."

An odd expression flickered over her face. As if, far from comforting her, his reassurance had somehow wounded. But it vanished in an instant and he wondered if he had imagined such a fanciful notion.

"I know." Infinite sadness threaded through her words, belying the smile she offered. "I wasn't going to tell you. But then I thought, why not? It's the truth. And I would rather you know the truth than ever have any doubt as to how much you mean to me."

Unease flickered deep inside although he couldn't fathom why. "The truth?"

She gripped her fingers together. "Yes. I love you. It's the reason I came to your bedchamber. The reason I shared your bed. I will always love you. And if you ever think of me, please always remember that."

If he ever thought of her? He would never cease to think of her. Would never forget this night when she had given him what he so desired.

A laugh rumbled deep inside and he claimed the small step that separated them. Strangely she retreated a corresponding step that brought her back against the stone wall of the palace.

"I promise," he said, again wishing there was more light so he could see every detail of her lovely face. "I will always remember."

Another uneven sigh whispered from her lips, as though his promise reassured her. Had she truly been concerned he could ever think of her with anything but pleasure?

"Then I should go." But her words lacked conviction and where did she think she was going anyway? He cradled her chilled face and pressed his body against hers. Even through his plaid and her gown she would feel the extent of his arousal.

"You're not going anywhere. Not yet." Before she could respond, his mouth claimed hers and his tongue invaded her parted lips. He thrust into her and her wet heat embraced as he angled himself more thoroughly against her, his cock hard as iron. Wanted, needed, to penetrate her more intimately. To prove to her, beyond reason, how much he returned her love.

Still holding her face with one hand, his other trailed the length of her jaw, her neck, and molded the curve of her breast. God, this was torture. His blood was on fire, his cock in agony. Her scent invaded his senses, her skin entranced him. Her tiny moans of pleasure sent him spiraling into insanity.

His thumb caressed the hard peak of her nipple. He imagined ripping her gown from her, taking her succulent nipple into his mouth. Lifting her skirts and impaling her where she stood.

He dragged his mouth from her and panted into her face. He might want her up against a wall, but it wouldn't be an outside wall. Wouldn't be where anyone might pass by and see them. See *her*. Hell no. She was his and her body was for his eyes only.

"Aila." His voice was ragged. "I want you." He was incapable of explaining further, but it didn't matter. She knew how he felt. Knew what he meant. They needed privacy, so he could show her in ways that words never could.

With surprising force, she flattened her palms against his chest and shoved. He didn't relinquish her face or her breast, but he eased back a fraction, an unwilling concession to her obvious demand.

"Don't." Her voice was breathless. Shock stabbed through him. She sounded on the verge of tears. "Don't tarnish what we had by doing this."

Tarnish? Did she think he was going to ravish her as though he were an undisciplined bastard?

"I'd no intention of taking you out here." Damn, but it was hard to speak when all he could think about was parting her thighs and sinking into her beautiful, welcoming body.

She curled her fingers around his wrist and attempted to tug his hand from her breast. And because he had no idea why she was doing it, he allowed her to.

"I have to go." There was a tremble in her voice, yet she still managed to sound immovable. And despite his lust, he knew she was right. She had to go back. Had to see out the rest of the night. But later—later she would find a way to come to him.

Something occurred to him. He struggled to batten down his need, and focus on facts.

"Have you told your father yet?" His thumb stroked her heated cheek. "Do you want me with you when you do?" He risked his neck, but if she wanted him by her side when she confronted the Pictish king, then nothing would keep him away.

Her eyes widened in horror. "Of course I haven't. I never will. I'd never put your life in such danger."

He managed a halfhearted grin. "Aye, well I didn't mean go into the details of the other night." He wound his fingers around one plait and let the silken rope slide against his palm. "I meant when you tell him—if you haven't already—that you're breaking the betrothal."

The silence after his words was more than a pause. It sank into the night around them, blacker and deeper than any abyss. A silence that shrieked louder than any scream of protest.

He stared into her eyes. Refused to acknowledge the insidious whisper of truth that gnawed through his mind. Refused to even contemplate the possibility.

Thrust the kernel of doubt aside.

"Well?" His demand was harsh.

She stiffened. "Why do you assume I'm breaking the betrothal?"

He refused to think. Refused to analyze. Focused entirely on this moment.

"Because you're here."

"Yes, I'm here. Because I had to see you. To make sure you understood what you mean to me."

She was speaking his language, as she had since the first time they had met. There was no misunderstanding between them. Her words were clear. But they made no sense. How could she stand there, tell him she loved him and not be prepared to break the betrothal?

"I understand what I mean to you." It would do no good to vent his impatience on her. She was clearly confused by events. "That's why you can't marry Fergus."

"I've given my word." Her voice was low, yet so regal, as if she were a queen explaining something fundamental to a mere peasant.

The analogy stung and he braced his palms on the wall on either side of her shoulders, a blatant reminder she was out here alone with him. So close he could feel her breath on his face and yet the icy conviction gripped him that she was as distant as she had been for these last five days.

Slowly, deliberately, he pressed his body against hers, and her curves molded to him as if they belonged together. Because they did belong together. And why she couldn't see that was beyond him.

"You're a woman." Their lips almost brushed. He slid one knee between her legs and exerted pressure against the tempting juncture of her thighs. Felt her startled gasp caress his mouth. Desire thrummed in his blood, clouded his reason. The thought of her pledging her loyalty to Fergus knotted his guts. "Tell your father you've heard sick tales of the prince." Her father loved her. That was the reason he had asked so many questions of the proposed bridegroom. And Connor had told him what he had wanted to hear. The knowledge that he was responsible for mac Lutin accepting Fergus for his daughter enraged him. "Tell him you've changed your mind."

Her hands curled around his biceps. But she didn't try to push him away. It was as if she needed his strength.

God knew, she had it. "Would you go back on your word to your king?"

He stared at her, uncomprehending. "Why would I do that?" He was a warrior. A warrior didn't break his word to his king. "We're not talking about me, Aila. This is about you. Your future. Your life."

Her hands slid from his biceps, inched between their melded bodies, and flattened against his chest.

"My love." Her voice was gentle and the words he'd fantasized her saying to him eased his battered heart. At last, she had seen sense. He allowed the smallest smile of relief to touch his lips. "Is a woman's integrity worth less than a man's?"

And froze.

"What?" The word scraped between his teeth, incredulous. How could she ask him such a thing? How could she insinuate that he somehow thought her lacking simply because she didn't possess the honor of a warrior?

Her bottom lip trembled. But shadows or not, he couldn't see a hint of tears.

"How could I hope to keep your respect if I break my word so easily?"

"My respect?' He could scarcely articulate the word. "It's not my respect I'm offering you."

Except it was. He offered her everything. But unless she broke her word, there would never be even a chance of his offer being accepted.

"You once admired my loyalty."

His hands fisted, knuckles grazed against the unyielding stone. "So now you throw my words back in my face." Of course he admired her loyalty—but this was different. "He's my half-brother, for God's sake. You don't have the first idea what he's like."

Fergus would never be faithful to her. And while he might never hurt her physically, Aila would fade beneath his brother's brash insensitivity.

"Do you think I don't know that?" Raw pain vibrated through every word. And instead of victory that he'd finally touched her, all he felt was despair. "I'll spend the rest of my life knowing I'm with the wrong brother."

He seized on her confession. "Then end it now. It will cause a storm, but it'll soon pass. MacAlpin knows of your reputation as a recluse. Offense can be averted. There are ways around this, Aila, if you will just—"

"Just what? Compromise my honor?"

Frustration ripped through him. "No man will dare question your honor within my hearing." She looked at him but didn't respond. Her expression showed she knew he had subtly altered her interpretation of honor to suit himself.

He knew, as well as she, that her integrity would be questioned. Her reputation damaged.

But at least she wouldn't be wedded to Fergus.

He recalled the night they had shared. His reckless behavior. And seized on the one possibility that might—that had to—possess the power to change her mind. Even if that very possibility sent shards of terror deep into his soul.

"What if you're wrong?" His voice was harsh, racked between hope and fear that he was right. "About the other night? You could have conceived my child, Aila. You could be carrying my babe as we speak. Would you truly marry another man, knowing that's a real possibility?"

"I'm not with child." Her voice was strangely devoid of emotion.

"You can't know for certain." God knew, he didn't want her to be with child, but if it was the only way she would see sense—Christ, how could he wish this on her? But how could he not?

"I do. And I am not going to bear your child."

Wretched despair snaked through him. There was only one reason why she could be so sure. Her body had cleansed her womb of his seed with her blood.

"I may not be a warrior." Pain clouded her voice, but once again that regal resolve underpinned every word. "I don't ride into battle with broadsword and shield. But I made a vow on the memory of my husband Onuist that I would do whatever I could to help rid this land of the Viking invaders." She paused for one heartbreaking moment. "Would you have me break that oath simply because I find the means not to my liking?"

Her question, her accusation, thundered between them, opening a chasm impossible to breach with words or blood or even his heart laid at her feet.

She loved him. But she loved her dead husband more. The husband who had sacrificed his life for hers. Who had died a hero, and about whom bards sang.

He dragged himself upright, arms dropping to his sides. There was nothing else he could say to her. Aila was a woman, but her honor and integrity were as much a part of her as the color of her eyes or shade of her hair. If she sacrificed either, her worth would be diminished in her eyes, if not in his own.

Yet he loved her because of who she was. And she was Aila.

But he'd be damned if he'd stand by and watch her marry his half-brother.

CHAPTER 22

*a*ila kept her gaze straight ahead and tried to ignore the nervous churn of her stomach. Soon they would reach Dunadd, the royal stronghold of Dal Riada, and while she longed for this interminable journey to end, she dreaded its inevitable outcome.

For two weeks, they had traveled through glens and mountain passes. At night they'd stayed in various Pictish hillforts and palaces. And their numbers had increased as kings and nobles and warriors joined their progress.

The last few nights, after entering the Scots territory within Pictland, had been spent in foreign property. While they had been treated with nothing but respect, she'd felt like an oddity, an exhibit on display. She knew it would only get worse after arriving at Dunadd.

Connor kept his distance. His message couldn't be plainer. If he couldn't have her the way he wanted her, then he didn't want any part of her at all.

Drawn by an invisible thread her gaze tugged to the left. Connor and a group of Scots warriors were overtaking the ambling pace of the massively extended train. Again, her stomach pitched, although whether it was the sight of Connor on horseback or the knowledge that he was riding ahead in order to announce their imminent arrival at Dunadd, she couldn't say.

He didn't glance her way. He might have been entirely oblivious to her presence.

Her fingers tightened on the reins as she forcibly dragged her gaze from his retreating back. She knew the thought of her marrying his brother disgusted him. Would he be so enraged if her proposed husband was a different lord? Or was it the thought of her marrying—no matter whom—that so infuriated him?

But what did he expect from her?

It wasn't as though he'd ever spoken of his plans for the future to her. He'd taken the night she'd offered without any indication afterward of wanting to prolong their liaison. And while she cherished the words he'd whispered in the throes of passion, words that hugged her heart and filled her lonely soul, she knew it highly likely he didn't even remember them.

Hadn't he told her, that last night they had spoken, that what he said in the heat of the moment meant nothing?

As Dunadd became visible in the distance, on top of a mighty hill on the west coast of Pictland, a dark despair dug in poisoned claws. And lurking beneath the flimsy facade of piousness instilled over the last nine years she glimpsed the raw truth.

She wanted his love, even if she could never accept it. Even if it meant Connor, the man whose happiness she craved above all else, suffered agonies because of that love.

She tried to retract the thought, smother it. Pretend it had never touched her mind because it was selfish, cruel. *Pagan.*

But it made no difference. Whether she wanted to acknowledge it or not, ancient pagan blood ran through her veins and in this moment of clarity, she saw the unvarnished truth.

If given the choice between Connor loving her or having simply used her because she was available, she'd take his love.

Despite the pain it caused him.

~

THREE HOURS LATER, after having arrived at Dunadd, Connor watched Aila as the royal party was greeted by a noble council. For two weeks he'd avoided her, yet been excruciatingly aware of her every movement. For two weeks he'd formed plans and strategies only to discard them in disgust. And now the moment had arrived he was no clearer in his mind as to how he was going to persuade his king against this disastrous marriage.

"Connor." Ewan gripped his arm. "You aren't truly going to speak to MacAlpin about this matter, are you?"

In a moment of madness during the journey, Connor had confided in his oldest friend. And been offended by Ewan's horror of his intention to confront their king. He wrenched his arm free and sent Ewan a dark glare.

"What would you have me do? Stand by while Aila marries my brother?" Far from diminishing, the revulsion at such a future had magnified beyond endurance. "If she refuses to save herself, then I have no choice."

"Don't say I didn't warn you if your head ends up on a spike."

Connor turned on his heel and marched off. There was a chance he might infuriate the king, but he was sure his head was in no danger.

At least, as long as MacAlpin remained in ignorance of the night Connor had shared with the princess.

~

"MY LIEGE." Connor rose from his knee as MacAlpin beckoned him forward. They were in the war chamber and, miraculously, MacAlpin was not surrounded by his advisors.

"Why so grim?" MacAlpin slapped him on the shoulder, clearly well pleased. "Events are proceeding exactly as planned."

That was the problem.

"I have reservations." The words were out, stark and uncompromising. He'd had more than two weeks to perfect this speech and still the right damn words eluded him.

MacAlpin raised his eyebrows in obvious surprise. "Reservations?"

"Aye." His mouth dried. Christ, now what? From nowhere, his brain hooked on to the image of Aila with her father. The questions the Ce king had demanded Connor answer before agreeing to this alliance. "I've had time to watch the King of Ce. He is devoted to his daughter. I fear once he discovers Fergus' true nature toward women and fidelity, he'll demand a retraction of the betrothal."

MacAlpin didn't appear overly concerned. "Are you the King of Ce's mouthpiece? Did he send you here with this… threat?"

Threat? "No, my liege. I speak only from my personal observations." He spoke for Aila. Because she refused to speak for herself.

MacAlpin gave a short laugh devoid of mirth. "MacKenzie, all fathers are devoted to their daughters. We want them to make successful marriages and strengthen our alliances. The fidelity of their chosen husband is, I assure you, of little significance to us."

Sweat trickled along Connor's spine. He knew, without question, had he told the King of Ce about Fergus' predilection for young slave girls, his aversion to matrimony and distaste for tying himself to a wife, the king would never have agreed to the alliance.

"My liege, the Picts are different in the way they—"

"No, Connor." MacAlpin took one step toward him. "The Picts are no different from us in this matter. Only you, with your idealized vision of marriage, can't see it. And who are you to level such accusations against your brother?" MacAlpin narrowed his eyes. "Do you think me unaware of your liaisons these past four years? The married women you take to your bed? You're no better than any other noble in my court in that regard."

The accusation stung, but he wasn't talking of any other noble. Wasn't referring to any other political marriage. Impotent rage twisted through his blood. "At least I have never taken a woman against her will."

He thought MacAlpin was going to thrust his words aside. Slaves were of no account and a wife little better. But then the king drew back, as if seriously considering the matter.

"Fergus will never harm the princess. Her well-being is our priority. No matter what your brother does outside of the marriage bed, be assured the Ce king will have no complaint as to how his daughter is treated as the wife of a Dal Riadan prince."

Desperation clawed through Connor's guts. There had to be something he could say that would sway his king's mind. "My liege—"

"Enough." MacAlpin's command slashed through the chamber with the force of a battle-ax. "Your concern for the continuation of this alliance is commendable. However." MacAlpin's icy gaze froze the words of denial on Connor's tongue. "Take a care, Connor, that you always remember to whom you owe your loyalty."

WHEN AILA REACHED HER CHAMBERS, exhaustion overtook her and she sank onto the bed. Six noble ladies comprised her personal retinue and stood in a semicircle before her, awaiting instructions. They were older than was usual for a princess of her age, widowed and without young children. There were none of royal blood. Her mother, for all her influence, had failed to persuade any other king to relinquish a treasured daughter to accompany hers into an unknown future.

A feast was to be held in her honor, when she would meet MacAlpin and his cousin's son. Her betrothed. She stifled the knot of fear and gripped her fingers together. These ladies were not strangers to her, but none of them were close confidantes. She couldn't show her true feelings. She was their princess and they looked to her for guidance in this new life.

But who would she look to?

A knock on the antechamber door distracted her and as two of the ladies left the bedchamber, she hoped it was her dear faithful servant Floradh returning with refreshments. Floradh, who had refused to be left behind in Ce despite her advancing years.

Floradh, who was the closest thing to a friend she had in this strange new world.

Her ladies returned. "Madam," Cailleach said. "Lady Maeve Balfour wishes to extend her greetings to you." She paused, glanced at her companion. "She also brings refreshments."

God, she was in no fit state to play hostess. She wanted to be left alone until the last possible moment. Until she had to attend the feast this evening and once again be subjected to endless speculation.

She inclined her head. "Of course." She would have no Scot accuse a Pict of being ill-mannered. "Show her through."

Receiving visitors in her bedchamber was scarcely the correct protocol, but her antechamber was crowded with her and her ladies' traveling caskets and belongings that had yet to be sorted out.

And besides, she wasn't sure her legs would support her if she attempted to stand. The last few days of the journey had been especially tiring. She hoped Lady Maeve Balfour wouldn't stay long so she could try to rest before the dreaded feast.

She watched the Scot enter her chamber, and her spine stiffened further. She already knew, from the nights she'd spent in the Scot-owned hillforts, that the gowns of Scots ladies were very different from her own. It was another point of disparity between them. Another fact that made her stand out when all she wanted was to blend in.

It didn't help that all her gowns were highly embroidered at the bodice and sleeves in threads of gold and scarlet. The Scots' gowns were often a white plaid, with a few small stripes of black, blue, and red, girdled around the waist with elaborate silver buckles and jewels.

Not Lady Maeve Balfour though. Her gown, although in the same style as the other Scots ladies Aila had already met, was a vibrant blue and her buckle and brooch were of gold, set with precious gems.

Lady Maeve sank into a curtsey. "Welcome to Dunadd, Lady Devorgilla," she said in deeply accented Pictish. "I hope you find happiness with us."

The simple speech eased her terror in a way the formal greeting earlier had only managed to intensify. "Thank you," she said in her own language. And then something made her add, "I speak your tongue."

Relief flooded Lady Maeve's lovely face. "I'm glad, madam. I'm afraid my Pictish is very limited."

It may have been limited but at least she'd gone to the trouble of addressing Aila in her own language. That was more than the official welcoming council had done. In itself that didn't worry her. She could, after all, understand the Gaelic language. But it was the unshakable feeling that the Scots nobles had assumed she didn't comprehend their words—and they didn't care.

She'd seen the assessing glances they'd leveled her way. And because they clearly assumed she didn't speak Gaelic she hadn't deigned to enlighten them.

But it had done nothing to lighten her fears for the future. The fear that the rumors were true. That, with perhaps some exceptions, the men of Dal Riada did consider their womenfolk inferior in intellect.

She glanced at her ladies and they brought over a small table for the refreshments and a stool for Lady Maeve.

They passed a few pleasantries, remarking upon the length of the journey and the comfortable appointment of her chambers. Lady Maeve was even kind enough to admire the embroidery on Aila's gown. Embroidery that Finella had painstakingly labored over during the last week before she'd left Ce.

She couldn't think of Finella now. Couldn't face the possibility they would never see each other again. Only when she was alone would she ever be able to unfurl her heart. Embrace her loved ones' memories. Because when she did, she was not certain she'd be able to hold back the tears.

She had to change the subject.

"I look forward to meeting the prince tonight." That was a lie. But she would have to get used to lying. The rest of her life was going to be one great lie. She fixed a smile on her lips and picked up a cup of aromatic tea.

"Aye, madam. We are all very much looking forward to the alliance between our two peoples."

Aila sipped her herbal tea so she didn't have to keep smiling. Lady Maeve's accent reminded her of Connor's. Doubtless every person here possessed the same turn of phrase, the same inflection on their words.

"I know nothing of the prince." She hoped her voice was light and didn't sound as despairing to Lady Maeve as it did to her own ears. "He is a great warrior, I imagine?" With raven-black hair and stormy-gray eyes? She'd go insane if Fergus resembled Connor in looks as well as voice and accent.

"Indeed, madam. He's as brave and honorable a warrior as any in Dal Riada."

Of course he was. After all, he shared Connor's bloodline.

Desperate hope pierced her heart. Perhaps she and the prince could come to an arrangement after their wedding. Perhaps he would be agreeable to a marriage of political convenience only.

Perhaps, if Fergus shared his brother's sense of honor, she wouldn't be forced to submit to another man in her bed.

It was a slender, tenuous hope. But the only hope she had.

CONNOR KEPT his arms folded across his chest as Fergus, dripping sweat from his training session, marched toward him across the flattened grass, broadsword still in hand.

"You're back then?" The words were a snarl as he shoved his weapon at a servant to clean. "A pox on MacAlpin, going behind my back. Now I'm saddled with a cantankerous shrew. If he wanted me shackled, he could at least have found me a young malleable virgin."

Connor's hands fisted. Images of smashing his brother's jaw flashed through his mind. So visceral he could smell the iron tang of blood as it splattered across his knuckles.

"Princess Devorgilla of Ce is twenty-six." Where MacAlpin had got his information from Connor couldn't imagine. No one with eyes in his head could look at Aila and think her a belligerent hag.

"An old woman." Fergus glared, as if Aila's age was a personal affront. "Why should I get something another man's defiled? My bride should be untouched."

Dark rage pounded through Connor's chest, constricting the breath in his lungs, tightening his throat. And then, between one infuriated heartbeat and the next, lightning flashed across his brain, illuminating the black fog.

"You're right." His voice was harsh, and Fergus shot him a distrustful frown at the sudden agreement. "A prince of Dal Riada deserves a virgin bride."

"Aye." Fergus sounded slightly mollified by Connor's evident understanding of the matter. "Who knows what unsavory habits a woman of her age has acquired?"

Connor struggled to hold on to his unraveling threads of temper. Fergus was playing straight into his hand. All he had to do was feed his brother's sense of injustice, stoke the fire of rebellion and Fergus would request MacAlpin extricate him from the betrothal.

"It's likely," he said in response to his brother's remark, "she is as set in her ways as an elderly maiden aunt."

The silence was broken only by the clash of sword on sword as warriors practiced on the field. Fergus watched them for a moment before turning to Connor, his eyes narrowed against the afternoon sun.

"You've seen her, this betrothed of mine?" He sounded as though he spoke of a plague. "Is she as hideous as rumor has it?"

Connor stared at the fighting warriors but saw Aila in his mind. To agree with his brother was pointless since no man would find the princess hideous. Instead he shrugged, as if the matter was of little account. "She's attractive enough. But not your type."

Silence again. Then Fergus folded his arms. "Really? Tell me, Connor. Is she your type?"

Caught in his own trap, Connor rounded on his brother, disbelief and incredulity at his own stupidity pounding through his chest. How had Fergus jumped to that conclusion? He hadn't given any indication of how he felt. Had he?

Fergus regarded him, his face an implacable mask. Perhaps, after all, his brother only bantered and meant nothing by his pointed remark.

"I hadn't given the matter much thought."

"It appears to me you've given the matter a great deal of thought."

God's death, could this day get any worse?

"You're mistaken." Connor glowered across the field, fingers itching to draw his sword and release some of the hellish energy that thundered through his arteries. "I'm merely agreeing with your objections to this match."

"Aye. And that's what I find so..." Fergus paused, considering the matter. "Interesting."

Connor grunted. It seemed the safest answer since everything else he had uttered this day had been turned inside out and manipulated beyond all sense.

"I don't for one moment," Fergus said, "imagine you give a shit about my marital happiness. We both know a wife will hinder me not in the slightest in my pursuit of earthly pleasures."

Connor's chest constricted. Of course he knew that. And if he'd been honest with the King of Ce when answering the king's penetrating questions, then perhaps Aila would not now be in imminent danger of shackling herself to Fergus for the rest of her life.

Fergus appeared to be enjoying himself. "Therefore, I can only conclude it's the happiness of the princess that concerns you. Do you desire her for yourself?"

Connor glared at his smirking brother. He could deny the accusation but there was no point. Fergus would believe whatever he wanted to believe whether it was the truth or not.

"You don't want this marriage. You don't want the princess. Tell MacAlpin, Fergus. He'll find a way to free you from the obligation." He was clutching at insubstantial fantasies. But even the slenderest of hope was better than nothing.

"I didn't want this marriage," Fergus said. "But there's no way I'll ask MacAlpin to free me from this betrothal now." He laughed. "You want this princess, don't you? And she is destined to be *my* bride. Destined to bear *my* sons. And all you can do is stand by and watch."

CHAPTER 23

Connor had never seen so many bodies pressed into the great hall. A lower high table had been set up for the many royal guests, leaving the high table for MacAlpin's intimates and the immediate kin of Aila.

And now his king entered, leading the distinguished party that included his brother and his bride-to-be.

As she followed mac Lutin, a ripple of interest spread throughout the hall. Heads craned for a better look at this foreign princess, breath inhaled, whispers echoed. She looked as regal as the queen she might one day become as she sat on a carved chair, the sumptuous gold of her gown a stunning contrast to the scarlet embroidery at her bodice and along her sleeves. Her veil too was scarlet and once again she wore the gem-encrusted crown.

She could have been one of the mystical fae folk from ancient tales, who had stumbled by accident into the drab world of mortals.

He couldn't drag his wretched gaze from her.

MacAlpin's speech of welcome droned through Connor's brain, meaningless. Aila did not glance to her left or right, merely looked at some indefinable point in the distance, as if the purpose of this feast meant nothing to her.

And then mac Lutin responded, taking Aila's hand in a gesture of clear pride. Offering his daughter to Fergus MacKenzie in an alliance to bond both peoples of Pictland.

It was done. The cheering and stamping of feet pounded against Connor like waves in a storm. Yet unlike when navigating a stormy sea, he possessed no learned wisdom on how to deal with the acidic energy firing through his blood.

"The princess is quite beautiful," Maeve said as they finally sat, and extravagant dishes were brought in. He couldn't fathom why she'd decided to sit next to him when he'd broken their liaison. "At least Fergus no longer looks as if he wishes to rip the king's head off."

Unwillingly Connor glanced at Fergus. Although seated at the other end of the table from Aila he obviously liked what he'd seen of her, if the self-congratulatory grin on his face was anything to go by. But then, it no longer mattered to Fergus whether he liked the look of Aila or not. All that mattered was he had taken what Connor wanted.

He couldn't trust himself to answer. Instead he downed a tankard of mead, refusing to look in Aila's direction.

"I took it upon myself," Maeve said, "to visit the princess this afternoon."

Wariness prickled along his skin as he turned to look at her. Maeve had a smile on her lips as she toyed with the stem of her goblet, but he knew her too well. She was hiding something.

"And how did you find her?" He jerked his head at a servant for more mead and tried not to glare at Maeve nor glance at Aila. He only succeeded by draining his tankard once again.

Maeve hesitated before taking a deep breath. "I found her most courteous. I hope your brother appreciates how fortunate he is to wed such a princess. For all that she's a foreigner."

He grunted, considered downing a third tankard within as

many minutes and decided against it. "Fergus appreciates nothing of true value."

Even as the words spilled from him, he knew it was a lie. There was one thing Fergus valued above his royal blood. Something that had nothing to do with power and prestige.

He thrust the thought aside. Fergus had made him pay bitterly for such jealousies when they had been children. And now, when he'd thought his brother's power over him had long since faded, Fergus was taking the woman Connor loved.

"She's not at all how I imagined. How any of us imagined."

Maeve had no idea. He couldn't even summon the energy to grunt in response and instead stared blindly into his tankard.

Silence hummed between them, a silence punctuated by the incessant, bawdy conversation thudding against his ears from seemingly every person in the hall.

"Does she know?"

Maeve's low words pierced his mead-induced fog and he gave her a wary look. "Know what?"

Maeve was no longer smiling. She looked oddly haunted. "The princess, Connor. Does she know how you feel about her?"

Alarm whipped through him, instantly eliminating the encroaching fog. "I feel nothing for her." He'd spoken too swiftly. He struggled to sound less rabid. "Only a measure of sympathy that she's soon to be shackled to my faithless half-brother."

"Aye." Maeve's voice was soft. "I'm truly sorry, Connor."

Denial thundered through his brain. Maeve couldn't have guessed his true feelings. It was bad enough that Fergus knew. "There's nothing to be sorry about. I feel nothing for Aila. She's just a means to the end."

"Aila." Maeve said nothing else, simply looked at him, and he realized his fatal blunder.

The silence stretched between them and he knew that whatever he said, whatever he did, would make no difference. Maeve knew.

He released a tortured breath. "By the time I discovered who she truly was, it was too late."

Maeve's fingers tightened around the stem of her goblet. "Perhaps," she hesitated, and appeared to be struggling with her thoughts. "Did you consider the possibility of taking her as your mistress after she is wed?"

No, he hadn't considered it, because he'd spent the last weeks denying the possibility that this cursed marriage would go ahead. But barring an act of divine intervention, or Aila finally coming to her senses, it appeared she was destined to belong to his half-brother.

"Her sense of honor," his voice was bitter, and he couldn't help it, "would never allow her to be unfaithful to Fergus."

"Perhaps not at first. But after a while..." *After she had produced a legitimate heir.* The unspoken words hovered like a specter between them. "She may. If she loves you, Connor, why wouldn't she?"

He gave a mirthless laugh. "Aye. But this is Lady Aila we're talking about. She stood in front of me and said she loved me. And then told me she was going to marry my half-brother."

Confusion flashed over Maeve's face. "You hold that against her? But she had no choice once her father made the decision."

The rage he'd managed to suppress beneath his own frantic plans heaved, like a volcano stirring from a restless slumber. "No. It's different in the Pictish kingdoms, Maeve. Women have more freedom than in Dal Riada." The kings might rule the lands, but their queens were not merely chattels to produce royal heirs. He'd soon discovered the Queen of Ce had taken it as a personal insult against her honor when he had refused to divulge his purpose to anyone but the king.

And mac Lutin hadn't agreed to the match until after he'd spoken with Aila. If she had declined, there was no doubt in Connor's mind her father wouldn't have demanded her compliance.

But Aila had agreed. Despite the night they'd shared together. Even though she knew how he felt about her.

Even though she loved him.

"But a royal marriage—"

"She put duty above her own feelings." He glared at Maeve but saw Aila that night as she'd stood before him and thrown his love, his heart, back in his face.

"And because she's a woman, you find that incomprehensible." Maeve's voice was soft, but a thread of censure scraped against his flayed senses.

"Aye." He couldn't help a fleeting glance at Aila. She looked as remote and untouchable as an ice maiden. "She wasn't forced." Unlike so many noblewomen of Dal Riada who had no choice in the man they married, he knew—in his gut—Aila had been offered such a choice.

It didn't matter that, fundamentally, he respected her integrity. Because it didn't change the raw burn of rejection that, without even a semblance of a fight, she had chosen Fergus over him.

Finally, the feast ended. Aila smothered a sigh of relief and struggled not to let her facade crumble. People still glanced her way. Continued to assess her. Nothing in her life had prepared her for the way she had been on display tonight, and every nerve in her body was stretched so taut she feared at any moment she would shatter.

The long tables were shoved back to the walls and despair knotted her stomach as musicians took their playing positions and fine-tuned their harps. Beneath the high table, she gripped her fingers together and searched frantically for an elusive remnant of calm.

But instead her glance fell upon Connor. The one man she'd spent all night desperately trying to avoid looking at. Even though she knew exactly where he sat, how many tankards of mead he consumed and how animatedly he conversed with Lady Maeve Balfour by his side.

They stood together now. A striking couple and she couldn't shake the feeling that they were more than mere acquaintances. Acidic jealousy seared her gut, twisting like poisoned serpents.

Would Connor take Lady Maeve to his bedchamber tonight? Did she have any right to condemn him if he did?

She knew she had no right at all. And yet she would condemn him for taking another woman when all she wanted was for him to take *her*.

Her thoughts pounded against her temples, escalating the headache that had plagued her all night. Did she expect Connor to remain celibate for the rest of his life? Never look at another woman much less find pleasure in one?

No. Dear God, she wanted him to be happy. But even as she wanted that, the thought of him finding happiness with another tore her heart to shreds.

"Lady Devorgilla." The deep voice pulled her from her thoughts, and she realized Fergus was by her side, smiling down at her, and extending his hand. And speaking her language. "May I have the honor of the first dance?"

Panic churned through her. They had already been introduced, a brief cursory introduction before the feast. And the fear that had gripped her then returned in force.

Fergus looked nothing like Connor. For which she should be grateful. He possessed, like his brother, a hard warrior body, towered over her, and his face was handsome enough to make any maiden swoon. But his hair was blond, his eyes were blue and all she saw when she looked at him was the personification of every Viking she had ever encountered.

Only years of successfully hiding her true feelings prevented her from flinching. Instead she placed her hand in his and mentally gritted her teeth against the revulsion that crawled from the tips of her fingers and along the length of her arm at his touch.

"Thank you." She forced a smile to her lips. "I fear the journey has tired me. Would it please you to sit with me instead?" *And release your predatory hold on my hand.*

He looked momentarily surprised, as though her refusal to

accede to his wishes was unexpected. But he motioned a slave, who brought his chair over, then Fergus sat beside her without attempting to change her mind.

He still held on to her hand.

"The journey must have been arduous for a lady such as yourself." He smiled at her again. There was nothing evil or distasteful about his smile and yet she found nothing comforting in it. "I hope you manage to rest sufficiently between now and our upcoming wedding."

She tried to withdraw her hand, but Fergus' grip was unrelenting. It appeared he intended to ensure her hand, at least, remained within his power even if she'd refused him the right to hold her more intimately while dancing.

"I'm sure I will." Fergus would never guess how her stomach pitched at his words. At the look in his eyes. Her fragile hope that her future husband might be agreeable to a marriage in name only vanished like morning mist.

"Connor." Fergus beckoned with his free hand and Aila didn't dare follow his glance. "It appears you've exhausted my bride-to-be in your haste to return to Dal Riada."

She knew Connor was standing at the other side of the table. His body blocked out the rest of the hall. If she gave in to her weak desire to look at him, he would block out the rest of the world.

"I've no doubt Lady Devorgilla will recover," Connor said as she struggled against the overwhelming need to look at him. Feast upon him.

Fergus raised her hand to his lips and skimmed kisses over her knuckles.

"She is a delectable piece, isn't she?" He continued to look at her but spoke to his brother. In Gaelic. Clearly, he was as ignorant as his king's advisors as to her ability to understand his language.

"Fergus." Connor's voice was feral. She dared not look his way. If she did, she'd crumble.

Fergus finally released her hand and she buried it in her lap before he could change his mind.

"My preconceived notions were wrong." Fergus flashed Connor a grin that left her in no doubt as to what his preconceived notions might have been. "I think I'll enjoy having this princess warming my bed at nights. I'll be sure to let you know whether she pleases me or not."

From the corner of her eye, she saw Connor's hand fist against his thigh. Briefly she closed her eyes, but still it seemed the hall spun around her.

A legacy of how she'd been unable to swallow more than a few mouthfuls of the mighty feast.

When she once again opened her eyes, Fergus was regarding her as if she were a prized warhorse.

"You do look a little fatigued, madam." He spoke in Pictish and sounded solicitous. "Perhaps you should retire, to conserve your strength." Then he smiled. She was likely the only woman in Dal Riada who found nothing seductive about it. "I wish you to be fully rested in order to enjoy our wedding night as much as I."

She wouldn't think of the wedding night. She'd focus on the fact he'd given her an excuse to leave the hall.

To leave Connor.

She allowed Fergus to take her hand to help her rise from her chair.

"You're too thoughtful." She sounded as though she implied the opposite. Fortunately, Fergus didn't appear to notice.

"My thoughts are all for you, my lady." He sounded sincere and yet she didn't believe a word. "I trust you will sleep well." He bowed over her hand, a lavish, practiced gesture, and she was unable to respond in the accepted manner because all she could feel were Connor's eyes burning into her.

Without a backward glance, she walked to the door, her ladies surrounding her in a protective cocoon. But at the door, her resolve faltered, and she paused and glanced over her shoulder.

In that fleeting instant she saw Fergus, her future husband, the man whose thoughts were all for her, grab a young slave girl and haul her toward the outside doors. And she saw Connor, standing where she had left him and looking at her across the hall as if they were the only two people alive.

～

"I don't trust MacAlpin or any of his advisers."

Aila sighed and glanced at Talargan as he sat beside her on the hill. Her ladies were some distance from them, for privacy, as were the royal guard who shadowed her every move.

It had been three days since they had arrived in Dunadd. It felt like three years.

She stroked the tiny black kitten that slept on her lap. "I doubt any of them trust us either."

Her brother looked at her. "He seems to think the Kingdom of Fortriu is his by rights. That his coronation at Forteviot is a foregone conclusion." He took her hand. "I fear your sacrifice might not be enough to avert another battle between Pict and Scot, Aila."

"It has to be." What good was this marriage if it didn't bring the people of Pictland together? "We can't fight each other, Tal, if we want to vanquish the Vikings."

Instead of replying, Talargan's gaze slid beyond her and his glare intensified. Without turning she knew who approached. Her skin prickled in awareness and her chest tightened, constricting her lungs. It took every particle of willpower she possessed not to follow her brother's gaze and watch Connor stride toward them.

He stopped some distance from them and bowed. A stiff, perfunctory gesture that acknowledged their royal status. There was none of the graceful flourish he had exhibited before. No devastating smile that could melt her heart. But despite his cold stance, her heart still melted.

His black hair was tousled from the wind, his eyes as stormy as the first day they had met. Beneath his length of plaid, his linen shirt molded his muscled chest, and a tantalizing glimpse of tawny flesh beckoned where his shirt fastenings were undone.

Her fingers curled against the kitten and it wriggled in protest before burrowing its nose between her thighs. Connor's glance dropped to her lap before clashing with hers for one brief, agonized second.

And then he focused on Talargan.

"My lord. My king and yours request your presence as a matter of urgency in the war chamber."

"The war chamber?" She couldn't help the alarm in her voice and instinctively clutched at the kitten. Surely Pict and Scot were not planning war? "Why?"

With clear reluctance, Connor transferred his attention to her. "The Northumbrians require reminding as to the limits of their borders."

"You're going into battle against the Northumbrians?"

He was a warrior. She knew that. Fighting was his life. But she didn't want him riding into battle. Didn't want the agony of not knowing whether he would return or not.

"Aila." Her brother's low voice, speaking in Pictish, penetrated her rising distress. "The Scots don't believe in sharing such information with their women." His disdain was palpable. "I'll tell you of the plans when I return from this meeting."

As Talargan stood and helped her to her feet, she glanced at Connor. His jaw was rigid with fury and he looked as if he'd like nothing more than to throttle Talargan.

Oblivious, her brother marched back toward the stronghold. Connor didn't move.

She held the kitten close, drawing poor comfort from its

warmth. It wasn't Drun, but like her beloved deerhound, it had been cruelly treated.

Except unlike Drun, the kitten's pain hadn't been her fault.

"I see you have a new companion." His words were perfectly civil. And yet she detected censure in his tone, an accusation of abandoning Drun and taking another in his place.

Yet even that was untrue. She knew what he really accused her of. But she didn't want to argue with him. Didn't want bad blood between them. She hadn't even seen him since that first night after arriving in Dunadd. She'd pleaded exhaustion, feminine indisposition, anything that had excused her from attending another excruciating feast.

And now, when he prepared to ride south to engage the Northumbrians, she wanted desperately for him to look at her the way he had looked at her that morning in his bedchamber.

"Some boys thought it great sport to torture her with flame and water. They'd already drowned her two littermates. But at least I saved this one from such a fate."

She'd hoped to soften the glare directed her way with her attempt at conversation. Instead his glower intensified. "Not all Scots are barbarians, Aila. You can't judge an entire people by the actions of a few children."

Her hope withered. "I wasn't aware I had."

His gaze roved over her face, as if he couldn't help it but hated himself for such weakness. "Are you ill?" The words were harsh. "You haven't attended the feasts held in your honor."

"I'm quite well." Did he ask because he cared? Or only because he thought her bad-mannered to snub his countryfolk? "Merely tired."

"Still?" It was a growl, but with an unmistakable undercurrent of concern.

"It's been many years since I've undertaken any journey of significance. My exhaustion is to be expected." But she knew her exhaustion had nothing to do with the journey. It was the incessant nightmares that ravaged her every time she closed her eyes. The constant feeling of dread that gripped her as soon as the candles were doused.

The salt-tinged breeze rustled through the grass and whipped raven-black strands of hair across Connor's face. She clutched the kitten to her breast and foolishly imagined its silky-soft fur was her Scot's wild hair. And still his stormy gaze didn't waver from her.

She knew they were surrounded by a dozen people, every one of them engaged to attend and protect her. But none of them mattered. She might just as well be alone on this windy hilltop with Connor MacKenzie because when he looked at her nothing else existed.

He moved toward her then hesitated as if recalling where they were. Silently her heart wept for a touch she would never again enjoy. A touch she would never again have the right to expect.

"I wish you happiness, Aila." He sounded as though the words choked him, as if the world were ending. "But if you ever need me, I'll be there for you."

With that he swung on his heel and marched after her brother and storm clouds blotted out the sun.

CHAPTER 25

*S*ix days later, she stood before her father and the King of the Scots and the official marriage contract was signed. No earthquake split the land. No lightning forked from the heavens.

And no beloved Scot warrior tore her from Fergus' side and swept her into his eternal embrace.

Connor, Talargan and many other warriors both Pict and Scot had departed five days ago to subdue the Northumbrians. It was, all the kings agreed, a timely message to send their mutual enemies that Pict and Scot would now act as one.

Aila focused on maintaining her facade of calm. Her new husband took her hand and she forced herself to acknowledge the well-wishes of the nobles who had witnessed the joining.

There weren't many. Only the Pictish kings and the more senior nobles had remained behind with minimal warriors. The rest had accompanied a contingent of Scots. Although it seemed a great many Scot warriors remained in Dunadd.

A strange disconnect caused her stomach to heave. As if there was a deadly significance to the number of Picts who went with the Scots versus who stayed behind.

"Are you cold, my lady Devorgilla?" Fergus appeared not to have grasped the fundamental fact her personal name was Aila. Not that she'd corrected his assumption. She didn't care what he called her, because whatever he called her meant nothing. He raised her hand and brushed kisses across her knuckles. She tensed so he couldn't feel her shudder. "Tonight, my beloved wife, I shall warm you up most satisfactorily."

She would not think about tonight. And she most certainly would not speak of it.

Fergus obviously misunderstood her silence, as he pulled her close to his side. "Don't worry." His whisper against her ear was predatory. "I understand your reticence. After so many years without a man you are likely as fearful of our marriage bed as a virgin." He sounded as though the notion pleased him immensely.

Aila gave him her most regal glance. "Indeed, my lord, I am certainly no virgin and do not fear the marriage bed as if I were one."

A frown of irritation at her response carved his forehead but there was no time for his reply. Another interminable feast loomed where she was, yet again, to be on display like a rare acquisition from the Eastern Empire.

LATE THAT EVENING, after her ladies had washed her and re-braided her hair in readiness for her wedding night, she sat on a stool before the blazing fire, hugging her cloak about her with one hand and cradling the kitten with her other.

She didn't know how much longer she would have to wait for Fergus. He'd informed her, with barely concealed incredulity, that his king required his presence in the war chamber.

Fergus had been furious at the delay in claiming his rights. And instead of relief at the postponement, Aila battled against a rising sense of dark unease.

All day a suffocating fog of dread had clouded her mind. At first she'd imagined it was because of the coming night. But it was more than that. And separate from it. An intangible certainty that was, somehow, inexplicably entwined with the terrifying dreams she'd suffered since arriving in Dunadd.

Clutching the kitten, she stood, her cloak tumbling to the floor. She didn't know why but she couldn't remain in the chamber.

"My lady." Floradh hurried over to her. Her ladies had already retired for the night. "Can I get you anything?"

The image of Connor with his black hair tousled from the Highland wind invaded her mind. She hesitated as the seductive memory flowed through her senses, momentarily calming her unease.

His stormy-gray eyes captivated her. His devastating smile ensnared her. She blinked rapidly, attempting to dispel the illusion, and thrust the kitten into her servant's arms. The need to escape this chamber overrode every other thought and she hurried to the door. "I need to speak to my father."

"But why, my lady?"

She didn't know why. She had left it far too late to change her mind about this marriage now. And yet she needed to find him. "Because I must."

She stealthily descended the main spiral staircase, keeping to the wall, peering into the gloom below, where only a solitary lantern glowed. Although she wore only a light linen under gown —her bedgown—unnatural warmth pounded through her body and sweat slicked her palms.

The hall was empty. She took a few cautious steps and glanced toward the entrance of the great hall, but it too appeared deserted.

Even the dogs that normally prowled had vanished.

I have to go outside.

The thought came from nowhere and she glanced uncertainly at the main doors, barred against the outside world.

It made no sense. She had to find her father. But she couldn't drag her fascinated gaze from the main doors. As if they were waiting for her to throw back the bolts, run into the night and—

Into Connor's arms.

It took all the willpower she possessed to turn her back on the doors. Pain wrenched through her breast, compressed her lungs, but she gritted her teeth and forced her reluctant feet forward.

Connor wasn't here. And even if he were, she could never run into the comfort of his arms.

And then the muted sounds of battle hit her. She froze, terror skating through her. Had the Vikings penetrated Dunadd's defenses? Was that why the stronghold was deserted? Because everyone had been slaughtered in their beds?

Primeval warning pounded through every beat of her heart, every erratic gasp of her breath. A warning she didn't want to understand. A warning she couldn't comprehend. And yet a warning she could no longer disbelieve.

Images of slaughtered warriors seared her mind, scarlet blood spraying; the stink of betrayal twisting her stomach. She was back at the sacred standing stones, the day before she'd met Connor, battling the vision that wasn't a bad dream or suppressed memory.

It had been a premonition.

Heart hammering, she ran along the passageway, rejecting her thoughts, until she stumbled to a halt by an open door. The stone walls contracted, pressed onto her, squeezed the air from her lungs. Her brain fought to deny the carnage unfolding but the nightmare was reality. Scot fought fallen Pict, swords flashed in the flickering glow of lamps and blood drenched the straw-covered floor.

"Father." Her terrified scream ripped from her throat as she saw him knocked to the ground, defenseless against the armed

Scot who loomed over him. Heedless of the danger she staggered into the chamber, the sodden straw clinging to her bare feet in silent condemnation.

She flung herself at the Scot, using her body weight to push him off balance, before sinking to her knees and cradling her father's face between her hands. Dimly she was aware of the Scot's shocked curse at her appearance, his obvious reluctance to plunge his sword through her as he had so easily through her father.

The angry yells faded. All she could hear were the shuddering gasps as her father attempted to drag air into his lungs. All she could see was his beloved face and his eyes that tried to tell her what his voice could not.

"Be strong," she whispered against his blood-stained lips. "We will return to Ce and avenge this outrage." Scalding tears blurred her vision, but she would not allow them to fall. Not allow her father to see how hopeless vows of vengeance were. Because hope was all she could offer him in these last, futile moments.

"We were betrayed." His whisper drifted across her cheek. "Forgive me, my daughter. For bringing you here."

Corrosive guilt coiled around her weeping heart. *This is my fault.*

Rough hands grasped her arms and hauled her to her feet. Reacting on an instinct she hadn't relied on for more than nine years, she snatched the dagger from the Scot's belt.

"Devorgilla." Fergus dragged her sideways and she stumbled over another dead Pict before she could use Fergus' own weapon against him. "You shouldn't be here."

Blood streaked his face and there was a savage gleam of madness in his eyes. She reared back, dagger glinting, prepared to plunge the blade into his exposed throat. Instead his fingers gripped her wrist, holding her arm above her head in a merciless vise.

"Get her out of here, Fergus." The roar vibrated the stone walls. "Do your duty. The marriage is still valid."

Aila swung around, her arm imprisoned by Fergus' grip, and saw the Scot king glaring across the chamber.

"The marriage is void." She scarcely recognized her own voice. "Do you think I'll allow this treachery to go unchallenged?" Words and images tumbled through her mind, making it hard to think, hard to speak. "The King of Ce's murder will be avenged. Our people will never—"

Her promise of retribution was swiftly severed as Fergus dragged her bodily from the chamber, as if she were a slave, a woman without rights. His chattel.

Rage pumped through her and a distant thundering barely registered, except as a counterpoint to the thundering of blood pounding at her temples and hammering through her heart.

He released her as soon as they reached an unfamiliar passageway and stumbled back against the wall as if the exertion had exhausted him. But his eyes never left hers.

"You shouldn't have seen that."

Her father's lifeless body flashed through her mind. The blood. The stench of betrayal. Renewed rage flared through her, smothering the rising horror, the hovering specter of madness on her horizon.

"And that would make the slaughter acceptable?" She jabbed Fergus' dagger in his direction.

Fergus warily pushed himself upright. "We defended ourselves, Devorgilla. Your countrymen were defeated."

"You lie. My people would never attack their hosts in such a manner." She tried to calm her tangled thoughts, make plans. Strategize.

Escape. Before the cursed Scots murdered her as they had all her kin.

"This changes nothing." Fergus took an unsteady step toward her. "We still have an alliance between our two peoples."

Breath rasped in her throat. "You've murdered all my people." Fresh terror threatened to undo her. "I won't let you murder my brother." She had to warn him. Had to…

Get outside.

"Your brother is safe." Fergus sounded as if every word was an effort. "He's been taken hostage. Along with all the others. Only a handful of Picts died, my lady. As long as I remain alive your brother lives."

CHAPTER 26

After hammering on the thick timber doors for what seemed eternity, Connor bit back an impatient curse when they finally opened. It wasn't usual to arrive so late, but Aila's brother had insisted they continue to Dunadd instead of camping for the night. And because Connor had grown to respect the younger man over the last few days, he'd thrown his weight behind the request.

For one incredible moment as he and the other nobles stepped inside, Connor thought they were being attacked. Chaos reigned, or so his momentarily frozen mind assumed. But within a second, the impression of chaos vanished, and he realized what was truly happening.

The Picts he'd so recently ridden into battle with, men he'd begun to know, were now surrounded by MacAlpin's warriors who had stayed behind to guard Dunadd.

"What the devil's going on?" he demanded, grabbing the nearest warrior by the throat, and shoving him backward. "The Picts are our allies."

The warrior knocked his arm aside. "We've orders to take the Picts hostage. And take your damn hands off me."

Ice stabbed through his gut. "All the Picts?"

"Aye." The warrior frowned. "Some of their kings turned on MacAlpin. That's all I know, MacKenzie."

Connor glanced at Ewan, who was glaring at the scene as if he'd very much like to pitch in with the Picts. None of the men who'd just returned were lifting a finger to help their fellow Scots.

He pushed his way through the mass of bodies. One thought thundered through his head.

What had happened to Aila?

The stench of spilled blood hit him first. Another step and the sight of slaughtered bodies rammed into his brain, halting his advance. He stood by the door and stared at the carnage and incomprehension battered the edge of his mind.

"MacKenzie." The harsh voice hammered through his fractured thoughts and he turned to see his king striding toward him. "Thank God you're back."

"My liege." He bowed his head then looked back at the bloodied scene. "What happened?"

MacAlpin stood by his side. "Foul betrayal. We were attempting a civilized ratification of the line of succession of Fortriu and the Pictish nobles turned on us." He turned from the scene, clearly sickened. "Fortunately, the attack was contained. So long as the rest of the Pictish kingdoms accept my rule of Fortriu, I won't rescind on our alliance."

He believed his king. But suspicion coiled in his gut. There was something wrong about the position of the bodies. The lack of Scots fatalities.

Something. But he couldn't fathom what.

And then MacAlpin's assertion hit him.

"The alliance stands?"

"Aye. I haven't gone to all this trouble to let this," he jerked his head toward the war chamber, "stop me. Pictland needs a strong leader, MacKenzie. One to bring all the kingdoms together. And this is the first step."

"Has the princess been told?" He'd recognized the King of Ce as one of the dead. No matter what mac Lutin had said or done in the war chamber, his daughter didn't deserve to shoulder any blame. "She's not being held responsible for this?"

"Christ, no." MacAlpin shot him a dark glare. "She's our jewel. It's unfortunate she saw the aftermath of the massacre, but Fergus took care of her. At least I assume he's taking care of her."

Aila had witnessed this? God Almighty. And then his king's last flippant comment pierced his rising disgust.

Fergus was taking care of her? That meant only one thing. Black rage seared his reason and without another word to MacAlpin he turned and stormed toward his half-brother's bedchamber.

The balance had shifted. The King of Ce could no longer object to his daughter marrying a commoner. The alliance could still stand. This time he would convince MacAlpin to allow him to wed Aila, and Fergus could damn well take another princess of Pictland.

His brother had no right to drag her into his chamber. No right to force her to submit to his will.

No damn right to have her.

He didn't even bother knocking, just kicked the door open and marched inside the antechamber. Fergus sprawled on a chair by the blazing fire, his leg propped on a stool, and Aila stood by his side.

Aila.

His heart slammed as his throat tightened in horror. Her white gown was soaked with crimson.

How could she have lost so much blood and still be standing?

"You're injured." It wasn't a question. Every instinct he possessed thundered for him to go to her, drag her into his arms, tell her everything would be all right. But he remained frozen to the spot, unable to move a muscle.

"Just a scratch," Fergus said. "I'll live."

Connor dragged his gaze from Aila and stared blankly at his brother. Only then did he see the blood staining his leg.

Aila held a Scot-made dagger. Had she attacked Fergus? But if so, why was she standing by his side? Why hadn't she escaped his chamber?

Why was she looking at *him* as though she wanted to plunge her dagger into his flesh?

"You're not hurt?"

Her lip curled. The depth of derision in that one small gesture was as powerful as if she had spat in his face.

"There's nothing wrong with my wife, Connor," Fergus said with gloating emphasis. "And much as I appreciate your brotherly concern as to my welfare, I don't appreciate your company for my wedding night."

Fergus was playing a dangerous game. "The wedding is tomorrow."

"*Was* tomorrow." Fergus shifted on the chair. Connor glared at him, unwilling to believe yet knowing, in his heart, his brother spoke the truth. He was too late. "It was brought forward. Now." Fergus shot Aila a lascivious glance. Even now the stupid bastard had no idea his wife could understand every word he uttered. "I'd like to be alone with my lady." He looked back at Connor. "Watch her unbind her hair for me and strip for my pleasure." He paused, allowing that image to burn itself into Connor's mind. And then he gave a slow, satisfied smile and thrust the blade in up to its hilt. "A good fuck will improve my mood."

HUDDLED within the furs she'd taken from the bed last night, Aila sat on the chair before the dying fire, her gaze fixed on the figure of her husband. Like her, he had not had a restful night, tossing and turning in the bed as if demons stalked his black soul.

Beneath the furs, she gripped his dagger. How many times had she imagined plunging it into Fergus' heart as he snatched a few moments of sleep? And each time his words came back to haunt her.

Her brother would remain alive as long as Fergus lived.

And so she had washed and bound the wound in his thigh as a good wife should. And that had been the entire extent of wifely duties she had performed.

She tried to focus on Fergus. Because when she thought of him, she could keep other thoughts at bay.

But it was no good. Images of her slain father and the other nobles flickered through her mind, tormenting her with the knowledge she had seen their deaths foretold weeks ago. Had dreamed of the bloody massacre night after night and still not understood what she was being shown.

And this was why she loathed Bride. For cursing her to foresee events without the ability to comprehend what she was seeing. Without the means to prevent what was to unfold.

Fergus stirred on the bed. Turned and caught her staring at him. After a moment he heaved himself up, gritting his teeth.

She hoped his wound gave him great discomfort. She hoped it had been her father who had given him the injury. But much as she craved his death—the death of all Scots—she had to keep this one alive.

For Talargan.

He regarded her across the chamber, assessing her mood. "You could have shared my bed, Devorgilla," he said at last in Pictish, still laboring under the delusion she was ignorant of his language. "I gave you my word last night I wouldn't claim my rights."

Only because he feared reopening his wound with such exertion. "Your word means nothing to me."

His jaw clenched. "I don't blame you for your countrymen's treachery. How can you blame me for merely defending my king?"

They had already had this conversation. It didn't matter how many times Fergus told her how her people had betrayed his. She didn't believe a word.

He winced as he made to rise from the bed. "There's one other stipulation in return for your brother's continued good health."

She refused to acknowledge him. After a moment he appeared to realize.

"You will tell no one our marriage is as yet unconsummated." His voice was harsh. "If this marriage is declared void, I can't answer for your safety. Or that of your brother."

AILA and her ladies were not, as she had feared, prisoners confined to their chambers. It appeared she was allowed the same freedom she had enjoyed during the last week with one exception.

Her royal guard now comprised of Scots warriors, not those from Ce.

She walked aimlessly, holding her kitten close to her breast, her thoughts in turmoil. Lowborn Pictish warriors retained their freedom, if not their weapons, but she had yet to encounter any Pictish warrior of noble blood.

But then she hadn't expected to. Any noble who hadn't been murdered would be a hostage to their people's good behavior.

How many hostages were held? She had only Fergus' word that Talargan was among them and she trusted his word as little as she trusted his king's. Suppose in reality he had been one of the slain?

Yet she couldn't risk the possibility that he was still alive.

Awareness prickled over her skin, and she stopped dead as

Connor rounded a corner of the stronghold not four feet away. Impossible longing washed through her, tightening the breath in her breast, causing her heart to thud violently. He was the one man she had refused to think of. The only man she wanted to think of.

He also stopped dead when he saw her, and an incomprehensible expression flashed over his face. As if she was the last person he wanted to see. And yet the only person he wanted to see.

"My lady." His voice was low and despite everything she knew about his people, the pit of her stomach still fluttered in response to that darkly seductive accent.

His hair tangled about his shoulders as if he too had suffered a sleepless night. But she wouldn't think of his hair. Wouldn't recall how soft and silky it felt beneath her fingers, nor think of how she had once buried her face in that black mass and breathed his masculine essence into the soul of her being.

She wouldn't think on any of it. Because there lay true madness.

Raw silence screamed between them and in her peripheral vision she saw her ladies retreat, allowing them a degree of privacy.

"My lady." His voice dropped even lower, a dangerous caress along her savaged senses. "I'm sorry for your loss."

Her spine was so rigid she feared it would splinter. "I don't require your sympathy, MacKenzie." Unlike him, she spoke in Pictish and infused every word with the thousand years of her royal lineage. She couldn't let him see beneath her facade. Couldn't let him see just how desperately she craved his arms around her. His people had murdered hers and for that, how could she forgive?

"Whatever happened last night," he said, his accent twisting through her as he responded in her language, "I deeply regret you saw any of it. You didn't deserve that, Aila. If I could take it back, I would."

In her heart, she knew he meant every word. But why hadn't he stopped the massacre last night? Why hadn't he stood up to his treacherous king and saved her father?

She ignored his words of sympathy, as if by acknowledging his kindness she would, somehow, be desecrating the memory of her slain countrymen. *Irrational* hammered through her mind, but she ignored that too. "Is it true my brother is held hostage by your king?"

His jaw clenched. "Aye." He sounded as though he battled his temper, that the knowledge Talargan was being held offended his honor.

"I see." She didn't believe a word Fergus told her, but Connor would tell her the truth. "So he is held to ensure my cooperation in this farce of an alliance."

Connor's gaze didn't waver. "There are many hostages, Aila. In these situations there always are."

Her stomach roiled and her heart squeezed with pain. His people were treacherous barbarians and yet she couldn't hate Connor for what had happened. Only blame him for not somehow possessing the means to stop it. She knew he hadn't been in the war chamber when she'd stumbled into the carnage. He wasn't a participant of the massacre against her kin.

But he had already returned to Dunadd from Northumbria when the outrage occurred. How else had Talargan been taken hostage? How else had Connor stormed Fergus' bedchamber?

She attempted to offer him an icy smile but failed. "So the Scots often extend the hand of friendship only to betray that trust in the foulest manner?"

"Christ, no." He appeared to forget who they were, where they were, as he took a step toward her. It couldn't be possible and yet she felt the heat of his body reach for her, as though he wanted to cocoon her from the horrors of last night. "Aila, that isn't what happened. We defended ourselves against attack. But no one holds you accountable."

Blackness engulfed her soul. Connor was defending the Scots' act of cowardice by perpetrating the lies already fed to her by his half-brother.

She tilted her jaw at a regal angle, grateful for the soft fur of the kitten that hid the way her fingers trembled. "I am accountable, Connor MacKenzie. Never forget that. And no matter how your king attempts to manipulate the events of last night I will never believe my people attacked."

He stared at her with stormy-gray eyes that threatened to destroy the hastily erected barriers around her heart. Barriers that, once before, he had so easily demolished.

She wouldn't crumble before him. But she couldn't drag her gaze from him. Couldn't prevent seeing the shadows beneath his eyes, the overnight beard that darkened his jaw. The way he looked at her as if, even with everything that now lay between them, he battled the urge to take her in his arms and hold her close.

She had craved his love, even when she knew it would bring him nothing but heartache. And now she was paying for those selfish, pagan wishes.

But even that wasn't why nausea rose and the world spun. It was because, even now, despising his people as she did, her foolish love for him would not die.

CHAPTER 27

Connor found his brother leaning against the western wall of the stronghold, engaged in bawdy banter with another couple of warriors. Raucous laughter split the air. One of the warriors clapped Fergus on the shoulder.

Impotent rage churned Connor's gut. He pulled up short and attempted to batten down the feral urge to smash his fist into his brother's foul mouth.

Aila was Fergus' wife. But not just his wife. She was a princess, destined to be a queen, and deserved more respect than to be talked about in such a manner.

"Connor," one of the warriors said. "Your royal brother is mightily pleased with his new bride."

"Aye," said the one who'd clapped Fergus' shoulder. "You'd never think by looking at her she possessed so wild a nature beneath the furs."

Fergus said nothing, merely smirked in clear satisfaction of his night's work. Sudden nausea gripped Connor, dousing the rage, as the image of Aila submitting to his brother rammed through his mind.

An image that had plagued him through the endless night. An image he'd tried— and failed—to eradicate with mead.

An image he knew would haunt him until his dying day.

"Guard your tongue." His voice was harsh. "Princess Devorgilla of Ce deserves our respect even if her kin do not."

"My sainted brother speaks the truth." Fergus shifted his weight as he leaned one shoulder against the wall. "My royal wife is innocent of treason. And God willing, after our lively bed-sport last night, she's also with child."

The two warriors grinned salaciously but said nothing. Connor tried to block his brother's last words, but they remained firmly embedded in his mind.

He turned to Fergus. "I need to speak to you alone."

Fergus flapped his hand at the two warriors, and they sauntered off. "What do you want to know?" His eyes glittered with malice. "How many times I took my wife last night? How she screamed my name as I had her up against the wall?"

Again, the rage surfaced. Black and scarlet, clouding his vision, fogging his brain. Involuntarily his muscles tensed, and fists clenched, but still Fergus' mocking words echoed through his mind.

He gritted his teeth and fought the overpowering urge to wrap his hands around his brother's throat and squeeze the life from him. "Just tell me what happened in the war chamber last night."

Fergus rubbed his hand over his mouth and jaw, and the section of Connor's mind that didn't crave murder noted the sheen of sweat that covered his brother's face. Yet the day was cool.

"The Picts wouldn't acknowledge MacAlpin's uncontested right to Fortriu."

"So they attacked?" Something still didn't feel right. He knew, as they all knew, the seven Pictish tribes had a violent history of warring among themselves when a kingdom's ruler was in dispute. But it was old history, from generations long since dead.

They had traveled to Dunadd to ratify an alliance. If they wanted war with the Scots, to attack while in MacAlpin's war chamber—when a good portion of their own warriors were absent—made no strategic sense at all.

"Aye." Fergus' belligerent tone had vanished, and he tugged at the neck of his shirt, as though it constricted his breathing. "We had no choice. We had to kill them, or they would have killed MacAlpin, simply to remove his claim to their supreme kingdom."

"What the hell was—" Shit. He had almost called her Aila. "The princess doing there? Watching the massacre of her people could have turned her mind."

Fergus expelled a harsh breath. "She appeared out of nowhere. Went into hysterics. I had to carry her back to our bedchamber."

She'd been covered in blood. The blood, most likely, of her father.

No wonder she'd become hysterical. Except when he'd stormed in on them, she looked far from hysterical. She'd looked coldly furious. Regal.

"Soon."

He forced his attention back to Fergus. "What?"

"I said MacAlpin wants me to take the princess home. She'll be guarded well enough at Duncadha as she will here."

Duncadha. The stronghold of his forefathers. The place he'd grown up.

The future home of Aila.

He couldn't trust himself to answer. Fergus shifted again but didn't move away from the support of the wall. "You'll be returning to Dunbrae shortly?"

Where else would he go? Dunbrae had been his home for the last six years. "Aye."

Another silence. Fergus wiped his brow as if they were suffering a scorching southern summer. "I've a mind to accompany you. Introduce my bride to my lady mother."

Chills crawled over Connor's scalp at the notion of Aila coming to Dunbrae. Being introduced to his mother, as the wife of her husband's eldest son, Fergus. Sleeping beneath Connor's roof. With Fergus.

It all came back to Fergus.

Their father's blood flowed through both their veins, but in this moment all he saw when he looked at his brother was a man who had the one thing Connor most craved.

He turned away. He'd not give Fergus the satisfaction of seeing how badly the thought affected him. "You're always welcome at Dunbrae."

It was nothing less than the truth. His mother enjoyed Fergus' visits. Sometimes Connor wondered why she had moved from Duncadha after his father's death four years ago. Fergus had made it clear he had no objection to her remaining.

"I'll inform my wife to prepare for our departure," Fergus said. "As soon as possible. I sicken of Dunadd."

FERGUS WASN'T at the feast the following night. It didn't take much imagination as to what otherwise occupied his time. Savagely Connor bit into a chicken leg and ignored the seductive glances and attempts at flirtation from the young noblewoman by his side.

But what the hell? Maybe he'd take Ewan's advice. Maybe a mindless tumble would help cool his blood, balance his mood, eradicate Aila from his thoughts.

He turned to her and watched her face brighten at his sudden interest. She was pretty enough but her eyes weren't green, her hair wasn't an intriguing combination of gold and auburn and her voice held none of Aila's exquisitely enchanting accent.

Beneath the furs, none of that mattered. He didn't need to look in her eyes or spread her hair across his pillows. Didn't need her to open her mouth to talk.

All she had to do was part her thighs.

His cock remained entirely unmoved by the prospect.

"My lord."

The unfamiliar feminine voice from behind him pulled him back to the present. He turned and recognized one of Aila's ladies. Instantly all thoughts of how to rouse his cock's interest in a night of unbridled passion vanished.

"What is it?" His voice was sharp. Had something happened to Aila? "Is the princess unwell?" But if she was unwell, why would one of her ladies seek him out?

"My lady is well." The woman's voice was scarcely above a whisper. "But she asks that you accompany me to her chamber."

His heart kicked against his ribs. It didn't mean what he wanted it to mean. Aila wouldn't arrange an assignation with him on the third night of her marriage. But logic made no difference to his cock, as it jerked to attention against his thigh in agonized anticipation.

"She fears," the woman said, her voice so low he had to strain to hear her words, "for the prince's state of health."

Fergus. Again. He stood up and followed the woman from the hall but even knowing an illicit liaison was the last thing on Aila's mind did nothing to diminish the extent of his erection.

Torches blazed and common-rank warriors guarded every door. Even though all the noble Pictish warriors were locked up, MacAlpin was taking no chances. "What ails the prince?"

The woman gave a small shrug. He couldn't tell whether she meant she did not know, or she didn't care. Either way it was plain she had conveyed her message and had no intention of sharing anything else with him.

He marched through the antechamber into the bedchamber. Aila stood stiffly by the bed, where Fergus lay propped up against pillows, his face flushed and sweaty.

"Fergus?" Connor hovered over his brother as dread clamped deep in his chest. His brother didn't appear to hear him as his breath rasped unevenly and his eyes remained half closed.

Connor turned to Aila. She met his gaze but there was no warmth. Instead she jerked her head, as if he were a menial, before turning on her heel and going to the window.

With another glance at his brother, Connor followed her. "Aila, what—"

"My husband is not responding to treatment." Her voice was as icy as the glare she leveled his way. "I called you here to ask if you know of any other physician aside from MacLeod who can help him."

"MacLeod's MacAlpin's own physician." And if MacLeod was treating Fergus, that meant the king knew. And if the king knew, why hadn't he been informed of his brother's condition?

"Indeed." Aila sounded entirely unimpressed. "The fact remains your half-brother worsens by the hour."

"But what happened? He was all right yesterday." Yet even as he said the words, doubt prickled.

Fergus hadn't been all right. He'd been sweating. And unable to stand upright.

Only then did he recall the trickle of blood along Fergus' leg the other night. Fergus had said it was only a scratch. Connor hadn't thought twice about the injury since.

"His blood is poisoned." Aila glanced at the bed and just as swiftly glanced away. "Your MacLeod has bled him several times, but the wound remains noxious."

To die in battle was a clean death compared to the drawn-out agony of having your own body rot from the inside out. There had been times in his life when he'd wanted to kill Fergus. But he would never have raised his sword against him. And he would never have wished this fate upon him.

"Where's MacLeod now?" Aila might not think much of him, but he was the royal physician, the most learned of all. MacAlpin would allow no other to touch a member of his kin.

"Reporting to his master."

The scathing note in her voice pierced his tortured thoughts and he shot her a sharp look. She wasn't looking at him. She was looking over his shoulder at the wall beyond.

MacLeod entered the bedchamber, scarcely glanced at him or Aila, and went directly to Fergus and pulled back the linen sheet. Connor watched MacLeod pluck three fat leeches from Fergus's thigh and drop them into a bowl.

Fergus gave a rasping groan and instantly Aila was by his side. As a good wife should be. Connor flexed his fingers before following her over.

"Is he improving?" Aila's voice was haughty as she addressed MacLeod.

"I've done all I can, madam," MacLeod said, but not before he'd shot her a glance of intense dislike. "We must put our trust in the Lord now."

Fergus opened his eyes. "Connor." His voice rasped. "Never thought it would end like this."

Chest tight, Connor gripped his brother's limp hand. "Nothing has ended, Fergus."

Aila was so close her scent invaded his jagged senses. But she didn't look at him. She was focused on Fergus.

"You are not going to die." Rage threaded her words as if the thought of Fergus dying ripped her soul in two.

"My lords," MacLeod said. "I will fetch the monks."

Fergus shifted his glazed gaze to Aila. "Leave us."

Aila stiffened, clearly offended at the dismissal. But she didn't say anything. She turned and regally stalked into the antechamber, her ladies closing the door behind her.

Fergus stretched his lips in a parody of a smile. "Does a man's heart good to know how much his wife loves him."

Did Aila love Fergus? A dull pain twisted his gut. "Aye."

"Always envied you that." Fergus hitched in a strained breath. "With Fearchara."

"I find that hard to believe."

Fergus' eyes flickered. "She worshipped you. I wanted that."

For once Connor was speechless. Fergus had never shown any sign of wanting to settle down with one woman.

"Never found a woman I wanted that way. Not how you found Fearchara."

Connor shifted uneasily. Fergus had never spoken of such things before. He knew it was the fever loosening Fergus' tongue but nevertheless, Connor didn't want to hear it.

"I was lucky." The words were little more than a growl. Because right now he felt anything but lucky.

"Aye." Fergus' breath rattled. "You always were a lucky bastard. I hated you from the day you were born. The day you took my mother's love from me."

Heat speared through Connor's temples. As a child, he hadn't understood his beloved half-brother's rages. Only as he'd got older had he realized how deeply Fergus resented not being the true blood son of Connor's own mother.

Connor's mother was the one thing in the world Fergus adored more than his own royal lineage.

"I took nothing from you." Was he really having this conversation? And yet as much as he wanted to change the subject, speak of less torturous issues, he knew, in his heart, Fergus was dying. And Fergus wanted to speak of their mother. "She's always looked upon you as her own son."

"I shamed her." Fergus' eyes lost focus, as though he looked at something beyond mere mortal vision. "If she knew, she would forever turn her back on me."

"There's nothing you could do that would make our mother forsake you."

Fergus began to shiver, although his skin was burning. "MacAlpin knew the Picts would never willingly acquiesce."

MacAlpin? Damn it, Fergus was sinking into delirium. But then his words penetrated, took on significance. "You mean MacAlpin's claim to the Kingdom of Fortriu?"

"If they refused to acknowledge his right they were to be slaughtered without mercy. Without warning."

"The Picts didn't attack first?"

"Only the nine nobles who claimed matrilineal rights to Fortriu were summoned to the war chamber." Fergus gripped Connor's hand, but it was involuntary, as his entire body convulsed in spasms of pain. "MacAlpin's orders. A warrior obeys his king."

Pictland needs a strong leader, MacAlpin's angry words echoed in his mind. *One to bring all the kingdoms together.*

And this was the first step.

"MacAlpin planned this. From the start." Bitter rage roiled through him at the knowledge he'd been so deceived. At the realization his unformed suspicions had been true.

"Eliminate all rivals to the kingdom." Fergus gasped for breath as his convulsions ceased. "Fortriu first. The others will follow."

Connor glared down at his brother, but the anger wasn't for Fergus. It was for his king, for his advisers, for the way they had gone about eradicating all threat of a Pictish succession.

"And what of the princess?" His voice was harsh. "Why drag her into this when he had no intention of ratifying an alliance?"

Fergus' eyelids drooped as if he no longer had the energy to keep them open. "But he does need this alliance." The words were slurred, as Fergus hovered on the precipice of unconsciousness. "She's the bridge between our peoples. Through this alliance her son will inherit Ce, and the northern stronghold becomes a Scots-held territory."

Fergus was so sure he'd got Aila with child on their wedding night. But for the moment, that was a secondary concern. Because when Fergus died—and he would die, Connor knew the signs only too well—Aila would be vulnerable.

Of all the hostages held in Dunadd, she was the most valuable. The one MacAlpin would use ruthlessly to gain advantage with the wealthy Kingdom of Ce.

He'd watched her slip from his grasp once. But this time he'd do everything in his power—lie, flatter and sell his soul to the cursed devil—to persuade MacAlpin that the only logical answer for the problem that was the princess was for her to marry Connor MacKenzie.

CHAPTER 28

Connor stood by Aila's side as the monks chanted in the tongue of Rome over Fergus' body. As they anointed his brother with oil in the name of the Lord, Connor risked a sideways glance.

Her fierce glare didn't waver from the scene before them. She believed the healing ritual would work and Fergus would once again rise in full health.

He wished he shared that faith. But he knew of no one who'd survived the extreme unction. As far as he was concerned it was merely a prelude to death, despite how the monks believed otherwise.

Yet if Fergus survived, he would no longer be a true husband to Aila. He would be required to give up the pleasures of the flesh and dedicate his life to God. Not a life Fergus would relish.

And Aila would be tied to a husband who wasn't a husband, and still beyond his reach.

When, finally, MacLeod pronounced the inevitable, grief seared Connor's heart. For the brother he had hero-worshipped as a child and the brother he'd tolerated as a man.

Instinctively he turned to Aila to offer her comfort. He didn't know how or why, and it no longer mattered, but since her marriage she'd grown close to Fergus. Her determination that he should live proved that.

Not that Connor had any intention of letting that stand in his way. Aila had loved him once and she would love him again. And now when she entered Dunbrae it would be as *his* bride.

"My lord," MacLeod said.

Connor barely glanced at him. "Wait for me outside. I will be with you directly."

MacLeod offered a stiff bow, clearly offended, but Connor knew he would wait. Connor was Fergus' closest blood kin and as such was entitled to accompany the physician when he informed the king of Fergus' death.

Only when the door between bed and antechamber closed did Aila finally turn toward him. She looked deathly tired. So fragile he wanted to wrap her in his arms and never let her go.

But the fury in her eyes rendered him immobile.

"I did everything within my power to keep him alive." Her voice was low and trembled with emotion.

"I know." Her people had been betrayed but Aila's honor had never faltered. Shame crawled over his skin at what she had endured at the hands of his king. He owed her an apology for accusing her kin of attacking MacAlpin without provocation, for doubting her word and, damn it, for bringing her here in the first place.

Always remember to whom you owe your loyalty. MacAlpin's thinly veiled threat echoed in his mind. Until this week there had never been a doubt in his heart as to the strength of his loyalty to his king.

He no longer trusted his king.

It was tantamount to treason. Yet the conviction remained. MacAlpin was his king but Aila claimed his loyalty. As soon as he and Aila were wed, he would tell her the truth. As his wife, she would never betray his confidence. But until then he couldn't risk it.

"I'm sorry." The words sounded awkward. As if he didn't mean them. Yet he did and in so many ways she could not yet fathom. He gestured to the bed. "Do you want me to send your ladies in so you can attend to Fergus?"

She drew herself up even more regally, although he couldn't imagine how such a thing was possible. "Will my performing those rites ensure my brother lives?"

He stared at her, suddenly fearful this final tragedy had turned her brain. "Your brother?"

"Yes. My brother." The look she leveled his way suggested she thought he was being deliberately obtuse. "Talargan mac Bredei of Ce."

He tried to make sense of her question but failed. "Why would preparing Fergus' body have anything to do with your brother?"

His response obviously wasn't what she'd expected. "Do you truly not know?" Uncertainty threaded her voice.

"Aila." He gripped her shoulders and tugged her toward him. "What are you talking about?" She wasn't ignorant of politics. She knew how the hostage system worked. Why then did she imagine her brother to be in danger?

"Do you promise to guarantee his safety?" There was an undercurrent of desperation in her voice, as though she possessed no faith in his king's political machinations. Not that he could blame her for that.

"Aye." He infused the word with all the conviction he could. Talargan was valuable, but only as long as he was alive.

"Even though your brother died?"

"I don't see the connection. Lord Talargan is safe and will remain safe. You know how it is with royal hostages." She was one herself. He hoped, without conviction, she hadn't made that connection.

Her glance flickered to the bed then back to him.

"So he will be accorded the rights his status demands?" She sounded less despairing, as if his assurances eased her mind. "The death of Lord Fergus will not impact on my brother at all?"

What the hell had Fergus told her? His hands slowly slid from her shoulders, along her arms and clasped her limp fingers.

"I give you my word," he said. "Lord Talargan will not be harmed because of anything that happened in this chamber."

She stared at him, considering the worth of his word. Then she gave a small jerk of her head, accepting his guarantee, and pulled free from his grasp.

~

MacAlpin took the news of Fergus' death in thunderous silence. He glared at MacLeod as if he held him personally responsible and the physician withdrew as hastily as protocol allowed.

Connor watched his king clench his fists before rounding on his advisers and ordering them from the chamber. An unexpected bonus. Now the only one Connor had to face was MacAlpin when he put forth his outrageous suggestion.

Yet not so outrageous. Without a legitimate living heir, Fergus' property would go to Connor. Not only Duncadha but also Dunfodla, the stronghold his brother had inherited from his royal mother.

If Fergus was right and MacAlpin genuinely craved an alliance with the royal clan of Ce, then he needed to find a powerful husband for Aila.

And with his brother's death, Connor was now a noble of significant wealth. And precedent had been set.

His own father had once married a princess.

"My liege."

MacAlpin rounded on him, eyes blazing. He smashed his fist

onto his desk, on top of the marriage contract. "This will not deflect my purpose." His voice was eerily calm, at startling odds with the fury emanating from him. "Do you understand, MacKenzie?"

"Aye." He understood more about his king now than he wanted to. But MacAlpin was still his king. His word was law. Just because the slaughter of the Picts sickened Connor was irrelevant.

"The princess could be carrying Fergus' child."

It was possible. It was a fact he had to face, no matter how much the thought of it curdled his guts. But no matter how easily his brother had sired offspring with a multitude of women there was always a chance he had failed to impregnate Aila.

"The continuation of her line is imperative." MacAlpin glared at him. "Her child will inherit Dunfodla and Duncadha from his father and by Pict law have claim on Ce." He flattened his palms on his desk and leaned toward Connor. "I will not allow anything to interfere with that outcome."

Ice chilled Connor's blood. "What if the princess is not with child?"

"Aye." The word was low, the king's stare intense. "That's the question, isn't it? If Fergus didn't succeed in planting his seed. She's too valuable to be unwed, yet if another man sires her child within a month, its parentage will forever be in doubt."

Connor fought against the urge to grasp MacAlpin by his neck and thrust him up against the wall. He spoke of Aila as though she were a prize mare, as if her only worth was what her womb may or may not be nurturing.

He fisted his hands, stood his ground, and attempted to cool his thoughts sufficiently so MacAlpin would favorably consider his proposal. "My liege. The princess requires the protection of a strong husband, one who—"

"I've no intention of allowing Dunfodla to pass on to a child whose claim to Kenzie's blood is in doubt," MacAlpin said. "You don't have the royal lineage of Fergus, but you did share a father. Kenzie was like a brother to me." MacAlpin straightened and narrowed his eyes. "You'll wed the princess tomorrow. And by God, if she isn't already with child then ensure she is before the month ends."

CHAPTER 29

Once more in her own bedchamber, Aila stared blindly through the narrow window to the gray sea in the distance while her ladies whispered together in the antechamber. She knew they were fearful of the future now that their princess was, once again, a widow.

But this time she felt no overwhelming grief. No desire to follow her husband into whatever Otherworld he might travel to.

She didn't even feel grim pleasure that one of the cursed Scots who had lured and slaughtered her kin had received justice.

Because something else, something that even managed to paralyze the pain of seeing her father murdered, crippled her mind.

Gingerly she brushed her fingertips over her belly, ensuring her action could not be seen by her ladies.

It wasn't possible, of course. Her constant fatigue, her inability to keep food in her stomach, the tenderness of her breasts—all could be logically explained.

For two years she and Onuist had tried to conceive. She had used every pagan ritual and spell she knew, had offered sacrifice and tears but not once had there been even a hint of the longed-for babe.

Despite the tantalizing glimpses Bride had so often shown her of a future filled with beloved children, Aila had convinced herself she was barren. It had scarcely crossed her mind the fault might lay with Onuist.

She released a quivering breath and rested her forehead against the rough stone wall.

One night with Connor MacKenzie was all it had taken to shatter the foundations of her existence.

She squeezed her eyes shut. She was tired because of the long journey, the events that had unfolded since, the grief she had suppressed. She was sick because the food here choked her. And her breasts were tender because…

Bride turned, looked at her and smiled the unmistakable smile of victory.

Her eyes jerked open. No. It couldn't be. But her heart pounded, and stomach churned, as a memory hammered through her mind.

That night, she had wished with all her heart to conceive Connor's child. Knowing it could never happen, still she had longed for such a miracle. But more than that. She remembered now. Remembered how she would give anything to conceive his child.

Bride had been there. Bride had heard.

And Bride had granted her deepest wish.

For a price.

The nausea rose and she battled against it, refusing to succumb to her body's weakness. For nine years she had shut out the goddess, refused to worship the ancient ways. Had tried to live with the constant guilt of having watched Onuist die. The knowledge she was destined to never hold her own babe in her arms.

In one moment of fractured concentration, Bride had

entered. Witnessed her night of illicit passion. And, like all pagan gods throughout the history of mankind, she had exacted her own twisted revenge.

How better to punish a lapsed chosen one of the ancient gods than by using the seed of Aila's bitterest enemy to fill her womb? What exquisite vengeance Bride had bestowed. She had embraced Aila's deepest desire and answered her most fervent prayer.

By using the man whose kin might personally be responsible for slaughtering Aila's own beloved father.

Instinctively her fingers curved protectively against her belly. Guilt ate into her soul, but instead of accepting it, as she had accepted the guilt that had consumed her after Onuist had died, she fought against it.

It didn't matter who the father was. She was this child's mother and she would do everything to protect its fragile existence. Bride might laugh at the knowledge she had so cleverly distorted Aila's dearest wish. But Aila would take the tarnished gift. Take it and embrace it and love it with her entire heart.

She glanced over her shoulder, but her ladies were still distracted. Once again, she focused through the window, her mind no longer numb with grief. She couldn't afford to cocoon herself in such self-indulgent misery.

Not if she wanted her child born in freedom.

Now she was widowed, there was a chance—no matter how slender—that she might be allowed to return to Ce. But there was no mistaking that if the Scots king discovered she was with child, freedom was the last thing she would ever be granted.

And should his physicians discover the unlikelihood of Fergus having fathered the babe the chances of her surviving pregnancy, let alone childbirth, were remote.

With reluctance, she forced her hand from her belly and beckoned to her ladies. If she intended to confront MacAlpin, she would look every regal inch the Princess of Ce she was.

∼

MACALPIN, to her surprise, agreed to see her directly. She had expected him to be evasive, reluctant to face her. That he was not only reinforced the truth of his barbaric nature and lack of conscience.

She wore the gown of gold she'd worn to the betrothal, with the scarlet veil and royal crown of Ce. If MacAlpin expected to find her cowed and broken by his betrayal, he would be grievously disappointed.

Accompanied by her ladies and the Scots guard, she followed MacAlpin's messenger to the war chamber. She wouldn't recall the last time she had entered this chamber. Brutally she pushed the memories aside. She couldn't think of her father or the other nobles. She had to be strong. For the sake of her child.

She buried her hatred of MacAlpin. Of all Scots. Buried it deep so when the upstart king looked at her all he would see was a princess with a thousand-year lineage. A royal lineage that put his own paltry three-hundred-year heritage in Pictland to shame.

The second she was ushered into the chamber, she saw Connor standing by his king. For a moment, she remained paralyzed, disbelieving, unable to move let alone think.

Of every scenario that had played through her mind during the last hour, the possibility of Connor being present when she confronted MacAlpin had never occurred to her.

She'd tried not to think of Connor MacKenzie at all. Because whenever she did, her head warred with her heart and now, knowing she nurtured his child in her womb, all her carefully constructed walls of defense threatened to crumble.

She forced one foot in front of the other. Her spine was so rigid she feared it would snap. But better that than to sag with defeat, awash in the despicable knowledge that just one glance at MacKenzie could cause her heart to ache with hopeless love.

She didn't acknowledge the Scots who bowed as she walked

the length of the chamber. It took every shred of willpower she possessed to keep her gaze on MacAlpin, and not stray to Connor MacKenzie.

Yet it didn't matter where she focused. MacKenzie filled her vision regardless.

"Lady Devorgilla." MacAlpin spoke her language and bowed, as if this was a perfectly normal meeting. Her glance flickered, unwillingly, to the flagstone floor where remnants of bloodstains lingered. "We deeply regret these tragic circumstances."

Hatred flared. She doused it, with difficulty. But managed to keep all such emotion from showing on her face.

"As do I." Her voice was chilly, and she replied in Pictish, unwilling to reveal she understood Gaelic although his physician was only too aware of her fluency in the barbaric tongue.

"On behalf of all the people of Dal Riada," MacAlpin continued, "We want you to know none of us bear you any ill will for the events that transpired within these walls."

Goddess, strike him down.

The curse surged up from the core of her soul. The curse of pagans, a curse she meant with every fiber of her being.

The civilized veneer she had worked so hard to embrace during the last nine years shattered. Uuen's teachings fled and primal instinct cascaded through her blood.

She didn't forgive him. She would never forgive him. And if ever the chance presented itself for vengeance, she would grab it with both hands and revel in the bloodied outcome.

MacAlpin remained central to her unwavering gaze, but she saw Connor stiffen at the king's words. She had to stop looking at Connor. Except she wasn't, yet she remained vitally aware of every breath he took.

"My lady," Connor said, and his voice wrapped around her like a mantle of fur. She spared him only a fleeting glance but enough to see him grip a heavy, carved chair and bring it to her side. "Please be seated."

She maintained eye contact with the king. The bastard didn't even have the decency to lower his lying gaze.

"I prefer to remain standing." Did they think to intimidate her further by making her sit when they all towered over her? Why did Connor MacKenzie continue to stand so close to her? Did he think her unaware of his scrutiny?

For a second, she forgot where she was, why she was here. All she could see, in her mind, was Connor. Looking at her as he had looked at her when she had conceived his child.

Heat washed through her. What would MacAlpin do if he discovered whose child she carried? Would it be Connor's death sentence as well as her own?

CONNOR TIGHTENED his grip on the back of the chair. Aila had spared him scarcely a glance since she'd entered the chamber. It seemed his presence meant nothing to her, that she was barely aware of his existence.

She looked at MacAlpin with chilly indifference. He'd expected her to be distraught, perhaps accusatory. MacAlpin had certainly thought the reason Aila had insisted upon an audience was so she could level vitriol his way.

But Connor should have known better. Aila could hide her emotions if she chose to. But it twisted his guts that she needed to hide her emotions from him.

It would be different once they left Dunadd. Once she was free of the stench of betrayal that clung to every stone and lurked in every crevice of the stronghold.

"We have given great thought to your position here, madam," MacAlpin said. If Connor didn't know otherwise, he would have thought his king showed both deep respect and concern for Aila. But all MacAlpin wanted was to keep Aila's bride price and her potential heir to the Kingdom of Ce within his realm.

"So have I, my lord," Aila said. "The terms of the marriage contract between Ce and Dal Riada have been fulfilled. The alliance ratified."

She sounded so sincere. But he remembered the blood on her gown, and the savage gleam in her eyes as he'd burst into Fergus' bedchamber.

God damn MacAlpin. He ached to take her in his arms, to rip the burden of grief from her shoulders. But all he could do was offer her his silent support. Yet if she so much as glanced his way, he'd offer her so much more than that.

"My lady." MacAlpin approached and instinctively Connor stepped closer to Aila's side. If MacAlpin noticed, he chose to ignore the gesture. Aila didn't appear to notice at all. "Your courage and honor humbles us. A strong alliance between your people and mine is all we crave. Yet for that, we need more than blood oaths. We need physical union."

Aila's expression did not alter, but Conner had the uncanny sensation that ice spiked from her, freezing the air.

"Physical union?" She made the words sound obscene, yet her voice remained as even as ever.

"Between Scot and Pict," MacAlpin elaborated. Did he imagine Aila had not understood his meaning? "Under other circumstances you would, naturally, return to your kingdom. But these are unsettled times, my lady. We must work together to ensure peace prevails."

Connor saw Aila's lips flatten. But instantly she recovered herself. So instantly, Connor wondered whether MacAlpin had even noticed the offense he'd given.

"In Ce, I shall work tirelessly toward such end."

MacAlpin inclined his head. As if he intended to give her words serious consideration. Connor clenched his jaw and shot Aila a sideways glance. Why was MacAlpin playing with her emotions like this? If his king didn't spit it out soon, then God help him, he'd tell Aila himself.

"We hope, my lady," MacAlpin said, "you will continue to work tirelessly to such end despite remaining in Dal Riada."

"My lord," Aila said and Connor saw the way her fingers gripped the golden material of her gown, hidden from sight from his king but plainly visible to him. "You have no need to keep me as a hostage. You have my brother Talargan, royal prince of the Kingdom of Ce."

"And he shall be treated as such, madam. But, alas, we cannot allow you to leave and it would be remiss of us not to ensure you are suitably protected."

Connor saw her swallow, saw her fingers convulse within the folds of her gown. His patience unraveled. "My liege."

MacAlpin raised his hand without taking his gaze from Aila. "Your continued safety and happiness is our prime consideration. That is why we have arranged another marriage for you, to a warrior whose status befits your blood."

All hint of color drained from Aila's face and for one heart wrenching moment he thought she was going to faint. He slung an infuriated glare at his king, but MacAlpin appeared oblivious to anything but Aila.

"I will not—" Her voice was no longer cool, no longer even. Without thinking he slid his fingers between hers, disengaging her death grip on her gown, and pressed his arm against hers for any support she might require.

Her cold fingers remained lifeless within his grip, but she didn't try to pull away.

MacAlpin smiled, well satisfied. "Already your future husband is eager to comfort you, madam. Tomorrow you will wed Connor MacKenzie, lord of the royal stronghold of Dunfodla and lord of Duncadha and of Dunbrae."

His king faded into oblivion and he and Aila might have been the only two people in the chamber as she slowly turned to look at him. He began to smile, hoping to reassure her that once this day was over, he would do everything in his power to heal her pain. To promise she would never have to set foot in Dunadd again.

The smile froze on his lips. She looked at him not with relief or pleasure or even a wary uncertainty. For a second his brain could not comprehend the look in her eyes, the expression on her face.

But his brain didn't need to comprehend, because his heart recognized instantly. Bleak despair filled her eyes as if he had just plunged a sword through her breast and betrayed the fundamental core of her being.

As if the knowledge she was to be his wife wrenched open her soul.

CHAPTER 30

This could not be happening.

Even as MacAlpin officiated the joining, a section of Aila's mind refused to believe she was standing by Connor's side. Becoming his wife.

But of course it was true. She'd been unable to think of anything else all through the tortuous night. And what made it all worse was the humiliating knowledge that a despicable part of her craved this unholy alliance with a desperation that shamed her.

Back in Ce she'd harbored foolish dreams of a lifetime together with her Scot.

Now, once again, her deepest wish had been granted. Truly Bride's viciousness in her vengeance was horrific. What more could the goddess take from her, manipulate to her twisted will and fling back in her face, crushed beyond salvation?

Connor turned to her, raised her hand, and brushed his lips across her knuckles. She remained motionless, her gaze fixed on the gold brooch pinned to the plaid slung over his shoulder.

She knew the answer. Bride had no need to do anything else. She had sown the seeds already.

Her unborn child.

What rights did a mother have in Dal Riada? As the father, as her husband, would Connor take the babe from her if his king ordered it? Another hostage to ensure her continued compliance?

It didn't matter if the rest of the world assumed the child was Fergus'. Connor would know the truth.

The horror of the extent of power he wielded over her heart, over her sanity, blazed through her and for a moment reality blurred. How could she survive, living with a man she loved as much as she despised his king, a man who could believe such vicious lies about her people without a shred of proof?

"Be strong for just a little longer." The whispered words caressed her ear as Connor drew closer. His evocative scent of savage Scot and foreign spices invaded her senses, tainted her blood, and speared with desperate longing between her thighs. He cradled her hand against his chest as his body shielded her from view. As though he was her protector.

She stiffened, battling the urge to surrender to her body's treacherous need for Connor's touch. She would show no emotion in front of the Scots. They would not bear witness to her total degradation. She was a princess. The honor and pride of Ce, of Pictland herself, rested on her shoulders.

She turned her head very slightly. Tried to ignore how his strong jaw remained unyielding against her cheek.

"You may be assured no Scot will ever have justification for calling me weak."

"Aila." How could she still find the way he said her name so distressingly seductive? His lips grazed her earlobe and jagged tremors heated her blood. But she remained immobile, refusing to react. Despite how she ached to sink into his arms, how she desperately wanted to hear him admit her people were innocent of the accusations leveled against them. "You are the strongest woman I've ever known."

Damn him. How could she keep an emotional distance from

him when he could penetrate her defenses with just a few whispered words?

In memory of the slain, she could never allow him to guess how much she still cared.

"Yes." She drew back so their faces were no longer touching. "How fortunate I'm not prone to hysterics. It appears, after all, there was a reason for my past."

At fifteen, she hadn't possessed the ability to hide her feelings. At seventeen, she had wanted to die rather than confront her feelings.

But nine years of living with her memories, of battling with her guilt, had taught her one thing at least.

How to hide from the world behind a veneer of ice.

His gaze sharpened on her, as if he had no intention of letting that comment remain between them, but MacAlpin intervened. Hurrying the proceedings onward.

Another feast. But this time Connor sat by her side. This time, as goblets and tankards were raised, she felt his eyes upon her. As if she was the only one in the hall. The only one who mattered.

Beneath the table, she fisted her hands. If she wanted to retain the strength to survive this marriage, she had to face the fact Connor's loyalties were, and would forever remain, with his treacherous king. She couldn't afford to trust him no matter how her foolish heart ached to.

And she had to be strong. For her child.

CONNOR GLANCED AT AILA, where she sat beside him on a carved chair. She looked beautiful, regal, and so remote she might as well be residing on the moon itself.

But she was his wife. His chest tightened at the knowledge that, against all logical possibility, he had achieved this miracle.

He watched Aila imperiously wave aside another serving of

delicacies. Her plate remained empty. Had she eaten anything at all?

He leaned toward her. "Is there nothing I can tempt you with, my lady?"

When she turned to him, he offered her a smile. The look on her face suggested he had just offered her the contents of a chamber pot.

"Nothing at all." Her voice was polite, but chilled. And clearly intended to convey it wasn't only the food that failed to tempt her.

He couldn't even begin to imagine how she felt, once again sitting at the high table. Once again a bride.

In the stronghold where her kin had been murdered.

The sooner they left the better. First thing in the morning. But first, he had to get her out of here. He turned to his king.

"My liege." He waited until MacAlpin turned to him. "My wife is fatigued by recent events. I beg leave to retire for the night."

MacAlpin grinned in clear approval. "An eager bridegroom." He glanced at Aila before returning his attention to Connor. "She's reluctant, that's to be expected. But she'll come round in time. Once there's a child filling her belly her thoughts will be more usefully occupied."

"Aye." Connor forced the word between gritted teeth. He had no intention of impregnating Aila. And if she was already… that was something he'd have to face. "We'll be leaving for Dunbrae in the morning."

The king jerked his head in approval. "She'll be safe enough there. I've no need to remind you she remains our most valuable hostage. Ce will not dare rise against us while we hold the heirs to their kingdom."

Connor beckoned a servant and gave orders for an intimate banquet to be served in Aila's chambers before he returned his attention to her. "Shall we retire?"

She looked at him. Her eyes were curiously blank, as though

she had buried her emotions so deeply they no longer disturbed her. But as soon as they were alone, she would no longer feel the obligation to present this perfect facade.

With him she could be herself.

"If you wish." Again, perfectly polite. And edged with ice that scraped his nerves raw.

He stood and held her chair as she rose. Lascivious remarks and knowing laughs filled the hall and Aila froze. For one agonizing second he saw the pain, the shame, flood her face before she straightened her shoulders, tilted her head and prepared her regal exit.

All newlywed couples were subjected to such irreverence. But this time Connor found no humor in the tradition. For God's sake, were his countrymen so drunk they couldn't appreciate how Aila must be feeling?

He swept a black glare around the hall. A fleeting glare of condemnation but it was enough. Not one of the warriors who had traveled with him to Ce, nor those who had fought by his side so recently in Northumbria, were among the foul-mouthed revelers.

To hell with tradition. He didn't take her hand as custom expected. Instead he wrapped his arm around her shoulders, shielding her from the crowd with his body, and escorted her from the hall.

She didn't pull away from him. But neither did she relax against him. God, they needed to be alone so she could drop this pretense before she shattered.

In silence they returned to her chambers, her ladies following. But she would have no need of her ladies tonight. He intended to administer to her every wish himself. And then, when she was safely in his arms and soft and glowing after their loving, he would admit she had been right.

She walked through the antechamber and stood by the fire in the bedchamber and he watched the flames turn her hair into fascinating ribbons of fiery sunsets and golden sunrises. Her ladies fluttered around her, removing her crown and veil, but Aila appeared as unaware of them as she had of him. As servants filed in with covered platters and placed them on the small table, he followed her into the bedchamber.

"The princess does not require your assistance tonight, ladies."

Her ladies spun around, looked confused and glanced from Aila to him, as if wondering to whom they owed allegiance. But since Aila didn't object they finally departed in a flurry of curtsies and anxious glances to their silent mistress.

Before he could move toward her, an elderly servant rose from a stool on the far side of the fire. He hadn't even noticed her sitting there. In her arms was the tiny black kitten.

Aila roused from her reverie to cast a glance at the kitten before she jerked her attention back to the fire. Unease snaked through his gut. If she wanted the creature to remain, why didn't she say so?

But she didn't say a word. And the old woman shuffled toward the door, clearly reluctant to leave her princess alone with him.

He reached out and took the kitten and the woman shot him a startled glance before hurrying from the chamber.

They were alone. Now she could turn on him, tell him what she thought of his king, his people, this cursed land he had brought her to. Finally, she could grieve, and he would comfort her. In time he'd ease her heart. Make her smile. Remind her of the love she bore for him, no matter how deeply she'd buried it.

"Aila." He trailed his knuckles along the silk of her face and outlined her jaw with the back of his fingers. Desire stabbed through his groin, and he recalled just how long it had been since she had been in his bed.

Five weeks. It felt like five months. But now, now she was his wife and she would share his bed every night.

Blood thundered through his veins and his engorged cock ached for her touch, her heat, the exquisite sensation of sinking into her welcoming body. He tilted her face toward him and lost his soul in the haunting depths of her glittering eyes.

"Aila, Princess Devorgilla of Ce." His hand cradled her jaw, his fingertips grazed her bound tresses. "Lady Mistress of Duncadha and Dunfodla." She was mistress of Dunbrae also, but it felt wrong to grant her that title. She didn't need it, anyway. "My wife." The words were raw, and a flicker of some emotion heated her eyes and caused the breath to hitch in her breast. It was a small response but enough to reassure him. His fingers tightened and a mewl of protest emerged from the direction of his hip.

Aila jerked back and looked down, bemusement clear on her features. He gave a laugh, half rueful, half frustrated, and lifted the indignant kitten.

"Don't make me regret allowing you to stay," he told the oddly endearing creature before placing it into a basket by the fire.

"I didn't ask you to allow it to remain."

No longer encumbered by the kitten, he cupped Aila's face with both hands, drawing her into his warmth, reveling in the sensation of her body nestling against his.

Where she belonged.

"You didn't have to." It had been evident in the way she'd glanced at it when until that moment she had ignored every other living creature. His thumbs stroked the soft skin of her cheeks. She was his. He could scarcely believe it. "What did you call it?"

She blinked twice, as if his question made no sense. And it didn't make sense, because why was he speaking of an animal when he had Aila in his arms?

But he knew why. It was because it didn't matter of what they spoke. So long as they spoke. So long as Aila said anything to break the strained silence she had maintained since being informed of their marriage.

"Hope." She sounded reluctant to tell him.

Hope. He translated the word into Gaelic and decided he liked it. It gave him hope, also, that he and Aila could build a future together despite the tragedy of these past days.

His fingers trailed against her throat, pausing against the erratic flutter of her pulse. Her breath teased his jaw and he captured her lips in an open-mouthed kiss, a kiss he had feared he might never again savor.

She tasted of honey, of spices, of sunlight from heaven.

Feverishly his fingers tugged at the ties of her bodice. But they refused to comply and with a growl of frustration, he ripped the material from her breasts.

He felt her gasp in his mouth and it was darkly erotic. An exchange of breath, of life. He tore his lips from her and trailed kisses along the column of her throat as she arched in his embrace, offering herself to him.

Exposed by the ruins of her gown, her breasts taunted him, the rosy nipples erect. One hand splayed between her shoulders he cupped one breast in his other and flicked his thumb over her tempting nipple.

"I've ached for this." He sounded parched, as though he had barely survived a devastating drought and she was his only hope of sustenance. "For you." For five weeks. And yet it seemed he had hungered for her love for years.

He caught her gaze and her eyes were glazed with passion, yet they didn't flicker from his. As if in the sea of desire, he was her anchor.

As she was his.

He swept his tongue over her nipple, licking, tasting and she trembled in his arms. Impatient for her touch he pulled her gown from her shoulders, over her hips and it slid unceremoniously to the floor.

She was as beautiful as he recalled, although she seemed a little thinner. Damn, he had meant to feed her before he seduced her but there would be plenty of time to tempt her with delicacies afterward.

After he had claimed her as his wife.

With fingers that shook, he unknotted the ribbons in her hair and began to unbraid the silken threads. Dimly, far beyond the pounding that filled his brain, he wondered why she didn't drag his plaid from his body. Rip his shirt over his head. But it was a vague, unformed thought, a whisper in the thunder of his need, and his need in this moment consumed reason.

It didn't matter. She wanted him and that was everything.

Her hair cascaded over her shoulders and he dragged his fingers through the rippling silk, caressing her partially concealed breasts. He molded his hands around her waist, moving down to the curve of her hips then knelt before her and pressed his lips against her belly.

She trembled but her arms remained by her sides. He cupped her rounded buttocks, teased her navel with the tip of his tongue and another tremble rode her.

"Are you cold?" His voice was raw, and he looked up at her. A naked vision of pale flesh and vibrant hair, and she was looking at him but there was not enough light to see the glorious color of her eyes.

She shook her head once. He knew she wasn't cold. Her body was warm, inviting, yet he'd wanted to hear her speak.

He inched lower, aching to taste her evocative scent that tempted him to the edge of sanity.

"Do you want to lie down?" God, what was he saying? He doubted she cared whether they fell onto the bed or remained upright. It made no difference to him. But why wouldn't she answer him?

Again, she shook her head. Just one brief shake. As though words were beyond her.

Odd relief surged through him. Of course that was the reason. Like him she had wanted and waited and dreamed of this moment. Thinking it would never happen. And now that it had why was he consumed with the need to hear her tell him what she wanted?

It was obvious what she wanted.

He slid one hand from her bottom, over her hip and caressed the soft curls at the apex of her thighs. She didn't make a sound, but her legs parted.

Encouraged, he slipped one finger between her pouting lips. She was hot, wet and a strangled groan escaped his throat.

"Aila, my love." His tongue flicked the hood of her clit, and her fingers rammed into his skull, shocking, painful, and deliriously arousing. He dragged his finger from her tight warmth and slid his tongue into her. Tasting her essence, and she tasted of heaven.

He kissed her, deep, plunging, mimicking with his tongue what he soon intended to mirror with his cock. Her hips arched and fingernails tore his head.

He wanted her up against a wall, but the bed was nearer. Tearing his mouth from her, he stood and kissed her, wet and hungry, allowing her to taste herself on his tongue and breath and lips. Cradling the back of her head to keep her angled for his continued penetration, he walked her backward toward the bed.

Flat on her back on the furs, he continued to worship her with his mouth while he struggled to discard his shirt and plaid. But when her hand trailed over his naked chest, reason fled.

To hell with his plaid. He hiked the offending material up, kneed her thighs open and thrust into her.

She reared against him, her breath hot and erratic against his mouth. With a primal growl, he plunged his fingers through her shining hair, spilling the silken tresses across the pillows.

"My wife." *Not Fergus'.* He rammed into her, harder, deeper, as if he could erase all lingering trace of the last five weeks. Eradicate the memory of his brother. Annihilate the betrayal of his king. "Tell me, Aila. Tell me who I am."

Her fingers tangled in his hair. But she didn't reply. Didn't say, *"You are my husband."*

Bracing his weight on one hand, he cradled her head and captured her passion-filled gaze.

"Tell me." It was a demand. Her tight sheath quivered around him, and his hand fisted in sweet agony on the pillow.

"You," her voice was hoarse, "are a savage Scot, MacKenzie."

Her savage Scot. The tattered remnants of his control fled. Sensation flooded and beyond the thunder of his heart, he savored her choked gasps as she convulsed around his engorged cock.

With a roar of frustration, he pulled from her slick heat. His hard balls slammed in rhythmic fury against her wet slit, her juices sliding over his heavy sac.

He wanted to be inside her. But at least she was beneath him, her hands in his hair, her legs tangled with his. Her scent entranced him, her heat enslaved him and he savaged her willing mouth as he spilled his reckless seed.

He panted in her open mouth, body shuddering, satisfied yet not fully sated. Slowly he raised his head and stared at her. Thank God she was with him. This time nothing could take her from him.

No breath to speak, he offered her a grin before reaching for his shirt. Somehow, he managed to clean her without having to break bodily contact. She didn't attempt to assist, just lay there as her erratic gasps gradually slowed.

He tossed the soiled shirt aside. Hell, his damn plaid was in the way. Yet he couldn't find the energy to dispose of it just yet. But next time he wanted nothing between their bodies to hinder the feel of her skin against his.

He wound errant strands of her hair around his finger. "That was an enjoyable start to our married life, my lady."

She didn't answer but she shifted beneath him. Instantly he

braced his weight on his free hand, allowing her room to breathe more easily.

"Better?" He traced the line of her face. Still she didn't answer. And finally, a thread of unease stirred. "Aila? Is something wrong?" Had he hurt her? Surely not. But why wouldn't she speak to him? He'd enjoyed their flirting, that one night they had spent together in Ce. It had never occurred to him she wouldn't continue after they were wed.

"No." She shifted again and with reluctance, he rolled onto his side and lay on the bed facing her. "Of course there's nothing wrong." Then she looked directly at him and the shadows cast by the flickering flames of the fire gave her a strange, otherworldly expression.

Inexplicably a chill crawled along his spine. And then she drew in a deep breath and said, "I've been married enough times, Connor, to understand the importance of consummating such unions."

Silence roared through his head and punched through his chest. Words failed and all he could do was stare at the woman he loved. The woman he had assumed, in his ignorance, might still love him.

The woman who had, by a few cold words, reduced their loving this night to nothing more than a necessary act, to seal a contract between Scot and Pict.

CHAPTER 31

$\mathcal{A}$ila tightened her grip on the reins as Connor rode toward her. They had been traveling since yesterday morning at a slow, leisurely pace, as if he didn't want to exhaust her.

She braced herself as he drew alongside her mount. Perhaps he didn't want to overtire her. No matter how many times she reminded herself he was a Scot and his people were her enemy, he had yet to treat her with anything less than utmost consideration.

"We approach Dunbrae, my lady." He might have been addressing a respected stranger for all the warmth in his voice.

She inclined her head, not trusting herself to speak. Dunbrae, she had learned, was the hillfort Connor had acquired through marriage to Fearchara. And Fearchara's mother and Connor's mother both resided at Dunbrae.

Aila doubted either lady would take kindly to her presence. A foreign princess and usurper. They would have heard everything that had happened from the messenger Connor had sent on ahead to warn them of their arrival.

She stifled a shudder, refusing to face the thread of terror that wound through her heart. All she had ever wanted was a husband she loved and children to cherish.

She had a husband she loved. She would soon have a child she already cherished. How bitterly wishes could come to pass.

Connor rode off without a backward glance and despite her best intentions, she couldn't drag her gaze from him. On their wedding night it had taken every shred of willpower she possessed to keep her distance.

Why was she lying? She hadn't been able to keep any distance at all. When he had taken her, all her suppressed love had flooded through her and overfilled her heart.

If she had been a young, naive maid, she could have imagined he loved her that night. But it was lust. And a woman could feel lust, just as a man. Her dream-lover had taught her that. Her lust for Connor was something she could face him knowing. If he guessed the depth of her love, it would destroy her.

Dunbrae loomed ahead. Nerves gripped the pit of her stomach. Last night they had stayed in a small hillfort. Connor had shared her bed, but he hadn't said a word. And although his mouth and tongue and hands had thrilled her body, his silence had flayed her heart.

Afterward, when all she'd wanted was to curl into his embrace and weep for everything she'd lost, he had rolled off her. Turned his back.

And gone to sleep.

CONNOR HELPED HER DISMOUNT, as though she was infinitely precious. Of course she was precious. She was an invaluable hostage. Naturally he wouldn't wish any harm to befall her.

When she attempted to pull from his grasp, his fingers tightened around hers. Reminding her they were in public and protocol would be observed.

It was hard enough to remain aloof whenever Connor was near. But with him holding her hand how was she supposed to act as if none of this touched her at all?

The same as she always did. She straightened her shoulders and hid behind the regal facade of her Pictish heritage.

A raven-haired lady stepped forward to greet her on the threshold.

"Welcome, Princess Devorgilla of Ce." She spoke in Pictish and dipped a respectful curtsy. "I hope you'll be very happy with us."

"My lady Aila," Connor said, still holding her hand. Did he think she would run if he relinquished his grip? Where could she run? "This is my mother, Lady Ealasaid."

"My lady. I thank you." The words sounded stilted. But she couldn't help it. They all knew she was here against her will. That her kin had been murdered by their king.

And yet to survive they would all present a mask of civility.

"And this is Lady Nighean, mother of my first wife, Fearchara."

She smothered the nervous churn of her stomach, forced a polite smile, and inclined her head as Lady Nighean welcomed her into her home.

Connor's home. Her home now.

As they entered the hillfort, the conversation battered against her shields. But it didn't matter. They spoke to Connor, not her. Telling him the master chamber had been readied, that a feast —*not another feast*—had been prepared in their honor. That whenever the princess was ready, she would be shown around her new domain.

"I'll show my wife to our chambers so she can rest before the feast," Connor said. "There's time enough for her to explore Dunbrae."

He spoke as though she wasn't present. Yet what did it matter? She did need to rest. She could explore Dunbrae another time. But still, it stung that he didn't consider her worthy enough to consult.

She preceded him up the stairs and then he led her to their chambers.

"It's not as grand as you're used to."

She walked through the small antechamber into the bedchamber. Faded tapestries hung on the walls, two carved chairs were on either side of the large fireplace, and a plain chest was under the window. Had he shared these chambers with Fearchara?

"It's perfectly serviceable." She turned to look at him and saw the way he clenched his jaw, as though her answer had irritated him immensely.

"Yet hardly fit for a princess."

"Is there anywhere in Dal Riada fit for a Princess of Pictland?" The words escaped before she could prevent them. Damn. She didn't want him to know he had the power to rouse her temper. She swung away from him, before she saw triumph in his eyes. Before he saw the despair in hers.

"No." There was an odd note in his voice, as if far from triumph he was the one filled with despair. "We had to come here first, Aila. But our permanent home will be Duncadha, the stronghold of my forefathers. It's..." he paused, as though considering his words. She refused to glance over her shoulder at him. Despite how deeply she wanted to. "It's grander than Dunbrae. More suited to your status."

Her status?

"As a hostage, you mean?" She did turn then and offered him a brittle smile. Let him think she didn't care one way or the other that the only reason they were here together was because his king had commanded it.

He glared at her and she saw fury glinting in his eyes. Shock speared her at the realization of how deeply he hated the position into which his king had plunged her.

"You're not—" She thought he was going to deny she was a hostage although they both knew the truth. But then he appeared to realize how futile such a claim would be. "I wanted you to know you won't be expected to share your household with another woman. In Duncadha you will be the sole mistress."

Pain lanced her heart at how hard he was trying to make this marriage tolerable. How easy it would be to reach out her hand, thank him for his consideration and allow her love to blossom. Instead she gave a disdainful shrug. "If that is your wish."

Even from this distance, she heard the angry hiss of breath between his teeth. "Oui, madam." His words were brutal. "That is my wish. That you be mistress of my stronghold in Duncadha. But we'll remain here for the present. Is that acceptable to you?"

Despite their difference in height, she managed to look down her nose at him.

"Quite acceptable, my lord."

For a moment she thought he was going to take issue with her compliance, but he appeared to decide it wasn't worth the effort. "I'll send your ladies in to attend to you." With that, he offered her a stiff bow and marched from the chamber.

THE FEAST that night turned out to be an intimate gathering of only the other two Scots ladies and Connor. They didn't even sit in the hall but a small chamber that looked to be the private domain of Lady Ealasaid.

Aila hid her relief as effectively as she hid her trepidation. The entire populace of Dal Riada might consider her people treacherous, but no Scot she encountered would be able to fault her countenance.

"My lady," Connor's mother said as Connor held the carved chair for Aila. "We planned a great feast for your arrival, but Connor felt you would prefer something less public tonight. I hope you are not offended?"

Connor had requested this? She struggled not to shoot him a thankful glance.

"I appreciate your concern." She spoke in Gaelic since it was obvious Lady Ealasaid wasn't as fluent as her son in Pictish. "I'm a little fatigued after recent events."

As servants brought in dishes, Lady Nighean spoke directly to her for the first time.

"It's no wonder you are fatigued, my lady." She spoke in her own language, as if until this moment she'd been unaware Aila could understand. "If it will not offend, please accept my condolences on your loss."

Aila swallowed around the constriction in her throat and inadvertently caught the older woman's eyes. Instead of condemnation or anger that she had taken her daughter's rightful place, only compassion wreathed her face.

Beneath the table, she gripped her fingers together and struggled for some semblance of control. The only way she could function was if she didn't think about that night in MacAlpin's war chamber. But now, for one blood-soaked moment, it flooded her mind and threatened her facade of serenity.

She would not crumble. But when she managed to drag her gaze from Fearchara's mother and saw a sad smile of understanding from Lady Ealasaid, pain engulfed her heart.

They were being kind. She had not expected it. Yet kindness would undo her as cruel taunts and icy indifference never would.

CONNOR TOSSED BACK his third tankard of mead and tried, without success, to stop staring at Aila. She sat beside him, so close he had only to lean toward her to touch her, and yet she was as distant from him as if she still resided in Ce.

His mother and Lady Nighean kept up a constant stream of inconsequential conversation, as he knew they would, and Aila occasionally deigned to answer them. She hadn't appeared in the least relieved that he'd managed, at great inconvenience to all concerned, to avert another huge, public feast for her.

Maybe he shouldn't have bothered. Maybe she didn't give a damn who saw her or not. And yet he couldn't rid his mind of the bawdy comments at their wedding feast, nor the way Aila had fleetingly cringed beneath the onslaught.

Fool that he was, he thought she'd appreciate his gesture. That she'd look at him without that remote expression in her eyes. Look at him—as if she saw him.

But she'd ignored him as effortlessly as she had ignored him from the moment they had wed.

She rarely opened her mouth to him. Unless they were in bed. Dark lust gripped his loins, a torturous reminder of how eagerly she responded to his touch in the black of night. How she clawed his chest, dragged her fingers through his hair, dug her teeth into his flesh. She opened her mouth to him then, but only to drive him insane with need. She never uttered a single word.

"That's a beautiful cross, my lady," his mother said, leaning forward to admire the damn cross Aila never removed from her neck. Except in bed. His treacherous cock throbbed in remembrance of the last two nights, and in anticipation of the night to come. Another night when she would open to him, accept his touch, but refuse, ultimately, to give him anything of herself at all.

"Thank you."

He watched the way her fingers fluttered over the cross before dropping to her lap. He had the sudden vision of ripping it from her, slinging it into the fire, watching it blacken and finally melt.

As if destroying the cross would make any difference.

"It's very unusual," Nighean said. "I've never seen anything quite like it before."

"It's very old," Aila said. He glowered at the wall, despising the way he soaked up every word she spoke. Her accent enchanted him. Always had. "It was a wedding gift from my—my—"

"Her first husband." His harsh voice cut through her stumbled words. He offered an insincere grin to the three ladies who stared at him with varying degrees of interest. Aila, he noticed, showed the least interest of all. "I, alas, am only the Princess of Ce's third lord and master." And this time his self-loathing leer was directed only at her.

A blush seeped over her cheeks, but she didn't break eye contact. In his peripheral vision he saw his mother and Nighean become suddenly absorbed by the contents of their plates, but he hardly registered their presence.

It was Aila's response he wanted. Aila's retort. Aila's anger.

God damn it, why wouldn't she lose her temper with him? Why wouldn't she shout and scream and tell him how much she hated his king, his country? Why did she treat him with such indifference?

Except when they were in bed?

"Yes," she said. Was that a thread of passion he detected in her voice? "I fear I have a reputation for husbands dying on me shortly after the ceremony."

"Your fear is unfounded in my case."

Her green eyes glinted. He raised one eyebrow, goading her, daring her to respond. Hoping she wouldn't once again retreat behind that regal mask she wore like a shield.

She tilted her chin at him and the look she arrowed his way suggested she thought he was something disgusting one of the hounds had dragged in from the midden.

At last. He braced himself and hoped his mother and Nighean would grace them with privacy but mainly—hell, the only thing that mattered was that Aila would finally discard this infuriating masquerade.

"How reassuring." The smile she offered him could have frozen a loch in midsummer. And then she delivered her deadly thrust. "My lord."

CHAPTER 32

Aila lowered her knife and hoped neither lady would remark on her lack of appetite. But even the thought of eating turned her stomach. She'd scarcely managed to finish a meal since the night she'd conceived Connor's child.

"Aila." Connor's low growl in her ear quivered through her senses. It took everything she possessed not to turn toward him. "What are you attempting to accomplish by starving yourself?"

She looked at him then. She couldn't help herself. He had noticed?

"I'm simply not hungry." She kept her voice as low as his, as unwilling as he appeared to be for the older ladies to eavesdrop on their conversation.

His stormy eyes ensnared her. Despite how desperately she wished otherwise.

"You're thinner than you were in Ce."

He'd noticed that too? For a moment words failed her. And then her pride rescued her, as it had so often rescued her in the past.

"Indeed? Or perhaps you have merely tired of your new wife already." Her heart squeezed at the notion, but he would never know. Let him think she didn't care one way or the other how soon his lust for her cooled.

His lips were by her ear. She struggled, without success, to hide the tremor of awareness that licked over her sensitized flesh.

"Rest assured, my lady wife, I haven't tired of you yet. Nor do I anticipate doing so for quite some time."

Not forever, then. She turned her head very slightly so she could look into his eyes and yet still feel his breath against her face. *Tragic.*

"Then in that, at least, we are in accord." Her voice sounded chilly. "I have yet to tire of you also."

His breath hissed against her, dangerously erotic. Awareness skated over her, along her throat, across her breasts, and her nipples hardened, aching for his familiar touch.

"Aye, lady." It was a rumbled caress that ignited her blood. "Your ice melts when I part your thighs."

Goddess. The thought tumbled into her mind unbidden, as the vision of Connor parting her thighs flooded her senses.

"Such wifely duty is not unduly onerous." Her whisper was scarcely audible, but she knew he heard. And he was the only one who needed to hear.

His lips grazed her cheek. A fleeting caress that branded her his.

"When I claim you, duty is the last thing on your mind." The low words hammered into her, raw and primeval. She barely prevented herself from squirming as arousal throbbed through her swollen clitoris.

He drew back, but only far enough so he could look into her eyes. She knew she couldn't hide how much she wanted him and didn't even try. Perverse power flooded through her when his own eyes darkened with lust, when his breath caught in his throat, when he reached out and captured her hand in a hard, possessive grasp.

Without care for etiquette, he stood and pulled her to her feet.

"I beg your leave," he said to the older ladies, not releasing his grip on Aila's hand. "My wife and I have matters to discuss."

Aila barely heard the ladies' responses. All she was aware of was Connor's fingers threaded through hers. The way he looked at her as though he wanted to devour her. The urgency as he ushered her from the chamber toward the staircase.

He palmed her bottom as she climbed the stairs and Aila leaned into the curved wall, fearful she would lose her balance and tumble to her death. And then his strong arm encircled her waist and his solid body melded against her back and thighs, his hand molding her breast, teasing her nipple.

At their chambers he kicked open the door without relinquishing his hold on her. Floradh, mending a gown by candle and firelight in the bedchamber, leaped to her feet.

"Leave us." Connor's command brooked no argument and Floradh scooped up the kitten and hobbled from the chambers, casting Aila a troubled glance before she closed the door behind her.

Connor finally released her, and she turned to face him, not even attempting to regulate her uneven breath. Why should she? He attempted no such thing.

"Remove your gown." The order was harsh.

How dare he speak to her in such a manner? She, a Princess of Ce, when he was nothing but a commoner?

"Or what?" Her words were low, taunting, no matter how she chided herself to remain silent. "You will rip it from my body? Ruin another of my gowns?"

"Aye." As he spoke, he pulled his length of plaid over his shoulder, his eyes never leaving hers. "If that's the only way to strip you for my pleasure."

She gasped at his arrogance, but twisted desire curled around her clitoris and quivered through her wet sheath.

"You would have me dress in rags?" Why was she encouraging him? All she had to do was discard her gown, open her arms, and pretend they were back in Ce. There was no place in this life for the entrancing flirting they'd enjoyed that night.

He bared his teeth in a parody of the smile that had once captivated her foolish heart. "Madam, I can well afford to ensure you have a dozen new gowns for every one I… ruin."

Without thinking, she began to tug furiously at the ties of her bodice. "So you would clothe me in the way of your Scots ladies, would you?"

His leather belt skidded across the floor. "No." He began to unwind the plaid around his waist. "Your ladies would continue to clothe you in the manner of a Pictish princess."

Glaring at him, she pulled her gown over her shoulders. "At least sewing gowns will keep me occupied during my endless days of incarceration."

He froze, as though her taunt had struck a nerve. She couldn't imagine why. What did he think she would do with herself for hours on end? She might not be especially talented with a needle, but it would surely be better than enforced idleness.

With one last shove, her gown dropped to her feet. Connor's gaze licked over her, as hot as branding irons, as his plaid also dropped to the floor.

"Come here." He appeared determined to exert his rights as a husband this night. But she'd be damned if she'd behave like an obedient wife. She remained where she was.

"Remove your shirt."

The firelight distorted his features, because it appeared he smiled at her demand. A genuine smile, one that reminded her so forcefully of those he'd given her in Ce that a dull ache gripped her chest.

"As you wish." His deep voice sank into her, threatening to vanquish the fragile shields she'd tried so hard to erect around her heart. She clenched her teeth. She couldn't let her guard down. She had to remember what his people—his kin— had done.

His shirt landed on the edge of the bed and her breath rushed from her in a soundless sigh. His black hair tumbled around his powerful shoulders and in the flickering light his burnished skin and taut muscles glowed with an unearthly beauty.

Inevitably her gaze dropped to his magnificent cock and as her mouth dried and reason scattered, wet heat throbbed between her thighs.

"Aila." His rough voice wrapped around her senses as his strong arms wrapped around her shoulders. It would be so easy to rest her head on his shoulder, wind her arms around his waist and let the ache in her soul spill free.

Instead she pressed her hands against his chest and levered him toward the bed. He laughed and sorrow stabbed through her. She longed to laugh with him. To laugh and then weep and allow him to reassure her that everything would be all right.

He didn't protest as she shoved him back onto the furs. Instead he lay there, one knee raised, hands clasped behind his head, grinning as if—she could not quite fathom why he grinned at her so. But within the last few moments, his attitude had changed, so drastically she could scarcely comprehend why.

She didn't need to understand. Didn't want to. Because when he behaved like this, she found it all but impossible to remember the reasons why she couldn't simply offer him her heart.

Feverishly she climbed onto the bed, straddled his waist, and plunged her fingers through his hair. Shadows obscured the color of his eyes, but they were dark with lust.

"Do you enjoy having a fearless warrior at your mercy, my lady?"

Words trembled on her tongue. She pressed her lips together to keep them forever locked inside. She could love him with her body, and he could imagine all they shared was mutual lust. But if she allowed him to glimpse that she loved him with all her heart and soul—her pride would wither. And her pride was all she had to keep herself from drowning.

She slid down his hard body and he groaned, his gaze locked with hers.

"Your methods of torture slay me."

Why did he keep speaking to her? She didn't want him to speak. It reminded her of how easily she had offered him her trust. And how brutally that trust in his people had been betrayed.

She tilted her hips and teased her clitoris against his cock. Back and forth, her fingers gripping his shoulders for balance. His guttural moan of sensual pleasure quivered through her and slowly she lowered herself onto him.

He filled her tender flesh so wholly and completely. She expanded around him, accepting and worshipping his unyielding invasion, and a strangled sigh escaped when his hands cupped her breasts.

They were sensitive and yet she loved him to cradle her breasts and rub his thumbs over her hard nipples. She tightened her muscles around him, and his grip became painful.

"Sorry, my love." His erotic whisper threaded through her mind and she realized she had winced. He had noticed and drew her toward him and dragged his tongue over her ripe nipples.

She closed her eyes and relished the sensation of his mouth suckling her. His teeth grazing her. His cock inside her.

Need spiraled. She increased the tempo of her thrusts and he released her breast to allow her unhindered leverage. Tonight, she would have him. Tonight, he would take her as he had taken her that night in Ce. When want and need and desire had claimed him so completely, she had known all he had thought of was her.

Her fingernails gouged his flesh. Their hot, erratic breaths mingled. Their gazes meshed. The world narrowed until all that existed was Connor MacKenzie, this bed, this moment in time. *Tonight.*

Desire shattered and a choked cry tore from her throat as convulsions rippled through her core. Beyond the frenzied beat of her heart, she felt Connor's hands grip her hips, wrench her from him, toss her aside.

And pump his seed into his crumpled shirt.

Gasping, she wrapped her arms around her waist as a chill invaded where only seconds before an inferno had raged. Remnants of desire, of untamed orgasm, thudded through her blood but tainting all else the sting of rejection scorched her heart.

Connor had no compunction about bedding her. But he had no desire to father her child. Why else would he pull from her at the moment of his release? And not just once. Every time since they had wed.

Even in Ce he'd been mindful of conception, concerned that he had come inside her. In her ignorance she'd assumed he worried for her reputation. But it had been nothing of the kind. He had simply not wanted her to conceive.

As Connor sat on the edge of the bed, she curled into herself and dragged the sheet around her chilled body. He had no idea she already carried his child. But at least now she knew what to expect when he eventually discovered the truth.

The only child he wanted was the one he'd fathered with Fearchara. She squeezed her eyes shut and breathed through her mouth so he wouldn't hear her silent tears.

He pulled back the furs, slid beneath the linen and curved his body against her back. His lips nuzzled her behind her ear and his hand languidly caressed her breast. Her hip. Then rested possessively over her belly.

Over his child.

She could not bear it. Flinging back the sheet, she dislodged his embrace and left the bed.

"Aila." He propped himself up on his elbow and she could hear the frown in his voice as she frantically pulled on her gown. "What's the matter? Is something wrong?"

"No." Her voice was muffled. She hoped he hadn't noticed. "I need the garderobe."

"But the chamber pot—"

"I would rather not."

Blessed silence. She dared glance over her shoulder, but Connor hadn't lain back in the bed. Hadn't dismissed her and fallen into oblivion. Instead he remained upright and in the firelight his frown was pronounced.

"Are you ill?" He sounded tense.

"No." Perhaps she would be ill. Her stomach churned enough. But she certainly wouldn't reveal that to Connor. "I simply— prefer privacy."

Incredibly his tension vanished.

"Don't be long." He even grinned at her. "I'll keep the bed warm for your return."

CHAPTER 33

Aila stirred, sighed and then realization rushed through her like the northerly wind on a winter's night in Fidach. Why was she in the bed?

Last night she'd huddled in the freezing garderobe, attempting to quell the foolish tears and hopeless thoughts that continued to haunt her. Eventually, praying Connor had long since fallen asleep, she'd gone back to the bedchamber and curled up with a fur on one of the chairs.

It had reminded her, bleakly, of her wedding night with Fergus.

Gingerly she opened one eye, but Connor wasn't beside her. She remembered now. At the time she'd thought it nothing more than a fragmented dream.

But he really had scooped her up in his arms. Put her back to bed. And not attempted to seduce her.

She covered her eyes with her arm. She still wore the gown she had pulled on in the night. And now it was time to face another day. Face the man whose babe she carried, the man who could not have made it clearer to her that the thought of her bearing his child was abhorrent to him.

∼

LATER THAT AFTERNOON Connor discovered Aila and her ladies with his mother and Nighean in his mother's private chamber. They were embroidering and the sight of Aila with a needle and a pained expression on her lovely face twisted his guts.

But she would have no further need of sewing. Not unless she wanted to. And Aila, he knew, possessed talents that lay elsewhere.

"Ladies." He entered the chamber and wondered if he would ever get used to how Aila was always surrounded by her ladies. It had not been so in Ce. He often wished they had never had to leave Ce. "I have need of my wife."

When nine pairs of eyes pinned him to the spot, he realized how his words might be interpreted. And the look on Aila's face suggested the thought did not thrill her.

But just as any dutiful wife might, she didn't question him. She simply stood, placed her embroidery on her stool and excused herself.

He stared in disbelief when her ladies followed suit.

"My lady has no need for your services," he said hastily, which only served to earn him another look from all present. Christ, could he be any more gauche if he tried? He glanced at Aila but she refused to meet his eyes and so he merely allowed her to precede him before closing the door behind him.

He heaved a sigh of relief that evaporated when he glanced at Aila. She was staring along the stone corridor as if he wasn't even there.

"I want to show you something." His voice was harsh when he'd wanted to be gentle. But he couldn't be gentle with her when he wanted to grab her shoulders and shout at her. Shake her even. Hell, he'd do anything to get a reaction out of her. To understand what he had done last night that had caused her to retreat within her shell once again.

He'd thought finally she was thawing. She'd answered him back, taunted him and then taken him with such mind-blowing intensity he had almost come inside her.

Then she'd disappeared to the garderobe. And stayed there so long he'd become alarmed and had gone to see if she was all right.

But he didn't get the chance to ask her. He'd heard the stifled sobs, the muffled sniffles, the heartrending agony of a woman who wanted no one to hear how she suffered.

So he'd gone back to bed. And faced the bleak fact that, no matter how eager Aila was in the marriage bed, she still didn't trust him enough to open her heart.

In silence he led her toward his private chambers. He'd spent the morning clearing out and rearranging the antechamber, but now the moment had arrived to show Aila, he realized the odd sensation in the pit of his stomach was nerves.

He glowered at the door as she waited with entire indifference by his side. She clearly had no interest in why he'd summoned her from her needlework or taken her to a part of the dwelling where no woman had any reason to be.

Over the last nine years, he had faced down the Norse, Northumbrian and Pictish warriors. But none of them had managed to cause him such trepidation as the anticipated reaction of this one fragile female when he opened this damned door.

With a silent curse, he pushed it open and indicated for her to precede him. A part of him knew he was setting himself up for yet more heartache. But even if she turned up her nose, even if she merely inclined her head with regal thanks, he wouldn't regret it.

And there was always the chance that this would finally break through her icy reserve.

He heard her sharp gasp as she stepped into the small chamber. He glanced at his handiwork and hoped he hadn't inadvertently damaged anything. But he'd wanted to leave her in no doubt that, while in Dunbrae, she could consider this her own private domain.

Almost private.

"My illuminations." She sounded stunned. Then she looked at him and her eyes sparkled with unshed tears. "You have unpacked my illuminations."

"Aye." It came out as a growl. He wasn't sure what to do with his hands, so he folded his arms across his chest. "This chamber is for your use while we remain in Dunbrae. I thought you would prefer spending your time working on your people's history rather than embroidering gowns."

Her bottom lip trembled, and she hastily turned from him, walking toward the table he had dragged to the small window. She fingered the various implements he had placed on it as if reassuring herself they were real.

"Why?" Her voice was low, choked, and he stared at her, unsure how to respond. He hadn't expected her to ask *why*.

"Because…" He hesitated, unable to find the words to tell her that he had done this because he wanted to see her smile again. Wanted to prove to her not all Scots were treacherous bastards. That, in truth, he would do anything for her.

He couldn't tell her. He didn't know how.

"Because I thought it would please you."

"Oh." A small word. Filled with tears. He shifted uncomfortably and wrestled the need to go to her, to embrace her. It was obvious she didn't want him to do any such thing.

After all, it was not night. They were not in their bedchamber. Yet the urge to comfort her gnawed through his soul.

As the silence lengthened and she didn't move, he chanced taking a couple of steps toward her. "Does it please you?"

She straightened her shoulders and turned to him, holding a length of vellum in one hand. "Yes. Thank you, Connor. You don't know how much this means to me."

He did now. But she would never know how much her calling

him Connor meant to him. Since their marriage, she had avoided calling him by his first name, unless she also affixed his second.

"I know you were," he swallowed, struggled to continue, "forced into this union, Aila. But the last thing I want is for you to be unhappy." His king had murdered her father. How could she not be unhappy?

But that wasn't what he meant. Yet how could explain what he meant?

Her gaze dropped and fixed upon her vellum. "Do you…" She hesitated and he watched her bite her lip. Then she appeared to reach a decision and looked at him. "Do you truly believe in this alliance between our people?"

Despite everything that had happened, he did still believe. He couldn't see how Aila could, but he wouldn't lie to her.

"Aye." He saw her pain, her loss, in her beautiful eyes, but she didn't look away. Didn't condemn him for his answer. "We need a strong alliance if we want to defeat the Norse. But I would never have wished this on you or your people. There had to have been another way."

His words were tantamount to treason. But his faith in his king was shaken and Aila was his wife. He had promised himself she deserved an apology, even if an apology could ultimately do nothing.

Yet until this moment, the words had always paralyzed his throat. He took another step toward her and cradled her hands. "I'm sorry. You were right. I only discovered the truth afterward. Your people were betrayed by mine."

She didn't move. For an endless moment he stared into her eyes but had the eeriest sensation she couldn't see him at all. Then she shuddered but didn't pull away from him.

"You admit… your king betrayed mine?" She sounded as though she couldn't quite believe his confession. That she'd expected him to take such knowledge with him to the grave.

"Aye." Did he dare confess his traitorous thought? "I don't

know what I could have done if I'd been in Dunadd, Aila, but hell. I would've tried to stop the massacre somehow."

"What?" The word was barely audible. And even though she hadn't moved, he felt her retreat within herself.

"It was your brother, Lord Talargan, who insisted we return that night. He felt something was—amiss." In truth, Talargan had insisted they continue onward to Dunadd because he was convinced his sister was in danger. And shit tactics or not, that had been the deciding factor in Connor's decision to back Talargan's demand.

"Talargan?" She sounded confused.

"There was nothing we could do, Aila. It was over by the time we returned. Your brother was taken hostage, but..." Hell, why stop now? He had already told her enough to get himself hanged should MacAlpin ever hear of his words. "None of us who had fought by his side in Northumbria assisted."

She looked at him as though he spoke the barbaric tongue of the Norsemen. Except, since she was Aila, he wouldn't be surprised if she could understand that language as well as she could his own.

He took her hand and pulled her toward the door to his inner sanctum. "When we arrive in Duncadha, you'll have your own chamber for your illuminations." He couldn't promise her she could work in the monastery. The monks would likely refuse to even consider the thought of a woman, even a princess, doing such sacred work within their hallowed halls. "But while we're here I fear you'll have to suffer my presence in the adjoining chamber."

It would be no hardship for him. And to hell with those who would be scandalized by the fact he'd installed his wife in his antechamber. A foreign wife who instead of spending her days with her needle spent them with vellum and paints.

A Dal Riadan wife had no business entering her husband's inner sanctum. But Aila was no ordinary wife. And there was something he wanted her to see. Something that would, perhaps, prove to her he was worthy of her hand despite his lack of royal blood.

He'd show her Thorstein Olafsson's broadsword. Tell her how he had beaten the Norseman four years ago and claimed the warrior's most prized possession. She would appreciate that. She would be sure to know how inextricably a Norseman's pride and sword were entwined.

He would omit the fact that, in that fleeting second when the Norseman had stumbled and Connor had claimed his sword, mutual respect had flared between them. Connor knew, as well as Olafsson, that if the battle hadn't ended at that precise moment, they would have continued their fight until one of them had slain the other.

But the battle had ended. The battle that he survived yet had claimed the lives of his and Ewan's fathers.

He pushed open the door.

AILA FOLLOWED, her fingers clasped in Connor's, her gaze fixed on his face, but she was no longer in this antechamber. She was back in the bedchamber at Dunadd when the image of Connor had soothed her agitated soul.

In the hall that night, she'd struggled against the compunction to open the main doors. If she had, would she have witnessed Connor's return? Known, from the start, he had not been in the stronghold when the massacre had occurred?

She could ignore the implications. Close her mind to the truth and her eyes to the inevitable. But that time had passed.

She'd tried to turn her back on her heritage. Bury the old ways when they had no longer suited her purpose. But Bride had never left her. Bride had not forsaken her.

When she'd needed proof, Bride had spoken. And Aila had ignored her.

As she had ignored her for so many years.

She had blamed Connor, irrationally, for not preventing the murder of her father. He might have been coerced into this marriage. He might not want her to bear his child. But he had not compromised his honor nor tarnished his integrity by failing to save her kin.

Connor was a Scot, but she would no longer condemn his blood for the actions of his barbarous king.

Bittersweet relief flooded her senses and she tightened her grip on his fingers as he led her into the chamber. He might not love her, but now she knew the full truth of that bloodied night she allowed herself to accept he cared.

It was obvious in the way he'd protected her from the jeering at their wedding feast. His consideration in setting the leisurely pace of their journey from Dunadd to Dunbrae. His thoughtfulness in rescuing her from attending yet another feast after arriving at his home.

The way he'd given her his own antechamber so she could continue with her beloved illuminations.

Tenderly she pressed her knuckles against her belly. In time, surely he would come to love their child. Now she could love him, without hating herself for loving her enemy, she would do everything in her power to rekindle the relationship they had barely begun in Ce.

He was speaking to her, but the words flowed over her, inconsequential. Tonight, after she made love to him the way she'd made love to him before he knew who she was, she would tell him of their babe.

Bride would not have brought her so far to have Connor fail them now.

Connor turned to her, still speaking, and she smiled up at him. For a moment he faltered.

"Is that an agreement?" He sounded unsure.

"Agreement to what?" She would agree to anything. The knowledge made her smile even more.

He offered her a guarded smile, clearly confused. "About the Halls of Valhalla. No Norseman is allowed entrance without his broadsword in his hand. Is that true?"

Her smile wavered. Why was he talking about Vikings? She had no interest in their barbaric beliefs and savage religious rituals.

Then Connor moved closer to her, looking intently at her as if he had suddenly realized something fundamental had changed. And from the corner of her eye, she saw something displayed on the wall behind him.

Time froze, splintered, and then rushed at her with the force of a stampeding horse. On the wall was a Viking broadsword. Its distinctive pommel, handle and quillion were ornately decorated with gold accents and inlays.

She knew that sword. It had haunted her nightmares for years, but in her dreams it did not gleam and glitter. In her dreams, it sliced through flesh and bone, dripped scarlet, delivered death.

In her nightmares, the owner of this broadsword bent over her, blue eyes searing into her ravaged soul, blond hair hanging in matted tangles over his shoulders.

The vellum dropped from lifeless fingers as her throat closed, her lungs contracted, and her heart hammered. *Nine years*. But she recalled every intricate detail of this broadsword. Every bloodied moment of that day.

Everything.

CHAPTER 34

Connor wrapped his arms around her, forced her backward and shoved her down on a stool. "What is it?" He gripped her hands and knelt before her. Stormy-gray eyes bored into her and raven-black hair filled her vision, obliterating blue and blond.

But still the putrid memories surged upward, swamping her reason, shattering the final fragments of her facade. She dug her nails into Connor's hands. *Connor.* She was with Connor now and there was no need to relive that day, those moments. But the images hammered through her mind, an incessant refrain, and to her horror, a terrified moan escaped.

"Aila." Connor sounded unnerved and glanced toward the door as if he hoped help might miraculously appear. But no one had miraculously appeared that day. Except the owner of that broadsword.

"How—why do you have Olafsson's sword?" Her voice sounded raw, as though she hadn't spoken in a year. *Nine years.* She forced herself not to drop her gaze, not to push Connor away, not to curl up into a ball and allow the screams in her head to escape between her lips.

"Olafsson's?" He sounded shocked that she knew the name. "I took it from him four years ago, bare seconds before the horns sounded to end the battle." His fingers tightened around hers. "How do you know of him?"

She didn't want to go through it again. Didn't want to think of it. Couldn't speak of it.

And yet the words seared her tongue.

"He was there. In Fidach. Nine years ago."

Comprehension dawned across Connor's face. Comprehension—and then horror.

"Olafsson killed Onuist?" He leaned closer to her. "If I'd known, I would have run him through with his own sword, battle over or not."

She was shivering. She couldn't stop herself. Still holding her hands, he wrapped one arm around her, rubbing her shoulder, trying to infuse her with heat.

"No." Her teeth were chattering. "Onuist had already been murdered."

The Viking raid that day had been swift, unexpected, and brutal. Caught unawares Onuist had attempted to defend them both but had been cut down within seconds.

And then the two leering Vikings had turned on her.

She closed her eyes, leaned against Connor's solid strength. Felt his hands holding her, his breath warming her. His anger sank into her wounded soul, a perverse healing.

But no matter what Olafsson had taken from her that day, he had still saved her.

"The bards sing of my Onuist's great bravery." She felt Connor stiffen, but he didn't pull away. 'He was scarcely nineteen, Connor, and had never been in battle. He was the youngest prince of Fidach—an artist. Not a warrior. Although he defended me with everything he was."

"I know." His words were muffled against her neck. "He killed those who would have dishonored you before he succumbed to his injuries."

"Yes." She breathed in the evocative essence of Connor, felt the roughness of his jaw against her cheek, the silk of his hair falling across her brow. "That's what I told everyone. So Onuist would be forever remembered and revered."

"Aye." He sounded oddly resigned. "He is a worthy hero, Aila."

Slowly she pulled back. There was a bleak look in Connor's eyes and his hand slid from her shoulder to clasp hers on her lap.

"He is." Her voice was faint as she tried not to recall how one of the savage devils had impaled Onuist's severed head on a spike while the other—

Her mind closed down.

"Connor." She waited until he looked at her. "He didn't kill them. After they murdered him, Drun attacked. They threw him against the wall and kicked him senseless. He almost died."

Understanding flickered across his face. Now he knew the origin of her beloved Drun's injuries. Drun, who had tried to defend her against the indefensible.

And then Connor began to frown as if, finally, he realized her words did not make sense. "Onuist didn't kill those Norsemen?" The words were guarded. He obviously wasn't sure how she might react to his question.

She started to shake again, although she wasn't cold in the depth of her soul. She hadn't been truly cold since Connor had entered her life.

"Olafsson found us." She couldn't tell Connor what had been happening when the Viking had found her. Some things could never be said aloud. "He—he decapitated both his countrymen without a second's hesitation. And then—"

Then he had knelt over her, blue eyes furious, blond hair hanging over his shoulders. He'd looked younger than she and instead of brutalizing her as his slain compatriots had, he'd straightened her torn gown while his broadsword dripped with Viking blood.

She swallowed. "He took my wedding casket."

Connor stared at her, his eyes dark with new knowledge. He had obviously guessed the entire sordid truth.

She'd told no one, but her mother, grandmother and the healers who had dragged her back to health knew what had happened without the need for explanations. Her father, she suspected, had guessed but he had never questioned her on details she had failed to clarify.

And so her version of events went into the annals. Onuist had died a hero's death while saving her from certain degradation. He had died at the hands of Vikings and she forever had to hide the fact she had survived only because of the actions of another Viking.

"Your wedding casket." He sounded grim and his words were so unexpected she merely stared at him in confusion. "The casket your cross completes."

"Yes." Of everything she had just confided, he questioned her on that?

He stood up, pulling her to her feet. "You look weary." He reached for her to cradle her face and then his hand dropped to his side, as if he'd thought better of it. "Perhaps you should rest before this evening's entertainment." His jaw clenched. "I couldn't put off the welcome feast for another night. I'm sorry."

She didn't relish being the center of attention at yet another feast, but the very fact Connor knew that, that he had tried to prevent such a happening, somehow made it entirely bearable.

"I have no wish to cause your mother or Lady Nighean offense." She attempted to smile at him, but his distracted countenance and the now-familiar waves of nausea that rocked her stomach caused the smile to fade almost instantly. "But thank you for trying."

He didn't answer, but he did take her hand and lead her out of the chambers.

Away from Olafsson's sword. And despite her best efforts to hide it, a relieved sigh escaped.

ARMS CROSSED, wind rippling the grasses at his feet and hair about his face, Connor glared across the glen. He was some distance from the hillfort, but still within sight of it. And although he wanted to leap on his horse and ride until his limbs ached and brain was numb, he knew he wouldn't.

He wouldn't leave Aila. In case she needed him.

Even if he knew, in his heart, she would never need him the way he wanted her to.

Just moments ago, he'd left her in their chambers. She hadn't argued about having a rest before that evening, which gnawed at him. No matter how he'd tried to ignore it over the last few days, she had an indefinable air of exhaustion about her.

He would get a physician to look at her. But he knew what she really needed. And he couldn't face it. Couldn't think of it.

Wouldn't contemplate it.

Besides, whether he liked it or not, Aila was a hostage and returning her to Ce was out of the question.

Finally, his rigid control shattered. Blood sizzled in his veins, volcanic and deadly. Leashed fury pounded against his temples. He tried to block the thoughts, suppress the images, but they were there. In his head. Driving him to the brink of insanity.

His beautiful, brave Aila, the woman whose facade of serenity had infuriated him over the last few days, had not only seen her husband murdered when she was a young bride.

She had been raped by his murderers. And he, Connor MacKenzie, who knew only too well the brutalities of war, hadn't managed to work out that fundamental fact.

But he should have. Things had not added up. The songs of the bards, the heroic acts of Onuist. Yet Aila had told him, weeks ago, that she had seen Onuist's head on a spike. How could she have if her young husband had killed their would-be attackers?

His fists clenched. The thought of her being so brutalized sickened him to the core. Now he understood her reserve. Now he understood why she retreated behind that icy facade whenever she felt threatened.

Now he understood why she had withdrawn from the world, why she had the erroneous reputation of being a recluse.

And because of his king's thirst for power, she'd been wrenched from her home. Her sanctuary. She had agreed because she believed, with all her heart, that Scot and Pict had to unite to defeat her bitterest enemy.

In return for her sacrifice, his king had betrayed her as brutally as any Norseman.

"Connor."

His mother's voice penetrated his black thoughts and he hissed out a breath before turning to her. "My lady."

She smiled, a sad, wistful smile, and placed her hand on his folded arm. They had spoken in private only once since his return and he knew she grieved for the loss of Fergus. And to ease her pain, and in memory of the boy he had once worshipped, Connor hadn't revealed his half-brother's involvement in MacAlpin's betrayal.

"My son." The words were soft. "Connor, I loved Fergus as my own. But you were always first in my heart."

The confession shook him. He didn't know how to respond. And so he merely grunted and glowered across the glen once more.

"I always believed you knew." His mother sighed, patted his arm, and relinquished her hold on him. "But it only occurred to me today that perhaps—you did not realize."

No, he hadn't realized. Fergus had idolized their mother,

often claiming her as his own despite his innate pride in his maternal royal heritage. And his mother had lavished her love upon her husband's firstborn son.

But not at the expense of her own. He'd always known that. And yet, as he had grown older, deep in his heart he'd often suspected Fergus was her favorite.

"It's hardly of importance now." He shot her a dark glare, because he didn't know how to tell her how much her words meant to him.

"Aye, it is." She ran her finger over his brooch, his father's brooch that she had given him, not Fergus, upon their father's death. "Sometimes things have to be said, no matter how unnecessary we believe them to be."

Not more confessions. He was a warrior, not a priest, and he was still struggling with the revelation of how much Aila had suffered in the past. And far from extending forgiveness to her rapists, he raged at the knowledge he could never exact retribution on her behalf.

Olafsson had seen to that. And for that, Connor owed him a debt no Scot should owe a Norseman.

"There's no need." He wanted to be alone. But he couldn't tell his mother that. Within weeks, he would leave for Duncadha and his mother, despite her status and right to live there, would remain in Dunbrae. Because he had promised Aila she would be the only mistress of his stronghold.

"You care for this Princess of Ce, don't you?"

"What?" He stared at her in disbelief. This conversation was becoming more torturous by the second. "I don't..." *Want to discuss it.*

"Connor." His mother's voice was gentle. "It's all right to love again. And when I see the way you look at the princess, it gives me hope that, at last, you've opened your heart to another."

Heat seared through him. Was he as transparent as that? He thought he'd managed to hide his love. But this was his mother.

Not Aila. And his mother, unlike Aila, would never throw his confession back in his face.

"It doesn't matter how I feel." He gave a bitter smile. "She was forced into this marriage."

She gave him an odd look, as if that fact was scarcely relevant. And of course it wasn't. Most marriages were arranged to strengthen alliances, but he wasn't talking about most marriages. He was talking about his marriage to Aila.

"Did she care for Fergus?"

Did she? Once he'd thought so. But after Fergus' death he'd got the strongest suspicion Aila had loathed his half-brother. "I don't know."

"I know you're planning to return to Duncadha shortly." His mother drew in a deep breath and Connor braced himself. Hell, did she think to accompany them? "But I believe it may be wise to remain here for the summer. And the winter."

She wanted him to remain for almost another year.

"I can't do that to Aila. MacAlpin looks on her as nothing but a hostage but she's a princess. She deserves to administer her own…"—*palace*—"stronghold at least."

"I understand." His mother stroked the length of plaid that hung over his shoulder, an oddly nervous gesture. "But I'm thinking of the princess's health, Connor. And if you don't wish to remain here, then allow me to return with you to Duncadha."

Her words thundered through his brain. "Her health?" What did his mother know that he did not? "Has she spoken to you?" But he knew Aila would have done no such thing. She did not confide easily.

"No." Finally his mother stopped fiddling with his plaid and looked up at him. Sorrow wreathed her face. "Connor, I may be wrong, and the princess has been very circumspect. And yet I suspect she is with child."

With child. The words thudded in his head. Knocked the air from his lungs. He stood on the hilltop with his mother by his side, but all he could see was Aila wincing when he touched her breasts. How she had stopped eating.

How she had been gut-wrenchingly sick after leaving his chambers earlier.

He wanted to deny it. With every enraged particle of his being. And yet he couldn't. Because, in his heart, he knew the truth.

His mother flattened her hand against his chest. "I know you haven't been married long enough for the babe to be yours." Her voice was soft, as if she knew how much, how selfishly, desperately, he wanted that child to be his. "But if she is with child, then this is the last link we will have with Fergus." She clutched his shirt, as though she feared he might storm off. "I should be there for the birth. And Connor…" She paused, forcing him to look at her. Forcing him to remain silent when he wanted to roar his despair to the heavens. "The child will still be linked to you by blood. You must always remember that."

"Aye." His voice was bitter. Did Aila know? How could she be feeling, knowing she bore the child of one brother while married to the other?

When she had been forced into both marriages? Had Fergus forced himself on her that night?

"I know how deeply you desire a son of your own." His mother's voice penetrated his thoughts and he wanted to tell her he desired no such thing. After that first reckless night he'd done everything he could to ensure Aila wouldn't conceive. He knew she hadn't fallen in Ce—she'd told him that in no uncertain terms the following day. And even if, in a dark corner of his soul, he did crave a child with her, he would never put her through such a deadly ordeal.

But it was too late. Fergus had already planted his seed. Fergus had already set Aila on the perilous path of childbirth.

"The princess is strong," his mother continued. "You and she will have your own children. Afterward."

But suppose Aila did not survive birthing Fergus' child?

His mother gripped his hand, as if something in his expression chilled her. "Connor." Her voice was urgent. "Do not think of it. Not all women die in childbirth."

He knew that. But it made no difference. Because all he could see in his mind was Aila in pain. Struggling to give birth to the child whose existence forged the future of this bloodied alliance.

And she would struggle in a foreign land, surrounded by people she considered her enemy. Far from the land she loved.

Aila sat on a stool in front of her mirror as Cailleach brushed her hair in preparation for the feast. She felt refreshed, strangely invigorated, and knew it had little to do with the rest she'd taken.

It was because Connor had not been in Dunadd as the massacre had occurred. It was because he respected her enough to apologize for the despicable actions of his barbarous king. It was because he had taken the trouble to give her a chamber of her own where she could once again enjoy her illuminations.

He was the Connor she'd fallen in love with in Ce and his blood was not tainted by the same duplicity that corroded the honor of his countrymen.

Unheeding of what Cailleach might think, she gently caressed her belly. Now she'd had a few hours to consider it, she could think of Olafsson's broadsword without seeing it dripping in blood. Could see it the way Connor had naturally assumed she would.

As a magnificent trophy of war.

Vikings did not relinquish their swords easily. To claim one in battle, from a Viking not even dead, was an astonishing feat.

No wonder Connor displayed it on his wall in pride of place.

As if summoned by her thoughts, Connor entered the chamber. Her ladies, as always, fluttered in agitation, unsure whether they should treat him with courtesy or disdain.

Connor didn't give them the chance to make up their minds this time. "Leave us."

She turned on the stool and watched her ladies depart. Connor waited until the door shut behind them before he faced her.

"Are you feeling any better, my lady?" His tone was oddly formal, and unease rippled through her stomach. Or perhaps it was simply a symptom of her condition.

"Much better, I thank you." She stood up, somehow not liking the distance between them. But the strangely shuttered look on his face prevented her from moving toward him.

"I'm glad to hear it." He could have been speaking to a stranger, not his wife. Not the woman he shared his bed with. The woman who carried his child.

The unease magnified. She clawed through her mind for something to say to him and could think of only banalities.

"I fear I'm not yet ready for the evening." She raked distracted fingers through her unbound hair and saw the way his eyes followed her action. "I didn't realize the hour was so late."

"It's not late." He dragged his gaze from her hair to look her in the eyes. "My lady, there is something I have to ask you. Please forgive me."

Ask her? Forgive him? Her stomach churned and it had nothing to do with her condition and everything to do with the sick unease that clenched her heart.

From the corner of her eye, she saw him flex his fingers before he folded his arms across his chest. And although he didn't move away from her, an invisible mountain loomed between them.

She hoped her anxiety didn't show on her face. "Of course." Or in her voice.

He remained silent, staring at her, his eyes dark as though he battled the urge to take her in his arms and to hell with the feast.

She hoped he would. She needed his arms around her. Wanted to shatter this unnatural formality. But most of all she wanted to confide in him. Tell him of their babe.

"Are you with child?" The question hit her with the force of a fist, punching through her mind, his harsh tone leaving no doubt as to what he hoped her answer would be.

The kernel of hope in her breast shriveled but she refused to crumple. And perhaps she was wrong. Perhaps Connor only looked as if her being with child was the worst catastrophe he could imagine. Perhaps, in reality, when she confirmed his suspicion he would be elated.

"I am." She infused each word with pride. No matter what Connor's feelings might be, she wanted this child. She loved this child. And her child's father would know that from the start.

He didn't move. And yet she felt his entire body flinch at her words, as his eyes darkened, jaw clenched, and muscles flexed beneath his shirt. He didn't say a word and he didn't have to. In that fleeting moment, his involuntary response said everything.

This wasn't how it was meant to be. The denial screamed through her mind but what did it matter? This was the reality. And the reality could not be clearer.

"Are you sure?" The words were stilted.

"Yes." Pride would sustain her until Connor left the chamber. "Do you require a catalogue of my symptoms?" Her voice grew colder with every word. It was the only way she could keep the scalding tears at bay.

"No." He sounded horrified by the idea that she might tell him of the physical manifestations his child had wrought. "Your word is enough for me." He swallowed and appeared transfixed by the kitten she held in one hand. "I will arrange for a physician to attend you."

"I don't require a Scot physician to tell me what I already know." But what did she expect? And what would happen when the babe was born? There were no Pictish healers here. Her mother and grandmother, her sister and cousins would not be in attendance.

She'd be surrounded by strangers. And only now, as Connor refused to meet her eyes, when it became excruciatingly plain that he wanted no part of their child, did the full force of that fact hit her.

The silence screeched along her nerves. Her legs began to shake but she wouldn't show any weakness before him. He glanced briefly at her face before once again fixing on the kitten.

"Is there anything else you require?" His voice was little more than a growl.

He didn't want a child. That was his choice. But the outcome of that night in Ce was the responsibility of them both. Not just her. And yet he behaved as if it was entirely her doing. "Besides my mother?" Her voice dripped scorn. "No, I don't believe so."

He looked at her then. And the bleak despair she saw in his eyes pierced her heart. "Aila, are you happy about this?" He sounded oddly uncertain. "Do you want this child?"

She bit back her instant response. *I want this child more than anything else in the world. As much as I want your love.*

"I do."

He jerked his head and a modicum of tension seeped from him, as if until this moment he honestly hadn't been certain how she felt about it.

"There's no need to attend the feast. I'll make your excuses."

Rage heated her blood, but it was more than rage. Deadlier than rage. *Rejection.*

"So now you are so ashamed of me you'll hide me away? What

do you intend to do, Connor, keep me hidden until this babe is born?"

"I thought you would prefer not to attend the feast." He scowled at the floor. "Of course I'm not ashamed of you. I'm… proud of you."

A bitter laugh escaped. She couldn't help it. "How gracious of you, my lord. I fear I cannot extend the same sentiment to you."

He stiffened at the insult to his integrity and finally caught and held her contemptuous gaze. "I'm sorry." His voice was as harsh as his glare. "For everything you've been through. But I can't change the past, Aila. I can only offer you a future."

"A future that includes this child." To emphasize her words, she splayed her fingers over her belly, daring him to ignore the fruit of their pleasure that night.

For a fleeting moment, anguish gripped his features.

"Aye. Of course I include the child. Did you think I would forsake him? Forsake you?" He appeared unaware of how she glared at him. "You're my wife, Aila."

Fury propelled her forward until she was standing so close to him, she could feel the heat of his body radiating from him.

"And this babe is of your blood." She fisted her free hand and battled the urge to hit him for his cruel coldness toward a child of his flesh.

"I know the babe is of my blood." His gazed raked over her face and then he stepped back as though he could no longer bear to be so close to her. "His heritage is not in question." He had the nerve to sound offended. "If it's a boy he will inherit Dunfodla. His bloodline will be unchallenged."

Did Connor really think she cared which primitive Scots' hill-fort her child would inherit?

She stiffened her spine and drew the pride of her ancestors about her like a protective cloak. "My child," she said with deliberate emphasis, "will inherit one thousand years of Pictish heritage and have claim on the kingships cf Ce and Circinn." She paused for one moment to allow her words to fully penetrate. "And isn't that what is really important here, Connor? How my child serves to strengthen MacAlpin's claim on my ancient lands?"

CHAPTER 36

It had been three weeks since Connor had discovered, and rejected, she carried his child. Aila attempted to ignore the dull ache in her lower back, knowing if she so much as stretched, word would get back to Connor. And he would insist they immediately make camp for the night.

They were only hours from Ce-eviot.

She still couldn't fathom it. After her last deadly thrust in their chambers, Connor had made no attempt to defend his king. He'd just looked at her as if she'd plunged a broadsword through his heart before he'd offered her a bow and left.

He had never returned.

Two days later he had informed her, with utmost civility, that he intended to return her to Ce to await the birth of her child.

Her child. Not theirs. But she'd been so astonished by the knowledge she would soon see her kin she'd failed to correct him on that fact. Or enquire what would become of her once their child was born.

Before they had left Dunbrae, he'd gathered a band of warriors to accompany them. She recognized many of them. They had accompanied Connor on his first visit to Ce.

He needed them. It was clear the nobles of Pictland would relish nothing more than to run through any Scot they encountered. Only the advance knowledge that Talargan and many of their young noble warriors were held hostage at Dunadd, and that the eldest Princess Devorgilla of Ce was being escorted to the land of her kin, prevented bloodshed, and ensured a roof over their heads.

Her ladies, riding by her side, were fairly glowing with excitement at the thought of returning home. And she too couldn't wait to see her mother and sister, grandmother, and cousins. The realization she wouldn't be alone among strangers when her time came reassured her beyond measure. And yet dark discontent gnawed through her soul.

For three weeks, Connor had been solicitous for the state of her health. Had ensured her comfort in every way he could. Had treated her with the respect her status demanded.

But he hadn't shared her bed. As though, upon discovering she nurtured his child, his desire for her had withered.

Yet she saw the furtive glances he arrowed her way when he thought no one aware. The raw hunger in his eyes, the leashed passion in his bearing. And as the journey progressed, and his reined desire became ever more apparent, a strange certainty coalesced.

Did Connor avoid her because he thought that was what *she* wanted? Was he concerned not so much that she was with child, but that the fact she was might lessen her desire for him?

As her beloved Ce-eviot finally came into view, her conviction strengthened. There was more to his strange attitude than him simply not wishing her to bear his child. Tonight, she'd ensure they shared the same chamber. Tonight, she would insist he explained his reasons for not wishing her to conceive.

Somehow, she would get through to him. Somehow, she would convince him. Because despite how he'd withdrawn from her, how could she possibly believe he didn't care for her?

She was MacAlpin's prized hostage. Her place was in Dal Riada, a guarantee that her people would not rise up and slaughter the treacherous Scots.

But Connor had brought her home. Because he knew how dearly she wanted to be with her kin for the birth. He'd brought her home without his king's knowledge and she could scarcely comprehend what MacAlpin's fury would be when he discovered it.

If those weren't the actions of a man who cared, then what were?

∼

EXHAUSTION all but crippled her and dusk had fallen as they reached Ce-eviot, and the contingent of warriors who met them radiated a potent force of welcome and antagonism. In the blazing torchlight she saw her mother and grandmother waiting on the threshold, their personal guard triple what it had been before she left.

Connor helped her dismount, his hand steady and sure in hers. She would have clung on to him, brought him with her to greet her kin, but as soon as she was safely on the ground, he broke contact. Stepped back. Allowed her to precede him, as befit her royal status.

Except Connor was her husband. He had the right to walk by her side in Ce. And yet she had no time to confront him because her mother and grandmother were there, holding her hands, their silence in the presence of their enemy piercing her heart.

For long moments nobody spoke. Nobody moved. And then her mother gave her hand a squeeze before releasing her and turning to Connor.

"Are you here to claim the Kingdom of Ce by force?" Her voice was cold, regal. Yet Aila knew, as acutely as all of them present, how depleted of warriors' Ce were. So many of them remained hostage to MacAlpin.

Connor bowed. Aila ached to go to him, to show her support, but her grandmother clung to her hand as though she would never let her go.

"Devorgilla, Queen Brilicie of Ce," he said, giving her mother her full title. Even now, in such dire circumstances, his accented Pictish still sent a tremor along Aila's spine. "Please accept my heartfelt sorrow at your loss." He glanced at Aila before once again focusing on her silent mother. "We have returned Aila, Princess Devorgilla of Ce to her homeland."

He made it sound as though MacAlpin had allowed her return. She would be sure to inform her mother of the truth.

"For that we are duly grateful." The Queen of Ce cast a disdainful glance over the Scots warriors. "We are in mourning for the murder of my king. There will be no celebratory feasts for your men."

"We did not expect such, madam. Will you allow us to make camp within your ramparts this night?"

"Certainly." The queen's voice was pure ice. Aila knew, as well as her mother, the request was a formality. And yet, unlike her mother, Aila knew if the request was denied, Connor would ensure his men camped outside the ramparts of Ce-eviot.

The queen turned her back and entered the palace. For one agonizing moment, Aila looked at Connor, wanting to tell him to follow them. But her grandmother dragged her away and besides, she would not invite him in without her mother's permission. In any case, Connor needed to supervise his men. There would be time enough for her mother to officially welcome him as her son-through-marriage.

She heard her mother order one of her guards to organize an all-night watch on the Scots. It didn't surprise her. The Scots would do the same, keeping a distrustful eye on their reluctant hosts.

Finally, they were alone in her mother's private chamber and the three of them clung together in silent sorrow. Her grandmother pulled back first, her eyes wet, a look of wonder on her face.

"Aila," her voice was hushed. "You are with child."

Her mother jerked back. "With child?" She glanced at Aila's belly then back at her mother. "So it has come to pass as you foretold."

You are the founding stone. For the bridge that will one day unite all our kingdoms.

Aila recalled the words as clearly as if they had been spoken only yesterday. But her grandmother had said them the morning after she had spent the night with Connor. Before she knew she'd conceived his child. At the time she'd hugged the words to her heart, thinking perhaps her dreams were not impossible after all. That it was acceptable to love again.

But it had meant so much more than that. How could she not see the words for what they truly were? A message from Bride. Telling her, with absolute clarity, that her child would bridge the divide between Pict and Scot.

She gasped, pulled away, and pressed both hands against her belly.

Until the Viking raid of Fidach, she had imagined her goddess showed her tantalizing visions of the children of Onuist. And then, as she recovered from her injuries, she saw only the goddess' malevolence. In taunting her with a family she knew would never be hers.

Yet Bride had always known. And Aila had refused to see beyond her own pain and disillusionment. Had turned her back and cast the goddess from her heart. Bride—who was part of her heritage. An intangible, essential part of her soul. It didn't matter whether Aila accepted her or not. But by denying her existence, the frost of rejection had consumed the core of her being. Only with the arrival of Connor had the goddess finally found her way back into Aila's heart. Yet even before that, Bride had prepared her to open her mind once again to the wonder of physical love.

By sending a mystical dream-lover.

"What is it?" Her mother's urgent voice catapulted her back to the present. "Aila, is it true? You were only wed to that—to the prince for such a short time."

"It's true." She looked at her grandmother, saw the wariness in her eyes. "This child is my husband's. Connor MacKenzie's."

"Connor MacKenzie's?" Her mother sounded horrified. "But how—Aila." She gripped her hand, agitation clear on her face. "Did he force you, my love? On the journey to Dal Riada?"

"No." Her voice was harsher than she intended. She knew why her mother was so confused. She'd been married to Connor for less than a month. That was scarcely time for her to realize she had conceived. "Mamma, you should know that MacAlpin thinks I'm still in Dal Riada. Connor brought me home to you so I might have our child surrounded by my kin."

"He disobeyed his king?" Her mother looked as if she might collapse. "For you?"

"It was always him," her grandmother said softly. "From the first time I saw him, I knew it was him. Devorgilla," she turned to her daughter, "Connor MacKenzie was chosen by the goddess long ago. He fulfilled his destiny by coming to Ce, but he was just as deceived by his king as we were."

Aila remembered her grandmother's gentle teasing in that week before her father had returned to Ce. As if she had known of Aila's secret rendezvous—and far from being furious she approved the liaison.

"Mamma." She waited until her mother's bemused gaze rested upon her. "My husband is an honorable man. Please welcome him as your son-through-marriage. For the sake of our child."

The Queen of Ce, widowed at the hand of Scots, relaxed her grip of Aila's hand. "He brought you to me, risking the displeasure of his despicable king. I will welcome him as your husband, Aila."

~

AILA STIRRED, waking slowly, reveling in the notion she was in her own bed. And then she frowned, rolled onto her side, and squinted at the untouched half of her bed.

Connor hadn't joined her last night after his audience with her mother.

She sighed and absently tickled the kitten. Last night she'd been so weary she'd retired before seeing Connor again. But her mother had promised he would be made welcome. Promised he would be allowed to join her as was his right as her husband.

He had decided not to. Goddess, this had gone far enough. If he needed to hear her tell him that she still desired him, then she would tell him. And perhaps, in time, she would even tell him once again how very much she loved him.

The early morning breeze was fresh as she left the palace, four guards tailing her. But she had no need of her cloak. Nor even her shawl. Because, since re-embracing Bride, her soul was no longer fractured and the chill in her bones that had been her constant companion for the last nine years had finally thawed.

Frowning, she scanned the surrounding area but could see no sign of a camp. Perhaps Connor had pitched farther away from the palace than she'd thought. With a sigh she turned toward the monastery. She had to see Uuen.

It was odd, walking such familiar ground without her faithful shadow, but Drun spent his nights with Finella now. She hadn't wanted to disturb her sister so early in the day.

She paused by one of the sacred standing stones and looked toward the monastery. It had been built more than two hundred years ago but compared to these stones that surrounded it in a gigantic circle, it was but a babe. As the new religion was just a child when compared to the gods of antiquity.

Uuen made no secret of his delight at her return. She might never have been away, except for the fact her father was now dead, she had been married twice and she was now with child.

"The queen is filled with bitterness at the death of our noble king," he said. "But now you're here I pray her pledges of vengeance will subside."

Instinctively Aila's hand covered her belly. "I also wish for vengeance." She recalled MacAlpin's arrogance in his war chamber and renewed fury flooded through her. "I won't rest until I see that upstart king slain, drowning in his own blood."

There was a silence and then Uuen sighed. "My lady, sometimes the only way forward is to extend forgiveness to our enemies."

No. She would not forgive. The ancient ways of her people did not forgive such outrage.

Her feelings must have shown on her face as Uuen, after a swift glance at her hand cradling her belly, said, "Not because MacAlpin deserves your forgiveness, my lady. But because living with the desire for vengeance will corrode your soul. Is that the legacy you want to leave your future generations? A blood feud?"

A blood feud? No, she didn't want that for her child. Her child, who was as much a Scot as a Pict. Did she want her child to hate his Scots heritage?

Much as she loathed the Dal Riadan king, she didn't hate all Scots. And she didn't want her child nurtured in an atmosphere of bitterness and dark plots of retribution.

Grudgingly she conceded Uuen and his ceaseless calls for forgiveness might have a point. And as he changed the subject and began to tell her of local gossip she had missed, she slowly relaxed.

Until he began to make plans for her to resume her teaching.

"Uuen, I was wrong. My goddess lives. I was only half alive while I denied her. I'm sorry."

Uuen's smile was sad. "Don't be sorry, my lady. God helped you through these last difficult years. He'll be there for you when you need Him again."

He didn't understand.

"I survived these last few years, Uuen. I only started living again when Connor MacKenzie arrived in Ce. When I allowed Bride to enter my heart and show me that it wasn't wrong to love again."

"My lady, it was never wrong for you to love again." He sighed. "For years I prayed that one day your burden of guilt would lift. It was never yours to bear."

Aila stared at him in shock. Uuen had wanted her to find love? Her grandmother had wanted her to find love also. Had she been wrong, all these years, when she'd been convinced everyone expected her to remain faithful in mind and deed to her dead, heroic husband?

"Oh. I… thank you." She glanced at the floor, wondering how she could possibly tell Uuen what must be said. "But you must see, Uuen. Now I've returned to Bride, I can no longer believe in your God."

"Ah," he said. "That doesn't matter, my lady. God always believes in you."

As Bride had always believed in her.

CHAPTER 37

As she left the monastery, intending to return to the palace and discover where, exactly, Connor was, she paused by a standing stone. It was the same one she'd stumbled against when Bride had sent her the vision of bloodshed and death.

Birdsong drifted on the breeze. It was hard to imagine so much had changed in so short a time when all around her the mountains and glens remained as they had for years without number.

Slowly she reached out her hand and flattened her palm against the ancient carvings. *Show me what I must do, Bride.* She held her breath, tensed her muscles, but her goddess sent no message.

She frowned and trailed her fingers over the sacred symbols. Why wouldn't Bride show her the future? Why wouldn't she give her a sign, warn her of what was to come?

A shiver scuttled over her arms and her fingers stilled against the stone. *Warnings.* As if a torch had been lit inside her brain, illumination flooded through her.

The massacre she had foreseen had not been a useless, empty vision. Its purpose had not been for her to rage against what could not be altered.

It had been a warning. And instinctively she'd utilized that warning by ensuring her mother and sister didn't travel to Dal Riada. How much worse would this be, if Finella had seen their father's murder? If Finella and their queen had also been taken hostage?

Her breath rushed from her lungs and she pressed her forehead against the stone. The world was changing. As the new God's religion spread, the old gods fought for survival. Acolytes born with the gift dwindled with each passing generation. When there was no one left alive to remember the gods of antiquity, would they die?

"Aila."

She turned, still leaning against the stone, and saw her mother and grandmother approaching, surrounded by their ladies and guards. She pushed herself upright, finally understanding the power and fragility of her gift. The legacy of her forebears and, she now hoped, one she might pass on to her descendants.

For a moment, the three of them looked at each other in silence. Then her mother took her hand.

"Connor MacKenzie left for Fidach at dawn."

"What?" She snatched her hand back and glared at her mother. "Why didn't you allow him to stay? *Fidach*?" Why would Connor travel north into Fidach? It made no sense.

"I left him in no doubt he was welcome to our hospitality. But he declined the offer of sharing your chamber and insisted he and his men would depart at first light." Her mother glanced at the dowager queen before adding, "He asked me to ensure you were made aware of his deepest regard."

His regard? She didn't want his regard. "Aila," her grandmother said. "He will return to you."

"Yes," her mother said. "He did say he would return to Ce before continuing back to Dal Riada."

Was this the real reason for Connor's journey? Was he, unknown to her, on a mission for MacAlpin in Fidach and he'd decided to bring her along so she might see her kin?

It made sense. Yet she didn't believe it.

"Very well." She began to march back toward the palace, her mother and grandmother hurrying to keep up. "But he needn't think I'm going to be waiting here patiently until he deigns to return. I shall meet with him in Fidach."

"You will do no such thing." Her mother sounded scandalized. "You'll remain here where you're safe."

"I shall be safe enough in Fi-eviot." The palace of Fi-eviot, royal stronghold of Fidach and childhood home of Onuist. If Connor was traveling to Fidach, where else would he go but to the king?

IT WAS the following midmorning before Aila and her small contingent of warriors arrived at the palace of Fi-eviot. Her mother hadn't stood a chance of keeping her in Ce-eviot, especially when her grandmother had tacitly taken her side.

There was, she was starting to realize, much power in her adult status as a Chosen One of Bride.

Onuist's kin greeted her with great warmth. Yet she saw no Scots warriors. But surely Connor had intended to come here? Where else would he go? The Pictish nobles she'd stayed with last night knew nothing of the Scots' journey, but that hadn't concerned her. After all, Connor wasn't hindered by a weak stomach or the need to travel at a sedate pace. He had likely reached his destination before night fell and had no need to detour to any hillfort en route.

Finally, she was alone with Onuist's eldest sister and her husband, the King of Fidach. Due to a hunting injury, he'd been unable to travel to Dal Riada and as such was the only Pictish king not held hostage or murdered in Dunadd.

"You have heard of my marriage to Connor MacKenzie." It wasn't a question. News traveled fast in the Highlands. "I had reason to believe he was traveling this way." She tried not to let her panic show. Because if Connor hadn't come this way, where else could she look? She would have to return to Ce and await him there. And somehow, that outcome scraped along her nerves.

"He did." The king's tone was harsh, and panic of another sort entirely flooded through her. "Bastard had the audacity to pay us his respects." The king narrowed his gaze. "Forgive me. He is your husband. But under duress, I know."

Aila looked at Onuist's sister then back at the king. These people had once been her kin through marriage and would forever hold a place in her heart. But she would allow no one to scorn Connor.

"He is my husband. But not under duress. And yes, he is a Scot but know this. I'll defend his honor with my last breath."

Silence reverberated around the chamber. Eventually Onuist's sister spoke.

"I hope he deserves your loyalty, Aila. But we fear his king plans to betray us yet further. Why else would MacKenzie plan on meeting with the Vikings in the north of our kingdom?"

"The Vikings?" That couldn't be true. They were mistaken. Why would Connor enter Viking territory? She would not believe he planned on betraying this alliance. However much she despised MacAlpin, she knew he wanted this alliance between Pict and Scot to flourish.

"However," there was grim amusement in the king's voice, "we've negotiated a tenuous truce with the jarl over the last few years. Olafsson sent word scarcely an hour ago that he would hold the Scots hostage if that is our desire."

She wasn't ignorant of politics. She'd known Thorstein Olafsson was now jarl of the lands the Vikings had annexed from Fidach nine years ago. She knew of the truce. Knew also how easily it could be broken, should the Viking kings decide they wanted more of Pictland for their own.

"Have you replied?" Despite her best intentions, terror threaded through every word. She didn't believe Connor was here on his king's orders. She was the reason he had traveled north and while she couldn't fathom why he'd continued into Olafsson's territory, if he was taken hostage why would MacAlpin have any inclination to preserve Connor's life?

"Not yet." The king regarded her then looked at his wife.

"We thought you might be able to enlighten us as to his mission," the queen said. "But as you cannot, all we can rely upon is your word that MacKenzie can be trusted."

"And there is something else." The king sounded reluctant. "Even if we tell Olafsson we don't require the Scots to be taken there's always the possibility the Vikings will hold them regardless. You know what they're like."

Yes, she knew what they were like. They could come upon a battle that had nothing to do with them and join the losing side. Simply to vanquish the presumed victors for no other reason than they could.

She blanked the image of his dripping broadsword from her mind and tried, with less success, to push aside the panic that clawed her. She focused on what she had to say. "Olafsson is an honorable man, for all that he's a Viking. If you asked for the Scots' release, surely he would honor your request?"

"I imagine," the queen said with a hint of frost, "that would depend not only on his mood at the time but how persuasive the request was. And I fear, Aila, that should Olafsson not be in a particularly accommodating frame of mind, we may not possess adequate methods of persuasion."

Do what you know in your heart is right.

Horror gripped her as her grandmother's words, the message from Bride, echoed in her mind.

She couldn't face going back there. Not to the place where Onuist had died. Where she had lost the innocence of her youth in that blood-soaked hell.

There had to be another solution. But there was no other solution. No one else in Fidach cared if Connor lived or died. They were only concerned for the welfare of the Pictish hostages MacAlpin held. That was the reason Connor could travel with relative safety throughout Pictland. But if Connor was here without his king's knowledge then would the Scot upstart be mindful of Connor's safety? And if not, why should the King of Fidach negotiate for the release of Viking-held hostages?

MacAlpin was single-minded in his determination to exert the full extent of his power. She had no doubt he would sacrifice Connor if it suited him, as a warning to others not to go against his will.

She had lost too much. She would not lose Connor as well. She'd follow him into hell if it could help secure his release, because what would her life be but hell without him? Before the fear could fully claim her and render her immobile, she stood. "I will personally ask Olafsson for the Scots' release."

"Absolutely not," the king said. He spoke as though she was still fifteen years old, when she had been a young bride and in awe of her husband's brother-through- marriage.

But she was no longer a girl who could be dictated to. She was Connor MacKenzie's wife, she nurtured his child in her womb, and she was a priestess of Bride.

A strange calm washed through her as she accepted her destiny. And it was only that destiny that would sway the king's mind.

"My lord," she said, "the goddess is with me."

Neither king nor queen moved, but there was a subtle shift in the balance of power in the chamber. They both knew of her gift.

Both also knew how she had repudiated it nine years ago. But as they looked at her, she saw the dawning realization on their faces. That she spoke the truth.

Even a king could not easily dismiss a direct imperative from a goddess.

The face of Connor MacKenzie was scorched into Thorstein Olafsson's mind. How could it not be, when the Scot had claimed the broadsword of his ancestors in that bloody battle four years ago?

And now the Scot was here, in Thorstein's territory, requesting an audience. The temptation to hold him hostage, in return for his sword, was great. But irrelevant. MacKenzie had won the sword that day and for that, and his prowess in battle, he had Thorstein's respect.

It hadn't stopped him sending a message to the Fidach king though. He knew of an alliance between Pict and Scot, but it would be interesting to discover how loyal Fidach was to MacAlpin's men when they were so far from Dal Riada.

Standing outside his longhouse, he fingered the hilt of his personal broadsword. It was of top quality, as befit his status, and had decapitated more than one man who had dared challenge his right to rule. But it wasn't the sword of his forefathers. And the loss was a constant thorn in his heart.

He narrowed his eyes as he surveyed his considerable estate. Some distance to the southeast the Scots were camped, awaiting his response. And while he'd very much like to make them wait a lot longer, his own curiosity as to what had brought MacKenzie into his domain refused to be ignored.

"Hakon." He jerked his head at the warrior who was like a brother to him. "Have MacKenzie sent to me in the hall."

~

THORSTEIN SAT on the only chair in the hall as the Scot, flanked by Norse, entered. Curious eyes followed their passage along the length of the building. It appeared the entire populace of his estate had found a reason to be inside at this particular moment.

MacKenzie, devoid of weapons, extended formal greetings in stilted Norse. Thorstein returned them with equal respect in somewhat more fluent Gaelic.

And then he got straight to the heart of the matter. "What message do you bring from your king, MacKenzie?"

"None," MacKenzie said, reverting to his own language. "I'm here on my own mission. And therefore of no use as a hostage to my king's favor."

Thorstein kept his face impassive while his brain analyzed that intriguing information. If one of his own warriors went into Dunadd without direct orders, Thorstein might consider it treason.

"For what purpose do you enter my territories?" He spoke in Gaelic. It offered a degree of privacy since only a few of those present understood the language.

"A matter of honor." MacKenzie hesitated, clearly irked by the crowded hall. Thorstein waited. The Scot would not dictate the conditions under which they conversed. "Regarding an incident that occurred here nine years ago. Involving the eldest Princess Devorgilla of Ce."

He held the Scot's unwavering gaze as he plunged back nine years in time. To his first raid, when he'd been a raw boy of fifteen. It should have been straightforward, a claiming of windswept land without undue bloodshed.

The scarce inhabitants hadn't put up much resistance. But a royal presence had proved an unexpected obstacle, although eventually defeated.

MacKenzie didn't refer to the raid. Nor the slaughter of the royal guard. He referred to the young girl Thorstein had stumbled across, being violently raped by two of his own countrymen.

She'd reminded him of his younger sister. Rage and disgust had turned his stomach. This wasn't a raid for plunder and enslaving. They wanted this land to settle and farm.

That was the day he had, unknown to most present, first earned the nickname he was now known by.

Thorstein the Beheader.

He stood. Gestured. His people, with clear reluctance, began to leave the hall until only Hakon and a few of his most trusted warriors remained.

He turned to Connor MacKenzie and using the knowledge gleaned from his spies made an educated guess. "The Princess of Ce is your wife?"

"Aye." MacKenzie's voice was uncompromising. "For what happened that day I owe you a debt of honor."

By Thor. This wasn't merely a marriage to unite Pict and Scot against the Norse. MacKenzie loved his princess.

Loved her enough to defy his king and enter enemy lands.

"Have no doubt," he said, "that one day I shall claim that debt."

"I have a proposition," the Scot said, as if they were on equal footing and he was not in a precarious position both politically and geographically. He would, Thorstein conceded, make a worthy Norseman. "And a request."

"Name them. I make no promises."

"I possess something I'm willing to return to its rightful owner." MacKenzie's gaze didn't waver. "As full discharge for my debt. And in exchange for something of equal value in your possession."

MacKenzie was offering to return his broadsword. The chances were high he had brought it north with him. He could order his warriors to ransack the Scots' camp until it was found. And risk great bloodshed on both sides.

Or he could negotiate.

"I'm listening."

"Nine years ago, you took something of great personal value from the princess. In exchange for your broadsword, I request the return of the Columba casket."

Silence thundered in the charged air. He'd taken that casket as a trophy, recognizing its great antiquity. And while he could have exchanged it for untold treasures, he'd held on to it. It intrigued him. It was exquisitely crafted yet something was missing. And while he knew the chances of ever reuniting the two pieces of the casket was remote, he'd refused to sell.

But compared to the return of the sword of his ancestors its value was of no consequence.

"You took a great risk, Connor MacKenzie, entering my lands with such a proposition. There's nothing to stop me running you through and claiming what is mine by force."

MacKenzie didn't move a muscle. "Only your honor, Thorstein Olafsson. Even enemies on the battlefield can recognize such in their opponent."

Thorstein took a step toward his enemy. A man who, under other circumstances, he would welcome as a friend.

"I will exchange the casket in return for my sword. All debts are repaid." He'd even let the Scots leave. Too bad if the King of Fidach wanted them kept as hostage. The Princess of Ce was MacKenzie's wife and he, Thorstein Olafsson, would not be responsible for keeping the man who loved her from her side.

Before MacKenzie could adequately express his gratitude, the great door opened, and a warrior strode up the hall toward him. Thorstein glared. He didn't appreciate being interrupted.

"My lord," the warrior said. "Forgive me." He stood some distance from MacKenzie and clearly wanted Thorstein to go to him so he could speak with a degree of privacy.

"This had better be good," Thorstein said so only the warrior could hear.

"It is." The warrior glanced at MacKenzie. "The eldest Princess of Ce has just arrived and requests audience with you."

Odin's balls. This day was turning into an entertaining saga.

"Have her taken to my private domain." He glanced at the Scot and pitched his voice low. "Keep MacKenzie in here for now. I don't want him knowing his princess has arrived."

Accompanied by one disarmed warrior from Ce, Aila followed one of the Vikings who had accosted her party before they had reached the Scots' camp. He showed her into a small room at the rear of the long building and informed her, with surprising civility, that the jarl would be with her shortly.

She tried to ignore the flutter of nerves in the pit of her stomach. Since leaving Fidach yesterday afternoon she'd existed in a cocoon of calm but now, when she needed it most, it was starting to crack.

The door swung open and in strode an enormous blond Viking. For a second, terror paralyzed her as that long-ago day flooded back. But this was not the boy who had loomed over her with fury etched on his young face.

This was a full-grown man, a seasoned warrior with whom Connor had fought, and although both facts should have served to increase her fear, oddly they managed to calm her.

"Princess of Ce, I welcome you." He gave a formal bow.

She inclined her head in acknowledgement. She was Aila, the

eldest Princess Devorgilla of Ce, and Bride was with her. Even if her head screamed that she was insane to cross into Viking territory her heart knew she was right.

"You know why I am here."

"Enlighten me."

Was it her imagination or did he sound amused? What chance did she stand of securing Connor's freedom if Olafsson found her amusing?

"You sent word to the King of Fidach that you would take the Scots hostage if it so pleased. I am here with the king's response."

Olafsson didn't answer but neither did he break eye contact.

She would allow no hint of her rising trepidation to color her voice. "The king requests the Scots be allowed to leave unhindered."

"I'm not interested in what the King of Fidach wants," Olafsson said and Aila's heart thudded painfully. He was going to keep Connor hostage. "What do you want, my lady, for the warrior known as Connor MacKenzie?"

He'd heard of their marriage. Of course he had. Spies were everywhere.

Should she pretend indifference? It was impossible to know what was behind the Viking's question. Yet she wasn't indifferent. And there was no guarantee that by pretending she was would be of any help to Connor's situation.

There was nothing she could say but the truth.

"I want his freedom."

There was a silence as Olafsson stared at her. He was a Viking, her enemy, and yet she didn't find his scrutiny abhorrent.

Because he had once served justice on her behalf.

"Tell me," he said. "What is MacKenzie's freedom worth to you?"

Everything.

"I'll give you my bride price." Everything she had taken into Dal Riada had returned with her to Ce-eviot. It might diminish her status in Connor's eyes, but what did that matter to her if it guaranteed his freedom?

Olafsson's eyes glinted in obvious interest and for a moment she thought she had won. And then a regretful smile quirked his lips.

"I have no interest in your bride price. I asked you what your husband's freedom is worth to you. What would you be willing to sacrifice?"

She was aware of the Ce warrior tensing by her side, clearly offended by the Viking's words. But there was no lustful overtone in Olafsson's question. And yet she knew that, for some reason, Connor's future hung on her answer.

She would forever love Onuist. He was a part of her childhood, her girlhood; her first love. He would live on, in a tender corner of her heart, but she wouldn't sacrifice Connor MacKenzie, the man she loved as she had loved no other, for the sake of misplaced guilt and old regrets.

"Nine years ago," she pushed the words past the obstruction in her throat and hoped the Viking couldn't see the way her fingers clutched at the folds of her gown, "you took a relic of Saint Columba. A casket." Goddess, please let him remember. Please let him not have sold or discarded it during the intervening years. "In exchange for the freedom of my husband and his men, I will give you the cross that completes the artifact."

With shaking fingers, she pulled the chain over her head and laid the cross on her palm to show him.

Olafsson appeared dumbstruck. A thread of panic inched through her. He had to accept. She had nothing else of worth to offer.

"Individually they are of great value. But together they are beyond price."

She shouldn't have said that. He was a Viking, he needed to know the price of everything. What use to him was something that could not be valued?

For a moment she didn't think he was going to accept. Then he reached out and took the cross from her. Finally, he looked up at her and there was an odd expression on his face. As if, at last, he was seeing her not as the girl he had once rescued but as the woman she had so recently become.

"I accept your exchange." His fingers curled around his prize. To her confusion amusement now glinted in his eyes. "Although I would equally have accepted had you simply told me you would sacrifice anything for the man you loved."

He would? Yet no regret speared through her at the knowledge she'd given up her beloved cross. Olafsson turned to the warrior who had followed him into the room.

"Hakon, bring MacKenzie in."

CHAPTER 39

Connor followed the Norseman to the rear of the longhouse that had been divided into smaller rooms. Now that the exchange had been agreed to, he just wanted to conclude their business and return the casket to Aila.

But if Olafsson extended hospitality, he had no choice but to accept.

The door opened and his thoughts collided. Aila stood in the middle of the room, by the side of Olafsson.

"What the hell?" His hand went for his sword before he recalled the weapon had been confiscated. How had Olafsson abducted her? When had he abducted her? He'd left her safely in Ce only yesterday.

Olafsson gestured and only then did Connor realize the Norseman who had brought him into the room had drawn his broadsword. With obvious reluctance, the Norseman stepped back.

"What treachery is this?" He glared at Olafsson. Had his trust been so badly misplaced? Had he, by his actions, brought devastation to Aila?

But what in the name of God was she doing there?

"Connor." Aila's voice dragged his attention back to her. Beside the massive Norseman she looked vulnerable and fragile. And she was with child. She needed rest and stability, not undue stress.

"Are you unharmed?" If the bastards had laid one hand on her, they would pay with their lives. Weaponless or not, he would not allow his wife's honor to go undefended.

"Of course I'm unharmed. Connor—"

A horrifying thought occurred to him. "Was Ce attacked after I left?" It was the only reasonable explanation. With so many warriors held in Dunadd, Ce was vulnerable. Had the remainder of Aila's kin been slaughtered?

"Attacked?" Aila stared at him as if he was insane. "Why would you think such a thing? Pict and Scot are allies now."

What? She was defending their alliance for the sake of appearances—he knew that. But she had also misunderstood his concern. It wasn't the Scots he'd accused of such attack.

"Then what are you doing here?" Now his initial shock was subsiding, he realized Aila wasn't behaving like a woman abducted. But then Aila was no ordinary woman. She could hide her feelings from the world. Hell, she could hide them from *him*.

But still things didn't strike true.

"I followed you."

He heard her words. Yet they were incomprehensible. She couldn't have followed him.

He knew his disbelief clearly showed on his face as she stepped toward him and reached out her hand. Only for her arm to drop to her side before she made contact.

"I left Ce-eviot yesterday morning, arrived at Fi-eviot earlier today and discovered you had continued north. And so I followed you."

Olafsson faded from view as Connor's entire focus arrowed on the woman standing in front of him. The woman who had just calmly announced she'd followed him into the land of her bitterest enemy.

"What the hell for?" Disbelief twisted into horror that she had knowingly placed herself in such danger. There was something she wasn't telling him. Had to be. If she hadn't been physically abducted, then somehow she'd been coerced.

"To negotiate your freedom."

There was a roaring in his ears, a pounding inside his head. His heart hammered as if it sought escape, and it took a second for him to recognize the source.

Fear. *Terror.* That Aila had undertaken such an unnecessary, foolhardy journey.

"My freedom?" He gripped her arms, wanting to shake her for taking such a risk, but mostly just wanting to touch her, to reassure himself she was here and safe. "There was no need for such negotiation. My safety was never in any doubt."

"There was." She flattened her hands against his chest and heat seeped into his heart. God, how could he bear to leave her at Ceeviot and return to Dal Riada without her? "Thorstein Olafsson sent word to the King of Fidach that he would keep you hostage if they so desired. I was the only chance you had for escaping that fate."

He wasn't much concerned by the possibility of the Norseman keeping him hostage. Once their agreement had been struck, it was a matter of honor for them both to keep their word.

But that was irrelevant.

"The Fidach king allowed you to leave?" Wait until he saw that incompetent fool. He'd ensure the king would never repeat such an error.

"No." Was that a touch of irritation in her voice? "I did not require his permission to leave. But yes, he gave me his blessing." Her fingers tightened on his shirt. "They didn't know why you traveled into Viking territory."

Her words were loaded with meaning. Aila was telling him the Fidach king wouldn't have cared if the Norse held him hostage, because they suspected his king of further treachery.

Was that what Aila thought? That he sought an alliance on behalf of his king with the Norse to undermine the alliance with the Picts?

It had never occurred to him she would think such a thing. Then again, it had never occurred to him she would discover where he'd gone after leaving Ce, until he returned and presented her with her beloved casket.

Heat seared through him. To give her the casket was one thing. To stand here, before two Norsemen and a Ce warrior and explain his reasoning was another. He ignored the third Norseman who entered the room and focused all his suppressed anger and relief onto Aila.

"What I do and where I go is none of Fidach's concern. But you—how dare you put yourself at risk by undertaking such a perilous journey?" Anything could have happened to her. He couldn't stand to think of it.

"If anything had happened to me," she said, sounding not incensed that he'd spoken to her in such a manner but, incomprehensibly, satisfied, "then you would be free again, Connor. Would that not please you?"

Had her condition addled her brain? He glared at her, because he couldn't tell her the bleak horror that crouched on his horizon at the very real thought of losing her.

"MacKenzie," Olafsson said, turning from the newcomer. With a rising sense of disbelief Connor saw a small, intricately carved casket in the Norseman's hand. "My part of our bargain is fulfilled. I await the return of what is rightfully mine."

He heard Aila's sharp, indrawn breath and instinctively loosened his grip on her and dragged her roughly into his arms. He wasn't going to give her the opportunity to retreat. Shooting the smirking Olafsson a black glare, he took the casket and held it awkwardly before Aila's shocked gaze.

"This is the reason I came north." He sounded feral. He couldn't help it. Not only did he need to explain himself to Aila, he needed to do it in front of an audience. "To reclaim your casket."

She didn't take it. When he pushed it toward her, she recoiled, pressing her body so tightly against his he feared she might well feel his erection even through the thickness of his plaid.

Finally, she looked at him. He didn't know what he'd expected. Tears of joy, perhaps? Gratitude? A promise in her eyes that, in spite of everything, they did have a chance of happiness together?

Fury glinted in her beautiful green eyes. She shoved at his chest with both hands and jerked herself free.

"You risked your life," she said. *Spat* might more accurately describe her delivery. "For that?"

He stiffened with affront and was humiliatingly aware of the avid interest of the other men in the room. He was a noble, a warrior, and had no need to explain himself to anyone but his king. Certainly not to a woman.

Least of all his wife.

But God help him. Aila was his wife.

"No." He growled the word at her. "For you."

"This," Olafsson said, "is the stuff of sagas but my honor decrees we should give you some privacy for a few moments." He turned to Aila. "Thank you, my lady. And MacKenzie, I expect my broadsword as soon as this domestic dispute is resolved." As he turned to Connor, he grinned and opened his palm to display Aila's cross. Before Connor could comprehend, the four other warriors left, leaving him alone with his wife who looked as speechless as he felt.

"His broadsword?" she said, regaining the use of her tongue

while he still floundered with the knowledge that Olafsson now possessed her beloved cross. "Why are you returning his broadsword? You won it in battle. It's yours."

Devil take the broadsword.

"You gave him your cross?" Even though he'd seen it with his own eyes, he still couldn't believe. "The cross you haven't taken off since the day your husband gave it to you?"

He thought she was going to argue with him. But then she appeared to reconsider. "Indeed, my lord, your memory is faulty. I removed my cross every night we spent together."

Once again words failed him as he recalled their nights of passion. No cross had come between them.

"Now, answer me." She sounded as regal as a queen issuing a demand to a peasant. "Why does Olafsson expect his broadsword returned?"

She had given Olafsson her cross. Somehow, with that revelation thundering through his mind, it was not so difficult to admit the truth.

"Because I owed him a debt of honor for how he defended you nine years ago. And because I needed something priceless with which to bargain for your casket."

She looked at him and this time her beautiful eyes shimmered with tears unshed. He battled the urge to go to her and take her in his arms, because there was something he needed to know. Was desperate to know. And only hearing Aila say the words would calm the storm raging in his heart.

"Aila." His voice was raw with need. What would he do if he was wrong? "Why did you give Olafsson your cross?"

Her bottom lip trembled. *Don't let me be wrong.*

"You know why." Her voice was low, oddly resigned. "I loved Onuist. But you are my husband. You are the man I love. Giving up my cross was a small sacrifice compared to what I might have lost otherwise."

She still loved him. Despite everything she had gone through. Bone-deep relief flooded him, and he went to her, intending to hold her close. And this time never let her go.

CHAPTER 40

She held him off by raising one hand, her fingertips grazing his chest and branding his heart.

Without taking his gaze from her, he put her casket on the desk and covered her hand that cradled his heart.

"I'm sorry you were forced into marriage with me."

Her words shattered his sense of wellbeing, the feeling of completeness, his rising desire.

"Forced?" Had he misunderstood? She was the one who had been forced. But surely, as she loved him, she couldn't regret they were wed?

"I know MacAlpin," her voice dripped derision as she said the name, "gave you no choice. I know you never intended to remarry."

How could she think that for even a second?

"Aila, I went to MacAlpin the day we arrived in Dunadd and tried to stop the marriage with Fergus." He saw her eyes widen at the knowledge he'd gone behind her back, but he wasn't going to apologize for it. "Because I wanted to marry you myself. And before my brother's body was even cold, I intended to fight MacAlpin for the right to claim your hand. But he'd already decided your fate. I know you were coerced and for that, I beg your forgiveness. But I can't regret the outcome of that day."

"You wanted to marry me?" She sounded astonished.

"Aye." Damn, did he really have to remind her? "I told you. The night before I discovered who you were." The night he realized just how much she meant to him.

Her frown intensified. "You meant everything you said that night?"

He resisted the urge to shuffle his feet and cast a surreptitious glance at the door. Just to ensure it was fully closed with no chance of them being overheard.

"Aye." It came out as a growl.

"I thought…" She hesitated and bit her lip. "I thought they were only words uttered in the heat of passion and meant nothing more."

He stared at her in disbelief, secretly offended by her confession. He'd told her she was his for all time. How much clearer did a man have to be?

"No." What else could he say?

A small smile tilted her lips. Lips he wanted to taste, and tease, and he could do neither while they remained in Norse territory. The sooner they returned to Ce the better. At least now he knew he would truly be welcomed in her bedchamber.

"Perhaps," she said, sounding oddly unsure, "one day you might grow to love me, Connor."

He laughed. And then saw the stricken look on her face, as though he'd just dealt her a mortal blow. Insane realization smashed through him. Had she been serious?

"What?" He sounded like a fool.

"Nothing." She pulled her hand free and gave him a brittle smile. "It doesn't matter."

He snatched her hand back and crushed her fingers. A deadly certainty snaked through him. "Aila, you do know how I feel about you, don't you?" He'd told her enough times. Hadn't he?

"Of course." She offered him another brittle smile but her eyes gleamed. "I understand Fearchara will always be first in your heart."

What the hell? Fearchara had nothing to do with how he felt about Aila. He had loved his first wife and she would always be a part of him. But Aila was—Christ, she was Aila. He couldn't imagine not sharing his life with her. Didn't want to imagine it.

Wouldn't think of it.

He stared into his beloved wife's eyes. Eyes that glistened with tears, and incomprehension warred within his soul. How could she think she was not first in his heart? How could she think he didn't love her with everything he was?

Sometimes things have to be said, no matter how unnecessary we believe them to be.

Unease inched along his spine as his mother's words haunted his mind. Even though it was blindingly obvious to him, did Aila not know how he felt because he *hadn't told her?*

He tugged her forward. The words would not come easily, but they needed to be said. Aila needed to hear them, to understand how very much she meant to him.

"Aila, even before the night we spent together in Ce I suspected I loved you. Even then I planned ways to convince you to leave your beloved homeland and come with me into Dal Riada."

A single tear spilled from one eye and trickled along her cheek. The sight tore his heart. His Aila, who had never cried in front of him despite everything she had suffered.

"It was the reason I went insane at the knowledge you were promised to my half-brother. The reason I tried to make you break your word."

"I didn't know," she whispered as her other hand tenderly cradled his jaw. "I thought it was merely your wounded pride."

He rested his forehead against hers, savored this moment, and tried not to let the impending darkness cloud his heart.

"Connor." Still cradling his face, she guided his other hand to press against her belly. The black fear roared once again, and this time would not be subdued. "Can you not find it in your heart to love our babe? I truly don't understand. Is it because you don't want a family with me?"

Every word scorched his soul. The horrifying vision of Aila, bloodied and sliced open, filled his tortured mind.

"I don't want to lose you." The words were raw. "But God forgive me. I'd give almost anything for you to safely bear my child."

"That's the reason?" She sounded stunned. "Goddess, is that the reason you withdraw?"

What other reason could she imagine? And had she just called upon a *goddess*?

"I'll ensure the best physicians attend you. They will travel to Ce for a royal birth." MacAlpin wouldn't argue when the fate of his blood-kin was at stake. Aila would survive. And then he recalled her other question and pain lashed through him. Was she concerned he could not—would not—accept this child? "Aila, there's something else you should know. I do love this child. How could I not? It's part of you. And part of my bloodline also."

She stared at him, the silence growing taut between them. He didn't know what else he could say, what else he could do, to convince her but then she shook her head, as if attempting to clear her thoughts.

"You told me this child would inherit Dunfodla if it was a boy." Her eyes were no longer shining with tears. "Why?"

Had she forgotten? "Because that's the stronghold of Fergus' forefathers, from his royal mother's side."

"Yes," Aila said. "I know that. But what does that have to do with this babe?"

Heat seared through him as her implication rammed into his brain. But it couldn't be. She had assured him that night it was safe. She'd been adamant in her denial after the feast, when he'd dared to assume his seed might have planted within her.

He'd believed her. Believed Fergus, his king, even his mother. But all along, he'd harbored the secret, despairing wish that her child was his.

Words failed. He pulled back and stared at her belly, as if the answer might miraculously appear before him.

"Oh, my love." Aila's sigh rippled through him. "I thought you knew and had rejected us both." She flattened her hands against his chest. "Connor, Fergus and I did not consummate our union. He was incapacitated and I was scarcely willing. He didn't touch me, do you understand? This child is yours, from our night together in Ce."

His. Protectiveness surged through him, protectiveness and pride and a love so wild he feared it might tear him apart. He took her hands, hoped she couldn't feel how they trembled, and lost himself in the green depths of her beautiful eyes.

"I love you." He couldn't hide the way his voice cracked, but what did it matter? Only Aila was here. And Aila was all that mattered. "I love our child. And I swear to you, I will never put you through this again. One child is more than I ever dared to hope for with you."

"Alas," she said, sounding as if she wanted to laugh, or perhaps cry, "we are destined to have five children. I've recently discovered there's no point in trying to alter some things. And this, I fear, is one of them."

"Five?" He crushed the spike of elation. "No. I won't tempt fate. We will have this one child and be thankful."

Her fingers tightened around his and a soft smile touched her lips. "I denied my goddess' wisdom for nine years. And now I know why she showed me those children. It wasn't for me at all. It was for you." She lifted his hand and brushed her lips across his knuckles. "To show you your future family. The children you will have with me."

He wanted to believe her. But the fear lingered. Perhaps it always would.

"After we reach Ce, I have to return to Dal Riada." But this time he had no intention of remaining there as he'd expected to before today. "But I'll be back with you long before the birth." He would not say such to Aila, although he knew she was fully aware, that with the death of King Bredei and imprisonment of Talargan, Connor was now the tacit King of Ce. He had a perfectly justifiable reason for traveling there without prior permission from MacAlpin, even if his king would not approve the relocation of his prized hostage.

But that didn't concern Connor. When MacAlpin discovered Aila was with child, her comfort and safe delivery was all that would interest him.

"I will accompany you to Dal Riada."

He dragged his knuckles, still clasped within her fingers, along her cheek.

"No. Stay with your kin. Where you belong."

"I belong by your side, my lord. And that is where I intend to remain. Whether that is Duncadha, stronghold of your forefathers, Dunbrae, home of Fearchara, or Ce-eviot, in the palace of my ancestors."

She had always possessed a regal air, a sense of serenity. But now, as he looked upon his wife, the mother of his unborn child, he was struck by a quiet aura of authority that he'd not been aware of before.

As though she had finally found her rightful place in the world.

His world.

Fierce pride and primal love gripped his heart and constricted his throat. "Our child will be born in the palace of his ancestors."

He cradled the face of his beautiful, brave Pictish Princess. The woman who had given him a new future to cherish. A new life to embrace.

Aila.

~

HER VENGEFUL SCOT

THE HIGHLAND WARRIOR CHRONICLES
BOOK 2

My enemies will pay for what they've done...

Cameron MacNeil pledges vengeance on the Pict noble who killed his sister. But he didn't expect to fall for the beautiful pagan princess – his enemy's widow, Elise.

A secret that could tear them apart forever...

When danger threatens her life, Cam risks everything to keep her safe from his king's machinations. He should be happy now his enemy is dead, but guilt cripples him at the secrets he must keep, for if Elise ever discovers the truth, he'll lose her forever.

An unwilling betrayal...

But Elise has a secret of her own, one she is blood bound never to reveal. Even if keeping it means she'll lose the only man she's ever loved.

HER BASEBORN SCOT

THE HIGHLAND WARRIOR CHRONICLES
BOOK 3

A warrior with cursed royal blood...

Commanded by his king to hunt down and marry the elusive Princess of Pictland, Finn Braeson is captivated by a mysterious Pict lady with secrets in her eyes. If only he were free to make her his.

A princess who must hide her identity...

Determined to avenge her people against the upstart king, Mairi cannot fall for the silken charms of a Scots warrior. Yet despite the dangers, she cannot resist his allure.

First love, only love...

But when betrayal rocks their fragile alliance, they must fight the political intrigues that surround them and put their trust in each other – or risk being torn apart forever.

ABOUT THE AUTHOR

Christina Phillips is an ex-pat Brit who now lives in sunny Western Australia with her high school sweetheart and their family. She enjoys writing historical fantasy, paranormal, and contemporary romance, where the stories sizzle and the heroine brings her hero to his knees.

She is addicted to good coffee, expensive chocolate, and bad boy heroes. She is also owned by three gorgeous cats who are convinced the universe revolves around their needs. They are not wrong.

Discover all of Christina's books on her website
ChristinaPhillips.com

ACKNOWLEDGMENTS

A special thanks to Sally Rigby and Amanda Ashby for all your encouragement, support, and cyber chocolate over the years—long may the fun continue! And to Mark and our marvelous children, I wouldn't be here without you all.

AUTHOR'S NOTE

Although Kenneth MacAlpin, King of the Scots of Dal Riada, became King of Pictland in 843 AD or thereabouts, this is a work of fiction based on myths, legends, and my own imagination.